REKINDLED

TERESA IRIZARRY

AuthorHouse™
1663 Liberty Drive
Bloomington, IN 47403
www.authorhouse.com
Phone: 1 (800) 839-8640

This is a work of fiction. All of the characters, names, incidents, organizations, and dialogue
in this novel are either the products of the author's imagination or are used fictitiously.

Published by AuthorHouse 08/11/2015

ISBN: 978-1-5049-1124-5 (sc)
ISBN: 978-1-5049-1123-8 (hc)
ISBN: 978-1-5049-1122-1 (e)

Library of Congress Control Number: 2015907228

Printed in the United States of America by BookMasters, Inc
Ashland OH
August 2015

Any people depicted in stock imagery provided by Thinkstock are models,
and such images are being used for illustrative purposes only.
Certain stock imagery © Thinkstock.

This book is printed on acid-free paper.

To an unnamed Christian in Syria 2015

In 1620 an essay was published in Holland about the wrongfulness of silencing people who are speaking their conscience. Four chapters of this essay surfaced independently in print in England in 1643, accompanied by the story of how these chapters were smuggled out of London's Newgate prison. The identity of the original author remains mysterious.

John Robinson, the pastor who sent a portion of his flock to America on the *Mayflower*, wrote long arguments attacking the 1620 version of the document. He supported the authority of church and state to discipline people's thoughts. John Cotton, the esteemed Puritan teacher in Boston, provided the first line of attack against the 1643 version.

Against all odds, this essay forms the basis for the principles of religious freedom that are established in the original charter of Rhode Island, the constitution of the United States, and the charters of other English colonies that peacefully gained their independence after the American Revolution.

PROLOGUE

Troas, AD 48

The two men walked along the dirt road, little more than a path, toward town. Their tense voices were quiet, but the disagreement was palpable.

"But good was done. How can it be wrong?" asked Paul.

"God builds even from evil to accomplish his ends. He will find ways to use your honest blunder to good ends. That does not change that it was wrong and that even more good may have been accomplished if you'd stayed in control. You cannot know. We will never know. The worst of it is that the powers of darkness may also build from this event. Do you really think a good end justifies your means?" asked the teacher and physician and good friend, Luke.

It was late evening now, after a long day of sailing, walking, and talking. Paul and Luke spent this day together, Paul telling Luke about his travels. Luke was a meticulous detective, and he would ask about events again and again from different angles, trying to picture them so that he could record them as if he had been present. They'd sailed together alone for a week and were now walking back to Troas. It was when Paul got to the part of the story that took place in Paphos with the magician Bar-Jesus that Luke's countenance had darkened.

Paul said to Luke, "Just hear me out. Barnabus and I were invited to a discussion with Sergius Paulus, an intelligent man who wanted to learn more about what I was teaching. Sergius Paulus was a disciple of Bar-Jesus, so the two showed up together. As I shared the stories of Jesus's life, Bar-Jesus would interrupt and twist my words. I became so frustrated after a time that I could not go on teaching until Bar-Jesus was dealt with."

Paul struggled with a handicap. In his personal encounter with Jesus on the side of the road over a decade before, the intense light was blinding. A partial blindness continued to irritate him mightily, especially when he was stressed.

Paul admitted "I focused intently on Bar-Jesus. With all my heart I called on the power of the Holy Spirit. I called him a son of the devil, and the enemy of all that is right, full of every sort of deceit and fraud. I said the hand of the Lord was upon him, and he would be blind, and unable to see for a time. The blinding effect was immediate, and Sergius Paulus was impressed."

Luke groaned.

"Sergius Paulus admitted he'd always been fascinated with magic and anything beyond what his own intelligence could figure out. He was immediately convinced of the power of the God we represent. He gave his heart to God that day, believed in Jesus, and was saved."

Luke said, "Do you see the problem?"

Paul shook his head, waiting to learn.

"I took Peter aside after a similar incident. A church member lied to Peter, and Peter wished him dead without even saying it aloud. Peter got a shock when God immediately struck the husband dead. Then, it happened again when the wife lied. I've been struggling with how to include that sad episode in my history—because I never saw Jesus cause any person physical harm. Not once. He only caused healing, the whole time I observed his ministry."

"And you were with him since there were only eighty followers. I do respect that," Paul admitted.

"Peter and you are both strong-willed, forceful, and prone to anger. But you have to learn the self-control that Jesus asks of us. Jesus always rebuked the disciples when they asked to use the powers given them against people who would not receive them. Peter knew that."

Paul pushed back, "But there was that fig tree he withered, and those pigs he ran into the sea. They were harmed."

"Those were temporal earthly creatures over which man has dominion and stewardship, whereas humans are created in the image of God. As a physician, I watched Jesus closely and came to believe that healing miracles were being performed before my eyes. When people did not believe, when they twisted Jesus's words and tried to trick him, Jesus began speaking in code—telling stories that only the disciples would be trained to understand, and Jesus released the unbelievers back to their temporal lives. In the end those people chose this life over the long-term plan, and Jesus knew they would perish soon enough. I think he felt sorry for them. Watching Jesus's patience in action convinced me more than anything else that a long-term plan really is possible for humans, that there is eternal life, and that I want to be a part of it."

Paul took Luke's words to God that night in prayer. He stood convicted and received again the forgiveness that made him a new creature. He went on in his evangelistic travels, and Luke never had to tell another story about Paul causing harm to any person.

Later, after Paul left, Luke agonized. How could he record the facts— he was committed to the most accurate accounting possible—and yet use them to illuminate the teaching of Jesus? Peter was the lead apostle, and Paul the lead evangelist of the day. Their actions were famous already, as they were told and retold by followers throughout the countryside. Yet Peter and Paul still made mistakes and freely admitted it to Luke when questioned. What should be recorded? Would Jesus's teachings be lost to human frailty if he did not record mistakes or lack of authority if he did record them? Luke prayed that nothing essential would be lost.

In the end, Luke recorded Jesus's admonition to the disciples in what would become <u>Luke 9:54</u>. He also recorded the stories of Peter and Paul as a historian, without comment—except for the subtle disapproval he gently expressed by not switching Paul's name from Saul to Paul at his conversion or even at his first missionary trip, but rather after the Bar-Jesus encounter and Paul's subsequent repentance about harming another purposefully, in anger.

Time passed, and the verses became recognized as scripture, words revealed by God. By AD 400 the cultural elite and the government adopted Christianity as the religion of state. By AD 1400 men, corrupt with power, were twisting verses to their own greedy ends—to justify all manner of torture, inquisition, and persecution in order to enforce the discipline of a corrupt church hardly recognizable as Christian. Brave individuals would retranslate the Bible and find that it didn't say what they had been taught at all. The Way was a lost code for over a thousand years. Now it was being rediscovered. The fight for the right to read the original language of The Way, and to make uncorrupted translations that could be read by all would cost many their lives.

CHAPTER 1

London, AD 1608

The young man loped easily through London, weaving in between the men and women carrying heavy burdens of merchandise. His burden was light and invisible—a letter from the schoolmaster to the leader of the small secret group that would meet in an hour. His mistake was slowing down as he reached unfamiliar territory on Bread Street, where the house gathering would take place. Suddenly out of nowhere boys bigger than he, meaner than he, and more English than he popped into view, surrounding him.

"Look, a Dutchie, a Stranger!"

"What do you think you're doing here?" taunted another.

"He thinks he's protected by some Privy Council act. We'll just see about that."

"I got his cap—hey, let's get his shirt too. We'll teach him to come to Bread Street alone!"

Hendric could not afford to lose the letter in his shirt. He struck the boy closest and made a run for it. He was caught by two others waiting around the corner. They easily held the lanky lad, who was more used to debating matters in his schoolbooks and interpretations of the Greek and Hebrew Bible at the Austin Friar school than to physical altercations. Unfortunately for Hendric, he was outnumbered and overpowered.

The boys did not beat him up long, for they decided that the reward might be greater if they dragged him to the magistrate.

"State your business now," the magistrate demanded. Hendric was silent, terrified. The scuffle exposed the top of the letter, and the boys had helped themselves to it, though it made no sense to them. The magistrate looked closely at it with trained eyes. Hendric's heart sank. He must never ever tell where he had been going with that letter nor who sent him. He felt alone. The officer's eyes shone with an evil glint as he began to realize what he had in his hands. This was a fair catch! He'd get a bonus for bringing this one in. He grabbed Hendric's collar, nodding brusquely to the boys to collect their reward and be off. Then it got worse.

"Where do you live? Who sent you? We'll give you a finder's fee for everyone you name." Hendric stayed silent, and he remained silent when they beat him. Eventually he woke up bruised, his shirt torn, bleeding from his nose and mouth in a dank, dark, rotten place called Newgate.

Hendric knew there was a long history between his ancestors and the English—a love-hate relationship that started when his merchant ancestors helped King Henry VIII in his wars. In return, the king allowed the Dutch merchants trading rights and religious harbor. It didn't hurt that King Henry VIII had it in for the pope over his divorce. In revenge, he sponsored the publication of an English Bible translated from German and Latin. Once the English Bible was published, all of England would see that there was no pope included in it.

Even so, the identity of the translator was a great family secret. Two years before King Henry VIII came to his decision to authorize a translation, the original translator, William Tynsdale, was strangled and then burned at the stake. No one wanted that fate. Even if a current monarch was supportive, the next one might not be. Only a select few knew that a key translator was a well-respected cloth merchant, Jacob van Meteren. Jacob was Hendric's grandfather. In addition to performing the translation work, he paid for the printing. The tracks had been covered well. The family waited for just the right moment to unveil the resulting document. While Henry VIII was at the peak of his anger at the pope, translators were able to receive an endorsement from Henry VIII, enabling publication as an instrument of the crown. The secret group of translators drew straws to elect a sacrificial lamb, Myles Coverdale—in case of future royal disapproval. Myles successfully insisted that it had been his work alone, never betraying his partners. Jacob took refuge in Germany for a time just to be sure.

Hendric knew what it was that drove his grandfather, a passionate desire for a more faithful translation. No one man could interpret the scriptures perfectly—and each successive interpretation if not from the original language lost more. The Latin Bible was corrupt with mistranslations that obscured the message; the German was not directly translated from the original Hebrew and Greek, either. The Van Meteren family became the key financier and architect of Austin Friar language education—the stated reason being so that the Strangers would continue to know Dutch; however, Greek and Hebrew were taught to all who would learn. The hope was that, with so many reading the original language translation of the Bible, the full revelation and authority of scripture would be rekindled to guide followers of the Way and that gaps in the Bibles in other languages would over time be eliminated.

The Dutch "Strangers" who produced Hendric were industrious and wealthy traders, putting English craftsman to shame with their superior technology. Their ties to the English Puritan community ran deep. The Puritans shared the belief in direct Bible reading as the primary way to keep the church the unstained Bride of Christ as she was intended to be. Puritanism was illegal. Dutch Strangers were tolerated because of their trade secrets and the wealth they brought to the crown. Ties between the Strangers and the Puritans were strictly forbidden.

As recently as 1561, Hendric's uncle, Emanuel Van Meteren, rescued an Austin Friar minister who was caught assisting Anabaptists. The trouble that followed threatened the welcome of the Dutch church in England. It was Emanuel himself, a clever negotiator, who suggested his own very public ex-communication, along with that of other supporters. In this way the Austin Friar church and school would be left alone. From then on, sources of financial support and all communication were carefully guarded secrets. The secret was so safely kept that all observing the decline in membership of Austin Friar assumed the decline was among poorer artisans, and not the wealthy merchant class, because the church budget did not go down. That fiction became a rumor that Emanuel and the three ministers at Austin Friar declined to deny.

Hendric worked hard at his studies, and on the first nights of his imprisonment his chief worry was falling behind the other students and losing ground toward winning a precious Austin Friar sponsorship to higher learning.

Hendric was getting hungry—stomach-hurting, brain-focusing hungry. He recalled a feast in the 260-person Draper's Hall that he served. He longed now for droppings from that table. Thick, hearty pea soup chock full of crunchy grilled salt pork served with rye bread and plenty of mustard. Smoked sausages cooked with parsnips, carrots, and onions, the vegetables perfectly caramelized in butter. Plenty of warm ale to wash it all down. Thin milk pudding with delicate sweet pastries—flaky on the outside while doughy on the inside. Oh, this thinking and remembering was making it far, far worse. Hendric was cold, it was dark, and there was no end in sight.

The English merchants resented the continued favor from the crown toward the Dutch Strangers and repeatedly harassed and sought injunctions against the trade of the Dutch. So it was no surprise how the young men of Bread Street felt about a Stranger. Newgate prison still seemed unbelievably bad fortune. How could it be? Hendric hadn't even done anything with his life yet—it was too soon to be tossed away. At the same time, he knew family history and that its consequence would be that Uncle Emanuel could not afford to help anyone in his position.

Just yesterday he'd been schoolmaster Abraham de Cerf's brightest student and one of minister Symon Ruytinck's best assistants in the Austin Friar church. The school was part of the church, and the church was protected with a charter. Hendric was fluent in Greek and Hebrew, was advanced in scripture interpretation, and enjoyed searching for places where translation errors masked The Way. He wanted to join his ancestors in cracking the "original code" of Hebrew and Greek meanings behind the inspired writing of underground followers of the Way from a thousand years prior. He and his pals were dedicated to seeing this code cracked completely and finding all the places the translation must therefore be changed. The danger of the adventure made it irresistible to a schoolboy and gave it all the greater air of importance. Yet, Hendric was just beginning to understand the vast difference between flirting with danger and the reality of actually being a prisoner.

The misery he found himself experiencing was not in itself an unacceptable or uncommon state for his time. The streets of London stank of sewage, hunger was common, and it was a full 150 years before happiness would even be recognized as one of the objectives in this life. Most were resigned to a fate of struggling against disease, stench, and death. His shock and incredulity stemmed more from his perception that his own brief life, his own bright purpose, the one he was so sure was ordained by God, seemed to be on hold or to have been tossed away.

London AD 1609

Joan Helwys was working through chores as fast as her hands would go, shelling peas, changing a diaper, when the knock came at the door. Agents of the magistrate stood outside. It was quite a surprise to see them in the midst of the large Broxtowe Hall Estate. As the surviving firstborn son, her husband now owned the estate. While he was away it was up to Joan to run the place. When the agents of the magistrate appeared at the door, Joan was not concerned at first, as her husband Thomas, whom she presumed they'd be after, was safely in the Netherlands. Their small church group was currently living in the Netherlands, supported by Helwys's wealth, just to avoid just such a magistrate's call. Yet Joan had not gone. Her home, the land she loved, as well as the animals they raised, the garden they loved, her parents, her friends, her extended family, and the family's servants were all here. Her seven children needed support, and she did not speak Dutch at all. She had no desire to live in the Netherlands in some shabby rooms where she could not even build a garden.

Mary, Joan's seventeen-year-old maidservant, opened the door and her eyes went wide.

"Joan Helwys, present yourself for arrest!" boomed the agent to Joan past Mary. Joan fell into shock.

"Johannes—you are in charge here," she yelled to her eldest son as she ráced to the door with her eyes fixed on Mary, who would need to assist him in running the place. Then, with no time for anything else, she cried, "Here I am; what is the trouble?"

"Come with us," demanded the two men—big, strong fellows with the physical authority to enforce their magistrate's authority. With that, she was gone.

Mary posted a letter from Johannes to his father in the Netherlands the following day, for they were in no position to run the estate without an adult. Johannes was but thirteen years old and just home from boarding school on weekends. Thomas needed to return home or give them instructions.

Several weeks later, Joan was brought before the judge and jury. At that time, there was not thought to be a need for a defense lawyer in such matters, since it was believed that an honest person should not need one. So Joan had no lawyer and no prior information on the charges against her. She was immediately asked to swear an oath: "I swear by Almighty God that the evidence I shall give shall be the truth, the whole truth, and nothing but the truth."

This she could not do. Separatists believed that no civil authority could dictate their relationship with God, and she could take no oath on God's name for a king or his magistrates and representatives. God to her was sovereign. The oath was forced worship and a blasphemy against God.

As a result, she was quickly found guilty and sentenced to banishment. In seventeenth-century London, a guilty woman could plead her belly, meaning that she was with child. Joan promptly did exactly that. This caused a jury of matrons to be scheduled to examine her. When she showed up to this jury the next week she brought all seven children with her. The matrons quickly supported her plea for her belly, and the proceeding was over. Her sentence would not be carried out, and she was released. How many of the matrons were secret separatists following the Way, no one will ever know.

Joan Helwys was relieved, but the situation was quite a scare and meant hardship for her family, especially as she had a miscarriage shortly thereafter. Thomas Helwys no longer believed his family safe, and he felt inordinately guilty for leaving them.

Thomas was dedicated to his small flock. He was sponsoring the relocation from England to the Netherlands, as he had helped a sister flock led by John Robinson and others. The Robinson church originally spawned the Helwys/Smyth congregation to reach new neighborhoods in England. The two congregations made a simultaneous decision to flee England as King James started to crack down on men who did not submit to the Church of England. It now seemed ironic that his wife was not with him. He owned a significant estate in England, however, and had presumed that his family was safe. Thomas Helwys, in turmoil, made a decision. He must stand up for his faith in England alongside his wife. Hiding in Amsterdam was not accomplishing anything for God. How could he sit there writing about perseverance in the face of persecution when he had run away? Helwys posted a letter to the king privately from the Netherlands and awaited a response.

King James took his role as Defender of the Anglican faith seriously. He famously took the time to converse at length with theologians—most frequently with orthodox teachers like Richard Neile and but sometimes with separatists. Discussions at court seemed promising for shaping the future of the Anglican Church to return to the Way now that it was fully separate from the Roman Catholic tradition. Puritans and Anabaptists wanted to convince the king to make the Anglican Church a pure church. All were aware that King James was deciding the sort of church that England would support, and Thomas Helwys wanted to influence the king.

London AD 1609

Hendric's mother, Orrelia, was beside herself. Hendric had not been seen for weeks. She was used to relying on Hendric for company, for physical strength, and as her sole connection to the intellectual world. While Orrelia could with labor read both books and maps, she could not write and relied on Hendric for all her outgoing correspondence. Hendric was also her link to the church. For Orrelia counted on Hendric to attend discussions, record them in detail in his excellent shorthand, and bring them home to her small group of women, most of whom could not read at all. Hendric read at her Bible studies and spoke to the group of women as they quilted and would then depart so that the women could speak together. Orrelia could not know the depth of the tragedy—Hendric was carrying a letter for one of her friends from her husband in exile.

Orrelia Hoste was Jacob Van Meteren's daughter and the daughter of Orrelia Orthellius, of the map-making family. Orrelia's husband was deeply involved in the cloth production business, as a part of the Draper's guild. Orrelia's most powerful relative was her brother Emanuel. He was her best hope for assistance, but he was also at great risk himself and therefore limited in his ability to help.

Orrelia came from a family rich in stories of narrow escape from authorities. Her fervent hope was that Hendric would someday be one of those successful escape stories. Her brother Emanuel was named "God with Us" because, when their mother Orrelia Orthellius van Meteren was pregnant with him, the house in Amsterdam was searched. With her husband Jacob away, there had been plenty to find. The authorities looked straight at the trunk that held their brother Leonard's Bible translations to date and her husband Jacob's printing implements, but they did not dig into the chest and did not realize what they had been looking at, because they were distracted. A beautiful woman with no husband in the house can be very distracting when she needs to be. They hadn't yet invented undergarments, so all it took was a fall to provide a diversion. She fell out of nervousness, apparently tripping over something, and that was all it took. You had to admire Mother for that.

Nothing was found. Leonard, Jacob, and Myles Coverdale survived to produce the Coverdale Bible.

Orrelia's husband was private, authoritarian, and austere. He had no patience with lost sons—lost to him as part of the business long before he disappeared. Hendric was his mother's boy, taking after her learned family and not after his father's business-oriented one. Dietrick Hoste had other, more promising sons. So Orrelia suffered alone and in silence.

The small group of mostly English women counted on the letter from the Austin Friar reverend for the plan of study for their Bible group. They counted on Hendric to read it. Without either the letter or Hendric, there was no backup connection method. Any connection at all between the Austin Friar school and the group that contained English women was strictly illegal, and the women watched and waited for an opportunity to reestablish their connection. They continued studying as best they could, however, reading aloud and discussing what they read. Their commitment to God did not waver, and their time passed in prayer for Hendric and the Austin Friar school. Without a list of names, no one could prove that the reverend had been spreading his knowledge to English families. The incendiary knowledge that the Dutch supported in that day was that a person—woman or man—could read the Bible for him or herself and think for him or herself, rather than relying on an official state church to tell them about God. Worse, they believed that the authority of the king was limited by God and did not extend to authority over God's relationship with a man.

Abraham de Cerf was nonplussed. Hendric was his best student, and Abraham's heart ached for a return to the quality of discussion, the passion for truth that spread across the classroom whenever Hendric participated. He knew that the shorthand had not been cracked and was unlikely to be detected. Not even Abraham, however, knew of the Helwys letter that Reverend Symon had given Hendric to carry, along with the coded instructions.

Reverend Symon Ruytinck's demeanor was unchanged. But his poker face was hiding stark fear, as he knew what Hendric had been carrying,

receive any answer. His heart sank, but the schoolmaster's wife seemed to expect him to continue. He began to train his mind to write. If he could not live life as he chose, he would write about why it was wrong to keep him here. Not a personal situation letter, but a puzzling out of what had gone wrong with the world that it interpreted scripture and abused power in this way, and how to get back to the Way.

CHAPTER 2

London AD 1610

Roger, focused as always, was deep in earnest conversation about John Smith's latest adventures with one of his father's favorite customers. As a result, he missed one of the charges that should have been put on the customer's bill.

It didn't take long for his father to catch the error. During a pause in customer traffic, his father often checked up on Roger this way.

"You might as well have given it away!" thundered the merchant to Roger. "You let them take advantage of us! Come, do these sums again. Your carelessness has cost me, and I intend to make sure it costs you." He fumed on "Now we'll be short at the end of the day."

Roger Williams hated the shop. He hated the bullying, he hated the heavy burdens, he hated the wheeling and dealing and endless carting of merchandise. The only part he didn't hate was talking to the customers when his father wasn't looking too closely.

"Yes, Father." Roger didn't know what he would be when was grown, but he did know he would not be a merchant. As soon as he could slip away, he did. Sometimes he retreated to the decades-old Great Bible in St. Sepulchre. In an age before books at home were common, the Bible was the main source of stories. The Bible was heavy, so tradition was to memorize chapters. Roger was an ace at that memorization and could recite more than most adults. His trick was to think up visions of each chapter, moving visions that told a story or rooms of a house that you could wander through that contained verses. Roger was very good at this and at age eight had detailed visions for over half the chapters of the Bible that he could use as guides to recite the chapters. After all, he'd been reading the Bible at St. Sepulchre to his mum after morning prayers since age six and then retelling the stories to his mum and his brothers, and sometimes Mum's friends, at night before bed.

This was not what every mum did. It was Roger's mum's discipline, a way to hear the Bible under the cover of teaching a son to read. Roger's mum owned a small inn, and as a result could not always make it to St. Sepulchre. She would instead meet at night with her friends and have Roger share his notes. Later, he'd share with the schoolmaster on Monday morning. Those sessions with a schoolmaster were never as intense as the sessions with Mum and her friends. The women did not all read, but they were all intelligent learners, and they would pepper Roger with questions and challenge his answers until he had it right, even if they had to send him back to St. Sepulchre to find the answers for the next week.

Roger hung out whenever he could down the road at the Austin Friar school. The schoolmaster made much quicker work of the women's questions than Roger could by poring over scripture in St. Sepulchre. The schoolmaster had a son, Johannes, two years older than Roger, and soon they were fast friends. Already fluent in Dutch, Roger was at home with these boys. The schoolmaster admitted him to the after-school English boy's school, though at a more tender age than most. His father was told he had a job collecting the large brass milk cans from the prison to get him out of merchant duties. There was such a job; the minister's wife did it and gave the can tops to the boys. Roger and Johannes deciphered the milk can caps, looking for writing. Not even the schoolmaster knew the full extent of the work they deciphered.

So it was at age eight that he ran out of his father's home-based merchant shop—down the street as fast as he could get away—and made record time to the back of his friend Johannes's house. There was a fresh cap with writing for the first time in two weeks!

"What do you have?" asked Roger in Dutch.

Johannes had the fire going and was checking the cap. "Lots of writing today; come and decipher it."

In the back room of the house, Roger and Johannes would pore over the can top, using the fire to make the words show. A challenge was to take the vague references written there in shorthand and to use their modern Dutch Bible to narrow in and place the reference in the deciphered version. They would write out the text and discuss it and then hide it. Each day was a clue.

The young boys pored over the writings, scribbling letter after letter, word after word. Sometime it was a little blurred, and they worked out together what it should have been.

To the boys it was a puzzle and a game. To Reverend Symon and the schoolmaster it was a teaching tool and a tragedy. Hendric was brash and brave and loyal, and when Miriam started the milk can search for prison brethren, they never dreamed they'd have to search for him. The first can tops that came back were miserable letters, and the Reverend Symon could not bear to read them. He blamed himself. The story of Hendric's capture came out over the can tops and Reverend Symon cried, even as Johannes and Roger sat by completely fascinated. The Reverend Symon could not bear it and left the boys to read alone. When the writing changed, Johannes and Roger were not really old enough to understand it. They had a sense of the greatness of the words and stored them away from everyone, promising each other to keep Hendric's writing safe and to treasure it until they could do something more.

While the boys deciphered, they talked across the fire. "Did you hear about John Smith?" exclaimed Roger. "He returned from Virginia a few months back to heal from a gunpowder accident. He's coming to St. Sepulchre tonight, and he's going to tell us all about it. We're all going to go—Father and Mum, Sydrach, and even Robert. Mum saw him; he's staying at her inn. She says he's going to be in fine form, with many stories. Mum says you can come too if you want—will you go?"

"Sure!" and after a moment, "Hey look at this ... this has to be a Bible reference, let's see if we can trace it. It seems to be 2 Timothy 2. Let's see ... 'The servant of the Lord must be gentle toward all men, suffering the evil men, instructing them with meekness that are contrary minded, proving if at any time God will give them repentance, that they may acknowledge the truth, and come to amendment out of the snare of the Devil.' And look at this shorthand. It looks like Hendric is getting beaten again."

The boys gazed intently, reading again and again and trying to see what was happening in the words and between the lines. Eventually they had to stop and run back to Roger's house, in order to get to St. Sepulchre on time. They didn't want to be late for John Smith.

John Smith was a leading parishioner at St. Sepulchre and a supplies coordinator for Jamestown in the New World. He was an outspoken man of tall tales with few adult friends, though respected for his exploration skills. Grievously wounded in a recent gunpowder accident on a boat in America, he was back in London. He first visited his financial sponsor and mentor, Emanuel van Meteren, to show him his maps and to thank him for his support, and together they'd hatched the plan for this fund-raising event. John Smith had debts to repay from his recent adventures, but more importantly wanted to raise money for a new exploration of New England. In the new venture, mapmaking would be the chief goal. Since the Virginia Company was expanded in May 1609 to include areas inland and far north of the original boundary, there was much potential for charts requiring new exploration. Another goal was to get the Virginia Company to increase logistical support for the colonists across the seas.

"John, your timing is impeccable. Henry Hudson is about to leave to find a passage to Asia. His planned route is southerly, but we both know he will have to deal with the wind and the ice. We'll give him a copy of your charts in case he finds them useful," said Emanuel.

"Emanuel, I don't feel like I have impeccable timing. When we first got to Jamestown, men died from the swamp-like conditions nearly every day. Fortunately I'd been sent inland to establish trading relations with the Algonquian. It seemed every time I'd return to town there would be tens of new colonists and no new supplies. They expected me to make up for that, and I did what I could, but it was unreasonable, and many died."

"Why didn't they settle where they could raise more crops?" asked Emanuel. "Shouldn't they be planning to be self-sufficient?"

"Maybe they should, but they haven't. They've been counting on striking it rich. I made them trade everything they owned for food. I've threatened people that they must work, or they won't eat. However, real rescue comes after many have starved and in the form of a ship with supplies every time. But the supply is short-lived because it always brings more people than food."

Emanuel nodded. "I'll do what I can. Sir Francis Bacon helped to draft Virginia's new charter, and I've got friends who are helping to supply his odd requests for his experiments in the prolongation of life. I imagine he's your best bet to get this under control."

Emanuel, as usual, was the crucial relationship builder on all fronts. Emanuel's extensive network of connections was expected at the event. Roger's father was included. At Uncle Emanuel's urging, Orrelia and her friends encouraged their families to attend with their children, for Emanuel promised the event would be memorable.

This was one of very few events attended by most of the Williams family (baby Katherine was left at home). Sydrach sat next to his father, James, and mimicked his posture and attitude exactly. Roger sat with Johannes as far from his father as possible. Robert sat on the other side of his mother.

John Smith had everyone's rapt attention for his outsize adventure stories.

Johannes and Roger sat with notepads out. They didn't intend to miss one word. John Smith started with tales from his early life, about running away after his father's death from the family farm, a feoffment. The feoffment was from Lord Willoughby's estate, and the estate had charter from the king. Feofees such as the Smiths paid fees to use this land and had rights to bequeath the property to their heirs. John Smith was thankful to have learned horsemanship skills on his father's feoffment but had no interest in tending it as his father's heir.

John Smith talked about going from runaway to indentured slave on a ship, only to be rescued when Perri Bertie, Lord Willoughby's second son, bought out his contract and freed him.

Then he launched into quite a tale of adventure—of traveling across France, getting robbed, winning sword fights, fighting wars where his horse was shot from under him, getting kidnapped by Turks and jumping overboard to swim to a desert island only to be rescued and to travel the Mediterranean. At one point his side lost the battle, and he remained among the many dead too long. He was kidnapped and enslaved by Turks and again escaped. Each of the boys was using the shorthand learned from Reverend Symon to record detailed notes. At the thirty-minute intermission they were approached by a tall, physically fit, well-dressed Sir Edward Coke, who politely asked that they each read back some of their notes for his amusement. And they did, a little awed by the rich man's stature and authority. Sir Edward watched and noted that the younger boy, Roger Williams, scribbled faster and read back more accurately. He gathered Roger's name and asked for an introduction to his parents, which Roger provided, though he didn't want to miss one second in which he might glimpse John Smith. He soon forgot the encounter.

The second half of the performance was about Virginia. There were stories of trading with the French and with the Algonquian Indians. Especially interesting to the boys was the story of how John placed his servant boys with the Algonquian in order to learn the language and act as liaisons.

John Smith's map-making skills were honed in his first encounter with Emanuel van Meteren, years back. At the time van Meteren was doing research for a book he was writing on the war John Smith was fighting. John learned from Emanuel that what you omit is as important as what you include. The lesson applied to more than maps. John's speech skipped over most of the controversial parts. There was no mention at all that he'd been sentenced to death for raiding in the Caribbean. The sentence was commuted when the sealed envelope was opened on landing, naming him a leader of the community. Interestingly, it was not until many years later that he spoke of the events that took place in 1607, in the tale of Pocohontas. Maybe they happened, but if they did, they were not deemed to be a help to his fund-raising cause at St. Sephulchre.

This speech was playing to the home crowd with every adventure put in its best light and nothing disturbing mentioned. Past and potential investors like Perri Bertie donned cleaned-up reputations, if they were mentioned at all. By prior arrangement, Emanuel's role as facilitator was kept private. Long afternoons drawing up careful maps did not quite make it into the story, nor did the scale of John's piracy. This was action-packed adventure with John Smith as hero from first scene to last.

The map on display told a separate story to Emanuel's practiced eye: John's skills were worth investment. The next venture would be funded.

Roger's father did not forget the encounter with Sir Edward Coke, for he'd been left Sir Coke's contact information and told to contact Sir Coke when Roger was older and ready to be apprenticed. Sir Coke was always on the outlook for talented clerks, and this offer was a huge opportunity, if a few years off. James Williams was less troubled from then on by his son Roger's lack of interest in the Merchant Taylor trade. From here on in, he would encourage the languages, the shorthand, the mysterious world his son seemed to have fallen into. He'd always planned to hand his own business to his eldest son, Sydrach, and now he had a plan to apprentice Roger. His gaze and focus of scrutiny would turn to mama's boy, Robert, who shuddered just then, though he did not know why.

John Smith's stories made it clear adventuring was hard work, needing both a sound body with which to battle nature and one's violent enemies and a quick mind to escape the complex political situations that inevitably followed a man of action. He who did not work hard, starved. The boys began to consider feats of strength from a whole new angle and to absorb how to create and maintain good physical condition to make their adventures possible. They did not figure they'd get training as cavalry like John Smith had. Were there really very many horses in America? They weren't sure. They began to notice political intrigue with a whole new eye. After all, if John Smith could escape so many times, so could they.

CHAPTER 3

New England AD 1612

The first snow was on the ground, and winter camp was a pleasant relief from the gathering of autumn. In the morning, the men returned with several deer and Oakana along with all the girls and women labored the afternoon to process the carcasses into venison. When the work was complete, they feasted. Oakana was eleven, with lean hard muscles and little fat to keep her warm. She curled up in furs near her mother and sisters listening to the twenty-eight-year-old brave named Yotan tell the tribe a story. Yotan, the sachem's eldest son, was in his element, telling a traditional tribal winter story to the people he hoped one day to lead as sachem.

"Rabbit was created with short ears and long legs, and a much longer nose than he has now. But he could not climb a tree. One day in winter rabbit was very hungry. He wanted to eat the growth he could see up high in the trees, but he couldn't reach it. He prayed and prayed for a way up that tree. Creator had pity on young rabbit, and that night it began to snow. For three days it snowed … and higher and higher the drift between the trees rose. Soon rabbit could tunnel up to the top of the snow and get into that tree. He ate his fill and fell fast asleep for the afternoon. The sun came out, and it was warm. Rabbit enjoyed the warm sunshine and his full belly and had many dreams. When evening descended, rabbit woke up. The snow was gone. He felt very precarious up in that tree and began to wobble. Rabbit fell out of the tree and began a long fall to earth. On the way down, branches caught his ears and stretched them long, and they slowed him a bit, saving his life. When he hit the earth, he broke his legs and smashed his nose. And that is why that rabbit looks the way he does even today."

Next up was the sachem's twelve-year-old nephew Miantonomoh. Miantonomoh was a tall and graceful athlete, dancing as he chanted. He told a story of the trip south they'd taken five years back, remembered through the telling of the story every year, first by his elders, and now by him. A good listener, he now felt as if he remembered every detail himself.

"We worked on our canoes all winter long, digging them out and making them seaworthy. As soon as the ice broke, we set out, our boats full of extra supplies from our magnificent harvest and hunting the prior fall and winter. We found so many towns to trade with that we passed most by, preferring to row as long as the weather held and get farther south than we ever had before. We passed four stretches of what felt like open ocean, but we could see the land come up to greet us; we were passing huge bays. Then we settled in to find people interested in our wares. We found not just Algonquian like ourselves, but also strange white people who had been adopted by this tribe. Those boys would buy anything and had steel knives and pots we much wanted to bring back. We brought a boatful of young women with us who were given to us by a Western tribe as tribute the year prior but who did not find good husbands in our tribe. We traded the women and their boat to this tribe so our journey back would be less arduous. We could not stay long; we wanted to ensure that we were back before the ice set in. When we left, the white boys tried to leave with us! We could not afford to take them, as they were not part of our negotiated treaty. They were ordered to return, and one did. The other we had to catch and return, to be executed in the most painful way so that all would remember the price of treachery. We then made our way back, stopping along the way to explore and trade metal pots and knives. Here is the knife I returned with. Feel its power."

At this, he went around letting the tribe examine his knife. When he got to Oakana, he watched her carefully while she ran her fingers along it. Miantonomoh was a high status brave, and Oakana's round eyes lingered as she admired him. Miantonomoh's brothers and cousins admired him too, and especially how Oakana, with her perfect complexion and well formed figure gazed into eyes. Miantonomoh had three younger brothers:

Weekan, Yotaash, and Cojonoquant. Yotaash's heart fell as he watched Oakana. He wished she looked at him that way.

Miantonomoh's cousins Yotan and Meiksah talked with Weekan and Cojonoquant long into the night, dreaming of a trip of their own. Meiksah wanted to head west this year, toward the Mohawk, where fur and wampum traded. Yotan wanted to repeat the trip south, a coastal trip to relatives that would have established European trade. As the argument went on it seemed likely the two would part ways, each to his desire. Weekan and Cojonoquant watched closely, as it would be up to them to choose whom to follow. In the end, it was Weekan and Cojonoquant that would be searching for wives. Yotan was happily married to Weko, and Meiksah was married to Magnus, Oakana's older sister, although he hoped to take additional wives that he would leave in the west. He turned to young Juanumo and whispered, "wives taken in the west can be left in the west, and a man with many wives has many towns with wigwams to sleep in when he travels. You must not repeat this to your sister Magnus, as it will not make her happy. You will want to plan this way yourself someday, if you like to travel," said Meiksah.

"The coastal women are more attractive," Yotan argued, "as clamming and agriculture make for fitter women. The inland women will still be preoccupied with making pottery, an endless muddy process that keeps them sedentary for long hours."

"That is all stories, and no one has gone far west for many years. We know what is south, including who our allies are. Miantonomoh went there already. To make new allegiances and explore new lands, including finding new women, we must go west," was Meiksah's stumbling answer.

Yotan won his followers in Weekan and Cojonoquant that night. Meiksah did not travel far the next season as a result. However, two eight-year-old boys, Miantonomoh's younger brother Yotaash and Oakana's brother Juanumo, listened closely to Meiksah and did not forget. Allegiances were more important than wives. Many wives could produce many allegiances. Someone needed to go west, but it did not seem like the older boys wanted to go. That message was reinforced when Meiksah did not even go west the next year.

London AD 1612

Thomas Helwys received no input from the king. He took the next step of publishing his work in England, calling the work "Short Declaration of the Mystery of Inequity."

King James had a history of pursuing the defense of the faith even with Dutchmen. He once demanded the resignation of an esteemed professor in Holland—an independent territory he did not own or control—because that professor denied the infinity of God. King James pursued the matter in letters to powers in Holland and had not ceased until the post was resigned. Thomas had been hoping for similar engagement from afar, but he had not gotten the attention of the king.

Holland was not a panacea. Thomas Helwys found his partner John Smythe to be recanting some of the most principled of their views about the baptism of believers being valid with the laying on of Christian hands, rather than the baptism being performed by a priest. Disgusted with Smythe and feeling guilty about leaving his family behind in England, given his wife's arrest, Thomas returned to England. Thomas Helwys began a new faith community in England that in the tradition of John the Baptist was dedicated to believer's baptism and voluntary worship—the first English Baptist church. This church was strictly illegal.

Because the relationship between individual and God was sacrosanct, no civil authority had jurisdiction over it, in Helwys's views. Thus the focus was on the individual's relationship with God, mimicking early Christian days when the faith was called the Way. This directly led to civil disobedience, given the king's belief that he and only he answered to God and that all subjects must answer to the king.

The Anglican Church had humble beginnings, given that it started by enabling Henry VIII to disobey clear edicts in scripture. King James aimed for higher ground. He was even sympathetically listening to the Puritans' insights as of 1603. He commissioned a fresh Bible translation because he believed God inspired the Puritan's complaints about the earlier versions of the Bible, which had margin notes not based in scripture. Work on that translation began in 1604.

King James had no shortage of heretics to contend with in England, however, and he differentiated carefully between theologies. He listened to the arguments of Bartholomew Legate in his own chambers and found them offensive, as Bartholomew denied that the three persons (God the father, Christ the son, and the Holy Spirit) were all one God. Then Legate sealed his fate when he admitted he had not prayed in seven years. In March 1612 Bartholomew Legate burned at the stake in Smithfield, and the burning was a public spectacle. The separatist community and the orthodox St. Sepulchre parishioners attended.

In April Edward Wightman was burned in Lichfield, and the spectacle was even more grisly, because Wightman recanted in the flames and had to be rescued. Edward and three rescuers suffered burns, and, to top it all off, within days Wightman began publicly speaking to large crowds repeating his heresies. Wightman was far more politically dangerous than the fringe heretic Legate, as he was a respected merchant and community leader. Yet his denial that Christ was God's incarnated son was clearly not in scripture. A few days later, the second burning was to the death, and it seemed that all England was talking about it. Had they in their apparent cruelty created a martyr who would attract followers, no matter how heretical his teaching?

The king read Thomas Helwys's "Short Declaration of the Mystery of Inequity" and asked two of his bishops to do so as well. He wanted help to determine whether a High Commission was in order. Bishop Richard Neile would sit on any High Commission that was called, and Bishop Lancelot Andrewes was overseeing the translation of the King James Bible. With them this evening was Robert Carr, King James's court favorite and confidant, acting as secretary.

"This Helwys is not like the last two we burned. He does not deny God; he clearly believes in the trinity, and he not only prays, but it is reported that he leads others in a prayerful church service, though an illegal one. He won't use the Book of Common Prayer, preferring individually inspired words. He would undermine God's appointed authorities—myself and yourselves," King James pointed out. "Still, he makes some good points about persecution and conscience. We cannot deny them; men's consciences are why we are translating the Bible in the first place."

The men nodded. Neither of them liked to contradict this king, but they were appalled. Helwys certainly believed in eliminating their priestly authority over what the laity was allowed to believe. Bishop Neile spoke up first, saying, "I don't believe you can allow God's appointed king to have his power limited to civil matters, as he suggests. The church needs a single leader."

King James bristled. "A single leader? The church needs inspired leaders, godly leaders. We'll not be going back to popery. Moreover, this Helwys fellow has only argued for supremacy of God over the king, which is not quite as offensive as this Sir Edward Coke fellow, who would have the law supreme over a king. These men both have a point; they are just naïve about the politics of men. After all, I believe in God supreme; I am just concerned that my subjects are loyal to me. If God speaks through groups of laity instead of through my authority, that isn't ideal. However, he has surely done it before. He did it with shepherds in a field, as I recall. Didn't tell King Herod a thing. I want to be like King David, not King Herod."

Bishop Andrewes maneuvered next. "Helwys has also disempowered church leadership with his conscience argument. All through the Bible, both the king and the church leaders represent God's authority. Consider the early church. Roman kings were to be respected, and the apostles were to be obeyed, in some cases under penalty of death. If the king is not a Christian, then limiting his authority to civil matters seems scripture-based, but when the king is a Christian, he is more like Peter. He must be obeyed."

"Yes, he must," agreed the king. Theological issues aside, there were practical matters to consider. "Still, he has a point on the persecution issue. I do not perceive your last burning to have served us well." This was aimed at the bishops, for it was bishops who sat on the consistory court responsible for assigning a burning as a punishment. "This burning riled up the people, as this man was more popular than you knew. You have created a martyr, but not one for God's good cause. I propose we cease all burning at the stake for religious heresy and leave them to rot quietly in Newgate, invisible if not unmolested."

That is what they quietly proceeded to do. No High Commission was called. No consistory court would be held. The sentence of indefinite imprisonment honored some of the spirit of Helwys's request, increased the strength of the king's rule, and silenced heresy all with one clever move. *Perhaps the role model should have been King Solomon, not King David,* he mused. *It was less bloody.*

Thomas Helwys could not know the discussion was over, and he continued to hope for an audience at court. The response came soon enough, but without discussion. He landed in Newgate.

Newgate AD 1612

Back at Newgate, Hendric was both in misery and in a trance so complete he did not know of his misery. After he drank his milk, he could always smell the rotten putrid ugliness of Newgate afresh. Beyond that, he was in pain. The welts on his back were swollen and infected, and he had a fever. The clanging of the chains echoed in his ears but did not reach his brain. It was a supernatural will that enabled him to concentrate as he wrote letter by letter, word by word, on the cover of his milk can. On a good day he now fit a paragraph. Usually he was content with a sentence. His need to cover up his writing was the cause of his beating last week—he kept at it a moment too long. The guard thought he was being unresponsive. That was good—the truth was worse. The writing on the milk can tops was not discovered, and Hendric's writing went on.

In prison you know nothing. Hendric had no support, no friends but the stopper on the milk can. Hendric hoped beyond hope that the woman who came to collect the milk cans was delivering them to a place where the tops could still be deciphered, but he wasn't sure. He wrote on.

Hendric studied the Bible as a Dutch boy at Austin Friar school. The translation was new and fresh, and the Bible was pored over and memorized as the subversive text that it really is. Good that it was memorized, for he surely did not have one now. The story of the weeds and the wheat, all left together till the harvest ... the story of the blind leading the blind into a ditch, and then Luke's story of Jesus chastising the disciples for wanting to cause harm.

Maybe if he'd been able to turn his other cheek he wouldn't have been here at all. But then he hadn't really hit the boy hard; it was the letter that got him here.

The guards were the ongoing challenge. For inmates with no money, the guards were very evil. He tried to live by 2 Timothy 2, which told him to be kind even to the most evil guard.

In Newgate with no money of any kind the days went very, very slowly. And the nights were even longer.

There was never any answer. Day after day the writing became more serious and complex ... and his hope that someone was reading grew.

The Dutch woman who brought the milk cans was taking them out of the prison and dropping them at a pickup point. The boy who came to carry the cans off to be washed and refilled replaced the cans tops daily, taking the dirty can tops that looked a little dirtier than most and replacing them with the prior day's can tops.

London, AD 1613

When nineteen-year-old Henry Spelman decided to return to England for his first visit home, John Smith arranged a letter of introduction to Emanuel van Meteren. He knew that, in his role of Dutch consul, Emanuel would be pleased to introduce the young man to his Dutch merchant connections.

Henry arrived in London at Emanuel's estate, letter in hand, and knocked at the door. A servant answered, "May I help you?"

"Yes, thanks. I'd like an appointment with Mr. Emanuel Van Meteren. Here is my letter of introduction." The servant took the letter and disappeared into the interior.

A few minutes later a gracious if sad woman, tall and emaciated, came to the door. "My name is Orrelia. Emanuel was my brother. He died last year, but I know he would like us to guide you on your way. How may I help you?"

Henry's story spilled out.

Remembering Hendric and knowing of Reverend Symon's love of languages, Orrelia remembered the Austin Friar school and arranged for Henry Spelman to speak to the boys.

Roger and Johannes were excited. They rushed through their studies and were at the ready to copy down every word uttered by Henry Spelman in their unique shorthand. Henry spoke of his life with the Algonquian since the age of fourteen, conveying his knowledge of their language and civil customs.

Henry was in his element. He knew the Algonquian, and he missed his own English adolescence. He stayed with the boys as long as he possibly could, lecturing and answering all their questions.

Henry told the story of Dutchman Sam.

"Dutchman Sam and I were apprenticed to the Algonquians. Sam didn't like it there at all. He convinced me to escape with him. When another tribe arrived we tried to join them as they left. The Algonquians didn't see it that way. We were not a part of the tribute or the gifts of the negotiations between the tribes. The tribe believed they had been double-crossed. I immediately returned to my own tribe and fell at the leader's feet asking forgiveness. I survived by returning to loyal service. The tribe's leader, called a sachem, sent a messenger to demand Sam return as well.

He refused. The visiting tribe handed him over as a prisoner and he was executed for his refusal to submit to both tribe's demands."

Henry impressed on the boys several key concepts during this talk. To Henry, the Algonquian were family now. They were clearly human, with human ethics, feelings, and a system of honor, though it was different from the English system. Henry described a culture without money, where land and other assets are communally owned. He taught them of family life, moving from summer home to winter home, and of men's role as hunters and warriors, and women's role in agriculture. Each gender had its own domain, and while no woman was a warrior, no man was clan head in camp. He talked of how there was not an Algonquian king, but rather a sachem chosen from among the people. The sachem did not inherit a throne but earned it. Like a king, the sachem had relations with neighboring leaders. Unlike a king, the sachem had responsibilities to a broad confederacy of sachems. Use of territory was divided and boundaries understood. Delegations visited back and forth. This was no uncivilized people.

Henry explained "When the Algonquian fight each other, there is often a brief, intense battle and then one side quickly concedes. Women and children are captured and inducted into the winning tribe, while men who do not concede honorably are tortured or killed. John Smith may have thought he was arranging an apprenticeship in return for supplies but in fact he was conceding defeat to the Algonquian and enabling them to adopt Dutchman Sam and me into the tribe. All of John Smith's supplies over the years were considered gifts to assure future alliance. This practice explained my treatment, as I was initially treated as a child prisoner and not as a man. After his escape, Dutchman Sam did not concede honorably when overpowered, and that was why he was tortured to the death."

The Algonquian language Henry Spelman introduced to the boys was one of many dialects on the eastern seaboard. It was an oral tradition language and included pitch, articulation, laughter, song, and chant rhythm. He gave them examples of each and explained some common expressions.

The boys were spellbound. If John Smith left the boys with a taste for adventure, Henry Spelman left them with a calling to learn to know the natives as a people. If John Smith taught them to be proactive and brave, Henry Spelman taught them to watch and learn how events would be understood and only then to choose their actions.

"How did you get as fit as an Indian?" asked a frail city kid.

Henry answered, "We run and climb trees and hunt and fish all day every day. We fight, we train on bow and arrow, and we row in boats. We eat very little, and what we eat tastes awful to an English boy. You get used to it, though."

"How did you finally get away from the Indians and back to England?"

"In 1610 an English captain came. He thought he bought my services from the Indians, but I was free to go as a full member of the tribe by then. I let him concede defeat with his supplies and then chose to join him. He used me as an interpreter, and I grew back into English culture from there, as I helped to trade copper for corn. I am not sure I am really 'back' from the Algonquian. I will surely return to them!"

"And what of God?" the boys asked Henry. "What did the Algonquian think of God?" Henry didn't have a good answer for that one. No one worried about God and Algonquian in his presence. It was all trade and politics and civil affairs. Henry wasn't even sure what he thought of God himself. The boys explained their Bible translation projects and how Henry too could read it. Henry wasn't sure he wanted to read a Bible, but he listened. They told of how he could have his own relationship with God. Henry had a headache at the end of this and was relieved to go back to his simpler existence interpreting more concretely visible topics.

Newgate, AD 1613

Hendric had been confined to Newgate for five years when the tall, clearly wealthy Thomas Helwys showed up and was assigned a cell nearby. Helwys was originally from London, and was well known as a leader in the Separatist faction of the church. Hendric knew of him from the Austin Friar days. Thomas's wife Joan and seven children had been among those in the meeting Hendric failed to reach. The two quickly found they could whisper through rat holes in their cells and have conversations to their hearts' content.

Thomas was coming to understanding in these conversations. "So you mean to say you were carrying a letter to Orrelia's that contained a private message for a Joan that was from Austin Friar in the late fall 1608? That would have been my letter for my wife! Oh no, how could I have left them here in London? How could I have written the letter that got her arrested? This makes it doubly troubling that I was away for so long." His guilt and shame over leaving his wife behind when he'd gone to the Netherlands hit him anew. But he realized almost immediately that Hendric was paying a terrible price for that letter. "Forgive me."

Hendric replied, "I forgave you long ago."

Thomas thought aloud. "So Joan was put on trial as a consequence of your capture. I wonder if it was my publication of the letter to the king or the illegal Baptist church I planted or my publications and letters while in the Netherlands or the authorities' rancor with Joan for having pleaded her belly to evade her sentence that got the magistrates to my door. I think we'll give you the code name HH, and I'll tell Joan to tell your mom. Maybe that will comfort our families a bit." Thomas could occasionally communicate to the outside because he could afford to bribe the guards.

Some in Thomas's church claimed it was a suicide mission in the first place to send the letter to the king. His risks were calculated. However, he had not counted on kin and friends being so caught up in the dragnet.

Whatever the cause of Thomas's imprisonment, it was an answer to Hendric's prayers. Here at last was a friend, a fellow believer, someone to talk to. Here at last was news of his distant family from the outside world.

A few weeks into Thomas Helwys's imprisonment, a visitor opened his cell door and quietly entered. "Gervase! What on earth … how in God's name have you got here in this uniform. Are you come with good news?"

Gervase replied, "God has had some tiny mercy on you I think, though the king will not let you go. You know he knighted me ten years back, and I've been a merchant, alderman, and sheriff since. Henry Howard, First Earl of Northampton, recommended me for this post. What motives he had, I am not yet certain. Our whole family helped raise the money to pay for it, Joan especially." Gervase had eight children to support, and a gambling habit. Gervase would not have had any funds to apply.

"So here I am, Lieutenant of the Tower of London for life! I am taking over your custody, Thomas, and you have just become a most eminent prisoner, my cousin."

Thomas replied, "Thanks be to God for this mercy. Gervase, my dear cousin, this is good fortune. Give Joan and all the children my love. Oh, how I miss them."

After a pause, Thomas continued. "Listen, Gervase. In the next cell is a fellow HH. He was carrying my message to Joan when he was arrested. Can you take him under your wing as well? I am sure Joan will compensate you for all your care."

"Certainly, Thomas, whatever you need. I will treat the boy as your son."

Gervase departed from Thomas and went to visit HH.

"Hello, son. Mr. Helwys has sent me to you and asked me to help. You are going to be moved to some nicer quarters today."

Life was immediately transformed for the two. They were moved to an apartment for eminent prisoners and could now get more frequent messages to Joan and the children and through Joan even to Hendric's mum Orrelia. She finally knew he was alive, and Joan and Orrelia became fast friends.

Better yet, money and connections made the chains disappear.

Money and connections provided better food.

Money and connections eliminated beatings.

Thomas and HH prayed together openly now. They celebrated God's glory and power. They knew they were tiny parts in a much bigger plan, and they sought to pray for that larger plan that their small parts might mean something for all time. They prayed for Joan and the children; they prayed for Hendric's mother, Orrelia; they prayed for Thomas's Dutch friends and for the audience that would read their writings—published on a press and published on a milk can top. They prayed for all the Strangers. And they sang. Some nights the Tower seemed to light up from their singing and joyous prayer. Hendric was a happier young man, and he and Thomas could not be contained.

Thomas shared with Hendric some of his own writings, and Hendric grew so excited about the scriptural basis for allowing worship according to conscience and for outlawing persecution, that he began to copy the writings, with Thomas's help, to his milk can caps, hoping the Austin Friar school would catch on and spread the fire of the Way throughout England. Gervase continued the delivery of can tops at HH's request, though he thought it a bit odd.

Thomas reminded Hendric when he was down that "Jesus spoke his conscience, and no authorities approved. John the Baptist sat in a prison much like the one we were in before."

Gervase was now keeper for all eminent, well-to-do prisoners. In one apartment Thomas lived with Hendric. In another, Sir Walter Raleigh was imprisoned since 1603 for his attempt against King James's life. King James did not want to have Raleigh executed, as exploration brought in assets that the crown purse sorely needed. Raleigh was stored away, but his claim to know where gold lay in the Americas was not forgotten.

Another prisoner Gervase took care of was Thomas Overbury. Thomas was at one time a good friend and advisor to Robert Carr, King James's court favorite. However, Overbury angered Carr's girl, Frances Howard, by actively campaigning against the match because she was married to someone else. To silence and punish him, in April of 1613 Overbury was put in the Tower of London while the two married. Over time Gervase realized that the Howard family was out to get Overbury. He took to changing out Thomas's food and watching over everything that went in and out of Thomas's cell. Then one day in September of 1613, while Gervase was called to court, Overbury was found dead of poisoning. Gervase knew he would be a suspect. He worried about what would happen next, and he watched his boss, the constable, with new fear.

CHAPTER 4

London, AD 1615

The boys were warming themselves by passing time around the fire. The days were short, and it was bitter cold and dark out. Johannes's father, Abraham, was in a good mood, so the boys coaxed a story from the schoolmaster. "Tell us a soldier story," they demanded.

"I've got a good one. Do you want to know how men in the northern countries travel as fast as cavalry in deep snow?"

"Yes, yes," the boys said simultaneously.

"Danish historian Saxo Grammaticus was the first to tell the story. He tells of battles against the Norwegians hundreds of years ago. The Danish soldiers had infantry and cavalry, but the snow is so deep all they can do is flounder about. Suddenly, over a hill, there are soldiers gliding toward them.

"At first the soldiers can't believe it. The gliding soldiers soon catch them, and there is a pitched battle. Afterward, the Danes looked carefully at what the Norwegians had on their feet, and this is what they found.

"Each man had long, flattened sticks tied to his feet. On the left was one as long as the man was tall. On the right the sticks were much shorter and wider. On the front of the left stick there was a curve up like the bow of a ship, which came up to fine point. The officers often had the figure of a God carved into that point. On the left stick, there was a wide bar in the back, for kicking off against the snow. Each stick was covered in leather and greased with animal fat.

"The men pushed with the right foot and glided with the left. They were very fast. When they retreated, no one, at first not even the horses, could catch them. Then we came to a rise in the land. Suddenly they were much slower.

"Up close, though, the skis cannot turn quickly, and the men are vulnerable unless they take them off, and they are vulnerable while they are detaching them. When the Danes could catch them, the Norwegians had to surrender. The victory was to the Danes!"

"Have you ever seen these feet sticks?" asked Roger, dubiously.

"No, but I hear there is a store of them for the Danish army for when we fight on snow, even to this day."

London, AD 1615

Gervase was a bitterly angry and sour man. He felt like a victim of Frances Howard; he felt his wife and children wanted to pick over his carcass for money; he felt despised by his boss; and he felt that, with his important title and successful merchant trade, he was entitled to some good times. Most weeknights Gervase did not go home but rather to the gambling house. He liked the games, he liked the drink, and he liked the young girls. He could take one up to a private room and have his good times with no questions asked, and no children to care for.

Tonight the girl was Lynn. She was a pretty, young, blonde thing, recently a house servant to a large estate. Like many servants, her master took advantage of her whenever he felt the urge. She'd gotten pregnant and been released. No decent household observing her condition would hire her, and the only career left to her now seemed to be hiring out her own body. In September, the French ambassador and his servants came to the inn, celebrating a recent audience with King James. She was well then, and they paid handsomely for her services. Like most girls in her line of work, she was soon sick. Most girls got syphilis, the big pox. Lynn's sickness was different. For several days she'd felt flu-like symptoms and was unable to work. Then she felt better but was left with a rash. She covered it over with low light and distraction and went about her business. The rash did not show in candlelight, and she needed the money. The rash slowly formed pustules like small pellets under her skin. She told the men it was a new sex style and encouraged them to touch them if they noticed. Gervase didn't notice anything but her soft breasts, her blonde hair, and her open legs. Lynn was suffering from smallpox, a recurring French import. It was contagious, and she passed it on to Gervase. Soon after, she would succumb to the disease, as this form of it was unusually deadly.

The Tower of London, AD 1615

Three weeks later, Gervase entered Thomas's apartment. His skin looked pale, his eyes wild, and he took Thomas to the side. "I'm worried, Thomas, really worried. This fellow Thomas Overbury was imprisoned here just before I was appointed to this position. From the beginning it seemed bad for him. He was involved in all kinds of court intrigue, and my mentor and appointer Henry Howard expected me to play along with their family's schemes. I took to checking on, and replacing, his food, for fear of poison. I fear I've been set up, for in September when I had to be in court, he was indeed found dead. Now they are getting ready to cast blame for his death, and they are pointing at me."

Thomas said, "I don't understand. You were at court. You are innocent! Justice will see you are cleared."

"No, I fear not, Thomas. I've racked up horrible gambling debt, some of it to the Howards. They are out to save their own souls, and they are earls. You do not imagine the vastness of the demands. They do not care about guilt or innocence. They care about clearing the earl's good name."

"We must pray then, Gervase." They gathered HH, and the three men locked hands and prayed:

"Lord, Gervase has been such a blessing in this foul place. Help him now to escape the intrigues of this court. Keep us all in your service, Lord. We know we are a part of your plan, and we ask you to keep us strong. We pray for a way out of this place, to be able to promote your

Will effectively. If there is no way out, conclude our lives quickly, Lord, and end our suffering in this miserable world. Have mercy on us. In Jesus's name, Amen."

The men hugged, and Gervase departed.

About four days later, Thomas and Hendric felt ill, whether with foreboding, stress, or the flu they were not certain.

Gervase especially resented Sir Walter Raleigh. This guy had an ego that would not stop, and he treated Gervase like a servant. He sat around writing poetry and looked to Gervase like every other player in the intrigues at court. Ever since Overbury's death, Gervase took special care around Sir Walter Raleigh, as many in the court hated Sir Raleigh as well. As Gervase began to watch more closely, and as it became clear that Gervase himself was the fall guy for those who killed Overbury, he came to resent the wealth and influence Sir Walter Raleigh represented. Today, though, Gervase was especially angry. Sir Raleigh was particularly nasty to him over a trivial matter of the temperature of his food, and Gervase spit in his next meal as an invisible, silent protest. Though the potency of his spit was unknown to Gervase, there is no better way to spread smallpox than through bodily fluids. Within the month, Sir Walter was ill.

Gervase was publicly executed in November 20, 1615 for the murder of Thomas Overbury. The entire administration of King James was embarrassed by this scandal. Helwys lost all protection. So did Hendric.

London, AD 1616

Joan and Orrelia met at Joan's estate. They often quilted together now. It was hard to bear outside company that did not share their private miseries.

"This is most awful news. I fear we will never hear from the men again. For it was Gervase who brought me all the news," said Joan.

"I spent years like this, not knowing whether Hendric was alive or dead. This is a return to that life of uncertainty. All we have is our prayers to help us bear it and our other children to keep us busy," replied Orrelia. "At least now we know of the milk can tops. I can ask Alice to check in on Roger to see whether his letters are coming still. That is a great mercy."

"I worry that the king's court is not finished. Thomas is Gervase's cousin, —don't forget. I don't think we will be untarnished by this awful scourge," said Joan.

Orrelia pondered this a while as they quilted. "It may be. And yet the king has many matters to attend to. The Overbury affair was two years old. And never forget they set up Gervase. They know they set up Gervase. Why should they come after you or your kin?"

"I hope you are right. I want my children to stay far away from matters involving court or fame, so we can live our lives quietly. Thomas would not think that is the right thing to do, but I feel we've had all the sorrow one family can bear during his long imprisonment," said Joan.

Newgate, AD 1616

In November, Thomas disappeared one night. Hendric was moved back to his cell in Newgate. The beatings became especially intense. Hendric once again had no support and no friend except the stopper on the milk can. Hendric hoped beyond hope that the woman who came to collect the milk cans would be Miriam, and sometimes to his feverish mind it seemed to be. He wrote on.

In Newgate, with no money of any kind, the days are long. And then the nights are longer. Somehow no money after protection is even worse than never having had money at all. The guards intimated that Thomas was dead; Hendric didn't know whether that was a scare tactic or a cover-up. He'd hoped Thomas's cousin could spring them both out of Newgate, but now the guards implied that Gervase was executed. While he hoped Thomas was on the outside, Hendric feared the worst.

Now Hendric wrote on with compulsion. It was his life. It was all he thought about. He hoped that his words would mean something somewhere to someone, but he wasn't sure to whom. As in the Tower, he signed his writing HH. With his family and schoolmates unable to write back to him, he felt utterly alone. Maybe he just imagined that someone was still taking care to decipher them. Maybe she just looked like the schoolmaster's wife. Hendric despaired. The last set of beatings left him with a fever and vomiting, and his whole body was festering with rashes and blisters.

When he was done writing, he lay down for the last time. The fever consumed him, and he lost consciousness. In the morning he was carried out, never to smell the harsh odors of Newgate again.

No one was notified, and the milk cans still came and went, and Miriam still collected them. The boys wondered about Hendric and waited for a new letter or chapter. Months went by and only silence. And then they suspected, but they could not know.

London, AD 1616

Shortly after Hendric's death of fever, in March 1616, Sir Walter Raleigh was released from the Tower. In Sir Walter's case, his rash was slow in developing. The blisters were largely hidden by his facial hair, which he now kept long. He claimed his welts were the result of his mistreatment during imprisonment, but in truth he still had scabs that seemed to take forever to heal. He was released from Newgate on the king's orders so that he could lead an expedition to Venezuela looking for gold, and he got right to it. King James was not getting the appropriations of funds that he was requesting from the Parliament, and he was desperate for cash. Robert Carr had confiscated a seaworthy vessel from some merchants, and the king decided that Sir Walter Raleigh was the man to set sail in the ship to search of gold.

Within the month, Sir Walter Raleigh took to the seas with a crew that included his son, Watt Raleigh. Everyone thought he was crazy with gold fever, but his real distress was his continuing case of smallpox. His continual exertions slowed his recovery. The voyage was made in pleasant weather, and transmission of smallpox occurred steadily but slowly during the warmer weather. He transmitted the disease to most of his ship. The winds whisked them rapidly to Cape Cod inside of two months, far north of where they wanted to explore. After all those years in prison, Sir Walter Raleigh and his son Watt felt ready for fun. They were not particularly loyal to King James and did not have hard work invested in the trip. The captain, his son, and the crew raped and plundered the villages around Cape Cod with abandon through the summer and autumn of 1616, taking advantage of the relative isolation of the women in the fields at harvest and acting like pirates. They hid the identity of the ship and kept no records. They had no care for relationships with these tribes, as long as they escaped with their lives. They had no plan to return to Cape Cod. From Cape Cod, Sir Walter made a straight course for Trinidad, just off the coast of Venezuela.

By the end of October 1616, many women whose summer camp was on the shore of Cape Cod fell ill with fever. As they appeared to recover and then formed rashes, their men were coming in from fishing and hunting expeditions, and that started a new round of infection. The disease spread through the Cape Cod region in its most potent form. As winter sets in, relationships are closer for the Algonquian. People gather for warmth and move to the closer quarters of winter camp. They have time to visit neighboring tribes for trade. The smallpox virus thrives because people feel fairly well during the contagious rash stage. After being isolated with the flu-like onset, they are ready to visit. In the Algonquian population, a much higher percentage eventually hemorrhaged and died from the disease, especially the young. Around Cape Cod whole tribes disappeared. The men away on hunting expedition when the disease was most infectious at home, upon returning and finding their homes devastated, scattered naturally to surrounding tribes where they had kin. The cycle would then repeat while the men were in the two-to-three-week incubation period, unaware of their illness, so each scattering produced new infections. The men returning home only had to get within ten feet of a contagious victim to be infected. And if they so much as kissed their wives or hugged their sick children, they were sure to be infected.

When Sir Walter Raleigh got to Trinidad, he was so weak that he stayed on the ship, ordering his crew, including his son, into town. In town a vicious fight ensued, and in their poor health the crew was no match for vigorous natives. As a result they lost the battle and did not take the town. Watt was fatally shot. When his crew returned, Sir Walter was viciously angry with them for losing his son, and at least one died as a result of the treatment they received at Sir Walter's hands. Back in England, Sir Walter would say the death was a suicide.

CHAPTER 5

London, AD 1617

"Roger, come sit down. I've got news for you." It was his father. All Roger's hairs stood on end. It could not be good news. "I've gotten you a position." Now Roger was horrified. Visions of merchant burdens flashed through his fifteen-year-old mind … but his father went on. "Lord Coke needs a scribe. He noticed you taking notes in St. Sepulchre on Sundays and when Captain John Smith was here, and he asked about your language training. You'll be living with him now in his office and doing his duties. You'll learn his ways. Maybe your languages will be your salvation, but you must work much harder than you ever did here. If you fail, it is the merchant business for you for sure. I know you think I want you to do work you hate. I don't. Go and make something of yourself, boy." Roger's father withdrew quickly, if gruffly. He was losing the chief translator for his clients, but he knew that only Sydrach would inherit the business, and these other boys needed to be apprenticed to learn to make their own way.

Roger was stunned. His life cavorting with Johannes would be over. His fun was at an end. Who wanted to be a lawyer? He didn't want to work. He wanted to have adventures and to explore. He cried himself to sleep that night and too soon, in the wee hours, his mother came for him, for he had to report for duty at 4:00 a.m.

"Roger, you are spoiled. You must learn to be thankful for what you have received. This may seem like a lot of work, but this is your ticket out of this neighborhood, onto the whole world's stage. Don't let it pass you by! I love you, and you will always be my little boy. Now go and give your new master all he is due," said his mum, Alice.

Roger Williams was deposited at 4:00 a.m. at his new home, as planned. He had his bundle of belongings, including his small Dutch Bible, his HH writings, and new clothes. Roger might not have appreciated his father's cloth merchant business, but his father and mother had been preparing for this moment since 1610 and ensured that Roger had plenty of fine clothes to wear to court. Sir Edward Coke's London quarters were cramped, with no plans for this new addition. Roger would sleep on a straw bed in the servant's quarters at first while in London, and his clothes would be his finest possession. Roger would look the young gentleman, though smaller and more boyish than the rest.

Coke had been preparing for this moment since 1609, when he purchased the Neals estate on the shore of the county Norfolk. He was three years into a position as chief justice when he decided to spend the rest of his life defending the principle of the rule of law—specifically that the king was both protected by the law and subject to the law. This was a high-risk position, and Neals was a place to be away from London's watching eyes and the busy court during times when Coke needed to be forgotten. In 1610 he discovered Austin Friar student shorthand as written at lectures by Roger and Johannes. That shorthand provided the inspiration to make a provisional plan for a way to attend court remotely. When he was moved to the King's Bench in 1613, a move plotted by his archrival Francis Bacon, he recognized the increased risk and pursued a second piece of his plan. He got himself appointed in 1614 as High Steward of Cambridge. Coke then organized the purchase of two seats for Cambridge's chosen representative at all parliamentary proceedings, and he would have the right to determine one of the two. Now, with Coke's dismissal last November and his suspension from attendance at Privy Court, Roger Williams's real job was to be Cambridge's representative at Privy Court.

Roger attended his first session at court the next day. Coke's carriage took him, Coke's Cambridge credentials got him entry, and there he was at age fifteen surrounded by young university men in their twenties scribbling words he had never heard before in furious shorthand. His language skills served him well, and even when he did not understand, his notes were accurate transliterations. Coke would explain the terms one by one. Coke had time on his hands, and no investment could serve his future career better. After a week, Coke realized his plan was working flawlessly. Roger was a perfect match for the job.

There was nothing unusual in being apprenticed at Roger's age to a wealthy family some distance from his middle-class home, especially given that he was not the oldest son and would not inherit his father's Merchant Taylor Guild membership or the family business. There was nothing unusual in Roger's living in the Coke household and being under Coke's care. There was a great deal unusual in a fifteen-year-old being at Privy Court. There was a great deal unusual in Roger's shorthand compared to the skills of the other boys.

Sir Edward Coke was an unusually wealthy and principled man involved in a long-term political battle he intended to win. Roger Williams found himself on the front line.

New England, AD 1617

Yotan was bulky and reticent as a thirty-four-year-old, no longer a serious contender for leadership among his peers of the tribe. He was more comfortable with children, and Weekan and Cojonoquant still followed his every word. He was growing unbearably restless as spring approached. He longed to travel and proposed a major trade exploration south. Canonicus was finally supportive, as it was time for Weekan, now fourteen years old, and Cojonoquant, now twelve years old, to explore and find wives. Yotan took the boys in his canoe, which was filled with goods, and set out, in early spring, heading east, as soon as the ice in the streams broke up.

At first they were rowing hard to stay warm and eating dense cakes made of corn and nuts, supplementing this with onions they gathered from the land. They were paddling off the shore of Cape Cod for four days when they stopped, hoping to visit their Wampanoag relatives. The tribes often intermarried, and the boys wanted to look over the young women in these tribes. Traditionally men often adopted the tribes of their women, unless they were leaders. None of the younger boys was an eldest son, and all hoped to extend the power of the Narragansett by marrying well and establishing kin ties for their tribe. Yotan was sent with the express assignment of arranging a future for the boys. Yotan intended to go home by winter to tend his own wife, Weko, and their children.

When they reached the south shore near Pocasset, south of Cape Cod, they beached the canoe and traveled inland. Cojonoquant was the first to speak. "It looks like they have not yet made summer camp on the shore. I see the signs of past camps, but all is abandoned! What is the story here?"

"Do you suppose they might have moved camp? Let's camp here and see if we can see signs of habitation in the area," replied Yotan. They camped and fished but saw no signs of anyone.

"How about we go up to winter camp and see what's there?" asked Weekan.

"Yes, something is exceedingly odd here," replied Yotan. "Let's follow the old trail."

Two days later they made the traditional camp of the Wampanoag, inland about fifteen miles. Here they found misery. The few women in camp were nursing the sick and were sick themselves. There were bodies piled up that they had not yet burned. There were signs of many prior burnings. The beautiful women whom the boys hoped to find were covered with scars, and many were bleeding from the nose.

"Help us!" they cried. "Help us burn our dead and leave this place." Yotan and the boys covered themselves and started to burn. Unfortunately, smallpox transmits through the air as well as through fluids. As careful as the boys were, Cojonoquant was exposed. Over the next three days they cleaned camp and moved the remaining people to a summer camp up on Cape Cod so that they could fish. They left the survivors with some of their own food, seeing as how the survivors were not in good shape and needed to get stronger.

As quickly as they could without being irresponsible, they hiked back through winter camp and down to Pocasset, returning to their canoe. They set off for the south, still disturbed.

It was two days later when Cojonoquant felt like he had the flu. Rowing became a torture, and he could not hold down his food. He was able to hide his condition for a day or two, but by day three he was in real trouble. Yotan was concerned, but he remembered the destruction he had seen. He did not want to go back home, where he had his own wife, Weko, and his children. He set course south, and the boys rowed to Long Island over the next week. By the time they made shore, Cojonoquant felt better and had a rash. The others did not touch him, but they did care for him. They camped near what is today New Haven, Connecticut, and the Quinnipiac soon found them. They consulted the sachem and the medicine priest in the tribe, but this disease was new. Yotan kept the boys far from camp, but the tribe was infected via airborne transmission from the boys and men who visited them. The Quinnipiac gave them instructions on how to cross the bay without encountering any kin, happy to send them away.

Early in the morning Yotan and the boys set off across the sound. They knocked out the thirty miles that day, arriving late at night in unknown territory, even though Cojonoquant was no longer rowing.

Later that evening, all were suffering from the day's exposure to sun. Cojonoquant began to hemorrhage. Now Yotan knew for sure that they were in real trouble. He did not seek out his distant kin among the Montauk, but the Montauk braves found him. As much as they needed to stay away, Yotan and Weekan were starved for company and were unaware of airborne transmission mechanics, and they spent the evening with the braves, trading stories. Cojonoquant was very ill, but he slowly began to recover. Yotan kept the party stationary to encourage Cojonoquant's recovery. He would never look the same, as he was heavily scarred. He no longer had the will to go on and wanted to return home. Yotan kept him until he was strong enough to walk and then sent him home.

Cojonoquant fished and searched for clams and slowly made his way home. He was much weakened and feared that he was too scarred, that he would lose respect in the tribe. When a local woman with equally low status provided comfort, he lived with her tribe. Soon he was drinking her rum. He stayed with her tribe for a few seasons, though he was not well liked.

From Long Island Yotan and Weekan made their way down the Jersey shore. Both had flu-like symptoms. Leni Lenape braves found them on the shore, sleeping in the sun. They did not share enough language commonality to make the braves understand quickly enough the importance of staying away. Days melded into weeks, and both of them got a rash as they made their way slowly down the New Jersey shore. It was midsummer now, and transmission of the virus was slower. They were bleeding, though, and stayed away from humans. They realized that they might not get home again.

After a wretched night of coughing up blood, Weekan died early in the morning. The sun was shining, and he was in Yotan's arms. Yotan felt he couldn't bear to go home and face his kin. He crossed the Chesapeake alone, slowly regaining strength. He camped alone. Eventually, when he believed he was well, he approached the Nanticoke, offered to support a woman, and was accepted as a husband. He settled down for the winter to learn the language. The Nanticoke were the tidewater people of the Chesapeake, and they were allied to the Powhatan of Virginia.

If Roger's life changed in 1617, the average Algonquian's life changed even more. Smallpox continued to ravage the East Coast of America for two more years. Families were disrupted, social structure was destroyed, and people became desperate, isolated nomads, fearful of interfamily contact that might spread disease. Indigenous American culture post-1617 contained a mere shadow of the prior organization.

Deer, small mammals, birds, and other game felt the impact of reduced predation. They multiplied greatly, and food became more available to the new settlers and the remaining Algonquian alike. There were not enough new settlers to balance the population, so certain species became overabundant. Wolf, eagle, and panther populations grew in response. The American coast changed from a tame garden controlled by periodic intentional burns to an overgrown, out-of-balance wilderness.

From here on out, when settlers encountered unknown Algonquian, they were more likely to be killed, including women and children and dogs. There was a deep anger in the Algonquian community, and raids on settlers for food expressed their collective rage. The settlers retaliated, and proactive self-defense became more common.

In contrast, when settlers encountered Algonquian they knew, especially Algonquian women and children without a man, they were more likely to be available for hire as servants. These individuals were on their way to assimilating into English/American culture.

The Wampanoag were driven to immediate offers of partnership with the English. Other coastal communities disappeared completely.

From Canonicus's point of view, his eldest son Yotan and his nephews might be establishing new kin connections for the tribe, or they might be dead. Weko feared that she had lost a husband when Yotan did not return by winter, as she knew his commitment to return. As they heard of the destruction around them, Canonicus, Meiksah, and Miantonomoh became determined to isolate their tribe and then to rebuild and prosper. They were ready to try novel approaches and liaisons, but they were not willing to cede their identity as a people. The smallpox plague largely spared the Narragansett, compared to the surrounding tribes, in part thanks to Yotan's brave decision not to return home in 1617.

When Cojonoquant decided to return to his father's tribe a couple of years later, his pregnant wife would not leave with him. He brought back only his entrenched rum habit on this trip, and his habit got worse when he found his father passed away while he was gone. His uncles Canonicus and Wekeum were dismayed, yet thankful that their late brother Mascus did not have to see his son in this condition. At least Weko knew now that Yotan was alive and had been going south when Cojonoquant left him.

London, AD 1619

Roger Williams was at Thomas Fone's apothecary shop waiting to pick up medicine for Sir Edward Coke, reviewing his notes on the cases for the day. John the Younger was back in school and watching the court after the recent burial of his Aunt Anne. He was in the shop to help out her bereaved husband, Uncle Thomas, at his apothecary shop and keeping an eye on the apothecary's seven-year-old daughter Martha. Martha's usual minder was Katherine, Roger's thirteen-year-old sister. The apothecary's other daughter was out making deliveries with Katherine along as a buddy for safety, and to keep her company.

"Hi. I'm John. They call me John the Younger. And you are...?"

"My name is Roger. So why should you be called the Younger? You are getting older every day!"

"My father has my same name. The whole family calls me Younger, since calling me John is confusing. It just stuck." They laughed together.

"I've seen you at court, and you've got some way of writing in code. What's in all that code?" asked John the Younger.

"I take notes at the court for my master, Sir Edward Coke," replied Roger. "I can write much faster this way, and I keep up as few others can."

"Prove it," said John the Younger. "Can you read me back this morning's first case?"

"Sure." Roger read off the case in more detail than John the Younger cared to fathom.

Always interested in a new invention, John the Younger offered, "I'll pay you to tutor me in that shorthand."

Roger considered this. *Was it a betrayal of his Austin Friar friends?* "Can you tell me more about yourself?"

John the Younger laughed heartily. "I want to do less work and get my notes taken. My dad's making sure I know the law, so that I can administer his estate. He'll likely push me to an elected government position if he can. At heart I'm a chemist. I'm much happier here learning from my uncle. I've got to make that legal education take as little time as possible, so I can get to studying how things work. I promise, if you teach me, I will use it only for myself and for messages to my immediate family or business. Is that good enough?"

"No, not really. This code is special and cannot be widely shared."

John wasn't used to being turned down, and Roger's answer intrigued him further.

"Why? What's the concern? I'm not going to share it with anyone."

"I'll let you figure it out on your own. Why would anyone need a special code?"

John looked at Roger closely. He appeared to be an average Germanic Englishman of the merchant class. *Would it be trade secrets? Would it be religious?*

"My family is Puritan, if that means anything to you."

That meant everything to Roger. He recalled that it was his mother who chose to place Katherine here, and that meant she trusted this family. The two began the work of making John the Younger fluent in Austin Friar's shorthand, and they were soon fast friends. Martha would watch, though it wasn't till much later that they figured out that she'd learned the shorthand at least as well as John the Younger. Neither expected a girl to pick it up, and she was happy to keep them in the dark. She was clever about getting her questions answered, maneuvering carefully to get John the Younger to do most of the talking.

Austin Friars, AD 1620

Johannes was looking at Roger's letters to him, noticing how they'd changed in tone over the last two years. Hendric had not written since 1616, and Johannes had been going to school in Leiden with Austin Friars's support since 1617. The two still wrote each other, and for memories' sake and the sake of secrecy, they still used the same milk can top shorthand system.

> *January 18, 1617*
> *Johannes*
>
> *I did my first day at court today. All those gentlemen from Cambridge looked at me sideways when I took my seat, but they had respect when they realized that my notes are more complete than theirs. Now they ask what they missed in the break.*
>
> *There is so much small detail handled here, and then in exactly the same tone of voice they put someone away prisoner at Newgate without visitation or take away his livelihood or put a warrant out for his arrest, or cancel one. It is a sight to behold all the connections and how they do as they please. One young man's warrant was cancelled because a Lord enjoyed his company. I dread to learn what he did to earn that.*
>
> *Of significance, you will be happy to learn that the Strangers were given means to go back into the cloth business today, just in time for some official function. Seems King James wants the best, and he knows the Strangers have the best dyes. Also there was a large loan made to the king. It appears the Dutch Strangers are the financiers for the court. They were in such a hurry to get them to work, they gave them leave to operate by the old charter till they could make a new one. This business of law is a business first of money, then of rules.*
>
> *My quarters here are small and meager. They call this place a dilapidated manse. However, Sir Edward tells me he has a much nicer place in the country, and I will someday accompany him there.*
>
> *Yours faithfully,*
> *Roger*

March 16, 1617
Johannes

    There is much tiresome discussion of money here. Seems King James must fine everyone to fund the crown sometimes or appoint him to a commission. The crown is most dogged when owed money.

    The export laws are especially profitable.

    They toss out punishment here as if it meant nothing. I wonder if Hendric's case came through this court.

Faithfully,
Roger

April 16, 1617
Johannes

    Sir Edward Coke has given me a copy of John Smith's "A description of New England" to read. Oh how I wish you were here to gaze at it with me. I told Sir Edward of our intent to go to America, and he is supportive. He says I must learn to canoe and to ride a horse, and I can do both up at Neals this summer. Neals is his hideaway several hours from London. There is a perfect calm place to learn to row called Abraham's Bosom, and rougher waters off the shore. It is apparently quite a huge estate with 150 rooms. He will teach me to ride himself. He says I must also swim and hike and act like a native if I hope to thrive there. The same must go for you as well.

Roger

August 1617
Johannes

    We've been to Neals every time there is a two-week break at council. I can sit a horse at trot now, and my swimming and canoeing are coming along nicely, at least in salt water. My arms, legs, and stomach look wholly differently now, with real muscle. I'm losing that pale scholar look, but the books are still inside. Sir Edward is out every morning putting me through a grueling routine even when we are in London. He says I must exercise daily if I hope to survive in the New World. I just hope to survive our next adventures at Neals. I've never been so exhausted and sore as I was after our very first visit. Avoiding that keeps me going during our workouts in London.

Robert was in court the other day. It was nice to see my little brother. Robert has been apprenticed to Lord Viscount Montague as his servant, and the Lord was getting permission to take his daughter and Robert his servant abroad. Routine matter, really, but it was good to see and hear of Robert.

Sir Edward is of the old school, for he has arranged for his daughter Frances to marry the brother of the king's favorite at court, George Villiers. He hopes that will help him win favor and get his position back. The daughter and her mother, however, are of the modern upper class, believing she should get to choose who she loves. They cannot stand the idea of this arranged marriage. There has been quite a row, and he even dragged her physically to the carriage when she refused to go. Now he's accused in court of kidnapping and beating her before the Privy Council. The council removed her from the household and then later restored her to his house, since all were claiming a truce was negotiated. No one seems to consult God in these things.

Sir Edward has taken on a terribly high-risk job. He thinks the king must follow the law. I don't notice in my day-to-day observances that the king respects anything but his own majesty as God's authority installed on earth. I don't think Coke is too sure of his own safety, but you have to admire his commitment. The daughter is selfish. I hope they marry her off as planned for the sake of the family. King James does treat his friends well. It is Sir Edward's best hope.

Faithfully
Roger

November 10, 1617
Johannes

The marriage connecting Frances to the court worked, at least for Sir Edward. Today Sir Edward Coke was restored to the Privy Council. Sir Edward seems to respect my work and tells me he will keep me on even though he'll be at Privy Council himself now. For that I am immensely grateful. The father of lights protects me.

May God help Frances accept her fate; she is still threatening to run off.

From here on out Sir Edward will have to find new work for me. He says possibly I'll take notes in the Star Chamber or he'll find me some administrative duties in the house.

Robert's trip abroad was not as routine as it appeared. It appears he's fallen in love and gotten married. Mother was surprised, but I could tell she was happy.

Faithfully
Roger

October 10, 1618
Johannes

I'm busy here between Neals and court. I will not be a lawyer, but it is good to learn how administration really works. It is all in your connections. Sir Edward Coke says the trick is to make good friends and avoid making enemies. He himself fails his test miserably. Sir Francis Bacon for one is constantly after him still, and he fights back so viciously that he assures revenge. Listen to what Coke said of Walter Raleigh in court in 1603, and I quote!

"Thou are the most vile and execrable creature that ever lived. Thou art a monster. Thou hast an English face and a Spanish heart and thy self, you art a spider of hell. There never lived a viler viper upon the face of the earth."[1]

Might that not incline one to be his enemy for life? No matter now, Raleigh was resentenced to execution October 29, *as the king said his expedition did not bring in the required treasure. Perhaps Sir Edward Coke will outlive this enemy.*

Yours faithfully,
Roger

September 15, 1620
Johannes,

Have you done anything with the HH papers? I think of Hendric all the time. I have not seen any case so miserable as his the whole time I have observed this court. I have looked carefully, and the laws that would have convicted him do still stand, though such persecutions seem less the king's fancy now. I wonder what happened behind the scenes. There is always a behind- the-scenes connection, and if we do not know it, we cannot really understand his fate.

I'm sure you are aware of the Star Council case against the Dutch merchants, claiming they exported more gold than has been manufactured in England in the last ten years. It seems they will use the large fines levied against the conjectured profits toward the king's debts. They are expecting that the church will raise the money, as they know they've fined some very poor men. They have them in Fleet prison until someone pays. I'm sure this is a huge topic of controversy there, but I can see no way out of prison for them except pay it. At least they will count the prior forced loan towards the debt. I understand that leaves the Dutch consul bankrupt, as he loaned the money to the Strangers. What a miserable piece of business this is for the Austin Friar Strangers. Everyone is on your side, but the king needs money, and unless he finds it elsewhere, the fines will stand.

Sir Edward Coke is having a productive year. First he was appointed Lord Commissioner of the Treasury, and now he is elected to Parliament. His restoration is well underway. He says he will get me into Charterhouse for a proper education, as he knows the headmaster. I am too old, what will that be like? My use here will soon be at an end. I must go on somewhere and make my own connections. *My father, as you may know, already has passed into Heaven, and so I feel the burden of making my own path. Sydrach will take the business now and has offered to take in our little brother Robert as apprentice to replace his own prior position, I having refused it when he offered it to me.*

Faithfully,
Roger

CHAPTER 6

Leiden, AD 1620

In July of 1620 about half of John Robinson's congregation departed on the *Speedwell* to rendezvous with the *Mayflower*. The half of the Leiden congregation that traveled to New England operated under the charter of the Plymouth Colony. John Robinson himself stayed behind to be pastor to the remainder until they could leave.

Johannes was gaining confidence and coming into his own by 1620 in Leiden as part of Robinson's church. He visited Orrelia's relatives in Antwerp on the way to and from school, and they became his extended family in the south. The Antwerp descendants of Jacob Van Meteren still had his printing equipment.

In the fall of 1620 Johannes printed Hendric's documents anonymously in Antwerp and carried them to Leiden to spark a discussion. Johannes spoke at both Puritan Separatist and Anabaptist gatherings. The writings were popular enough to be directly incorporated as chapters 6, 7, 8, and 9 of a 1620 Anabaptist confession of faith. This publication circulated in Holland but was not printed in England or America. By mere months, it missed being seen by those departing for New England.

The Antwerp relatives were in need of cash, and, in return for helping with the Anabaptist confession publication, they asked Johannes for his help in selling off the printing equipment. A connection led to a connection, and Perri Bertie, second son of Lord Willoughby and purchaser of John Smith's original apprenticeship, ended up at the Van Meteren estate in London speaking to Orrelia van Meteren Hoste, whose family now lived there.

"I understand you know of some old printing equipment in Holland the family would like to sell."

"Yes, it was my father's machine. It was used to print the original Myles Coverdale Bible, before King James authorized an English translation. It's quite valuable as a historical piece," said Orrelia. "The family in Antwerp has no use for it and has fallen into financial troubles and would like to sell it. Would you bring it to England?"

"No. We'll move it from Antwerp to our estate in France for now." The attractiveness of this particular press was that he could move the machine from Holland to France. His printing projects would be well away from Lord Willoughby's reputation and control.

In Antwerp, he spent some time with the machine and was able to see that it really did still operate. He paid the asking price and hauled it away, storing it in the dungeon of the Bertie Orleans estate. The only person that Perri involved in his secret printing career was his twelve-year-old nephew Montegu Bertie, who would someday be the next Lord Willoughby.

Pamphlet wars were how controversial conversations happened in England between 1588 and the early 1700s. Queen Elizabeth started the practice when she had a speech she'd made to the troops published as a pamphlet. Controversial pamphlets were authored anonymously and printed in secrecy, with the constable destroying printing presses found to be involved in the printing of positions contrary to that of the king. Perri's press was valuable because it was outside the control of the constable. His wealth allowed clandestine purchases of supplies. Through careful anonymous placement among his relatives and their friends, he could have access to a readership in the English upper class. He would never divulge to anyone other than his trustworthy nephew that the printer existed.

Austin Friars, AD 1622

Johannes studied intensely for his final exams in Leiden and was very focused on getting a graduate research position. He remained absorbed in his own world, out of touch with Roger and all his friends back home. When exams were complete, he went home to London.

It had been nearly a year since he'd heard from Roger, and he knew that Roger had moved. Now he was back home, for a visit, and he found two letters saved for him, in one package. Roger must have written the first and held on to it for some time.

September 30, 1621
Johannes
    There has been tumult here. How quickly the winds of fortune do change. Father's will did leave me funds, but Sir Edward Coke has paid for Charterhouse, and that is where I am now, thanks to the full support of Sir Edward. They must have made their decision to accept me a day or two before the recent events in court that put Sir Edward back on the outs politically. I am relieved Charterhouse has not reversed my admission. I am a Foundation Scholar here and intend to spend all my time studying. Most of the boys being so much younger, there are few who can carry an interesting conversation. What a change; I wonder if the Cambridge fellows beside me in court saw me as I now see these boys. I suppose they must have.
    Sir Edward's political career has been stopped cold. The king has been feuding with Parliament, and Sir Edward Coke made his most elegant defense of parliament based on the Magna Carta, which he interprets to mean all freemen have rights that a king must respect. The king does not buy in. I've read the Magna Carta and listened to Sir Edward, and I tell you he has rewritten the intent of the old document with a one-word definition change. The original Magna Carta protected barons. In the 1200s it was changed to protect all freemen, at that time the elite of society. Now freemen are most of the middle classes. Moreover, while it was clear that the king is not a baron, the king is a freeman. So Sir Edward claims that the king, as a freeman, is subject to the rule of law.
    It is admirable in a way, reminiscent of the days when he could be paid to argue that a mastiff is not a dog so that it can't be punished for entering the king's woods. But here so much more is at stake. He has declared there is a rule of common law

that a king must honor. I see no evidence of this in scripture; God sets all kings in place no matter their attention to the law. I would rather he was arguing that the king must submit to God as expressed in the consciences of his people. He does not.

He has really gone for the kill with Francis Bacon as well. He has got him fined and thrown in prison, for twenty-eight counts of misconduct. I am sure Francis has his connections appealing to the king at this moment.

Then, to top it all off, Sir Edward's daughter Frances has run off with another man. What a public embarrassment for the king's favorite at court. That one move effectively ended Sir Edward's protection from his enemies.

Now he has lost his positions, and I fear worse is yet to come.

I am glad to be away from it. This place is much more to my liking than court intrigue and theatrics. The building was a home for Carthusian monks, and there are many small cells where a man can study and pray. I'm so happy to be here studying scripture and the classics, instead of petty complaints that plague a government day to day.

I am renewing my dream to make the gospel reach the natives in America. I have been reading Augustine and his methods of interpreting scripture, seeking the ways to teach new cultures. I am becoming convinced that all reference to soldiering and war in the New Testament was allegory for the spiritual battles ahead, that Jesus had no use for government beyond civil safety. Each soul could and must accept the Lordship and resurrection of Jesus, as we are taught at Austin Friar; the government has no place to dictate it.

Mankind has graduated to a new level of capability in relating to God with the advent of Jesus. Before Jesus, God taught with physical examples of spiritual truths as a parent would physically show a child the meaning of arithmetic with blocks or sticks before expecting the child to learn algebra. I am determined to become a serious student of God's spiritual algebra and learn how to apply it to the new cultures we find in America.

Yours in Spirit,
Roger

January 1, 1622
Johannes

    On December 27 Sir Edward Coke became prisoner at Newgate, kept without communication to the outside world. Can you imagine? Sir Edward Coke, inspired lawyer and wealthy man, a prisoner. His ex-wife Elizabeth must be laughing now, for he made her sit a spell in prison while he was getting Frances's marriage arranged, so that she had to agree. Sir Francis Bacon must feel he has gotten some revenge. He also spent a few days at Newgate this year after Sir Edward accused him of corruption, given the magnificent gifts he accepted from his clients. I hope Sir Edward's stay will be as brief. This is a sorrowful day.

    It seems all men of action may be destined for Newgate. Hendric and Sir Edward, a child and a man in his prime, both brought to the same place. What a miserable world this is.

Spero Meliora
Roger

Roger's father passed on. Sir Edward was in Newgate.

Roger was having a rough time of it. That was a lot of news. Johannes wrote a moving reply meant to comfort Roger. In so doing, Johannes utterly forgot to update Roger on the publication of HH writings. When Johannes realized this later, he thought, *There will be a better time.*

Sir Edward Coke remained in prison for three months before getting communication—and then visitation—privileges. After six months he was allowed house arrest, and finally he was freed.

Jamestown, AD 1622

Yotan and his new wife, Sawhoog, traveled south together the summer after they were married, continuing to trade Yotan's goods from New

England. When she was ready to give birth, they settled in with her relatives in the Powahatan tribe. Like many others in the tribe, he took a plot of land in Jamestown, donned English clothing, and submitted to the civil authorities of the town in outward appearance. His new family remained healthy, and one day led to another until he'd been in the area for five years. On his plot of land in town he grew tobacco, as did most of his peers. He spoke English about as well as he spoke the Powhatan dialect of Algonquian. He also encouraged his wife to tend food crops in the woods, not wanting to depend on English food supplies.

Over the five years, relations with the English had deteriorated. The English gentry never liked the work rules John Smith established, and they strayed from them as soon as he left in 1609. His successor, John Rolfe, was married to a Powhatan sachem's daughter named Matoaka, renamed Rebeccah upon her conversion to Anglican Christianity. John Rolfe relied on Rebeccah's excellent tribal connections to obtain food when English supplies were slow in coming. The Algonquians loyal to her as princess knew she most appreciated food as tribute. Adequate food supply enabled all of Jamestown to focus their production on tobacco. Tobacco was a cash crop, and on paper and in currency the Jamestown English were wealthy. Rolfe did not learn the tobacco art from the Algonquian; he imported Spanish seed purchased from Dunkirkers who pirated in the Indies. His wife helped him improve his crop, however, using Algonquian methods for backcrossing to get desired traits. His tobacco, first sold in London in 1614, was the finest in the world, and the colonists were very proud of their success.

By 1619, with ten tons of tobacco sold, the currency was being used to import slaves from Africa for labor so the gentry could cease working the fields. In addition, destitute women were recruited off the streets in England and promised a life that the Virginians had no intention of delivering. An English woman fresh off the boat cost £120, about a year's salary for a skilled tradesman back in London. The people of Jamestown were the elite and proud property owners of humans, of livestock, and land. Yotan was disgusted. Algonquian traded wives captured from other tribes. They were treated with respect, however, and became the core of the tribe's future. These English girls were used and abused and rarely lasted a year. *We should be killing men for treating women of their tribe this way, but the boats keep coming and human property keeps drawing tobacco-generated currency, and the owners do not care.*

Jamestown residents still lived in a swamp, and dysentery was a repeated challenge. There was little fresh water, and even less natural food supply. The arrogance of the English was daily taken out on the slaves, the women, and the Algonquian. The policy was to integrate the Algonquian, Christianize them as they had Rebeccah, and encourage them to live in town. There was a prejudice, however, that each Algonquian felt, including Yotan. His children were not treated like English children, he saw them learning how to be subservient to the English, and it angered him. He was a proud Narragansett, and he decided to return home. He wondered whether he should take Sawhoog and the children. His heart ached when he thought of his wife, Weko, back home. Perhaps he would tell Sawhoog he was off on an expedition and find out whether Weko still wanted him. If she was not waiting, he would return for this family. It would not be traditional to move a wife or her children. It would be more conventional for a powerful brave to have a wife and children in more than one tribal unit, but he did not like the way the English here were treating his children. The conflict kept him from making a move. He watched and waited.

Opechancanough was sachem for about a year when he, too, decided that the subservience must end. He planned with his most trusted braves. Yotan was not included in the planning, for he was an outsider. His fighting skills were respected, though, and the night before the planned events, a son of Opechancanough finally briefed him deep in the woods, far from town.

"Tomorrow is the end of Jamestown peace," the brave began. "Opechancanough requests you be there with us to fight."

"What would he have me do?" asked Yotan, surprised.

"We will be extra friendly tomorrow morning, taking the English fruit and treating them as they wish. Then, on this signal, we change," the brave demonstrated a subtle hand signal. "Repeat the signal to others, and attack whatever English are near. Have your family far from town this day to prevent retaliation. This is not an Algonquian traditional fight. This time we will fight like the English until they are massacred."

"We are proud Powhatan, Nanticoke, and Narragansett, and I will do this with you," declared Yotan. Here was a chance to seek justice on behalf of the Algonquian, the slaves, and the women.

That evening he went to find Sawhoog and told her that she must take the children and gather strawberries in the far fields. She was compliant and left early in the morning.

The following morning a young Powahatan boy tried to warn his English teacher of the impending battle. The boy was frequently excitable, and the teacher believed the boy was making it up.

He wasn't.

After their lunches, 347 Jamestown residents, mostly men, were massacred. Simultaneously, most of the food supply of the town was destroyed. Remaining residents fell back to the fort. That summer the Algonquian continued to destroy crops, and by winter the situation was so severe that 400 more English, especially women and children, died of hunger.

By the next spring, the colonists were resupplied on a war footing. Half their company owners were in England and from a distance, ignorant of the inhuman behaviors in the town, they vowed revenge. Sawhoog and the children were killed in one of the first waves of retaliatory massacres while Yotan was off on a hunt. When he heard of it, he immediately set out alone for Narragansett country. He was finished with Jamestown. The English disgusted him as immoral.

Yotan was once again a nomad. He spent the summer traveling, gathering food, and trading, using his canoe to transport goods. He was in no rush and enjoyed fishing and the open country, making it back to Weko just as the first snows fell.

After seven years, Weko was very glad that she had waited. She had not gone traveling; she had not taken another man. Yotan's children were healthy and strong. He was home, and his scars were not as disfiguring as Cojonoquant's. There was great celebration.

He returned with a valuable knowledge of English, of Powhatan, and of tobacco. His disgust for the English was disturbing, given the alliances formed in his absence, and it detracted even further from his ability to serve the tribe in a leadership role. While he was allowed to teach English by Canonicus, he had no desire to deal with white men and every motive to invest in keeping his people's ways. He would be the first in the tribe to understand the danger when the English tried to settle his people on tracts of land and the first to warn of the dangers of becoming English servants, indentured slaves. He told his stories of human bondage and massacre on the coldest nights. The stories horrified and warned, eroding trust in the Europeans. He encouraged them to be crafty, to take advantage of the Englishmen and not to give anything of permanence.

Meiksah and Yotaash felt justified in not going south, but they were also skeptical of his distrust of the Europeans as a whole. Juanumo on the other hand believed every word and took Yotan's warnings to heart.

London, AD 1622

Sydrach wished his father were here to see him marry Ann. He thought his father would be proud of him so far. He thought back over the key events in his life, realizing that today would be on the list from here on out.

He remembered as a child when he first had a little brother and sister, and losing both of them when he was eight years old. The plague swept through London that year, through the tenements his mom rented out.

As soon as one of her tenants was sick, she'd sequestered herself over in the tenement, because she had to take care of them. The two little ones stayed with her during the day, as his father said they were too young to stay with him in the shop downstairs in the house, for the maids could not control them. They were only four and two years, and they soon were ill and then gone. Everyone was relieved when Roger was born alive, as they knew his mother must have been pregnant while exposed to the disease. Roger was a miracle baby, born in the plague year.

Sydrach had to go motherless till she and the town recovered. It had been scary times, but that one move might have saved his life, he knew now. He had been one angry nine-year-old when the next child arrived, and they reused the name of his little brother. The new baby was also Robert. He was more used to it when they did the same thing with the next daughter, naming her Katherine, just as the prior daughter had been named.

He moved from schoolboy to apprentice at the age of fifteen, working for his father. He was lucky to be the eldest boy, since all the other children had been shipped out to strangers by that age. When he was eighteen, he graduated to being his father's assistant alongside his good friend William Clobbery. William and he traveled together several times to Turkey and Asia, establishing connections and getting supplies for the business.

When Father had gotten ill and passed, they'd brought Robert back into the business. Robert had married young and had a child already. Father had disapproved, and Robert stayed away while Father was well. Robert might never be wealthy, but his family would not starve working for Sydrach. Because Robert was a family man, and Sydrach knew the Italian, Turkish, and Asian connections, Sydrach continued to travel and focused Robert on maintaining the home front. Now that Sydrach hoped to be a family man, arrangements might need to change. Perhaps they really would send Robert to Virginia someday and hire a younger man to travel with William. In any case, Sydrach would stay at home more often.

Ann was a beautiful girl his mother had found for him, and he adored her from their first brief meeting. She was a Helwys daughter, and a Baptist. Mum always had her secret little friend circle, and Sydrach didn't like to ask questions. He supposed his wife would be the same way now, though she had promised to attend St. Sepulchre publicly with him. He hoped her family would learn from Mum to keep her private worship secret, as he hoped that Mum would not emulate the Helwys family—their behavior seemed like suicide by inquisition to Sydrach.

Sydrach knew about inquisitors. While traveling in Italy he'd been imprisoned for being Anglican and encountered an inquisitor. He'd said what needed to be said to earn freedom. He would not choose to repeat the experience. He shuddered. Now Sydrach was a St. Sepulchre parishioner, dutiful but not deep thinking. There was business to attend to.

He was ready now. He nodded to William Clobbery, his best man, and they entered the church.

CHAPTER 7

London, AD 1623

Roger's mother, Alice, proudly brought the roast to the table. This gathering was in Roger's honor, celebrating his graduation from Charterhouse as an exemplary scholar. He'd won a £16 stipend from Charterhouse to continue his education and a scholarship from Pembroke for his advanced skills in Greek, Latin, and Hebrew. Cambridge was the center of separatist thought in learned circles, and his mother was proud that her son would join them. She was wearing her best petticoat, commissioned for her by James years ago from his finest purple cloth.

Sydrach, along with his wife Ann and their baby son, James, arrived early to settle in. Robert, his wife Sarah, and their five-year-old daughter, Sarah the Younger, arrived next. Johannes de Cerf was home from Leiden on break and so was able to join them. Roger's mom's friends Joan Helwys and Orrelia Hoste were there as well. Katherine was indentured, working for the Fones, and they were all up at Groton for a funeral.

Sydrach was the head of the family now and offered a prayer of thanks:

"Dear Lord
Thanks for your bountiful employment and success in trade for all of us. We dedicate our brother Roger to your service, and thank you for his success to date. We ask your blessing on our trade in the forthcoming trip to Turkey. Finally may you bless Katherine and the family she is serving, and prosper their trade as well. Amen."

"So when will you leave for Turkey?" asked Johannes.

"Within two years I hope to establish direct connections and trading partners. Operating through the middlemen we've been using since our last trip takes out any profit for us. We must go directly and establish our relationships."

"Why Turkey, instead of Holland? The Strangers have the best technology and finest cloth," pressed Johannes.

"Have you seen how King James has been taxing the Dutch? Sometimes it appears that the entire crown is funded by the levies the Strangers pay. He has shorn the Dutch of their entire fortune," replied Roger, from his experience watching the ins and outs of the court. "Yet I did not see one levy against Turkey. His Majesty knows they would never pay, and trade would simply cease."

"What will the Turks buy from you, Sydrach? Your wool is too warm for those hot climates, is it not?" noted Orrelia.

"From Turkey I can obtain alum. I need a steady supply of alum for the dyes. I will make whatever cloth they want to wear, to get alum as a free and fair trade. I understand I may be able to market hemp rope," said Sydrach.

Orrelia nodded. "You know, Sydrach, Emanuel had many contacts for the Strangers in the Turkish world. I have all his papers. Would you care to study them for follow-up? Perhaps you will find some old friends who can help you make your way in this business."

Sydrach recognized that this was not an opportunity to pass up lightly. He knew that Dutch to Turkish trade was more established than the English, and he could leverage this connection. "Thanks, Orrelia. Let's do that together."

"Roger, so what are your plans for study at Pembroke?" Sydrach asked to change the subject.

"My study will be theology, with intention to become a minister of the Lord," answered Roger.

"So you will not become a lawyer after Sir Edward's tradition?"

"And end up in Newgate over some insignificant squabble with a king over money? I think not," replied Roger. "If I take a stand, it will be for something worth fighting about, in service of the Lord."

"Hmmm, I see my prayer's arrow sank deeper than I could know," answered Sydrach. "Where will you hope to settle?"

"You know America is my dream. That has never changed." Robert nodded along with Roger. Each shared that dream.

"You go first, Roger, and maybe we will send Robert after you. America seems to be a great source of cotton, and the Turks are more likely to wear cotton and silk, don't you think? We'll put American fabric with European dyes and trade it to the Turks."

"Now that sounds like a plan." Robert's eyes lit up with possibilities.

"Not so fast. I've got studies to finish first," said Roger, laughing, but he too liked the sound of the plan. His last exams were complete, and in a few days, as of June 9, he would officially matriculate as a Pembroke pensioner. Being a pensioner meant he was a middle-class student, below the nobles that the likes of Sir Edward's son might have been, but above the subsizers who worked for their board. "Johannes, I hear you've turned quite the scholar now as well?"

"The University of Leiden is doing well by me. I am working part-time for board and going to university full-time as of next fall. If all goes well, I'll be a full minister in the Dutch Church by 1630," said Johannes.

"You don't want to go to America?" asked Sydrach.

"No, I am called to shepherd our Strangers here, Sydrach. All that adventure is not for me. Our strength training never made me very strong, that much was quickly clear."

"Aren't you worried about Bishop Laud, now on the Privy Council, stirring up hate for all our separatist peoples?" interjected Roger.

"Who is Bishop Laud?" asked Johannes.

"Bishop Laud is rising in power every day. First ordained in 1601, just before we were born, he is the son of Merchant Taylor William Laud. Sydrach, you remember Father used to aspire to be like the senior Laud, right?"

"Yes, he was very wealthy," Sydrach said, nodding.

"Bishop Richard Neile is one of the men who condemned Bartholomew Legate to burn at the stake, and probably the one who condemned Hendric as well. He recommended Bishop Laud to the king. He attended some royal trips as chaplain, and the next we knew he was chaplain to George Villiers, a man everyone knows is the king's favorite at court. Bishop Laud has now been appointed to the Privy Council where Sir Edward sat, and his views are anti-Puritan, anti-Presbyterian, and vehemently anti-Separatist. Sometimes they almost sound popish. He wants to tell the king what the church approves and to use the king as his enforcer. He is building a power structure in the Anglican Church to rival the pope, and he intends to enforce uniformity everywhere he can reach. He is the opposite of all that Hendric and Thomas Helwys stood for, and he has got the king's ear," said Roger.

"The Dutch Strangers have special protection. I'm sure we'll be fine," was Johannes naïve reply.

"Enough," intervened Alice. "God will prevail. Put your trust in him. All these evil men and their kingdoms will pass soon enough."

A warm silence ensued while all focused on their food. After dinner, Alice brought out her surprise finish for the midday meal, a syllabub with trifles. The small spoonfuls of syllabub were rich, homemade cream curdled with homemade fermented cider. The more voluminous trifles were a cream-based custard, with chunks of cider-soaked cake, jelly, and dried fruit. The syllabub was only served at the most special celebration, and the trifle was meant to leave no belly unfilled.

Johannes asked, "Roger, you look so oddly fit for a scholar. Are you still going to Neals?"

"Yes, Sir Edward likes to take me up to Neals during summer breaks. Often we stop to visit his friends in Essex on the way there or back. Sometimes I stay and return on a later trip when school is not in session. I am becoming quite the ocean rower."

The whole family laughed. None of the rest of them could canoe, and none wanted to, except Robert. Robert wished he could tag along. His duties called. There was no such thing as a vacation in the merchant tailor business.

London, AD 1623

Roger enjoyed the rowing on the river Cam, which wound around his school. One of his rowing buddies was Montegu Bertie. Often they rowed in silence, two young athletes from very different backgrounds with a common objective. Sometimes they told stories.

Montegu was in a grim mood this morning. "I'm likely to leave Cambridge soon, you know."

"No, how can that be? You just arrived this term," Roger replied.

"Yes, but I'm a soldier at heart, not a scholar. My Uncle James is the master of Sidney Sussex College of Cambridge, and he let me in as a favor to my mother, but really I've never wanted to study. I don't think he can keep me here when I don't make the grades. Soon my parents will have to face up to the truth that I will never be a lawyer."

"So your uncle is James Montagu, the champion for getting Hobson's conduit built?" asked Roger in surprise. Hobson's conduit was supposed to keep Cambridge safe from the plague. It carried fresh water in pipes from nine wells directly into Cambridge, where it was released as a clean fountain, and construction was completed in 1614. Since 1614 the plague had not touched Cambridge University, and all were hopeful that the project was a success. Part of the reason Roger liked Pembroke College was that the freshest water supply terminated there.

"Yes, and my father Robert Bertie is big into engineering the draining of Boston in Lincolnshire. My family on both sides is fascinated with the management of water. I think it comes from the miserable times our protégé John Smith had in Jamestown with the swamps and disease. We've been studying water ever since."

"What do you mean, your protégé John Smith?" asked Roger, with interest.

"My Uncle Perri claims to have invested in John Smith when he was nothing but an indentured slave on a ship. He provided the means for John to escape and adventure, and Uncle Perri claims credit for all of John's travels. In fact, he did the research to find the printers for John and financed his first books. Uncle Perri's nothing but an old drunk, though, so I'm never sure how much to believe of his bragging. I've never actually met John Smith. Have you?"

"Only as his audience … he was my boyhood hero. He attended St. Sepulchre, and I remember when he came to speak at our church. In fact, I was scribbling notes so furiously that I was noticed by Sir Edward Coke, and that landed me my own first indentured servant position."

"Uncle Perri will be taking credit for your career as well, then, while he drinks away his life. I want first printing rights on all your work," quipped Montegu. He was only half-joking. "Seriously, though, what did you do for Sir Edward Coke?"

Roger launched into stories of what he'd seen at court, with all the intrigue related to the rise and fall and rise again of Sir Edward Coke. The stories were so enchanting that Montegu could imagine himself there in the Parliament—when he wasn't fighting as a soldier. Montegu had the connections to get a position in the House of Commons through his father, and Roger had the hard-earned knowledge that just might keep Montegu Bertie alive in a world where wealthy heirs were more likely to be executed for speeches in Parliament than for soldiering on a losing side. After all, in soldiering, valuable prisoners were kept and traded. Montegu left Cambridge and was elected Member of Parliament representing Lincolnshire in 1624. With Roger's stories in his head, he was careful—very, very careful.

He and Roger resolved to stay in touch, one way or another. Each sensed usefulness in the connection that he hoped to be able to leverage later.

Leiden, AD 1624

Austin Friar leadership did not approve of Johannes de Cerf associating with the Anabaptists. The Dutch in London never admitted to Johannes to seeing any copies of HH writings published for the Anabaptists, yet they seemed to be out to punish him. When they understood that he'd preached to the Scrooby Baptist congregation, they expressed special displeasure. Austin Friar ministers suggested that Johannes's time would have been better spent with Presbyterians. While Presbyterians, Anabaptists, and Austin Friars were all Calvinist Protestant, Austin Friars liked the Presbyterians' confirmed order and hierarchy within the church and took a dim view of believer's baptism and the laying on of hands for succession.

Meantime, on the Puritan side, John Robinson felt compelled to answer the Anabaptist treatise that included HH's work with a discussion of his own in 1624. These writings, along with many others, were in the swirl of debate about churches and separation from the Church of the King of England. In John Robinson's vision, the Puritan government would be a unified force and would banish all evil from the garden of Christians.

HH's views as championed by Johannes were dangerous, in John Robinson's mind—they would lead to disorder and anarchy and ruin the promise of the New England/New Israel dream. Johannes's views never became particularly famous or influential largely because John Robinson convinced people they should not.

Johannes de Cerf found himself blacklisted in the Dutch and English communities. He was accused of all forms of immoral behavior that would merit severe punishment in the Austin Friar church, including drunkenness and failure to repay debts. In London, special government privileges accrued to the Dutch church as a body. If a Stranger violated the church's moral or other rules, he or she was banished and lost the right to privileges like working papers. As a Dutch stranger in London without those privileges, Johannes would become unemployable. Even so, he left Leiden and returned to London. He was declared unfit to be a minister, and some suggested he look for a job outside England as a schoolmaster. Depressed and jobless, Johannes struggled to get through each day.

John Robinson grew ill and died on March 1, 1625. With both Johannes and John Robinson gone from Leiden, the controversy over HH's writings about persecution for beliefs being a practice not intended in scripture faded from attention.

London, 1625 AD

From the summer into the fall, the fleas are especially active, and they travel between rats and people. Fleas spread bubonic plague. The plague of 1625 killed 25 percent of London's population. Because the plague is not transmitted through drinking water, the Hobson conduit did not slow the spread of the plague through Pembroke.

A university by definition has students in close quarters. College men's eating and cleaning habits having not changed much over the centuries, and there was a plump rat population, so the fleas multiplied. The plague went on a rampage. To stop it, the school dispersed the students to their families. Roger, with Sir Edward Coke's blessing, retired to the shore at Neals. School would not resume classes till winter, when they expected the plague season to have passed.

Johannes de Cerf had been home from Leiden now for six months. His throat seemed swollen. By day's end, lymph nodes in his armpits, under his elbow, and in his groin were swollen, and he knew he was in trouble. Within days his lips, nose, and fingers were black, and he was not moving from the house. His family was afraid to come near, and he died in his bed alone.

Similar stories were pouring in from all over London. Roger's brother Robert had been married for eight years, and he lost his wife, Sarah, and their seven-year-old daughter, Sarah the younger. Now Robert was left to care for the remaining baby, a daughter named Anna Grace, alone. Anna Grace had been nursing when Sarah was ill, and everyone expected the baby to sicken and die, but she didn't. She survived a mild version of the illness. Sometimes a mother seemed to be able to help her babies even when she was too far gone to save herself. Roger's mother was once again cloistered in her tenements, caring for the ill and dying. Sydrach's wife, Ann, was not as lucky as Roger's mum. She was pregnant when the plague was all around her, and they decided to name the baby Roger, in hopes that he would survive. Her son James survived, but baby Roger was taken.

Alice Pemberton Williams lost two of her four grandchildren to the plague of 1625. She lost many more tenants, each family a miserable, sad story.

The mood altered for Roger at Cambridge. Many classmates and professors were gone, and he grieved Johannes's passing.

Court life intruded again into Roger's world. King James died. King James's royal favorite, the Duke of Buckingham, needed a position, and the new King Charles was determined to get him an appointment that at once kept him close enough at hand to consult, and far enough away to show Charles's independence from James. The royal court connections worked in concert to get the duke the job as Chancellor of Cambridge University, even while assigning him to distant military campaigns at their convenience.

Roger didn't want any part of the new court intrigue to affect his personal ambitions. He rather hoped he was forgotten as a minor player in Sir Edward Coke's support system. He kept his head down and worked toward graduation. Roger signed papers to be considered for his Bachelor of Arts degree in March 1626.

All the students were assembled for the ceremony. To be approved for a degree, each student was asked to sign in the presence of the University Registrar a loyalty oath that King James personally designed in 1623. Signing was a nonnegotiable degree requirement.

This document specified that:

1) the king was the only authority in the entire realm, including dominion in spiritual and ecclesiastical matters;
2) the student believed the book of Common Prayer contained nothing against the word of God and that he himself would use it and no other form of worship;
3) the student recognized that the book of articles of the bishops agreed with the word of God.

Roger signed.

London, AD 1626

Montegu was in his third term at the House of Commons, where he was behaving circumspectly and conservatively and attracting no untoward attention, when his father Robert Bertie became Earl of Lindsey. Montegu now inherited the title Lord Willoughby and gladly retired from Parliament. Montegu continued his father's soldiering tradition, and they often trained together. On the advice of his father, Montegu took a retinue of cavalry soldiers to serve in the Low Countries for a season. All professional soldiers needed experience protecting against Spanish expansionism into the countries bordering the English Channel, those being Belgium and the Netherlands.

Upon his return, and at the strong urging of his father, Montegu set out to find a suitably stationed wife. Within the year he married a widow, the former Countess of Holderness, Martha Ramsey Cockayne.

In every way the public Montegu appeared to be conforming. The private Montegu continued his passion for printing controversial material, undiscovered.

CHAPTER 8

London, AD 1627

By spring 1627 Roger was finishing his final classes during the last semester of his senior year.

For his younger sister, Katherine, now twenty-one, wedding bells were ringing. It would be a small ceremony in the house. She and her maid of honor, Elizabeth (Bess) Fones, were upstairs getting ready. The two had grown close over the last six years. Bess was four years Katherine's senior, though Katherine was the stabilizing influence on the pair. Katherine and Bess remembered many shared adventures delivering medicines for Bess's father. Neither, however, had managed a proposal from a doctor out of the experience. They had been a little too wild for that.

"Remember the time we told your father we'd deliver medicines and snuck up to Parliament to see Roger at work?" said Katherine.

"Yes, who knew then they were all old men with no humor whatsoever," said Bess.

"The Cambridge men weren't old," replied Katherine.

"True enough, and neither were the Inner Court men," mused Bess, thinking of John the Younger. "But all those men who chased you out sure were old. And humorless."

"Your groom, Robert Wightman, is a nice, conservative merchant tailor. Do you think you'll ever do anything exciting again?" asked Bess.

"I hope to have many children, and I'm sure they will be quite exciting enough. I'll also be helping Mum from time to time, and that is never dull."

"How many people have named their children after your mum, now?" teased Bess.

"Hmmm, two that I know of, and there could be others. Only one actually named her as godmother. She helped out a friend from childhood and now that goddaughter, Alice Ballard, is to have a baby of her own. The other was even longer ago, and that Alice has three children now. Mum always stays in touch with them at Christmastime in some way. Mum is a hard-nosed proprietor when the tenant has money, but put a destitute woman on her doorstep, and Mum melts," mused Katherine.

"No shortage of destitute women around, are there now?" replied Bess as she started on Katherine's hair. "It's a wonder she has any profit at all."

"Mum always says, 'There is a sea of those who need rescue, and each of us is but a cup of water, but God will call us to account if we spill our cup and quench no thirst.' She always makes sure there is someone. I think I'll choose to do the same."

"Robert best watch his purse, then!" laughed Bess. "He'll be blaming Sydrach for introducing the two of you once you've given away his riches."

"I'll make my own way. The Pemberton women always have, and I've got Mum's Pemberton in me."

"Does Robert ever talk about his cousin?" asked Bess. Robert's cousin Ed Wightman was, notoriously, the last religious martyr burned at the stake in England back in 1612, over in Lichfield.

"He was dismayed to hear of our house church meetings at first," said Katherine. "I thought I'd lost him, as he's a dutiful Anglican by nature."

Just then Martha arrived with the flowers fresh cut from the woods outside town. If Bess was the adventurous one, Martha was the observant one. She knew just what to get this time of year and where to go find it. She was carrying primrose and English bluebells woven into a mat-like pillow covering for the bride to carry.

It was a spring wedding, full of hope. At the reception back at the Harrow Inn, Bess caught the flowers. She wondered to herself, is this how it starts? For it was not at all obvious whom she would marry.

The family celebration completed, Roger was on his way to Neals with Sir Edward Coke for Easter break. "I've signed the loyalty oath. I feel sick about it. I don't believe any of the three points, but if I hadn't signed, I wouldn't be getting a degree." There, he'd said it aloud, even knowing Coke was a staunch Anglican.

Roger went on. "When I got to Pembroke they were busy burning books by Pareaus. A student, William Knight, was imprisoned just for publicly referencing his work. William Knight implied that a freeman could lawfully resist the king if the king were unlawfully threatening him. He said nothing more than you've said in court, frankly, but he did not have your connections or your funds. Even when you demand that the king respect and be protected by common law, your liberty is threatened whenever your court relationships are frayed," continued Roger. "I see how the real world works. To get an idea implemented in the real world requires more than speaking in public or losing one's life. Our lives are too fragile, the court too all-powerful, and our ideas too sacred to waste ourselves forever in this manner. There has to be a better way."

The two fell silent for a time, and finally Roger concluded, "At this point in my life, I've made a strategic decision that this was not the time or place to object. Having watched court life and the struggles of the university itself, and knowing the outlook of the duke personally, I decided this was not a battle I have the ammunition or artillery to fight at this time. But I worry, have I lost my soul?"

Sir Edward replied, "Now Roger, there is a time and place for all things. I've argued more ridiculous proposals for clients than I can even count. I've argued that our mastiff hunting dogs are not dogs after all.

What pride could be left after that? It was only later in life when there was less life, less that could be taken away—after my fortune was made, my children grown, and my first beloved wife passed, that I could afford to be principled. You know that, and you know that even scripture tells you to be shrewd in your work for God. You have to work your way up with cunning and practical moves, without losing sight of your goal. What is your goal? If you don't have a goal, you have already lost."

"My goal is no different than when we met ten years back. I want to be God's minister. I will go to America and share the gospel with the native peoples and be a part of establishing a church with honest and heartfelt worship. I want to learn the languages of the natives and know their ways, and give them the opportunity to know their true status as the cherished children of God."

Sir Edward Coke thought for a bit. "I'm glad you signed. With your BA degree you'll be eligible for a post as chaplain. Unfortunately, with the current political climate, you may have to wait a bit. I suggest that in this climate you continue your studies, and let's keep options open. Why don't you study law for a time to supplement all this religious study? The New World is a blank sheet of paper, and you'll need rule of law."

"What's so special about the current climate? I'm not planning to be a lawyer. You study law as if it were scripture," lamented Roger. He'd been focused heads-down on his studies and had not been carefully monitoring the swirl of court activity.

"There's a war to fund," started Sir Edward.

"There's always a war to fund," replied Roger.

Sir Edward smiled. "King Charles has made it worse. King James was a religious man. He always had a place in his heart for Puritan consciences, for Presbyterian elders, as well as the Anglican's common prayer book. Anything but popery. Charles is different. He does not care about consciences; he cares about consolidating power and funding his wars. He'll go Catholic if he must, we fear, for he married a Catholic.

He proposed to continue to fund the war against the Hapsburgs when everyone was hoping he'd cut it back. Parliament has not funded him, and in fact it refused him the funding source allocated to every prior king for life: tonnage and poundage. There was a proposal to fund him for one year as a stopgap, but the Duke of Buckingham refused it, raising the stakes. So he was funded nothing at all. The taxes on imported wine and on all imported and exported merchandise were not renewed at all. King Charles was furious, and the merchants grew rich.

"Not getting any support whatsoever from Parliament, he has dissolved it. Every time he brings it back, we make his actions violating traditional English freedoms the issue and demand protections. Then he dissolves it again."

"That's about as dysfunctional as a government can get, don't you think?" interjected Roger.

Sir Edward just went on. "Finally in October, King Charles had the bright idea to force all his noblemen to loan him money until Parliament provides the funds. Over seventy men refused, and they were all thrown into Marshalsea."

Roger thought this over. "Of course, being aristocrats, they can pay for privileges there. I don't imagine their conditions are actually like a prison." Marshalsea was famous for being a fee-based system, even more so than the Tower.

"Perhaps not. But consider one of my clients, Sir Francis Barrington. He's about as noble as they come, descended from George, Duke of Clarence. He's got estates of thousands of acres, but he is sitting in Marshalsea at this moment with pneumonia. His wife Joan volunteered to stay with him and has been his nurse, but she reports he is failing. We've petitioned the king for relief. And he is one of over seventy similar men."

Roger could feel some empathy. Still, in his mind, HH was a far greater tragedy. Sir Francis Barrington lived a full life with decades in Parliament and hundreds of committees and appointments. The authorities stole HH's life. Once more, Roger was glad that he had signed the oath. What was a piece of paper against a life of opportunity? A little knowledge of the law couldn't hurt.

They rode on in silence for a while.

"So, if the war is not funded, there must be military consequences?" asked Roger.

"King Charles has changed English alignments significantly, part of why Parliament is so reluctant to fund. He is too friendly with the Catholics. One question is which side of the war he is really on. All these wars were started as Protestants against Catholics. It is fair to say the Catholic territories are gaining ground."

"The sweet irony of the whole situation is that it was the Duke of Buckingham who nixed the one year of funding, and it is the Duke of Buckingham who has been hung out to dry without the troops or resources he needs to fight the battles he's been sent to win. The Cadiz affair in Spain was a disaster. Now, as we speak, the duke is gearing up to attack France, just off the shores of La Rochelle. He's gathered eighty ships. He'll likely want for resupply. His ships are going to be picked off one by one, as the Royal French Navy is expecting them. I have to remind myself that we are supposed to want England to win."

Roger could only shake his head.

Roger's Bachelor of Arts degree was conferred in July of 1627.

Sir Francis Barrington got partial relief. The king allowed him to live out his imprisonment anywhere in Sussex. He and Lady Joan took a small garden house in Sussex and served out the rest of the year.

The battle between Parliament and the king raged on.

CHAPTER 9

Off the Coast of La Rochelle, France, AD 1627

Given the state of Parliament, the Duke of Buckingham resorted to resupply from Ireland and Scotland. Word came in via messenger that thirty Scottish relief vessels carrying 5,000 men and supplies had broken up off the coast of Norfolk and would not be arriving as expected. He owed the men back pay and knew Parliament would not approve what he needed. He was desperate.

The siege of St. Martin de Ré, a fortress city on the island Ré off the coast of La Rochelle, France, was three months old. According to Buckingham's spies, the dunes at the landing sites at times hid 1,200 infantry and 200 cavalry. In the last attempted landing he lost twelve officers and one hundred infantry to establish a beachhead and begin a siege. Now his men were sick and dying, and one could have questioned who was holding whom under siege.

The duke's original plan was for the English to assist the islanders' revolt against the French. The citizens of La Rochelle at first did not admit to a quarrel with the French government at all. Two months into the siege, hostilities were reported, so perhaps all was not lost. If an attack was not ordered now, his forces would be weaker, his supplies diminished.

Events three weeks ago seemed the last straw. The Royal French Navy mustered thirty-five ships—a combination of naval and mercenary cargo vessels, and his men were only able to sink six of them before they slipped through the blockade. So now twenty-nine ships were resupplying St. Martin de Ré.

Marney was captain of one of the twenty-nine French ships. As a Dunkirker pirate, John Smith had once been in his crew when he captained a ship for Balthazar Cordes. He knew John Smith didn't talk about that part of his background now, but he was proud of his connection to English fame nonetheless. Still, he preferred working for a military that he believed could win, and right now that looked like the French.

John Smith had abandoned the old Dunkirker crew without saying good-bye just before Cordes left for the New World anyway.

Marney had gone on with Cordes to cross the Atlantic and pirate tobacco in the West Indies and South America. Marney was back on the European side of the Atlantic now only because Cordes had been taken prisoner in South America. In addition, the West Indies had generally ceded their tobacco trade to Jamestown, and Jamestown had invested in ordinance fully capable of a strong defense. Marney, for the first time, took an honorable job, working for a legitimate army. In this, he was copying a play in the book of his mentor, Balthazar Cordes, and using the trip to watch for good recruits when he returned to his more traditional role as Dunkirker pirate.

John Winthrop the Younger was twenty-one years old and working as secretary to freshly commissioned Captain Henry on the ship *Due Repulse*. The preceding captain had been lost in battle. John's first major battle was coming up, and he often kept his field notes for the captain in Roger's shorthand, translating them to English when they returned to the officers' tent.

The captain was fighting his first major battle, his commission purchased by his wealthy father. One of the captain's soldiers was Johnny Felton, a thirty-five-year-old veteran, cynical about his young officer but unable to blame him for his woes. Johnny was hoping for the post himself. This was the second time that the position had been filled that year. When the crew for the fleet from England was recruited, he applied for the post and was passed over. The winner of the post had been killed three months earlier at St. Martin, and the position opened once again. This time, the Duke of Buckingham chose a fellow wet behind the ears and brash beyond tolerance instead of promoting Johnny. It rankled. Johnny had been a professional soldier and knew what should be done. Henry had to be told. And yet, Johnny would help Henry. All their lives were at stake. His anger was reserved for the top of the line—the duke.

John the Younger accompanied the captain as he led his troops into battle. By the time they reached the stone walls around the town, John the Younger and Johnny Felton had both killed French soldiers. But the ladders were too short to scale the wall. Retreat was the only option. Johnny was furious. Had no one planned this battle? Had no one thought they would get this far? On the retreat, Johnny was covering for the captain and was stabbed deeply in the leg. He returned to Portsmouth to recover. John the Younger also made it back to his ship safely.

Unfortunately, because Parliament and the king were still fighting over the appropriation of war funds, the army had no funds to pay Johnny Felton the £80 he was owed in pay. The money would have made his recovery much more comfortable.

The duke was soundly defeated. The campaign lost five thousand out of seven thousand men. John the Younger was fortunate to be able to complete his commission without injury. He did not renew.

With his father's money, he decided to travel to Italy.

The duke, on the other hand, returned to Portsmouth and began to plan the next campaign to La Rochelle. The idea was popular with no one.

Marney worked his way back to the Atlantic and began to explore farther north of his usual routes, as he had heard that the ships up north had more supplies and less artillery.

Cambridge, AD 1628

Roger stayed on at Pembroke and began to broaden his studies. His heart was not in the law. His classes were a pale shadow of the drama he'd watched taking notes for Sir Edward Coke. He began watching and waiting for the right chaplain position. To get ready, he wanted to improve his Hebrew.

An eight-minute walk from Pembroke was the Christ's College of Cambridge, and a thirty-five-minute walk brought them to the boathouse. Both colleges had rowing teams. John Milton was five years younger than Roger, and neither was very talented at rowing, but they both enjoyed the river. In informal competitions they'd discovered each other's mutual love of languages and the study of God. Today they rowed together in practice and then planned to study together. John Milton was an expert at Hebrew and was learning Dutch from Roger. In return John was shoring up Roger's Hebrew.

As they walked back from the river, John said, "I hear you actually knew this Duke of Buckingham."

"'Know' is a vast overstatement. I surely did watch him control the court by being in the ear of the king for several years. I am afraid England is not ruled by law but by who can gain the king's eyes and ears," said Roger. "I heard you wrote a poem denouncing classes in Latin."

"Yes, I did, in a tongue-in-cheek sort of way. I'm more concerned about the loyalty oath. Should I make fun of that in a poem or just sign it when the time comes? There's far more at stake," said John.

"I detested the loyalty oath. My mother is a separatist Puritan, and even she would not have approved my taking a stand now at the cost of losing the degree. I have to consider my mentor's investment. The school's scholarship investment would also have to be paid back. Standing on principle would mean losing all prospects for a future right now. I decided it would be wise to choose a different battle, one more likely to have an impact. My family is merchant at its core, and they expect some profit, if not in dollars, then in souls. I signed the oath," said Roger.

"My family is Presbyterian—no common prayer book for us, either. But you're right. We are destined to do great things, and we cannot be stopped by petty oaths that are used as conditions for awarding us our degrees. I've fired tutors I disagreed with, but spurning Cambridge may be too big a risk. My career might never recover," said John.

"When I was very young, Bartholomew Legate was burned at the stake. I watched as the brightest pupil at Austin Friar languished away in prison. I watched the Baptist Thomas Helwys languish and die and all but destroy his family by writing unasked to the king in broad daylight and then foolishly publishing it in his own name. Here at Cambridge I watched William Knight toss his life away carelessly by speaking plainly with passion."

John nodded, and Roger continued.

"But I've also watched Sir Edward Coke, who bit his tongue for decades, and is now in a fight he may yet win for the same principles that William Knight espoused. I watched him get removed from power and yet pull out and recover. Over and over again he has done whatever it takes to invest in relationships and connections and to find a way back. As a lawyer, he is expected to maneuver with cunning. Why can we not find a way to be cunning for the Lord, in his service?"

John replied, "I am trying to decide whether that is a godly idea or not. Certainly Jesus bit his tongue many times, like when he paid the Temple tax, even though as the Son of God he knew he should be exempt—in Matthew 17. And in Matthew 16 he actually told the disciples to 'be on guard.' In any fight, being on guard would require one to maneuver to protect oneself, which is a bit like cunning."

Roger replied, "I will bite my tongue now, but I mean to be the Sir Edward Coke of ministry someday, ensuring that no king rules over the relationship a man has with God. As Coke fought for the rule of law, I will fight with all God's weapons for the collective power of honest men's consciences joined in heartfelt worship."

"Yes, I think you are right. I, too, will sign the loyalty oaths—no matter how onerous they get—and keep my reservations to myself. May we live long enough to garner real power and speak with voices no one can silence," agreed John.

A minute passed while they finished their walk.

As they reached the gate, John said, "All honest men? I think that needs to be all honest Christian men."

"The minute you add that, you put some earthly monarch or church administrator who is by definition affected by the curse and not capable of error-free decisions in charge of knowing who God has called to his elect. God didn't put man in charge of doing his electing. We are all flawed and fallen and cannot be trusted in practice," replied Roger.

At that moment they went through the gate at Christ's College, ran into some friends, and left the issue unresolved, as they went upstairs to John's rooms to study.

Essex, AD 1628

On January 2, 1628, all the men incarcerated over refusal to pay King Charles's forced loans were freed, including Sir Francis Barrington. There was an air of hope in the land. He immediately went back to work. The community reelected him to serve as senior knight for Essex, and he joined thirty-four committees and one joint conference during 1628.

June 7, after a dance of maneuvers that not even Roger fully followed, Sir Edward Coke saw his crown achievement, the Petition of Right, approved by Parliament and by the king.

The Petition, in its final form, declared:

1) Taxes must be approved by Parliament.

   This meant an end to forced loans.

2) Freemen are not to be forced to house soldiers.

This meant an end to King Charles's ability to cope with the ongoing war without funding by requiring Englishmen to support the army in their homes.

3) Cause within the law is required for imprisonment.

This was a blow to Charles's power and authority. He imprisoned men when forced loans to the crown were not paid, loans not authorized in any law passed by Parliament, and he also routinely imprisoned anyone who was a threat to his authority.

4) Restrictions are placed on the use of martial law.

Martial law was common before this edict, used by Charles to suspend normal rule of law so that freemen were subject to the rule of local military commanders.

In short, every creative measure the king put in play to accumulate cash in order to prosecute the war was now illegal. Lord Francis Barrington was vindicated, and he and his lawyer, Sir Edward Coke, were in a justifiably celebratory mood.

Clashes began again almost immediately, however, and within the month, on June 28, Parliament was once again discontinued and the Petition of Right ignored. Hope for near-term justice foundered in England. In disappointment, Sir Francis Barrington died on July 3, 1628.

Portsmouth, AD August 23, 1628

A beautiful summer day dawned. Classes had not yet started, and the school administration was still away on summer break. The Duke of Buckingham was on a working vacation of sorts in Portsmouth, England. Portsmouth was an island city, and the duke's warships were docked there for supply. The duke was happy to be away from his political battles and happy not to be stranded in Spain or France. He was working on plans for his next campaign, since he planned to make certain that supplies were sufficient before he started. Supplies had been the bane of his efforts the past few years, the cause of two lost battles.

The duke was spending the evening at "The Spotted Dog," building relationships with connections for his supplies. He started drinking around 3:00 p.m., in anticipation of tea and a light supper. Countless waiters served the duke and the ten men with him; many people were in and out of their private room.

Johnny Felton entered the establishment through the kitchen and donned a waiter's uniform. He did not work there but was hoping to pass unnoticed. He spent some time sharpening a knife and watching. Then he followed a group of servants into the dining room. He successfully slipped into the duke's private room and made as if to fill the duke's water glass. He wanted to be face-to-face, nose-to-nose, with the source of all his misery. Their eyes met.

Johnny plunged his cheap but well-sharpened knife into the duke's heart. He left immediately and returned to the kitchen like any other servant, no blood on his hands. It happened very fast, and Johnny's body obstructed the other guests' view of the action, so the first hint that anything was wrong was when the duke stood unexpectedly and shouted "Villain!" and then keeled over dead.

Johnny felt avenged for being passed over, for being owed eighty pounds of back pay, and most of all for having been put in harm's way without the resources to succeed in the field of battle. He blamed his chief officer, the duke, for all the crimes of ill supply and lack of resources, and for his remaining pain. He had no intention of escaping long, and he had written two notes of explanation and apology and secured them in his hatband in case he was killed during capture.

The king's men closed off all the exits and found Johnny still in the kitchen. Upon being questioned, he said, "I am the man." He hoped to prevent the torture of all the servants, which otherwise would have happened. He gave them his hat and pointed out his notes. He explained that he was patriot, a gentleman, and a soldier. He quoted Parliament's

1628 chastisement of the duke to support his case. The men arrested him as required, but they felt more like congratulating him.

Otes, AD 1628

"Roger, come in and make yourself comfortable," said Sir William Masham.

Roger was far from comfortable. He was on the vast Otes estate next door to the Hatfield Broad Oak estate that formerly belonged to Sir Francis Barrington. There were tens of family members, connections, and friends coming and going. There were over three hundred servants to take care of them. Roger was applying for the position of chaplain on this winter day. Neals might have prepared him for this, for the mansion had over a hundred rooms, except that Sir Edward Coke kept most of Neals closed up, unfurnished, and unused. Otes, on the other hand was a self-sufficient estate. Otes's main house consisted of forty fully furnished and often occupied rooms, with a servant responsible for the upkeep in each. The working rooms and outbuildings included a brew house, a milk house, a cheese loft, and an apple loft. Sir William Masham's brother-in-law Thomas Barrington was now Lord of the much larger estate next door. In reality, Lady Joan Barrington, Sir Francis Barrington's widow, ran both estates. The families of the two estates shared the dairy, buttery, pastry house, drying chamber, barns, silos, orchards, and vegetable fields of the larger estate.

Robert, Roger's brother, had been apprenticed at fifteen as a servant in such an estate, but Roger's closest experience was Neals. He decided on the spot that if he got the job, he'd consult Robert, as it was clear that there were many written and unwritten rules. Was the chaplain a servant? It wasn't quite clear. The chaplain was paid like a servant and had duties like a servant, but he also had ministerial authority over the property owners. Roger had a degree and felt himself a gentleman, being accustomed to working side by side with Sir Edward Coke.

Sir William continued, "Sir Edward tells me you have some experience taking notes for him in a form not easily readable by unfriendly eyes?"

"Yes, sir," replied Roger. *Where was this headed? It didn't sound like a minister's duty,* he thought.

"In this family there are three members of Parliament, and Parliament is destined to be contentious—it has already been contentious to the point of arrest. We want you to record the events for us, preferably in indecipherable form. Bring them back and read them to whoever is assembled here to provide support. Will you be able to accomplish this as part of you ministerial duties?" said Sir William.

"Certainly." Sir Edward Coke must have told Sir William about his shorthand code.

"You are hired. Can you move in before the New Year?"

"It will be arranged," replied a relieved Roger Williams.

"Let me have someone give you the tour and show you to your quarters. Welcome aboard."

London, AD 1628

Johnny Felton was tortured until they were certain he acted alone. The authorities then required him to confess publicly and repent at the gallows, which he happily did. He was hung November 29, 1628. His body was sent to Portsmouth, where it was supposed to rot in chains. The, site, however, attracted repeated, if clandestine, acts of veneration, like the bestowing of flowers and other mementos, and was soon removed.

Johnny Felton was a hero.

King Charles was publicly mourning the duke's death. In private, he was relieved. The duke restrained Charles's impulses to rule without parliament multiple times. Now his rule would become his own. He had no patience for these parliamentary antics. He was king; he would rule. He was not subject to any law.

On religious matters, King Charles consulted Bishop Laud directly, with no tempering voices to intrude.

All those who were happy that the duke was gone would come to wish he would return.

London, AD 1628

"Robert, you must teach me all about how the estate ran under Viscount Montagu. I'm to be chaplain at Otes." The Williams brothers, Robert and Roger, were in a carriage making deliveries for Sydrach's business. Robert had become a quiet man since his family had been stolen by the plague, and even before he became so quiet, he had never talked about life as the servant of a viscount.

"Well, I can surely show you how the estate ran. I've still got the rules. Can you believe that? There was actually a thirty-page book of rules written in 1595 for exactly how the servants' jobs were done and how we were to operate. They told us where to sit at dinner, where to get our supplies, and every last detail of what we were and were not to do."

"May I borrow it?"

"Sure, but Roger, it's not going to do you any good. Viscount Montagu was a Roman Catholic. Your job did not exist, and the traditions are all very different."

"Good point. I'd still like to read it, since it must give one some view of this life, which is so far removed from any I've ever known. I do know I'll be expected to ride a great deal. It's a good thing Sir Edward taught me to sit a horse. Who knew that would be his most relevant training for a chaplain's position?"

"Just remember you work at their pleasure. If they trust you, everything will go well. Except never be alone with one of the mistresses, or you can be accused of all kinds of things. First thing you know, one of the nobles gets a girl pregnant, and they ask you to marry her. Avoid that if you can.

Although Sarah made me a good enough wife, that's for sure. When you saw me in court, they knew they were going to have us marry, but first they sent us abroad so it would appear I had done it. I have never been so set up, but then again, as I said, she made me a good wife. When she died I was very sorry."

"Robert, I had no idea. I always assumed ..."

"Yes, and you must continue to appear to assume ... as I was sworn to secrecy, and the viscount has long arms. You need to know the truth, though, so that you understand how you are entirely at their mercy. They can write the rest of your life at their whim and frankly, in a more compelling way than our poor father ever could have done."

A silence ensued while they prepared to make the next delivery.

When they were traveling to the next stop, Robert continued the conversation. "Roger, did you really think I'd have married so young voluntarily? I hadn't even finished the apprenticeship. Once I married her, they were kind to us both, and no one would ever tell which gentlemen had done it, not even Sarah. Especially if anyone sneered at me a little, I always wondered if it was he who had slept with Sarah, and—worse—if he continued to take advantage of her. That is often the arrangement, you know. She never mentioned anything, and honestly I was afraid to ask. It would have seemed an insult to her honor."

"I do know this," Robert continued. "We were both very happy to be able to leave and set up an independent household after Father passed. Sydrach has been good to us. Those years working for Sydrach with my family to support were the best years of my life. I am happy to work for him now, but I don't know if I'll marry again. My life is Anna Grace for now. She keeps me chasing her, that's for sure. She is into everything—the most curious child I ever met." Anna Grace was three years old, a robust child, and she already had her doting dad wrapped around her little finger.

Roger nodded. He was adjusting to all the news as they delivered the remaining carpets while discussing less weighty topics.

CHAPTER 10

The Road to London, AD 1629

The good thing about a winter horseback ride to London was that the extra clothes you wore gave a bit of extra padding for the bumps. Roger's saddle sores had been weeks in the making and were slowly receding, as his riding muscles developed. Parliament had been in session since January, and it was a four-hour trip each way. His rides with Sir Edward Coke at Neals had served their purpose but had been far too short to keep him from being sore now. The on-the-job endurance training was excruciatingly painful for the first week, but he was improving rapidly.

The three people of the Otes and Hatfield Broad Oak estate who were in Parliament were his primary audience. One was Roger's boss, Sir William Masham, husband to Lady Joan's daughter Elizabeth. The other two were her sons, Thomas and Robert Barrington. Lady Joan was unwilling to lose all three men at once, having already lost her husband Francis to the deadly dance between the king, the gentry, and the Parliament. Thus Roger's real job was to take notes for those who were back home and to tell the story at Otes. The men alternated, so the pattern was not obvious, and Roger was constantly back and forth.

When Parliament convened in January, they were unanimously furious that every part of the Petition of Right was being ignored. Then things got worse.

In England the state headed the church. King Charles reduced the differences between the Anglican Church and Roman Catholicism to please his wife, on the one hand, and Bishop Laud, on the other. The king encouraged Laud to crack down hard on any worship that deviated from the revised Common Prayer Book dictating a new High Anglican order of worship.

To Laud, the advocates for voluntary inspired worship were revolutionary enough. He did not believe laymen were qualified to interpret scripture and so studying it would be fruitless. Now, however, an even more extreme view was taking hold in the people. In this view, each man contained within an inner light, so that the free will of this inner light reigned supreme. As Laud saw it, laymen were confusing their inner desires with the calling of the Holy Spirit. This view was counter to scripture in that it ignored the need for collective confirmation in the body of Christ, and it seemed dangerous to all forms of civil and church authority. The extreme views triggered a wide dragnet that caught people who espoused Bible-consistent views along with teachers of heresy. The reaction of Bishop Laud and the king was to force conformity, with little respect for honest inquiry of the heart and little care for individual commitment to a personal relationship with God.

The secret Austin Friar note-taking system was once again useful to hide communications from prying authorities, now personified in Bishop Laud and his spies.

Parliament and the king's forces came to physical blows that March, and Roger Williams reported the entire ordeal back to Otes. With the king's forces pounding at the door, Parliament passed three items, two of which opposed the king's ability to raise funds without Parliament, and one of which opposed King Charles's changes to the Anglican order of worship. Parliament made the crimes capital offenses. The king dissolved the Parliament, ignored the taxation-related measures, made peace with Spain and France to avoid needing extra funds from Parliament, and mercilessly punished failure to conform to prescribed Anglican worship.

Lady Joan Barrington was happy that all her family had returned home without having made a target of themselves, and none were in jail. Their self-sufficient bubble of an estate lived on, with worship unaffected for now by all the new rules.

In the land a general toleration of Catholic mass resumed, alongside the Anglican order. Bishop Laud forbade the hiring of new private chaplains in favor of forcing the people to come to the public churches for worship, where he and his spies could monitor activities. This made Roger William's position secure, in that to replace him would be illegal. It also eliminated the option of moving from one estate to another, should things become uncomfortable at Otes.

Otes, AD 1629

Her eyes were an intense crystalline blue with a hint of steel, which mirrored the discipline of her thought. Her skin was the pale, unmarked, transparent organ of protected youth that only the rich could afford to produce in their daughters of marriageable age. And the wonder of it for this new chaplain at the Otes manor was that when he looked at her, transfixed, she was usually looking back at him with a smile.

Jane was no less than Lady Joan Barrington's niece. Lady Joan was a religious and highly disciplined woman, and Roger was the chaplain for both ladies. Lady Joan was stern with those around her, able to hold a grudge for years, and not one to be reckoned with lightly. This was not the role model of an Anglican woman, and her chaplains uniformly called on her in correspondence to be wary of her gray hairs and advancing age and to repent before it was too late. She should assume the role God intended as a subservient, meek daughter of God at the service of her son Thomas, who should be running the estate now. Did they dare say the same to her face? Most did not, but Roger did. Roger could irritate and agitate like no other, holding to his principle no matter the cost.

Jane spent every free moment over at Otes these days. Sir William's wife, Elizabeth, noticed the budding romance and encouraged it. Most of the chaplains in this age arrived single and left married or about to be married.

Roger and Jane were riding over the manor. It was spring now, with flowers in bloom and the entire world echoing the promise of new life. Roger seemed distracted. In hopes of bringing him back to the present,

Jane galloped off, forcing him to chase her or lose her company. Follow he did. As the horses slowed, she asked, "Why the frown?"

"It was a long night in London two nights ago. I fear I've overstepped now. We were all there—Lord Coke, Sir William Masham, Reverend Cotton, and several others. We were discussing the ridiculous state of affairs in the nation, with the Anglican Church being changed to be more like Roman Catholicism every day. The number of differences in worship formats has been reduced from thirty-eight to eight by Charles's court. All fear it will change fully back again at the whim of the next king. What true faith can there be when you are told one minute to bow to Pope and the next minute to bow to King and that the Pope is now evil? What a mockery of faith! The government should not be in charge of the church; it is Christ's alone."

"Lord Coke doesn't buy that, does he?" Jane teased.

"That is an understatement. I think he will disown me now. He has been my mentor, a father, and my financial support since I was a child, and I have worked with him toward causes we did and did not agree on. I surely owe him. He fights for the rule of law. Our Puritan fight is for the rule of God over each man's heart. The worst thing that ever happened to the church was when they let Constantine adopt it and make it the religion of the Roman state. It has wrought over a thousand years of madness. Now, with America, we've a chance to make a new land, one with Christ returned to be the head of the church as was intended."

"Bite your tongue. Bishop Laud will have your head if you talk like that!"

Roger smiled. "You're right. The time will come, but it is not now. Let's go eat. I'm famished."

That evening after supper they sat in the parlor, Jane and Lady Elizabeth sewing and Roger pretending to read. Jane was her most beautiful in candlelight, and Roger had trouble taking his eyes off her.

"I hear you've been offered a position in the colonies," Elizabeth said to Roger.

"Yes," Roger replied, watching Jane's interest level closely. "I've turned it down, though. I'm not ready to leave Otes, and this is a merchant trip. They just want a chaplain to bless their merchant profits. I'll be letting them sail without me." The room grew quiet.

"I'm going to New England someday," ventured Jane. "I don't know when or how, but I must, I just must!"

"Have you told your aunt? I'd have thought I would have heard repercussions if you had." Elizabeth smiled. "I believe she seeks a match for you in London. She has it all worked out you know, a life in London as a lady."

Jane looked miserable. "I haven't yet," she admitted. "I cannot bear the thought of London. I love the countryside, the fresh air, the birds, and the horses. I just cannot bear the thought of parlors and harpsichords and dressing every day for tea."

Lady Elizabeth laughed. "Yes, I was lucky to marry Sir William."

They left it there that night.

Roger tossed and turned. He knew his calling was to the New World, and he hungered to look after the Indians' souls. He was madly in love with Jane and could not bear the thought of leaving her. He was torn, and now he knew that she hungered for the New World as well.

London, AD 1629

Bess's excitement would not be contained on this cold March evening. Her cousin John the Younger was back from Turkey, and she was throwing a dinner for him with her little sister, Martha. Family friend Katherine and her husband Robert Wightman agreed to get a babysitter and come out for once. Robert had been down with tooth pain, so this would be a rare night out for the couple.

Sydrach and Anne were expected as well, along with Sydrach's brother Robert.

At Katherine's suggestion, Roger had been added to the party. He was in London, down from Otes, because of Parliament.

When John the Younger arrived, Bess had a surprise for him. "John, did you know Henry is here? He's been staying with us since he got back from Barbados, and he's been an immense help since father died."

"I had heard. Your father made his displeasure well known, I'm afraid. Are you hiding Martha here somewhere, I hope?" teased John. He'd had a license since February to marry Bess's sister Martha.

"I'll find her," said Bess.

"Henry!" said John. "You look good. Barbados has treated you well."

"Yes, it treated me quite well, except for my finances," replied Henry with a laugh.

They settled in, and before long the others arrived. They brought out the cider, and soon the conversation was unstoppable.

The night flowed on with good food and conversation. Eventually Bess caught Henry in the kitchen. "I did miss the cooking back home. You have done a fine job tonight, Bess," said Henry. Bess's smile lit up the room.

"Henry, it's been so good to have you in the household since father died. You know your father is now in charge of our finances, right? With my mum gone since I was nine, and father's inheritance going to his son with my stepmum, I'm on my own now. It is so frustrating that your father, as my mum's brother, controls all my and Martha's inheritance till I marry or turn twenty-one. I'm bound and determined to marry quickly. He won't even send an allowance unless I can prove I've been to church. He's so strict!"

Henry laughed. "That, he is! So who will you marry?"

"I haven't figured that out yet," Bess replied, laughing. "I've an offer, but he's so boring. I can't bear the thought of it. What do you think?"

"So all you have to do is marry to get your inheritance?" asked Henry. His mind was racing now. This beautiful girl who wanted to marry brought an inheritance. To a lonely, bankrupt fellow, she looked like salvation.

"Yes."

"Do you think I'm boring?" asked Henry. His eyes were locked on hers.

"No," replied Bess. He kissed her.

When they returned from the kitchen, the men had settled in the parlor to smoke, and the women in the sitting room, to sew.

"So, were you able to follow up on any of Emanuel's contacts for us while in Turkey?" asked Sydrach.

John the Younger nodded. "Yes, I did. I found two were deceased, but someone else was running the business for them. Several of the businesses were just gone. I've got the names and addresses for the ones I did find, and they are very anxious to reestablish connections in London. Seems the Spanish blockade has been brutally effective since 1625, and their business with Holland has come to an end. So, they are really hurting for business and welcomed me grandly. I don't think my reception would have been nearly as warm if I weren't representing merchant tailors."

"That's really quite remarkable to hear," ventured Roger. "When I was scribing for Sir Edward, the Dutch had the technology edge, and the Spanish couldn't keep up with either the Dutch or the English at sea. The king would levy extra taxes on the Strangers just to slow them down, and while he got his poundage, it didn't slow them much. How quickly it all changed."

"The value of an effective blockade," agreed John the Younger. "Too bad the duke couldn't conjure one up against the French. Now it looks like we need lessons from the Spanish."

"So why are you not still in Barbados, Henry?" asked Roger. "Our generation at Otes and several in Parliament are abuzz with excitement to invest in the John Pym and Nathaniel Rich expedition to the Indies, also backed by Lord Say and Lord Brook. They have started the Providence Company for just this purpose. What do you think about such an expedition?"

"We were growing tobacco and exporting it back to Europe. We found that disease was infesting our crops and that we could not compete with the Chesapeake Bay tobacco growers. They are still subsidized by the crown. More important, their winters are more severe, killing off some of the pests that plagued us mercilessly. If I return, I am thinking of planting sugar instead, and for that I'll need to raise new capital. In the meantime, I'm thinking of expanding to New England," replied Henry.

"Another swift change in trade," said Roger. "Have you heard of this Providence Company?" He'd turned down the Providence Company because he did not want to leave Jane. How he wished she were sitting with the women in this house this moment.

"No. I've been sequestered on Barbados, so tell me about it," replied Henry.

"It's a merchant expedition, intent on growing tobacco and cotton off the mosquito coast and disrupting Spanish trade. The investors are all Puritan and seek to set up a God-fearing ideal community. They are apparently unhappy with the current chaplain and are looking to replace him already, even though he's only been there a few months. Apparently the colony looks like little more than Dunkirkers in spirit and needs some fortitude injected," said Roger.

"Let me see. So this would be the Puritan version of a Dunkirker expedition?" John the Younger found this amusing.

"Sounds like a paradox to me," added Henry. "Besides, if they want to make any money, they'll have to find another crop. Possibly sugar cane, which will bring rum. I wish that poor chaplain luck."

"Roger, I've never known you to be one for form instead of content. I fear they only want a chaplain for the form. You sound like you are still thinking of joining them?" asked John the Younger. "Aren't your parliament days over? I thought Charles dissolved the whole thing. What's the story there?"

"I turned down the Providence Company. On March 10, King Charles personally showed up and dissolved Parliament. He says he doesn't need it, though that means he'll be limited in how he goes to war. He can't raise money, given the Petition of Right. That's one way to keep the peace abroad!" said Roger. He continued, "Sir Edward Coke is retiring. He'll stand on the Petition of Right as his legacy. He won't change his mind even if Parliament returns, but he doubts if they will call another Parliament in his lifetime. He says it is time to retire to his horses and estates, and he'll focus on his children and grandchildren."

John the Younger mused, "I wonder how long England without Parliament will last. The era of personal rule has begun."

Personal rule would in fact last a terrifying eleven years and would be Charles's revenge for having been forced into the Petition of Right. The Petition of Right, as the foundation for the 1689 English Bill of Rights and later the United States' Bill of Rights, would last over 386 years, and the counting continues. But John the Younger could only look toward the future with something like a shudder at horrors to come. His planning was much closer at hand.

"I've been working on convincing father we should all go to New England," continued John. "I think he's starting to see how it could make sense, especially as distance from Charles seems to be a good idea at this point."

"You make good points. That was part of the temptation of the Providence Company," agreed Roger.

"We can do better than that," said Henry. The men all agreed with him.

In the sitting room the women were also chatting as they did their handiwork.

Bess asked, "So how is Robert? He looks so pale."

"He is not well," replied Katherine. "He struggles to complete his daily work and then collapses. Even then, less is being sold than in past years, and finances are tight. The two babies keep me occupied, and we've a third on the way, though I'm not showing just yet."

"I wish Father were still alive. He'd know just what to do for Robert," said Martha.

"We've been through every remedy. We even had the tooth worm pulled, but his mouth is infected and raw, and the pain is into his jaw and does not want to heal," fretted Katherine. She was worried because tooth worm was a very common cause of death, as it was caused by a tooth infection that spread into the root of the tooth and then on to the jaw and often the brain.

"Let me send you home with a concoction to kill his pain from father's supplies," Martha suggested.

"That would be most welcome," answered Katherine.

"Take joy in your strong babies, Katherine. You are blessed. Our James is four now, and he's strong. The next two, little Roger and Elizabeth, were like quick-blooming flowers, here and then gone," said Anne.

"Will you be like Mum and Father and name another baby after each of them?" asked Katherine. Katherine knew she was the second by that name in her family, as the first died while a toddler.

"No, I prefer a new name. If you reuse the name, you can't even talk about or remember ones gone. I prefer to honor each one as a child of God," said Ann. Her house church roots were showing.

"Why aren't you and John the Younger married yet?" asked Katherine of Martha. She knew they'd gotten their license.

"Father got sick, and it didn't seem right. I didn't think he'd pass on, though. Now, in hindsight, it seems silly. But he is gone, and now we are in dire straits, as none of the children can access the inheritance till we marry. I wanted a big wedding, not a small sad one."

Just then the two Roberts poked their heads in. "Katherine, gather up your things. We'll be departing shortly. I've offered your brother Robert a ride home as well." Robert nodded to the ladies.

"Martha, Bess, Anne, it's been wonderful to spend this evening with you. Such times are so rare. I'll treasure it. Blessings on you all," said Katherine.

As Katherine gathered her things, Martha made a quick trip down to her father's office rooms and prepared a powerful painkiller for Robert.

Later, John the Younger and Henry departed as well. Henry quietly repeated the information about Martha and Bess's predicament to John the Younger. Then he made a bold proposal. "I know you are planning on marrying Martha, but you are solvent. If I quickly marry Bess, you can wait and have a proper wedding with Martha. If I don't, I fear our cousins will do something extremely foolish soon."

"Interesting. There is no need to let these beautiful women and their inheritance out of the family, is there, now? We Winthrops know first-rate women when we see them, don't we?" mused John the Younger. "You know Father will not approve."

"Father, Father, Father. We'll let him vent his ire on my match, and you keep yours nice and proper. In the end he won't mind keeping his sister's money in the family."

"It's a deal. You know, we could do much worse. Bess is always up for adventure and will do you well in New England. Martha is smarter than most men. And there's not a prettier pair in all of London. Not to mention Anne Winthrop's inheritance. Interesting as venture capital for an ironworks or windmill production to me, but since you have spent a small fortune on rotten tobacco, the difference between solvency as a freeman and becoming a debtor to you. Do try not to destroy another fortune, Henry."

Henry's smile made him look guilty as charged.

John the Younger paused before going on, "Henry, I really don't think you should take Bess to Barbados, though. Come with Father and me to New England first, and make some real fortune back and then return."

"I'll think about it. Once Bess has her inheritance, we'll have options, but I do like what I hear of New England," replied Henry. The two rode on in silence, each deep in contemplation of his hopes for the future.

John the Younger decided to stay in London to follow up with Sydrach and perhaps to travel back to Turkey in order to carry return correspondence. Martha would not like the continued separation, but he knew she was perfectly capable of staying busy on her own.

Martha did stay busy, with wedding planning. She chose St. Sepulchre as the venue and set out to make up for lost time with a grand ceremony followed by an even grander reception.

John did not return home to Groton until August. By then the wedding plans were set, with reservations and deposits, and he went along.

CHAPTER 11

London, AD 1629

Spring deepened, and daffodils gave way to irises and then lilacs and dogwoods. Roger grew close to all the Otes and Hatfield Broad Oak residents. He was at home there now, and his relationship with Jane was deeper than ever. He received encouragement from the family and had high expectations. He resolved to make his case to the Lady Barrington in a letter. "I've turned down a position, intending to stay locally," he wrote in an effort to appease the old woman. *The calling could wait, couldn't it?*

Knowing that such a letter might arrive, the still grieving and impatient Lady Barrington had begun, some time ago, to look seriously into the young man's background. The merchant background did not impress her. Worse, though, was the young man's irritatingly confident manner. He would never rise far, she feared, for such an annoying personage would quickly be swatted down in this cruel world. She was ready to reply upon receipt, and her reply was swift and devastating to the young couple. She was determined to end this romance once and for all.

"But Aunt Joan," pleaded Jane, "you have destroyed my whole life."

"To the contrary, young lady, I have preserved it," parried Lady Barrington. They were alone in her chambers, and Jane, in tears and angry, was devastated.

"Aunt Joan, you don't know what you are saying," cried Jane. It all spilled out, for the two women were close. The dreams of America, the calling to be a chaplain's wife, all came tumbling out; there was no use in holding back now. All was already lost.

Lady Barrington ruled the manor with a firm hand, and there was no chance at all that she would change her mind. But she empathized with her niece, and in fact resolved privately to find a different sort of match for her than she'd previously planned. This Roger, however, would never do. But perhaps there was another … she kept her thoughts to herself and let Jane cry her heart out. Steel is forged in fire, and Lady Joan knew well that the fire of discipline would instill character in Jane that otherwise would never have developed.

William Hooke soon found a willing audience in Jane for his dreams of America. A bit more well-to-do than Roger, a great deal more genteel, this young chaplain now began courting at Hatfield Broad Oak, perhaps sensing his chance.

It was a summer full of romance at the Barrington estate, and Roger could only watch in jealous anger from afar. Oliver St. John courted Lady Elizabeth's daughter from her first marriage, Jug, and all hoped it would become serious. He wasn't perfect, as he had a bastard father, but Jug lacked suitors due to issues with her inheritance. All were anxious to see her married. Oliver and Roger were grand friends and had spent many an evening together. It hurt now to be without a date and therefore off to the side, as Oliver focused on Jug.

Sir Gerard Gilbert courted Lady Joan's daughter Mary. The laughter and merriment of the three couples inspired the manor, but Roger was left inconsolably alone, and he focused on his duties.

It was a summer full of aspirations for a New World as John Pym, a local merchant, backed the Providence expedition to the West Indies. The young Barrington crowd was growing deeply involved in formulating plans to join and/or support the Providence Company. Roger wanted no part of it, having been born to merchant trade and having rejected it. A bought ministry was not for him. Nevertheless, traveling with the planners was the activity of the summer, and the chaplain was expected to attend. So attend he did. Visions of wealth and freedom danced in the hearts of the young Barrington crowd, and Jane and William were committed to the travel.

As if to rub it in, Elizabeth Fones agreed to marry Henry Winthrop. The two married right away in a house wedding, and the Williams crew was invited. Henry was already planning to leave for New England later that year with his father and other family members. Anne Winthrop's money would back the venture, and John Winthrop Senior would be recorded as a major investor. John the Younger was traveling and missed the wedding. His own wedding was postponed until 1630.

It seemed that the whole world was pairing off.

Roger found company and solace in the long discussions and debates he had with his compatriots: John Winthrop Senior, John Cotton, and Thomas Hooker. Long rides to Sepringham for planning made for comfortable times among the four men. John Winthrop Senior was planning to bypass the Providence Company to leave for New England with the Massachusetts Bay Company.

The Massachusetts Bay Company was a new company formed in the hopes of fixing some of the problems experienced by the settlers of the Plymouth Company, the London Company, and the Dorchester Company that preceded it. As far as King Charles was concerned, the Massachusetts Bay Company was a business for profit led by wealthy London merchants, among them Simon Bradstreet and William Coddington. Secretly, however, the Massachusetts Bay Company investors intended from the start to emigrate, taking control of the company with them. If an investor did not manage to emigrate, his options would be either to invest passively or to sell to those who did emigrate. The most interesting aspect of the charter was that it did not specify where the controlling council would meet. As soon as could be arranged, it would be meeting in New England. In April 1629 John Winthrop was elected first governor of the Massachusetts Bay Colony, and he set his sights on sending a large flotilla in 1630. His hidden purpose was to enable a Puritan settlement with little control by King Charles.

John Cotton was twenty years Roger's senior, working as the teaching reverend in Alford, Lincolnshire. John championed enabling members of a church to determine who could join, who should be banished, and other matters, as the body of Christ. This was in direct opposition to Bishop Laud, who believed in a strict hierarchy of authority. Bishop Laud was therefore already watching John Cotton closely. Thomas Hooker had been a close friend of John Cotton since they'd been together at Emanuel College at Cambridge; Thomas had been only two years behind John. Thomas Hooker was an excellent, persuasive speaker and was currently hired as lecturer at the Chelmsford Cathedral. John Winthrop Senior, Thomas, and Roger would take off on horseback to meet up with John, and they would then join John in his carriage for the rest of the ride in, with their horses left behind to rest for the ride home.

Roger, John Cotton, John Winthrop Senior, and Thomas were bumping along in the carriage enjoying the summer breeze.

"You can see the commitment to toleration in 1 Corinthians 7, when heathen are kept in the family after one converts." Roger was expounding on the scriptural basis for the good treatment and toleration of the native peoples in America, even if they did not convert.

"Yes, but you are ignoring completely 1 Corinthians 5:5, when evil is in our midst: 'You must deliver this man to Satan for the destruction of his flesh that his spirit may be saved in the day of the Lord Jesus.'" Cotton went on, "What is destruction of his flesh but death itself? In the New Israel, those not compliant with the Puritan ideal should be put to death."

"That's just not what it means!" Roger was excited, as he'd caught Cotton in an error by knowing the Greek the verses came from. "Deliver, not kill, deliver—as in, take him to Satan. If his motives are sinful, Satan will drag him down and then the burden bearer will be so miserable that he will be most likely to confess and repent. 'Destruction of his flesh', means 'destruction of his health and worldly gain'. The whole point of ejecting the evil-doer from the garden of God's worshipers is to effect repentance so that he will be saved. Tell him the Gospel and deprive him of resources and fellowship, and await repentance, don't kill him. How will you help God save him after you kill him? God loves that heathen as much as he loves you."

Thomas whispered to Roger with a laugh, "Keep going! I do believe you'll convince him yet!"

On and on they went while Thomas Hooker dozed off, for the moment happily safe among good friends.

At the end of the summer, Jane entreated Aunt Joan for forgiveness of her brash behavior after the Roger affair, and she was restored to full honor, the threat of a long grudge having passed. The next letter for her hand was accepted, and only six months after Roger's dismissal as Jane's suitor, William Hooke was her husband. Lady Barrington felt fully justified and pleased. Her niece would fulfill both women's highest aspirations. Jug and Oliver were married in grand style by fall. Lady Barrington could check two good matches off her list of to-dos.

Political powers were not interested in these couples but rather were restless about the religious romance the Essex chaplain hotheads promoted. As summer ended, Bishop Laud engineered a private chat with loyal Anglicans as he toured from London to Norwich. In Finchinfield he met with Sir William Martin, a merchant neighbor to the Masham estate. With leaves swirling around in the breeze, they walked around the gardens while their coaches took a break. After pleasantries, the bishop got down to business. "I am looking over the private chaplains at the estates around the country to find suitable men for good positions. I'd like you to take some Sunday visits to key estates nearby and report back to me on services you experience and the content of the sermons. Can you do this for me?" asked Bishop Laud.

"I'm honored that you'd trust me with such a task. How will I know what to report about?" replied William Martin, a little shaken. As a merchant in the area, he dared not refuse the bishop. He counted on church families to buy the shoes he imported.

"Just take careful notes on the sermon and the order of the worship, and report the facts to me. No need for commentary, but be sure to include anything unusual or inspiring that you find," replied Bishop Laud evenly.

"Are there particular estates you most want me to visit?" asked Sir William.

"No, I'm sure your friends will lead you to their most inspiring chaplains without my help. If I knew who I was looking for, I'd go myself," the Bishop told him. He didn't want to scare anyone off. At the same time, merchants were vulnerable to trade disruption, so they were most easily controlled.

Sir William Martin's fall Sunday visit to Otes followed soon after. He'd heard great things from Sir William Masham about his chaplain, Roger Williams, though Lady Joan had not been as positive. The chaplain dared to allude to her advanced age and mortality in an effort to get her to pray more vigilantly, Sir William Masham confided as explanation for her opinion. Sir William Martin was curious.

That Sunday Roger preached on the subject of prayer. He preached from Isaiah 66:3–6, focusing on how false prayer was a stench to God, more foul than prayer to idols. He lambasted forced prayer of one man upon another, common memorized prayer, and public ritual prayer. He asked his listeners to search their hearts and offer heartfelt, earnest prayer to the Lord.

Sir William Martin was both inspired to prayer and at the same time dubious about the condemnation of ritual prayers in the common prayer book. After all, he'd prayed them all his life, and they were a part of each day's worship. He believed they inspired earnest reflection. He wrote of his concern that Roger could be prone to error, describing it as much less settled than what he'd actually heard, and embedding his concerns in much praise for the scriptural basis and passionate fire he'd heard from Roger that day. It was enough to get Roger on what was turning out to be a lengthy list of chaplains whom Bishop Laud meant to pressure toward correction or silence.

Bishop Laud watched the dissent from the Anglican orthodoxy growing and organizing itself. He saw more threat than the young preachers, including Roger, imagined. By fall Bishop Laud resolved to stamp out this

Puritan nonsense. The easiest way to do so was to stamp out the position of chaplain in these private manors altogether. Let the rich come to a proper church with everyone else.

A private visit from Sir Edward Coke provided a word of warning to Roger. A staunch Anglican himself, Sir Edward expressed with some disappointment the reports he'd heard about Roger. At this stage of his career, Roger needed to garner respect, not controversy. He encouraged Roger both to recover his relationship with the bishop and to conform in order to advance in position.

Bishop Laud continued to expand his crackdown. He observed that it was the lecturing ministers who were the driving force of the Puritan movement, inciting people to read Bibles. He eliminated the position of lecturer wherever he found it, including at Chelmsford Cathedral, to force the uniform, prescribed worship he sought. Even after retiring from his position as lecturer, Thomas Hooker's acquaintances and his public persuasiveness got him noticed by the court. Instead of enjoying a quiet retirement, the middle-aged Thomas was considering running to Holland.

All the men felt the pressure, and continued long rides to Sepringham created a relief valve in their lives.

Otes, AD 1629

As the autumn deepened, Roger grew very ill. A fever raged in him, and Sir Masham's family feared for his life. Much of his time was spent in a coma or delirium.

Roger, when conscious, felt that all the world weighed him down. He did not want to move. He felt dizzy, and the least movement made him queasy, and noise, though close by, seemed to come from many rooms away. While he could hear voices, it was as a small child, without understanding.

Sometime during this period the news was brought of the death of Robert Wightman, Katherine's husband, from fevers brought on by his tooth worm malady. Roger was too ill to attend the funeral.

During Roger's fevers, William Hooke accepted a post as chaplain on the ship sailing for the Providence Company to the West Indies. William and Jane would go as a newly married couple. Chaplain Hooke would replace a German Calvinist minister sent home in disgrace for singing inappropriate songs on Sunday. With his hope for Jane gone, Roger began a slow recovery.

Roger dreamed ... and Johannes called out to him repeatedly in these dreams. "Roger, where are the Indians? I'm in Heaven waiting, and you promised me you'd introduce me to the Indian Americans. You're not welcome yet up here at the gates of Paradise. Roger, go back and find the Indians. They are waiting for you."

Another time: "Roger, where are you? HH is here, and he's so proud to know we got his letters to the end. What will you do with the letter, Roger? How will you honor it?"

There was no respite from these dreams, and the fever raged on.

The task of nursing the delirious Roger fell to Mary, Jug's maid. Mary Barnard was as plain as Jane was exquisite. She came from a solid family, and placement with the big manor as maid was considered an honor. Mary was Jug's best friend and her closest companion, but with all the time Jug now spent with Oliver, Mary found herself sewing alone more and more often. Mary was compassionate, and she nursed Roger well, with cooling cloths and frequent baths. She sat by his bedside often and prayed for him, for how could a chaplain pray for himself?

One morning in late fall, as Mary sat in her now accustomed spot darning socks, Roger woke up, finally lucid for a bit. Quietly he watched Mary. She reminded him now of his mum, with her quiet, steady hands and her care for others.

His dreams of Johannes shook him, when he remembered them. Apparently he cried out often, for Mary began to inquire about Johannes.

"Who was Johannes?"

"A childhood friend." The guarded answer showed that Roger was not happy, and he wondered what of his deepest secrets he had divulged while incoherent. It was an uncomfortable feeling in a dangerous world. Mary understood and quelled the questions in her heart. It took a while, but Roger learned that Mary was not talking to others about his past, had not allowed anyone else close when he was delirious, and was deserving of his trust.

While he lay, weakened and recovering, they talked of everything—of the social life of the manor and the marriages all around them, of Bishop Laud's rumored threats and actions, and of native souls in America.

Roger learned that Mary wanted eight children, having raised her four brothers with her father after her mother's early death. Her father was a separatist minister, and an author. He'd taught Mary how to read a little, but never to write. She read the Bible, but her father's books were beyond her ability to enjoy. Roger asked for one of the books, and she dutifully brought "The Isle of Man." It put him soundly to sleep.

By the time Roger was up and about, Mary and he were fast friends.

"There is a ship being planned, you know, to head for New England sometime next year. Why not be on it?" suggested Mary.

The more Roger considered and prayed, the more he became certain that God was willing his departure for New England. He was grateful to Mary and began to look at her differently. Finally he went to visit her father, Richard, and asked for her hand in marriage. This time his offer was readily accepted.

Mary and Roger were married quietly on December 15, 1629, at the High Laver church a mile and a half from Otes. Alice Pemberton Williams watched as her last surviving child married for the first time. Sydrach was the best man, and Jug, the maid of honor.

That would leave Robert as the bachelor brother and single dad, though in truth Anna Grace was left more and more with Sydrach's family. Robert was happy enough with a trip to the inn from time to time, and had no intention of taking responsibility again for more family soon. In this he was not traditional, since men of means often married within a year of losing a wife, especially if there were children. Robert loved Anna Grace, as did Ann and Sydrach. Ann and Sydrach's house was an environment suitable to children, and Robert enjoyed feeling unencumbered. He enjoyed traveling to support Sydrach's business.

Roger and Mary continued their employment at Otes through the next year. Slowly Roger regained strength and resolve. He continued his friendships with Winthrop Senior and with John the Younger, Cotton, and Hooker. Mary spent her time getting to know Rebecca Throckmorton, a maid she worked with at the pastry house Hatfield Broad Oak shared with Otes.

"Sorry I'm late, my daughter was ill, and it was hard to leave her," said Rebecca breathlessly.

"So you have children already?" asked Mary.

"Yes," she sighed. "I've been married to John since he finished his scrivener's apprenticeship in 1627. I got pregnant right away and had twins. John is healthy, but Patience gets every illness that goes around."

"How is it that you can still work here then?" asked Mary.

"John doesn't much like being a scrivener. He has big dreams. I work here, and he keeps the children while I work, and then he does his work from the house when I get home. We are saving every penny for passage to New England, where John intends to have ships of trade. He can get investors for the ship and pay them back from trade he claims, but we must raise passage for the family. I don't want him to go alone, like so many do. I want to be there with him building our dreams."

"Roger and I will also be traveling to New England. We're saving for a passage right now and trying to time the best departure," said Mary. "Maybe we'll go together!"

CHAPTER 12

Alford, Lincolnshire, AD 1629

Anne Hutchinson was in love with God and hung on John Cotton's every word, whenever and wherever she could hear him. Often she and her husband took off on horseback to ride twenty-one miles to hear Cotton preach on Sundays at St. Botoloph, where he was minister. Anne's family included seven children, and another one on the way, so she didn't always get to go as often as she would have liked.

Others claimed that Reverend Cotton's sermons were dry—some fell asleep—but Anne loved them. Anne, as a woman, was educated at home. Her father was a minister, so the books in the house were about theology, and that was her reading material, along with the Bible. Anne was a brilliant child, and her father found a great deal of inspiration in the questions she'd ask while he taught her, and so he was willing to feed this dry sponge all the liquid it would hold. Now John Cotton had taken over the role as her teacher.

Anne married Will Hutchinson, a merchant, in 1612 at the age of twenty-one. She had her first child a year later. Just this year, 1630, they'd lost two daughters: Susanna, at the age of sixteen, and Elizabeth at age nine after a fever. During the sickness, Anne and eleven-year-old Bridget were nurses in shifts and did not leave the house at all.

After that loss, Anne immersed herself even more deeply in the Church. Cotton had been counselor as well as minister to her. Anne often wished it had been she the Lord had taken and not her precious daughters. Now, with rumors that Bishop Laud would oust John Cotton, she was concerned for his future as well and wanted to plan to follow wherever he might go.

She hoped he would not retire and cease preaching, as she felt he was the best she had ever encountered.

The announcer at worship said at the end of the service, "You are invited on a special pilgrimage. It will be two hundred miles to Southampton to hear John Cotton give a special address to our parishioners and others leaving for New England."

On the way back home, Anne worked to convince her husband to watch over the family and to invest in a ticket for her to join them. She could not bear the thought of being left behind, and eventually her husband too realized that he did not want to deal with the disappointment of an Anne who had been left behind. He supported her and donated generously to the expedition, hoping that in return his pregnant wife would be well cared for during her absence from home.

Bristol, England AD 1630

Much as John Robinson blessed the departure of Holland's Pilgrims, headed for the *Mayflower* in 1620, Cotton delivered the blessing for the Massachusetts Bay Colony eleven-fleet expedition. A crowd of thousands was gathered on April 8—families of those departing and supporters who hoped to follow if the plantation was successful. Much was at stake. King Charles looked to Bishop Laud for the stewardship of the church, ensuring tremendous and continuing persecution in England.

John Cotton's persuasive oratorical skills were immense. The sermon argued that settling the New World was a divine calling on a par with the calling of Israel to settle Canaan. Cotton's sermon was titled "God's Promise to His Plantation." Cotton explained the experiences of Biblical emigrations and translated them to what should be expected in New England. God blessed the emigrants by giving them victory at war with prior inhabitants, as with David, or he made the inhabitants willing to sell their land, as with Abraham, or to give riches to the newcomers, as Pharaoh gave the land of Goshen to Jacob's son, or he would make the land empty before they arrived, as he did for Noah. He set up the emigrants to look for any and all of these behaviors as signs of his blessing.

He went on to lay out Biblical reasons to immigrate to the New World. He was working from an outline on parchment he'd prepared as notes. The outline read:

1) To emigrate on a temporary basis, for learning, as when the Queen of Sheba visited Solomon;

2) To search for valuable merchandise like the merchant searching for pearls in <u>Matthew 13:45–46</u> and <u>Proverbs 31:14</u>. Cotton took special care to note that Jesus never asked his followers to emulate the sinful parts of the humans in his stories, only the admirable parts—as all humans contain both a sinful portion and a godly portion. Thus the merchant searching for valuable pearls is engaging in godly behavior, since Jesus asked his followers to copy this behavior when searching for souls in need of salvation;

3) To plant a colony when prior civilizations have grown too full, giving the example of such a colony prospering in <u>Acts 16:12</u>;

4) To remove to a new place, as one's talents and gifts are better utilized there, especially if he is not otherwise bound. For this example he used the story of Joseph remaining in Egypt as told in <u>Genesis chapters 37-46</u>.

5) To remove from a jurisdiction with unjust laws. Here Cotton spent the most time, as he was approaching the central reason most Puritans would leave. He followed with many examples from religious, economic, and civil realms.

   a. Religious

      i. When leaders force worship of anything other than God, as with Jeroboam encouraging worship of golden calves and dismissing priests who would not follow him, causing those priests to leave his jurisdiction. <u>2 Chronicles 11:13–15</u>

      ii. When evil or grievous sin as defined in scripture is made legal and approved, and God's people are asked not to teach what the Bible says is true anymore. <u>Micah 2:6–11</u>

      iii. When persecution of God's people for their faith must be escaped in order to survive. <u>Acts 13:46–47</u>

b. Economic

    i. To be absolved of the debts of an unjust creditor, or to avoid an unjust tax. <u>1 Thessalonians 4:6</u>

    ii. To avoid miseries of debt, a form of bankruptcy <u>1 Samuel 22:1–2</u>

c. Civil

    i. To be sent as one in command of a new colony by the existing civil authorities or by God's authorities. <u>Matthew 8:9</u>

    ii. To leverage civil incentives offered for purpose of transplantation.

In conclusion, Cotton promised, "If you are godly in your behavior, God himself will protect you and assure that the colony takes root."

The desire to immigrate to New England was implanted in many hearts that day.

Anne Hutchinson's was one of those hearts. The idea seemed preposterous, as her husband's family and merchant business had deep roots in Lincolnshire, but it was intriguing and mesmerizing and would grow compelling.

Among the departing receiving goodbyes were John Winthrop Senior, three of his sons, and his brother-in-law, Arthur Tyndale. His son Stephen was eleven, and Adam was ten, and they climbed aboard hand in hand with their father on the *Arabella*. Henry on the other hand, was with friends and boarded at the last minute. In all, seven hundred Puritans departed for New England, along with over a hundred seamen. Both John Winthrop Senior and Henry left family behind. The families were expected to follow once affairs were settled, and babies were born.

The *Arabella* first sailed along the coast from the Isle of Wight to Yarmouth, making stops for supplies. At the first stop, John Winthrop Senior sent Henry, one of Henry's friends, and some servants ashore in small pinnaces to pick up an ox and a herd of cattle. On the way back to the ship, the winds were against the small boats, making it difficult to catch the *Arabella*. The servants made it back with the ox. Henry and his friends stayed out later in the night, having one last entertaining evening ashore, and they were unable with the cattle to catch the *Arabella*. They had to settle for catching the *Talbot*, the ship that was second in command. Henry wasn't disappointed in creating distance between his strict father and his friends for the passage.

Bristol, England AD 1630

After the departure, John Winthrop the Younger, twenty-four years of age, returned to Groton in Suffolk and was immediately in charge of the wide-ranging Winthrop affairs in England. He was tasked with resolving legal affairs with respect to selling properties in England, which resulted in his spending a good bit of time in London. He was also charged, with his stepmother's assistance, with looking out for the extended family. That family included his own wife, Martha, his full brother, Forth, aged twenty-one, and his stepbrothers, Deane, age eight, and William, age three, as well as his stepsister Mary, Deane's twin. Finally there was Bess. John found himself lord of a significant estate. He was immediately embroiled in his father's complex business affairs. He was left with less time than he wanted to plan his own emigration.

John Winthrop the Younger and his wife Martha made a powerful team. She'd already taught her husband doctoring, and she'd already picked up the Austin Friar shorthand. John the Younger told his military and travel stories to the younger children, and Martha told stories of doctors and patients and the apothecary and trips to the woods to gather herbal supplies. Both were intellectual and constantly learning new skills, and they enjoyed involved discussions that only Forth made the effort to follow, when he was around.

Forth was studying at Exeter for the ministry. He was engaged to yet another Fones cousin, Ursula. He was so deep into his own affairs that he did not write to his father in New England. Soon he was the only family member that had not written.

Back at Otes, Roger noticed that discussions more frequently turned to common ceremonies and forced worship. Roger put forth his arguments against common prayer, being convinced it was deep sin to join in them. If the Gospel was not preached directly, according to Paul it was some other gospel, an idol, and they must leave, shaking the sand off their sandals as they went. Cotton and Hooker were more equivocal, recognizing the falsity of dragging citizens to church for unfelt prayer, but wanting lost souls exposed to faith over and over until they were able to believe. No child wanted to learn rote lessons, but no adult could read Greek or Latin without those lessons. Neither was convinced that the common prayer book was a false gospel, and so they did not agree with the graveness of the error of using accepted rituals, though they preferred, when able, to depart from them. The debates raged all the way to London and back again, week after week.

Bishop Laud, forcing the issue, threatened Roger's employment at Otes. The good ship *Lyon*, departing November 1630, became not only a desired goal for Roger, but also a source of escape.

New England, AD 1630

Eighty cold and—according to the children—boring days after departure, the *Arabella* arrived in New England. The first days were spent sailing up the coast catching mackerel one day and cod the next. The fish were so plentiful in these waters that the men only needed a couple of hours with line and hook to feed the entire boat a dinner of fresh fish, which was much appreciated, as provisions on board were very low.

The prior settlers were, as always, glad of resupply but a little shocked that so many would soon join them. Waves of immigrants had been arriving for a year now, and as they arrived, groups of settlers were encouraged to leave and start new settlements elsewhere. It seemed that each ship brought more people than food.

The elder men went off to plan who would settle where. They sent groups of settlers north to the Saugus River and south to Dorchester. They also introduced the new charter. Meanwhile, the boys wanted to explore.

A group of young men not yet freeholders headed upriver a ways, and when they stopped, some younger boys kept going. They were happy to be on land. Stephen and Adam were among them. In the woods they came across a meadow full of wild strawberries. They sent word back, and soon many from the ship were spending the afternoon picking strawberries, eating all they could and taking some back for the remaining passengers.

That evening the newcomers were treated to venison pasty and beer. The men and boys slept on the ship, but the well-to-do women were taken in by the town, and they slept in homes.

Two weeks later the *Talbot* arrived, having lost fourteen passengers on the way. Henry survived the trip but did not see his father before heading off the next day to explore with his brothers. In the moonlight before dawn, they headed upriver by boat with others. They headed for the mouth of a smaller stream they wished to explore, and travelled up this stream as far it was navigable.

By daybreak on July 1 they were hiking up the stream, and it was a hot, muggy day. By noon the group stopped for lunch near a large, deep pool. Newly reunited, Henry and his brothers Stephen and Adam moved on alone upstream past the falls that created the pool. By midafternoon they were far inland near a Massachusetts Algonquian village. The stream was a little narrower now, fifteen feet across, full of rocks and rushing fresh water. The boys were all thinking of a nice swim to cool off.

"Look!" shouted Stephen. "A canoe." There was a beach on the far side and, sure enough, a traditional dugout canoe was beached there.

"That looks like an Indian's canoe," said Henry. "I don't see anyone around, though. If we can nab that canoe, we can float back downstream to the others in no time. I'm going in."

The boys all stripped off their clothes and got ready to climb in. The younger boys didn't try to follow Henry, though, as they didn't know how to swim. The water was way deeper than they expected and the footing more treacherous than they were ready to tackle, and they decided to sit on the bank with their feet in the water and watch Henry's progress.

Henry jumped right in.

"Don't you think the owners will want that canoe back?" asked Adam of Stephen. "What if we make them mad, and they have bows and arrows?"

"Don't worry. Henry's been all over. He knows what he's doing. We won't ride it far. I'm sure they will find it again."

The current was very swift on this side of the river, and Henry was immediately pushed downstream way faster than he anticipated. Soon he was trying to swim upstream to get back to where the canoe lay. He tired quickly, still weak from days of limited provisions, and the water felt cold. Soon he was making no progress toward the canoe and was being washed downstream with the current. There was no standing in this swift current, and there was no moving to either bank. In the center of the stream, it was all Henry could do to keep afloat.

The boys grabbed their clothes, and they ran downstream after Henry. In the blink of an eye, as they were picking up the clothes, Henry disappeared. He was farther downstream than they could see, and they ran after him.

The boys ran till they were exhausted, and there was no sign of Henry. Finally they reached the rapids, followed by two-foot falls, and below it was the quiet pool where the other young men were last seen napping peacefully, but the area seemed eerily empty.

"He couldn't have gotten this far, could he?" asked Adam.

"I don't think so. Let's sit and think a minute, and get our clothes on in case others are still at the pool. I don't like being out here anymore," said Stephen.

The boys dressed. While they were dressing, Henry's naked, lifeless body shot down the falls and into the pool. For a minute he went under and then he popped up again. He was still out of reach of the boys. They stared in disbelief.

"Do you think we can fish him out?" Adam asked with a shudder.

"I think Father will not want to lose more than one son today, Adam. We'd better go find the others."

The boys headed off downstream. The other young men were hiking downstream as well, and it took some time for the boys to catch up to them.

Weekan and Aunan, also eleven and ten years old, heard the commotion in the bush near their canoe while they were gathering strawberries. They were on the other side of the stream, watching in the trees as Henry jumped in. These boys knew the currents and how they played on the far side of the beach, and they were amazed at first. Then they watched and realized that there was no need for amazement; he was just foolish. After the English boys disappeared from sight, they gathered the canoe. They knew the last spot to beach before the falls and how to portage around them. When they reached the quiet pool below the falls, the younger boys were already gone. They pulled Henry into their canoe, dragged him on the portage upstream of the falls, and took him home to the tribe.

The boys found their mother. They knew their father was off on a hunt.

"Mom, we have a dead English in our canoe who drowned in the river. He has no clothes. What should we do with him?"

Chapter 13

Naumkeag, AD 1630

Oonue knew that Miantonomoh would not want the boys to start trouble with the English. Visiting their cousins for a few years to help a struggling tribe, they'd primarily brought young men with them to provide labor. They also intended, however, to learn this Massachusetts tribe's technological improvements in wampum manufacture. Because wampum production is a woman's job, Miantonomoh brought his wife Oakana, called Oonue now that she was married, and his children on the trip, even though it was unusual. Oonue, as a guest of the tribe, went off to find the old Squaw Sachem Jole. Soon there was a crowd at the boat staring at the ugly dead English.

Jole, Nanepashemet's widow, was sachem over the northern range of the Massachusetts tribes, including most of eastern Massachusetts, north of Boston. Nanepashement and his children were spared the plague because, while it was spreading in their land in 1615, they were suffering a siege and were effectively quarantined in a fort structure surrounded by Tarrantine. When food supplies were finally dangerously low, Nanepashement planned a diversion that got him killed but let his boys escape the siege. After Jole's sons escaped the siege, they lived the nomadic life of their remote ancestors and spent most of their energy evading capture or worse.

Wampum is a woven material made of shells. The white beads are ground from northern whelk, and the purple beads from quahog. Each bead is about 5.5mm in length and 4mm in width, with a 1-mm hole though the length. Beads were threaded into cloth. The iron tools sped up the production process, compared with the stone drills used before the Europeans arrived, and they enabled more accuracy in drilling the holes. White wampum symbolizes purity, light, and joy. Purple wampum symbolizes sorrow, serious loss, and the need for recovery and new growth. Often the two are mixed, symbolizing the balance that is most highly valued. Originally wampum was made by hand and, as highly valued art or sacred objects, it was routinely gifted at ceremony.

With the arrival of the Dutch, trade using wampum as currency began, and the need for wampum skyrocketed. The Dutch brought tools to improve the manufacture of wampum and began to trade the tools along with other desirable European goods, to obtain wampum. They then used the wampum to obtain furs from tribes farther west, often Iroquois. As the situation with English competition escalated, the Dutch began to trade firearms as well. A previously peaceful set of Algonquian relationships was disrupted, as the power balance changed. The arrival of the English in Salem drove the Dutch north, shifting the power balance yet again.

Now that the Tarrantine were vacating the land called Namkeag near Salem to follow the Dutch north, Jole's tribe was ready to rebuild and recover. They reclaimed the old wampum-building site and reactivated it first with the iron tools obtained in Tarrantine raids, and were soon augmenting with tools obtained in trade with the English.

Jole leveraged kinship ties with other tribes to rebuild in the Algonquian way. She sent a request for support to her brother, Canonicus. Miantonomoh and Oonue arrived with extended family in response in 1628.

The expectation was that Miantonomoh's expedition would stay long enough to stabilize, create a food supply, and find wives for Jole's remaining braves. Jole hoped that some of the visiting young men would decide to stay, further populating her tribe. It was customary for boys to travel and to join the tribes of their chosen wives. It was also customary to take wives as property in negotiated settlements, and Miantonomoh would be expected to acquire wives in this way for the braves, since Jole's tribe had few suitable women.

Canonicus's choice of Miantonomoh was shrewd, as it got him away from Canonicus's sons, Yotan and Meiksah, to let him develop independent leadership skills. The young men were like young bulls, very aggressive and always fighting for status. Canonicus did not want Yotan's attitude about the English to pervade the tribe so deeply that strategic options were cut off.

Canonicus also expected Oonue and her daughters to study the manufacture of wampum. Oonue's tribe had collected shellfish and made shellfish fabric, or wampum, for thousands of years. Oonue recalled how Canonicus had explained it to her and Miantonomoh before they left.

"The trade with the European visitors has fundamentally changed the demand for wampum. They have an insatiable need for beaver skins and other furs. They are willing to go far inland to obtain fur, and all the inland people are always hungry for wampum. Jole acquired iron tools and knows how to use them. If you come back with these tools and the skills to use them, I will set you up as your own tribal unit and enable you to prosper as a part of my confederation. You will become your own 'little sachem,' or Manisses." Oonue fully expected her daughters to return home with the family at the end of the expedition, and she knew this meant that Miantonomoh must be successful in finding wives for the boys who could regenerate Jole's people. She feared there would likely be intertribal battle over this issue.

Jole wanted no trouble with the English. Her numbers were too small, and the English were her chosen protection from the Tarrantine. She sent some of Miantonomoh's braves downstream with the body and an interpreter. The braves had instructions to find Endicott if they could not catch the hikers to ensure that the body was properly returned without any blame falling on her tribe. She wished the boys could have saved the man. A life preserved would have been of more value to the tribe.

The braves with Henry's corpse caught up to a group of young Englishmen returning to the pool to look for Henry. Dismayed, the men clothed Henry's body and returned in silence to the ship.

Upon hearing the news from his boys, John Winthrop Senior cried out the first of several laments: "Oh, my poor, poor son!"

The young men, the new governor, John Winthrop Senior, and ex-Governor Endicott dug a grave and buried Henry. John Winthrop Senior wrote his wife, Forth, and John Winthrop the Younger private notes of sorrow.

John Winthrop Senior's brother-in-law Arthur Tyndale was shocked both by Henry's death and by how many of Arthur's own friends on prior voyages had not survived. He wanted to go home. His visions of happiness were dashed. He decided to arrange a return on the first ship to leave New England. The *Lyon* set sail for England a week later, and Arthur Tyndale was on it, bearer of news and letters.

London, AD 1630

"Mum, I don't know what I'm supposed to do. There's no food in the house, and I've no money, and my babies are hungry. Robert's meager leavings paid the rent this month, but I don't know what we'll do next. Can I move back home?"

Alice Pemberton Williams wasn't falling for this. She needed her daughter to buck up and get some Pemberton back into her. She thought for a bit before responding, trying to think of some options in real time.

"Katherine, daughter, let's think harder here. Look at how quickly your Fone friends married off once their father died. What you need is a man to support you. You are young. You can still bear him children. Have you any prospects?"

Katherine burst into tears.

"Mum, the babies have me occupied every minute. When am I to find a man? Have you a match for me?" she asked, enough Pemberton finally intruding to have her at least turn the tables.

"Hmmm … actually, perhaps I do. Let me investigate some options on your behalf, okay? We'll arrange this the old-fashioned way, if love has not found you a mate," Alice replied.

Over the next few days, Alice looked for a chance to talk to John Davies alone when he was not in a hurry to do her books.

"John, have you a wife yet?" Alice knew the answer, but she wanted to hear whether there were plans.

"Why of course not, ma'am. I work too many hours to find a wife!" he replied with a smile.

"I think you would do better work with a wife," Alice proposed, watching him carefully. "My daughter needs a husband, and she will make a good wife. She's a hard worker. Would you consider her?"

John's eyes went wide. He saw potential, not to mention job security. To his own surprise, he wondered why he hadn't thought of it first. He hadn't thought she would be interested.

"Would she have me, ma'am?" he asked softly.

"I'll let you know," Alice replied.

That afternoon she saw Katherine again, and she promoted John Davies. "John has been my clerk for five years now. He is solid and honest. Most important, he is healthy. He wants to know whether, if he asks, you will say yes. He's very shy."

"Oh, Mum, you know right now I'd marry a horse if he could provide for us," said Katherine. "Don't tell him that, of course. Tell him yes."

The deal was done, and the two were quietly married within the month so that Roger and Mary could attend before they had to leave for the *Lyon*.

By year's end Katherine was pregnant with John's child, and the older children were calling him Father.

Naumkeag, AD 1630

Oonue was proud of the wampum factory production. She measured the factory output by the tens of fathoms. Because she wanted her factory worker daughters to return south with her, she convinced Miantonomoh to take wampum and attempt to trade it for young wives, thinking this would be a safer path than expecting women as spoils of war. It would need to be a tribe with many women and too few men, else no tribe would be willing to relinquish their women. Miantonomoh and Oonue weren't sure where to find such tribes, but Jole knew. She sent Miantonomoh due west. Miantonomoh remembered Meiksah's desire to go west years ago, and how Yotan talked him out of it. *This could be my moment*, he thought. *If I survive.*

Miantonomoh was dubious that any tribe would relinquish its valuable, hardworking women, or that any potential wife would be willing to return with them. With reservations, he took a group of braves and set off west as the fall of 1630 arrived.

The Connecticut River Valley was a powder keg of conflict waiting for a spark to set war in motion. The beaver were scarce because of overhunting. Normal Algonquian behavior was to use every part of the beaver and to leave beavers in the land to reproduce. At first, as fur demand rose, there was an overabundance of meat because of the desire for the fur. The Algonquian then neglected their horticulture in favor of a more nomadic existence that would allow them to find more fur. When they grew short on plant-based foods, they could trade wampum for food. This worked well for a few years, but now the beaver and other small, edible fur-producing animals were very scarce. The abundance was followed by a famine. The inland tribes had been trading furs for wampum, which they could then use to barter for food from other tribes. The men in the tribes had also been skirmishing, using the firearms that the French traded directly for furs. They had been picking each other off, leaving more women than men in all three neighboring tribes. Now, as the furs grew scarce, famine threatened. The people recognized that the natural balance had been lost, and they must get back in balance to survive.

Miantonomoh arrived in the Connecticut River Valley with winter coming on quickly just as the sachems of these fur-focused tribes realized they were facing famine. While Miantonomoh did not carry food in great stores, he did have wampum that could be traded for food with other tribes farther west. He was quickly able to negotiate wampum for young future wives, a double win from the sachems' perspective, as each woman gone was one less mouth to feed. Miantonomoh was more successful than he had dared to hope and returned home with thirty young potential wives of Pequot, Mohegan, and Nipmuc origin. Of course, they might not have been the hardest workers of each tribe, but they would learn. He tried to get them young, so they would be easier to train. His sweep of the women and his gifts of wampum ironically brought a peace that lasted several years before the balance once again disrupted the tribes' lives and led to war. Meeting Jole's needs in this win-win manner gained Miantonomoh respect with Jole, the Pequot grand sachem Tatobem, and other more minor sachems. Canonicus heard of the success and was well pleased.

The Squaw Sachem Jole was triumphant at Miantonomoh's return with the girls and women. A matching process began, part the couple's choice but overseen by Jole so that there was balance and harmony in the overall result. Jole's three sons and the men Miantonomoh brought from Canonicus's tribe were ceremonially attached to women from the west, and Jole's tribe was strong again. Weekan and Aunan both begged to stay, and Miantonomoh agreed as long as Weekan would choose the highest-status bride: Ale, Jole's granddaughter. Weekan agreed, the pairings were set for the future, and the boys were set to stay.

Miantonomoh decided to return to Canonicus before winter with Oonue and their daughters, Sochepo age nine and Capat age eight, and the younger children. Both Sochepo and Capat were now experts at wampum production, as was Ale. Since they had just added thirty hungry mouths, it was good that eight mouths would leave and not deplete the food over the winter. Jole was a wise sachem, but thirty women was more than even she was prepared to receive.

Before she blessed the departure, Jole asked Oonue to train the new brides in wampum production. Oonue complied, but they were rather slow students, as this was far from their interest, and they did not like the shell dust or the cold water used to dampen the dust. There was a language barrier that slowed the process as well. She taught them enough to produce, but she didn't teach them everything she knew. At the outset, before anyone was paying too much attention, she packed the best three sets of tools for travel. She spent some time with Ale as well, getting her ready to lead the women and inherit Oonue's role. Ale was the same age as many of the brides, and at first they had a hard time respecting her. Jole started spending time at the factory to add some authority to Ale's leadership.

The walk home was a rare, memorable journey for the family. It was traditional that Algonquian men went on expeditions with other men and boys. It was equally traditional that groups of women moved along the coast and traveled to lands where they were encouraging crop growth or harvesting edible plants. It was also frequent for an entire tribe to move between summer coastal harvesting areas and inland hunting grounds protected from winter storms. It was highly unusual for a single-family unit to travel alone. Oonue was carrying the baby on a board, Miantonomoh was carrying the five-year-old-boy, Canonchet, piggyback, and the girls each carried a younger sibling on her back. Sochepo carried four-year-old Neechipog, and Capat carried three-year-old Seip. Each parent was also pulling a dugout canoe filled with supplies and gifts, and sometimes in quiet waters they let the children ride atop it. In marshes they tended to make multiple trips from one dry shore to the next, ferrying people and goods. Often they stopped and hunted.

Miantonomoh missed Weekan and Aunan as hunting help. Given that they had taken wives, they were likely to be valuable liaisons and were not likely to return home.

He hoped that he had done the right thing by leaving them behind. They were already stronger men than Jole's sons, and they were forceful personalities. He believed they could develop into leaders, even though they were not first in line for succession, and their prospects were better here in a small but rapidly growing tribe with weak leadership and many enemies to conquer. There was great opportunity for them to make a name, if they so chose.

Miantonomoh began to train Sochepo with the bow and arrow. Sochepo was a graceful child, and her aim was true. It was a great honor to have a high-status man train a girl to hunt, and Sochepo wanted to learn all she could before Canonchet was old enough to be a real help. Canonchet tagged along and learned what he could. He certainly didn't think he was too young. Miantonomoh noticed this little fellow's assertive nature for the first time and smiled. His prospects were brighter with his older brothers placed so far away. Perhaps it was a good plan after all.

The distance they covered would be a fifteen-hour walk as the bird flies, but that was not the route chosen. Instead they followed the shore, where the land was flat, and food was plentiful, and the smaller members could sometimes ride in the canoe with the supplies. They took their time, enjoying each other and the fall weather. Sochepo and Capat were very happy not to be making wampum every day, as was Oonue. All knew they were likely to return to this business soon enough.

The family turned west and took the portage between the Manomet and Scusset rivers and then resumed the coastal walk/canoe. Their route covered three times the straight-line distance—forty-five hours of solid walking at adult speeds. They were part walking, part lugging, and part riding in the canoes. They arrived back at the home tribe in about a month and a half, just as the weather was crisp, and there was frost at night and dense fog in the morning.

There was great joy at their return. Yotan and Weko planned a great ceremonial jubilation, remembering the joy Yotan's own return brought after years of absence. There was a fire and a dance and feasting, and many stories of the successful restoration of Jole's tribe. In front of the whole tribe, Canonicus proclaimed the trip a major success; and, as a reward, the family and some friends of the couple's choice would be set up on what the English called Adrian Block Island come spring. Meiksah was relieved. He was not genuinely happy about the return of Miantonomoh, who was growing very strong and popular. While Yotan was not an engaging leader and therefore not a serious contender to succeed Canonicus, Meiksah intended to be a contender. Going west had been Meiksah's idea, but now Miantonomoh was bringing news of success leveraging relationships in the west. Meiksah was married to a high-status woman in Magnus, now called Matantuck. He was respected, and his wife was very popular with the women. It was a tricky business. Sachems must be popular leaders. If they are not, the people will go to another sachem. Meiksah admired the popularity Miantonomoh could inspire, recognized Matantuck's sister Oonue as an equally powerful wife. It smarted that Miantonomoh was so successful and had not even gone very far west. Meiksah liked the idea of Miantonomoh on the island, out of sight.

Adrian Block Island lies thirteen miles off the coast of Canonicus's Narragansett tribal summer camp lands. It was named for the Dutch explorer who charted it in 1614. The Niantic, once an independent tribe, claimed it. Now the Niantic tribe was decimated and divided into two sets of people. The western people were allying with the Pequot to rebuild, whereas the eastern group, including most of the group on Adrian Block Island, was allied with Canonicus. Miantonomoh transferred his skills from assisting Jole to leading and rebuilding this group of Niantic and Narragansett people. The existing up-and-coming Niantic leaders—even Juanumo, a blood cousin of Miantonomoh—were all suspected to have deep Pequot ties. Canonicus hoped that Miantonomoh would gain the trust of these people.

CHAPTER 14

Groton, AD 1630

Arthur Tyndale arrived in Groton in October with the terrible news of Henry's death.

Unexpectedly, in early November Forth Winthrop returned home to Groton and took to his bed with fever. After a few days and many passionate speeches about God, his love of the family, and his love for Ursula, he passed away. These speeches were very similar to—and possibly modeled on—the speeches that had impacted him deeply when his father's eloquent second wife was bedridden with mortal fevers when he was only six years old. Forth was dead at twenty-one years of age.

As Roger and Mary were preparing to leave Otes for the final time, word came that John the Younger's brother Forth had passed away and would be buried November 23. This was on top of the news of Henry's death. Roger and Mary changed direction and traveled northwest to Groton to help to bury Forth there. John the Younger was in the process of selling Groton, yet there was no other family place in England more appropriate to bury him.

"Henry and Forth are gone, both in the prime of life, now entering heaven from opposite sides of the Atlantic," Mary commented.

"He'll never even meet Martha Johanna, our daughter," sobbed Bess. The women surrounded her and removed to the kitchen, leaving the men to their separate grief in the parlor.

Martha, John the Younger's wife and close partner in all affairs, and Mary, Roger's wife, organized the food and the mourning to support John the Younger and Bess in their double grief. In performing simple daily tasks in sorrowful silence, the two women grew very close.

Later, Roger offered to carry letters from Margaret, Martha, and Bess across the sea to John Winthrop Senior. Margaret professed jealousy that Martha and John the Younger often played in their secret code when separated, with intervening letter carriers and readers none the wiser. Margaret's letters to John Winthrop Senior were plain to all who saw them and so took a more serious tone. Roger was surprised and asked Martha to show him an example of the code. He could see that Martha knew the Austin Friar shorthand very well, and she was the first and only woman ever to learn it, as far as he knew.

"John, how many people have you taught the shorthand?" Roger was furious.

"Only Martha! She is flesh of my flesh now, Roger. I travel a great deal, and we communicate using your shorthand. I really haven't taught anyone separate from myself. And I wouldn't—it would limit what I can say to Martha safely. I understand the need for privacy well," replied John the Younger. "Martha is one of the smartest people either of us will ever encounter. I know you don't approve of women's education, but Martha is a real exception to the rule. Besides, you taught her most of the code while she was watching you teach it to me. You just didn't know. Trust me on this. You'll learn its value in the New World."

Roger acquiesced for now in deference to John the Younger's losses. He would never have taught Mary the shorthand or involved her in any political business, and he did not approve, but he would respect John the Younger's right to organize his own household the way he wanted to. Besides, Mary would never have figured out the code on her own.

Turning to the matters at hand, following the Puritan tradition, they now focused on forcing themselves to give thanks, as Roger prayed, "Lord, comfort us in our afflictions, and draw us close to you in your Word, as we give thanks for:

- Bess and Margaret having survived childbirth, which is a great cause for celebration;
- the twenty-one years of quiet life granted to Forth, and the blessing of knowing him;
- Bess's new baby, Martha Johanna, and Margaret's new baby, Anne;
- the safe passage of the eleven ships in the fleet, and the new ventures John Winthrop Senior is undertaking;
- the twenty-three years of adventure granted to Henry, and the brief time he and Bess were allowed together;
- the good health and youthful exuberance of Deane and William."

The ocean loomed large between the halves of the Winthrop family, while they suffered the pain of grief and the demands of the newborns.

Their last evening together Roger and John the Younger were in the parlor after tea, while the women retired to the sitting room.

"What languages have you been studying lately?" asked Roger, knowing John the Younger was always learning.

"Persian has fascinated me since I spent time in Turkey. Not many know it, but I am still brokering messages for Sydrach and enjoy corresponding with the Turkish side in Persian directly," said John the Younger. "What have you been studying?"

"My focus has been on Hebrew and Greek Bible studies while at Otes. Most who come through are Puritan, so most of the discussion turns theological," replied Roger. "In my leisure time, though, I still read John Smith. I've read all of his fourteen books so far. He has much to say on colonization and planning."

"Loan me your latest Smith. I'll try to read it before I go. With all the business to conduct, I don't get too much time anymore. I enjoy retreating to the library with a good book, though. I just finished the second edition of Johannes Keplar's *Cosmic Mystery, the Secret of the World*," said John the Younger.

"Sure, give it back to me when we are both in New England, if you like. And Keplar's secret is …?" asked Roger. He viewed most non-Biblical wisdom with some skepticism, especially someone claiming to have the secret of the world.

"It's all about how to calculate and explain the orbits of the planets around the sun," said John the Younger. "The second edition is half again as long as the first. The new story seems to be in the footnotes. Come look."

The two became happily absorbed for hours in exploring the polygons of Keplar's theories and the Platonic solid model of the solar system. It was a respite from their present-day worries.

Eventually they came back to practical affairs as they prepared to part. "I'm thinking to follow Father to New England in the summer. He has been writing letters about supplies. His first list was for all the luxuries he missed—butter, oatmeal, peas, fruit—and telling us in great detail how to store things so they don't spoil. I can read in each instruction some pricey incident of loss. He wants the eggs stored in salt so they will not break. The liquids must be in hogsheads, as many of their casks are broken, and so on. I think they are often cold, as he warns over and over about the need for coming with many layers of warm clothes.

"His next letter was more basic. He wanted basic foods in greater volume and again in containers that would prevent spoilage. He also asked for building supplies like tar and liquids requiring fermentation like vinegar, and more livestock. He wants grain meals and specifies to air it for three days before packing. He seems to be under a lot of pressure. He warns that there must be a year and half of provisions for every person sent. Finally, and most important, he says not to travel on any other ship than the *Lyon*, and to leave in summer to avoid the worst of the cold on passage. That will have us arrive in New England with provisions as the winter sets in, and they will be much relieved by this. It would seem that Captain William Pierce of the *Lyon* plans ahead well and always arrives with healthier passengers than the other ships."

Roger grew serious. "Mary and I are on our way to the *Lyon*, to set sail soon. Give us the lists. We'll get him what is needed before we go if you assist by funding it. We'll shore up our own and the other passengers' supplies as well. I feel God's blessing that we've planned on the *Lyon*; we'll ensure the warm clothing, but I cannot risk imprisonment by waiting till summer voyage."

They studied John Winthrop Senior's letters to his son in detail. "This is really helpful," said Roger when they were done.

"There's one other thing," said John the Younger. "I want to show you a contraption I've designed, based on all I've heard of New England and their troubles." He showed Roger the basic design of a vertical axis windmill. "I wrote to Father about this; it is a combination of designs I saw in Turkey with what we have here. I want this to be the New England version of the mill. What do you think?"

"Interesting. How do you know it will work?" asked Roger.

"I build miniature models and experiment. I've read my Francis Bacon, and per his approach, I set up artificial tests," said John the Younger. "Things could change at scale of course, but I'm fairly certain this will work."

"Impressive," said Roger. "Bacon, now there's a familiar old name, bless his soul. He never did get a fair shake in the political sphere; Coke and other powerful men were always out to get him. Perhaps his experimentation techniques will last longer than his politics, if you, my favorite naturalist, are still quoting him."

After they left Groton, Roger and Mary went to London to say their own quick good-byes to Mum, Sydrach and family, Robert, and Katherine and her family. They felt now how soon that same ocean would loom large for them. There were tearful good-byes. Next they traveled back to Essex to say good-bye to Mary's father and brothers. Finally they were on their way, heading to Bristol and the *Lyon* with all their belongings, including their wedding gift, a bed, as well as a cow, two goats, two horses, and Roger's books.

Roger also brought along a cousin named Thomas Agnell, indentured as Roger's servant for the next seven years in return for passage. They could really only afford one servant, and he and Mary decided that male labor in the wilderness might be more valuable.

When Roger arrived, he reviewed the provision plans with Captain William Pierce. The captain was way ahead of them. In July when prices were low, Captain Pierce bought 281 pounds of wheat, peas, oatmeal, beef, pork, cheese, butter, suet, barley seed, and rye seed for the colonies. Now they asked any willing passengers to wait for the next voyage and added more warm clothing in all sizes, improved the storage containers for many supplies, and added the rest of the supply requests on John Winthrop Senior's lists. Lemon juice, vinegar, dried fruits, and wine were among the late additions.

The *Lyon* left the bay December 30, 1630, with over two hundred tons of food and other goods.

CHAPTER 15

The Sea, AD 1631

Marney was waiting and watching in port. The word was that the *Lyon* would leave with few men, loaded down with goods. It was the perfect target for his raid. He decided to follow.

The *Lyon* got underway with a brisk tail wind and immediately achieved a high speed. Marney set off just within sight behind her and tried to follow her course. Soon, however, he realized that he'd lost her somehow, as she was no longer visible, and he focused on getting to New England.

During the night Captain William Pierce had to slow and modify course when the spirit sail needed repair, and the seamen on board set to it. This unexpected event put Marney in front of the *Lyon* instead of behind, without his realizing it. As Marney rushed to find her, he was getting farther and farther ahead of her.

During the repairs, a sudden change in wind direction caused a lurch, and one of the seamen, a young man named Way, was knocked from his perch, landing in the sea. Way was a strong swimmer, and Captain William Pierce was fiercely dedicated to his men. For fifteen minutes the men struggled. Way was swimming in ice-cold water, bobbing up and down in the waves, and getting farther away with each passing minute.

Pierce's men desperately sought to lower a skiff for a rescue. The winds were high, and they needed a break in the winds in order to let the men down safely. As the men struggled to get the skiff in the water, Way went under and did not reappear. A collective gasp rose from all those watching, horrified, on deck. The rescue attempt was fruitless.

This incident set a somber mood that pervaded the crossing, even as they kept the tailwind and made excellent progress. Captain Pierce did not like losing men, and he resolved not to lose any more. Ship procedures were tightened, and everyone spent a good bit of the trip below deck as a result.

The *Lyon* became for Roger what Newgate had been for Hendric. There were no chains, and the duration was thirty-eight days, not eight years, but God was not so sensitive to these details. The wretched smells down below were worse than those in the prison. For as any good mortician knows, the way to adjust in the presence of bad smells is not to switch to fresh air but to let the body naturally become numb to the odor. On the boat Roger habitually found a sheltered corner upwind to think and write, even though it was bitter January cold, and his fingers and toes would grow numb. As a result, the return to life in the present involved becoming aware of the overpowering odor anew, which made it all the more gut-wrenching.

There was much time to contemplate his losses: Jane, the comfortable friendships and support of the Otes manor, the sheer decency of civilization and clearing of the head from a good gallop. Depression sank into his bones, making his brain more able to focus on his studies, causing him to see distant and complex patterns that he had not before understood. Finally he even dug out the HH writing, something he hadn't done in his adult life. *The Polish King Stephen admitted he was the king of bodies, not of souls. The king of Bohemia declared men's consciences should not be violated, urged, or constrained. Yet Bishop Laud could run Roger out of the land, just for having friends with consciences.* For as far as Roger knew, Bishop Laud had no direct evidence of Roger's own views.

In prayer he came to a renewed commitment to his calling. Bishop Laud's threats focused Roger on his priorities. His mission would be to tend to the Indians' souls and to promote God's own enabling, conscience-felt worship, as opposed to rote rituals. In time, Jane came to represent temptation, tempting him away from his calling. Mary came with his obedience to God and brought him joy.

As ship's chaplain, Roger shared a private room with Mary—one of the few on the ship. Most slept in rows of cots down below, one level above the animals. The private room was small and dark, smelly and windless, however, and both were prone to retch if they stayed too long below. Private cabin or no, biting cold up above or no, it was up above they wanted to be whenever the captain would allow it. It was a stormy crossing, made stressful by the knowledge that ships before them had foundered, forcing them to make landfall and settle in places like Bermuda instead of the Virginia and Massachusetts destinations they'd planned. Prayer came easily to the twenty passengers crossing in midwinter.

Roger was a good minister to these people and became fast friends with most on board. Each morning there was a service, with friendly discussion after.

One morning Roger learned that his cow had died. He approached the captain.

"Captain Pierce, have you a minute for me?" asked Roger.

"Certainly. How can I help you?" was the warm response.

"My cow has passed on, and I think we should eat it. How about a big fresh steak dinner tomorrow noon for all aboard? I don't think we want to open the salt containers if we can eat and freeze this meat until it is consumed."

The captain was elated. Nothing would keep his passengers healthier in the middle of winter than fresh food of any kind.

"That's an excellent suggestion, if this calm holds. You'll want help to butcher and prepare. I'll let the cook know."

"Is there something we should celebrate—that is, other than the immense blessing of our continued life?" asked Roger.

"The sightings today say we can call this the halfway point, so that's something to celebrate! This crossing may be rough and the ship operating with temporary repairs, but at least so far it has also been the fastest. We are with the currents and the wind, and if we can keep them, the second half might go as quickly as the first. Keep those prayers coming," replied the captain. With that, he was off to his next set of chores.

The steak dinner was served on deck in calm if cold, clear weather. The cook roasted the cow over open coals, and the taste was beyond anything the passengers expected to be eating even after landfall. Cows were very precious, and in New England their main job was to produce more cows and milk, not steak, in these years.

John Throckmorton, between bites, was involved with Roger in a discussion of free will versus election, with Roger asserting that God's call to his elect was required before a man would voluntarily choose to worship. John was asserting that each man has a free choice and an embedded conscience, that every man could listen to that conscience but has free will to choose to do so or not.

Their wives, Mary and Rebecca, grew tired of this discussion and began one of their own. Rebecca had twenty-one-month-old twins, and Mary frequently helped her with them.

"It is so nice to have a good friend on the boat. With toddlers, I'm surprised you came so soon," said Mary.

"We wanted to come with you, but it also would have been nice to wait another year. We've been saving for our passage, but we'd like to have brought more supplies. We didn't really have a choice," said Rebecca. "I held house meetings for the women to study scripture at our home. I don't read well, and I got one of the boys in town to read to us. His father mentioned us to the minister back home. The minister must have mentioned it to the bishop, because we were asked to stop," said Rebecca.

"That seems so severe," said Mary. "Roger is a minister and in a private position; the Anglican hierarchy is bound and determined to eliminate all such positions. Your husband is a businessman, and there are women's house churches all over England. Why you?"

"I suppose it is because John is from Anglican country. I am from Hatfield Broad Oak, but John's family was in Norfolk. That's only part of the story, though. Because John is a merchant, he always dreamed of investing in shipping up and down the coast in the New World. When we heard that our neighbor William Parke would make the move, it seemed like our opportunity. His parents have already left, and they've promised to invest in John's first ship to be built in New England. The longer we stay with these children in England, the more tied down we'll be. We decided to move now and grow our roots in New England," continued Rebecca. "William is a cousin to the governor, and he says we'll be well connected to get whatever we need. The start of that was the jobs that John got for us in Hatfield Broad Oak while we raised our passage."

Mary wished she was pregnant. Her eight children were not coming fast enough for her taste. She cuddled little Patience while Rebecca chased John. Toddlers are hard to control on a ship, especially robust ones like John.

The dinner was an unqualified success, and it improved the mood for the rest of the trip.

Another morning Roger was sick as a dog down below, and Mary went up to the deck to get away from it for a break. She found herself chatting with Judith Perkins.

"So you have five children! I'm hoping for eight children, but we have none as of yet," said Mary.

"Yes, and we are really fortunate how spread out they are. The eldest, Elizabeth, is twenty, and she's of great help with Jacob, our three-year-old," replied Judith. John and Judith Perkins were in their forties.

"You are brave to bring them all at once. What made you choose that instead of sending ahead like the Parke family did?" asked Mary.

"We are separatist Puritans. Our small church is all under threat of imprisonment. Our minister was Samuel Skelton, and he and many others came out with the Higginson expedition last year. We didn't want to come last year, as I was with child, but we lost the baby anyway. When that happened we realized we were meant to emigrate, and we decided to follow our friends and our Church. We are hoping things are a bit more civilized now, for we've no desire for wild adventure. I really want to be where there is food and order."

"Skelton is the minister in Salem now, though I understand the center of the colony has moved south to the Charles River under Governor Winthrop, and they are calling it Boston. We know his son well, and he has a brilliant mind. He says there is fresh water and arable land along the banks of the Charles, and a much larger population will thrive there. Perhaps you are meant for Boston," replied Mary.

"That sounds right. We will surely look into it. Will you stay in Boston?" asked Judith.

"I doubt it. I want to live on a farm, not in a city. We want to be near the native peoples. Roger intends to learn their language and to minister to them as well as to the English," replied Mary.

"I see. Perhaps you can introduce us to your friends in Boston, for all my friends are in Salem. I want my children to survive, and I've heard awful things about the Salem swamps," said Judith.

"I'd be happy to," said Mary. With that, she went back down to check on Roger.

It was thirty-seven days into the voyage on a sunny, cold Sunday afternoon, and Roger was relaxing quietly on deck after having given what he hoped was a great sermon. He'd spoken about how the image of Moses crossing the Red Sea was meant to teach about conversion, going from death to new life.

The Throckmortons were huddled in a protected corner on the deck, and Mary approached. Rebecca and Mary hoped to be neighbors, and they were discussing practical matters, like what they would grow in their gardens in the new world.

The Onge family was on deck as well. They mostly stuck to themselves. Today, Judith Perkins struck up a conversation with the only other woman her age on deck.

"That's my Thomas over there playing with your Simon. He tells me you have many children at home, as well the ones on the boat?" asked Judith.

"I've had thirteen, though five are passed on. The older girls stayed back to run the shop, and we left a toddler with them for now. Originally we planned to come as a family, but my husband Edmund died of fever along with three of the youngest children last year," said the widow Onge.

"I'm so sorry," said Judith. "My, you are brave to come anyway."

"My choices were all bad. I could stay home and be miserable without Edmund, reminded of him daily at the shop. Alternatively, I could set out for the new life we'd dreamed of and make all our dreams still count for something. I chose the latter."

"That makes sense. Do you know anyone in New England?"

"No, we are the first. I hope to set up shop in a Charles River town upstream of the current population, a place the Indians could bring furs to buy shop goods, as I can process and send finished furs back to the shop in Lavenham. I'd like to set up trade between my shop in Lavenham and a shop here. Our business was in bad shape because the cloth industry we relied on has been displaced with New World furs. We decided we could grow or go out of business. My nephew here with me took Edmund's place on the roster and will help me set up and get connected, and then he will return—laden, we hope, with supplies for the shop in England."

"That sounds really smart. We'll have to come visit your shop. I'm sure we'll quickly find things we did not bring. We hope to stay in the Boston area," replied Judith.

"As you find things you'd like to have shipped, let me know. Francis will go back with a list, and then my daughter Mary hopes to come out with the supplies and bring Isaac, my youngest. We can bring almost anything you can imagine," said the widow Onge.

"I feel better about this new life already," said Judith. "It is not nearly the end of the earth that it seemed if there will be frequent trade back and forth."

The widow Onge laughed. "I personally hope it *is* the end of earth. I am looking forward to a homestead plot near the edge of town and a milk cow, and growing my own vegetables in the sunshine, and a big bell a customer can ring to call me in when I'm needed at the shop. I have been in a shop in a smelly city all day with youngsters at my side for over twenty years. It was successful, but I will be happy for something new to look at."

William Parke was chatting with Nicholas Bailey, who was also traveling alone. "I'm looking forward to this landfall. This was a thoroughly unexpected trip for me. The things parents get their children into!" said William.

"How did that happen?" asked Nicholas, laughing. The two were about the same age and traveling alone, but Nicholas already had a wife named Margaret and children whom he expected to follow him.

"My dad knows John Winthrop, now the governor. When he heard John was going, he hoped we could join him. He is afraid of Laud, of course. Everyone we know wants out. I was sent to get last-minute supplies and ran into some old friends. It's a long story, but I missed that boat, as the messages were slow going back and forth. I caught this next boat out. My dad and my brother Thomas made the boat and are setting up trade on the narrow strip of land all must pass between ships in the harbor and the town called Roxbury. I've been trying to convince the widow Onge to set up upstream a good ways to get some diversification, as Dad will have the harbor covered, and there's no need to drive each other out of business with a whole country to cover," said William.

"So, if your family knows the governor, can you get a word in for me? I'd like to serve as bailiff or in a militia or in some way use my training as a soldier," said Nicholas. He figured these military skills would be valuable in this new and dangerous wilderness, especially if the Indians became hostile. His skill as a vintner, passed down from his grandfather, might get him in trouble with all these Puritans. Their strictness was not something he'd planned on, so he was also looking to get away from Boston as soon as there was a good opportunity.

"I'll look into it," promised William Parke.

The seamen were also up top, making repairs and watching for landfall.

Over half of the twenty voyagers were up on deck, even with the cold. It was better than the alternatives. They'd all been cooped up down below for most of the previous four days, as a storm raged, and the seas were high. Another week, and they expected to make landfall. It was hard to believe in this small boat tossed by such big waves that they'd be making landfall in a particular place, but the captain said they were aiming for Boston harbor and that, if anything, they were ahead of schedule.

Toward evening of this glorious sunny day, all above deck heard the loud, clear words of the seaman up top of the spirit sail: "Land Ho." Long Island was in sight. Joy and excitement spread through the boat, and all strained to see what he was talking about before it disappeared.

They steered directly toward Boston. This ship had provisions to deliver, the passengers had eaten steak midway, and there would be plenty of time for fishing once their cargo was safely ashore. This voyage of the *Lyon* was blessed with one of the fastest crossings recorded—fifty-three days from first passenger on in England till unloading day in Boston. Marney also achieved landfall safely, but well north of Salem. He sat off the coast and began a correction south, watching and waiting, not sure whether he was ahead or behind.

Adrian Block Island, AD 1631

Springtime meant fresh scallions across the landscape, the first harvestable green food. Oonue and Sochepo were gathering while Capat watched the younger children back at camp. For Oonue, the winter went quickly, between reacquainting herself with old friends and family, and preparing for Adrian Block Island. Miantonomoh asked her to think about which women would be willing to migrate with them to learn the wampum production methods. Oonue had been training a large group of the tribe's young, unattached women.

Miantonomoh was a handsome warrior, large in stature, gregarious in nature, and a disciplined athlete. His leadership skills came naturally, and many young men gathered around him and supported whatever activity he was organizing. Block Island would be no different.

"I want to fortify the island. We'll build wampum in the shadows of a cliff on a rock shelf we'll work to expand. Over time we will seek to have a shallow ditch that becomes a tunnel for access from above. I want that factory impregnable to Pequot, Mohegan, and to English. We start today."

Twenty of Canonicus's braves accompanied Miantonomoh as they scouted the island, set their location, and began to build. Block Island was ten miles long and four miles wide. Its hills were covered with impenetrable scrub oak, with only narrow trails through the brush. Miantonomoh selected a spot for the wampum factory in a natural cave off the southeastern bluffs facing the roughest seas. He ordered that access be dug from a point deep in the forest—a small, shallow tunnel to just inland of a flat beach where they could easily offload supplies and that could be completely camouflaged with brush. The opening from the sea was invisible from above and from most vantages below, as it was deep in shadow. It was a steep climb up, but an easy drop down for the finished product at low tide.

When the younger, unattached men saw how many young women followed Oonue, they climbed on board as well. Soon, out of Canonicus's five-thousand-plus tribe, about three hundred wanted to move to Block Island, and Miantonomoh had his pick of men. He could support about twenty families, in addition to the twenty Niantic families living there. At the western end there were also western Niantic families that he wanted to woo.

Miantonomoh welcomed each family. Each family unit that offered loyalty was rewarded with privileges. Soon there was a plan for one unified tribe between the eastern Niantic and the Narragansett. Anyone who did not follow Miantonomoh was soon left with only one alternative: join the Pequot sachems recruiting the Niantic. For all practical purposes, the island's Niantic, as an independent tribe, were gone, melded into the Narragansett and the Pequot. On the mainland, Miantonomoh's cousin Juanumo was on a similar mission with the mainland Niantic, and Meiksah with the Nipmuc.

A few families would live inside the fortified town center next to the factory; Oonue's family was one of them. Most would live further inland, and the women would walk up to work. Block Island became the Fort Knox of the Canonicus confederacy. Upward of thirty people could work in the factory at one time. Because so many people had moved to Block Island, there were plenty of workers, and each worked about three hours a day and then reverted to more traditional activities. Oonue did not want to face a food shortage and have her daughters become vulnerable like the Connecticut Valley young women.

The wampum produced on Block Island was of high quality and great quantity. It catapulted Canonicus and the Narragansett tribe into a position of wealth and status among Algonquians and Europeans alike. Because of the Narragansett trade with the English, the English also gained status and relatively safe travel in the territory controlled by Canonicus.

John Winthrop Senior initiated a strategy of setting up trading posts upstream of Dutch establishments, and his great desire was to set up a fort on the Connecticut River. He was not aware of the wampum factory, but his strategy fit nicely with Miantonomoh's strategy, because the trading post would utilize wampum as its currency. Algonquian customers could pay in wampum and receive steel tools or brightly colored wool in return. Winthrop's intent was to drive the Dutch to abandon their posts and move farther north or west and cede territory to the English. Each time the Dutch abandoned a post, the Abenaki continued to follow them north, and the Narragansett and Massachusetts territory expanded in turn.

CHAPTER 16

Boston, AD 1631

John Winthrop Senior climbed aboard the *Lyon* and greeted Captain William Pierce warmly. Then he turned to Roger.

"I have never been so relieved to see a godly minister. It must have been your prayers, alongside ours, that delivered you today."

"It was a fast crossing, if choppy," replied Roger. Governor Winthrop looked a great deal older than when they had last seen each other at John the Younger's wedding.

"No, you don't understand. The colony has no food. Last night I handed out the last meager rations of bread, and we dropped to our knees in prayer. Your arrival means our lives," replied the governor. Each life was sacred to him, as leader of this small colony, and each death a reminder of how small and dependent humanity is on God.

"It's been a long, hard year, Roger. Within the first six months in Salem's swampy mess, two hundred of our seven hundred were dead of the fevers, including Lady Arabella and her husband. We moved as many people as would go south to Boston for better lowland soil, plentiful fishing, and freshwater access. I started six small towns in the area, each with some independence, hoping that, when a disease wiped out one, the harm to the others could be limited. Provisions rotted, crops did not always prosper, and we've learned hard lessons here," he continued.

"Yes, let's give thanks to God for this passage, for our arrival just in time," replied Roger. Those on deck gathered around, and Roger led them in prayer for the next hour.

Roger gave John Winthrop Senior a hug after the impromptu service. "John the Younger shared some of your letters with me. We've taken care to bring what you requested and more. I bring you his love, and he hopes to join us by fall. He'll be heeding your advice not to leave until summer with the children. Many of the families on board this ship are known Puritans who have come to the attention of Bishop Laud. We are each convinced that he is after our lives. We dare not leave family behind after the Helwys affair. King Charles seems more likely than King James was to go after families. So here we are. Hooker and others could not prepare large families so quickly for overseas travel and have removed to Holland. Cotton is in hiding. I believe they may come yet."

"Roger, John Wilson, teacher in First Church of Boston, is going to return to England. He says he will return with his wife, but in the meantime we'll need a teacher. You will take the interim position, of course," said the governor. It was less a question than an assumption. John Wilson's passage was on the *Lyon*'s return trip to England, leaving a most prestigious position open in Boston. Without discussing it with Roger, John Winthrop Senior had campaigned to select him for this post and succeeded. Proudly he offered Roger the job, fully expecting to work closely with him once again, as they had in England.

Roger needed employment and said, "I'll pray about it."

Boston was growing rapidly. Roger had seen that few Algonquian desired to live close to the center of the Europeans' purview, and he knew his calling. He had also seen that the church in Boston had refused to separate from the Church in England and to Roger this meant the perpetuation of a deeply flawed system that he intended to see replaced. Within the week, he went to John Winthrop Senior in private to decline the job.

"Governor, I just cannot do this. It would set me up for life as a city man. Boston will grow, and this church will be the St. Sepulchre of the New World. I know that is not where God intends me to be," said Roger. "I eventually want to be down in Plymouth, near the larger, more important native routes. Mary wants to live on a farm. What do you think?" asked Roger, for he respected John highly.

"I am disappointed, but I understand. I don't agree with you on separation, but Endicott does. I need men who can communicate with the Algonquian, and you are like John the Younger with languages. Go and learn with my blessing. I will find another plan here. But you should know that there are many here who do not see Algonquian souls as fully human. For them, this will seem folly. Can you keep that part of your mission quiet for now? We will say you have declined in order to go to the separatist churches. That way, I will get points in England for having chosen another, and we will keep Bishop Laud off all our backs."

"Surely you cannot worry about the bishop all the way out here?" asked Roger.

"I can, and I do. He threatens to banish all Puritans from New England now. This I will not support. We must take care. It is the king's charter, and we are best out of sight and out of mind."

The rest of the winter both old and new residents of Boston survived on the provisions from the *Lyon*. During this time Roger was studying his options and first set his eye on Plymouth.

On up the Charles River where the swampland gave way to solid farmland sat the outpost of Watertown. The widow Onge staked her claim there. She was allowed to stake claim for the four family members she had with her, as well as two who had tickets to come out in future, so she got six acres in her claim. William Parkes joined his father and brother in Roxbury. The normal course of action for a ship like the *Lyon* was to spend a few days or weeks on shore ferrying passengers up and down the coast before heading out again. On this trip, however, more urgent matters awaited. Captain William Pierce had no sooner unloaded his passengers and lifesaving goods than he set off for Newfoundland to rescue the foundered *Ambrose* and tow her in for repairs.

Marney continued to examine his copy of John Smith's maps, and he was now watching and waiting. Finally, he observed the *Lyon* heading north, but he could tell it was alone and empty by the way it sat in the water. Winthrop didn't even know how blessed he was that Marney had not arrived in time to catch the ship with two hundred tons of goods.

Marney continued to head south, looking for a next opportunity. He found it on February 18, as the *Charles*, the *Success*, and the *Whale* were together arriving in Plymouth and were low in the water. He made his move. He and his men ambushed the *Whale* first and temporarily took command, using her ordinance on the *Charles*. The fight was long. Marney and his men managed to remove most of the supplies and kill many men. Marney's boat was unscathed, and they quickly made their escape without sinking any of the ships.

The remainder of the English crew limped into port at Plymouth. The *Charles* was very torn up, and none of the three ships had more than a pittance of supplies for the colony. Plymouth was in trouble. The governor, William Bradford, encouraged new arrivals to head for Salem or Boston to enable self-sufficiency and prevent hunger. He discouraged movement inward. The population of three hundred would not grow significantly in 1631, and Roger would need to wait till they were able to recover to join them.

Roger formally declined the job in Boston, not mentioning his calling but only the correction he wanted to see from the church. Since there was no position currently open in Plymouth, Roger took an offer of an unpaid position in Salem, a separated church. In Salem Roger would wait in hopes that Plymouth would recover the food supply and reopen to new settlers.

Several other passengers were housed in Charleston, just north of Boston, or on the peninsula itself, while they arranged for employment and looked at options. The Perkinses were exploring Boston as well as Salem and decided to travel with the Williams and Throckmorton families to look Salem over. It would be a good reunion with their congregation from England. Nicholas Bailey decided to go south to seek his kin in New Amsterdam.

Salem, AD 1631

"It is so good to see you, Judith," said Suzanna. She and her husband, the Reverend Skelton, gave each Perkin a hug.

"And you." Judith thought Suzanna had aged five years in the one since they'd seen one another. "I am so sorry to hear about the Reverend Higginson passing. The fever took many."

"Yes, it is very hard here. Many have moved south to Boston to avoid the swamp fevers that seem to start here. We will stay here to minister to this smaller town. We've grown roots, and our old parish is much of the town. Now, introduce us to your friends," said the Reverend Skelton.

Judith introduced the Williamses and the Throckmortons. The men and women naturally separated into separate groups, and Sam Skelton Jr., age seven, took the five young adult Perkinses outside and showed them around. Elizabeth, twenty-two, and Mary, fifteen, took the youngest Perkins, three, and the youngest Skelton into their arms for the trek.

The men in the room were Reverend Skelton, Reverend Williams, John Perkins, and John Throckmorton. John Perkins started a frank discussion of the issues his family faced.

"Judith does not want to live in the wilderness. We've five children, and she fears for us all. I am not sure it is better in one place than another, and most of our church brothers are here."

"There is choice here, and there are risks both ways. If you go to Boston, there is higher ground, more fresh water, and more arable land. Most of the political power has gone to Boston, and the church there is committed to staying a part of the Church of England, not to separate for purposes of continuity," said Reverend Skelton.

"Yes," noted Roger. "I did not come here to be caught up in ceremony. I came here to minister to souls, including native souls. I am convinced that the common prayer book encourages false worship, and I want to be in a separated church."

"I agree," said John Throckmorton.

"The Salem church has been Separatist since 1630. That is how John Endicott wanted it, and that is how we will stay," said Reverend Skelton. "It is a quiet yet independent group in Plymouth now, and neither Plymouth nor Salem tolerates any in the settlement who would promote the Book of Common Prayer."

Roger's attention spiked at that. Use of the Book of Common Prayer was something he'd despised in the likes of Cotton and Hooker. They claimed to pick only the best prayers, but they evaded the truth of their convictions. They were willing to hire an associate to kneel for them, so that they would not have to kneel. But how is asking others to commit false worship or idolatrous acts a good thing? Roger wanted a true community dedicated to pure worship.

If a man truly wanted to worship with the Book of Common Prayer, however, Roger would not have punished him. He would tolerate Anglicans, while trying to convince them of the error of their ways.

While Roger and John Throckmorton were keen on moving to one of these colonies, John Perkins looked concerned. "We came here to avoid persecution. We want to live a peaceful life, allowed to worship and read the Bible directly as Puritans within the Church. I think we can do that in Boston. I fear the bishop will target Salem and that Boston will eventually target Salem if you go in this direction. I see the old conflicts arriving at these new shores," John put forward.

Reverend Skelton looked older. "Yes, the pristine New World has practical challenges. What you say may be so, but this is my calling. You are free to settle as you choose for the safety and peace of your family. Go in friendship, John, and with my blessing on you, your wife, and all your children."

"I have already declined a position in Boston. I have no desire to be an agent of a church that would let any king but Christ rule over it," declared Roger.

"You are welcome to stay here and join me in this ministry, Roger," said Reverend Skelton. "With Reverend Higginson gone now, I can use the help."

"I want to be honest with you. I am hoping for a position in Plymouth. Those who came a decade ago specifically set up a Church not beholden to any state structure. The Robinson pilgrims now worship alongside more recent Puritans, but that church retains a better structure of relationship to government. They have no opening now, but should one occur, I would jump at it," Roger told Skelton.

"We can make you visiting teacher here, for now, until a replacement comes."

"Excellent. I would enjoy that."

John Perkins turned to John Throckmorton.

"If you are dependent on William Parkes's investment, won't you need to locate down near Roxbury?"

"No, it's all worked out. Mr. Parkes found a master shipwright here. His name is Robert Mouton. I'm commissioning a ship here in Salem and want to watch it while it's under construction. I've got my own family money and the investment from Mr. Parkes. Robert Moulton will carry a share of the first boat. I'll be in debt again—I worked a long seven years as a scrivener to gain my freedom the first time—but this time it's a business I want to own."

"So you'll not be a freeman for some time, even with your family and your land?" asked Reverend Skelton. Most churchmen became freemen so they could vote and be full participants in the town. Men who were indentured or otherwise in debt could not.

"I project being a free man again in 1638. I will live like this now so that long term I'll be in the business we want to be in."

"You are courageous. I'd not have ever thought to go into that kind of debt, and you started out with more than we did," noted John Perkins.

"I learned from my father that no risk means no reward," said John. "However, I'm not sure why he thought I needed scrivener skills. I think he wanted to make sure I paid attention to every painful detail," John said with a sigh.

The men laughed and went on to other topics.

Roger was quickly elected to the church in Salem, and the establishment he had spurned in Boston formally objected in writing to Endicott. In Salem, rejection by colony authorities had the opposite effect of that intended, in that it endeared Roger to the people. He was legitimized as a follower in Higginson's separatist footsteps. Both Higginson and Williams had given lip service to the authorities back in England when their lives depended on it. Higginson did so in a speech from a ship with the bishop listening in, and Roger had done so in his signed loyalty statement at Cambridge. Both had broken rank and stated their real principles on landing in the New World.

In Boston, Roger was persuasive enough that a debate was sparked about church separation. To quell it, John Winthrop Senior put out a handwritten tract to all church members. The tract reminded them that yes, as Puritans they were seeking to correct ways in which the church had been defiled over the centuries, but no, they should not separate. The churches were all churches of Christ, and must remain unified, as Jesus himself requested in John 17:23. It would be a sin to cause further separation, even though the church had faults.

Roger was biding his time, awaiting an opportunity in Plymouth. By summer the colony's food supply was secure, and Plymouth's minister Ralph Smith extended an invitation to assist him. The position offered Roger was more humble than what he'd left behind in Boston and Salem, but it was suited in fundamental ways to his needs if he was to be the person he meant to become. Plymouth matched Roger's objectives in two significant ways: it was fully separated from the English Church, and it was near Algonquian settlements.

The Throckmortons stayed at Salem, so Mary was separated from her good friend Rebecca with the move.

At Sea to Boston, AD 1631

John Winthrop the Younger heaved a sigh of relief. It was a warm day in August, and the family was on board the *Lyon*, the trusted Captain William Pierce at the helm. Groton had been sold, legal matters had been concluded, and he was on his way to New England, just as planned. His stepmother, Margaret, and his sister-in-law, Bess, had babies in their arms. Infant Anne was aunt to infant Martha Johanna. John the Younger's wife, Martha, stood proudly at his side, along with his stepbrothers Deane, age nine, and William, age four. There were one hundred people on this summer voyage, about seventy of them passengers. There were not nearly as many provisions on this voyage as were on the previous winter trip.

John the Younger passed many an afternoon reading peacefully in the sun on the deck of the ship. John Smith's death just a couple of months before the ship embarked made reading his last book seem a fitting way to honor and remember the man. The book was subtitled *The Pathway to Experience to Erect a Plantation*. John felt the adventure and responsibility of exploring and planning passing from the Smith generation to his own. Smith sparked John the Younger's interest in the lands north of Salem with their rich potential.

Whenever Martha wasn't helping tend the babies, she was snatching John the Younger's book out from under him and was reading it as well. As closely as John was reading for engineering and planning tips, Martha was reading for knowledge of plants, Algonquian culture, and healing strategies in this new world. Smith was a close observer of peoples and a clever, skilled dealmaker. Martha formed many questions to be answered on arrival through her own observations of Algonquian ways. For the first time, she realized her father's medicine recipes would need augmentation, as the species of plant life would be new to her.

John Eliot, a twenty-seven-year-old conservative Christian from a devout, religious family, with a Jesus College Cambridge education and a heart for native souls, was also on the boat. His last job in England was as teaching assistant to Thomas Hooker, of the Sepringham rides. When Hooker fled to Holland, John Eliot began making his own plans to emigrate. John Eliot was a single man, traveling alone. His reputation was as a straightforward Anglican Puritan, believing in direct Bible reading, but he was no separatist. He was in fact a strong believer in theocracy, conformity, and authority. Yet, John Eliot feared Bishop Laud because of his association with Cambridge, a Puritan center, and with Reverend Hooker.

In October, Captain William Pierce and the *Lyon* sighted land for the first time, and on November 5 the passengers disembarked in Boston. They'd seen whales, so close that they wondered at their immensity and were concerned for their own safety. They'd seen schools of mackerel that made it seem food would be plentiful. They arrived to the most glorious autumn colors New England could offer. Yet this trip was not without its sorrows. Baby Anne perished en route. The governor had a daughter in heaven whom he would not meet on this earth. Of the seventy passengers departing England, in all only sixty were still alive when the ship arrived in Boston.

John Eliot spent some time in Boston and by April moved to lead the First Church of Roxbury. He hired servants from the Massachusetts and Mohegan tribes and began diligent work with them to learn their language. Bess Fones Winthrop, herself a widow, had an invitation to join the widow Onge in Watertown and graciously accepted.

John the Younger joined John Senior for a time, assisting in running the colony. He was quickly convinced by his father of the importance of setting up villages upstream of the Dutch to gain footing in the fur trade. He wanted to explore the north anyway, based on Smith's writings, and within the year he organized, recruited, and led an expedition to settle

Agawam, Massachusetts, in an area Smith described as particularly rich in bountiful shellfish and opportunity for industry—even though it was currently a large swamp and would require construction.

Martha spent her time in the woods north of Boston watching and learning. She befriended the women of Jole's tribe by quietly watching and sitting with them and emulating their behavior. Her knowledge of their language focused on plant life and horticultural techniques and their use of herbs as medicines. One day a woman pointed out a plant in the woods, signaling that one would make tea with it and drink it, and pointed to her belly, clearly indicating that it would help Martha get pregnant. Martha wanted nothing more than to be pregnant, and she tried out the tea.

Over time, Martha augmented her father's recipes for healing concoctions with Algonquian formulas. She scribbled out her findings in the shorthand she used with John, whenever she could construct or find surfaces to write on.

CHAPTER 17

Watertown, AD 1631

The widow Onge left Bess in charge of the trading post in Watertown while she made the first of many trips around the greater Boston area to scout for items worth trading back in England. Onge was so quickly successful and happy in Watertown that she planned to retrieve more of her children and investigate whether the London operation should be sold to finance expansion in New England.

Bess admired the widow Onge, with all her children and a successful independent business of her own. She had no intention, however, of remaining a widow and felt the need to get on with life post-Henry, while she could still have more children.

Lieutenant Robert Feake was a goldsmith by seven years of apprentice training, but a soldier and landowner in practice. He served as a deputy to Watertown and had claim to one hundred and fifty acres, including several acres suitable for homes in town, that he had not taken time to develop. His handsome, fit—if stiff—figure distracted most from his lofty, compassionate, and artistic approach. Today he entered the Onge establishment, ostensibly to see what gold and iron items were on hand; in reality, however, he was looking at Bess.

Robert was ready to settle and needed an adventurous, business-oriented wife if he was to succeed—someone to complement his skills and manage their property. John Winthrop Senior did not believe in staying unmarried himself, or in leaving his children, most especially dependent daughters-in-law, unmarried for long. He had mentioned his niece Bess to Robert some time back, and Robert wanted a better look. He watched her as he looked about the shop, and she chatted with other customers, and she smiled back at him.

Bess's passion for life still came through, and her spunk and adventurous spirit made her beautiful to Robert. Without a word said, he was smitten and reported his offer of marriage back to John Winthrop Senior. The matter was quickly arranged, and Elizabeth Fones Winthrop was married to Lieutenant Robert Feake on December 2, 1631, in Roxbury. Even though they would settle in Watertown, Roxbury was the center of commerce and was easier for all to reach. Robert's best man was his ranking superior, Captain Daniel Patrick.

It wasn't long after the wedding that Bess realized how dependent Robert really was on Captain Patrick. It seemed that Robert not only fought lawlessness and the Pequot with Captain Patrick, but that their personal lives were intertwined. Captain Patrick was the only person who had really surveyed Robert's land, and it was he who had ideas on how it should be developed. Bess found herself alone as much as she was before she was married, and Lieutenant Feake wasn't even traveling across the sea. Bess set to work, using her considerable charm, to befriend both Captain Patrick and his peer Captain John Underhill. She quickly took over the practical reigns of the Feake businesses and staffed it with her own competent help, purchasing the apprenticeship of the sixteen-year-old indentured servant William Hallett from William Parkes.

Plymouth, AD 1632

Mary Williams finally began to think of Plymouth as home, not a place she was traveling through. She took charge here, for this wilderness was surely her forte, not Roger's. It was she who organized the running of the farm, ordering and breaking down the labor into doable steps. It was Mary who was out at 5:00 a.m. doing the daily farm chores, tending to the care of the animals and spending the morning planting and the afternoon foraging, and it was Mary who assigned field work to their servant, Thomas Agnell. The days were long and the work exhausting but satisfying.

Men in town taught Roger stone masonry, logging, and other construction techniques. Roger developed trading relationships with both Algonquian and English. To Mary's dismay, he often used Thomas Agnell to staff the trading post and do much of the cleaning and stocking. The homestead was near the edge of the town and upstream of the other traders on the Manomet River, for easier access by the Algonquian peoples. Roger stocked all manner of English provisions, which he eventually traded for furs and wampum. He traded the Algonquian axes and knives for a fine dugout canoe, which he used as his main form of transportation, enabling the transport of goods effectively in Algonquian style. Roger was thankful for Sir Edward Coke's foresight in having him learn to row. The canoe was also useful for his own forays into Algonquian country, as he was intent on learning the language and the culture. To learn effectively he chose to observe the Algonquian in their own habitat to be able to see how communication flowed. His respect for the Algonquian soul and his respect for their customs were soon apparent, and he was given access far greater than any other Europeans, other than children adopted by the tribe.

Early mornings found Roger paddling upstream on business with the Algonquian or downstream into town to do business with the English. Roger's business dealings often went through midday and then in the heat of the day he rested. Often he spent his evenings on his construction projects or other needed heavy labor around the farm. Late evening found him and Mary in prayer and study. Roger often slept lightly and woke in the wee hours. By candlelight, in the silence of the night, he would write.

In due time, the couple was admitted to the church, and soon after that Roger Williams was asked whether he would volunteer to help teach.

The Reverend Ralph Smith was a grave and careful man, and a very erudite—though for most, unmemorable—speaker. He was quiet, and his own life was private. He welcomed assistance from Roger, though he didn't always approve of Roger's willingness to confront. Plymouth's independent survival as a small town relied on maintaining good relations all around. Those out to make quick money had long ago moved on, and those remaining were intent on respect for their separatist forms, but also committed to internal unity. To Reverend Smith, whether or not a book of prayers was in use did not matter as much as the ability to keep souls and bodies fed, and that required unity. Reverend Smith's most memorable acts included banishing children and adults for publically criticizing his practices and for endangering others. His model was not so much separation on principle, as autonomy and quiet coexistence. He and Roger got along by teaching scriptural lessons and staying away from church/government politics.

It was a typical summer Sunday in Plymouth, though the visitors were more distinguished than on the average Sunday. The governor of the Massachusetts Bay Colony, John Winthrop Senior, was visiting the governor of the Plymouth Colony, William Bradford.

Reverend Smith had Roger ask a question, and the answer was Reverend Smith's sermon. Then the two set up a formal debate. Today's discussion was about treatment of people of foreign cultures, such as the Algonquian. Roger's dark hair and eyes conveyed his focus. As a fit young man, eloquent in speech and passionate in delivery he was pleasant to watch. He set out his position memorably, in a rhythmic cadence that resembled that of verse:

"In <u>Deuteronomy 24</u> it pleased the Lord to permit the many evils against his own honorable ordinance of marriage in the world to suffer that sin of many wives of Abraham, Jacob, David, and Solomon with an expression that seems to give approbation.

In <u>2 Samuel 12</u>
Though we find him sometimes dispensing with his law,
We never find him denying himself
Or uttering a falsehood

Therefore it crosseth not an absolute rule
To permit and tolerate
Toleration will not hinder our being Holy as he is Holy in all manner
of conservation

Even the permission of the souls and consciences of all men in the world

God suffers men like fishes to devour each other <u>Habakkuk 1</u>

The wicked to flourish <u>Jeremiah 12</u>

Sends the tyrants of the world to destroy the Nations and plunder them of their riches

<u>Isaiah 10</u>

Two sorts of commands

Moses gave positive rules both spiritual and civil

He also gave some not positive but permissive for the common good e.g., Bills of Divorcement

So the Lord Jesus expoundeth on it

<u>Matthew 6, 7, 8</u>

Moses for the hardness of your hearts suffered or permitted, a toleration."

It was left to Reverend Smith then to set out the more conservative position:

"The children of God are his roses

To be kept in the garden and pruned.

To protect healthy growth and eliminate sly mold and bold flying devourers

To keep a rock wall separating them from evil weeds outside.

Pruning does not tolerate, it cuts off into a fire.

If not the fire, then tossed outside the wall into the weeds and wilderness."

Roger responded:

"The children of God are his roses,

and all peoples are God's children.

All need the protection of Gospel, the nourishment of his Word.

But only some will open the door when he knocks.

All with thorns, all with a wicked rottenness in their hearts
All reliant on God's grace,
All requiring pruning.

God's roses are not in a circle in a pretty English Garden
They are strewn across all his creation
All must be taught
But only those who answer when he calls will learn

Those who will not open the door
Have not the hearts for worship
And must not enter his church

They must remain in the world where they can hear the Gospel
And we pray for them
The garden of the heart will be choked lest they open the door to his knocking
God's judgment will execute a controlled burn
Not man."

If Reverend Smith had a response, no one remembered it. Years later, Roger's words remained in people's hearts, as words from the Lord.

Roger quickly became well respected and loved, as he had been in Salem, including by the elected governors and magistrates. Roger was not getting paid for these services, so he and Mary were making their living as traditional traders. Roger leveraged all his friends in his own business dealings, including with the governor's family, as an aspect of developing trade relationships.

It was a bright, sunny, end-of-summer morning when Ed Winslow showed up at Roger's trading post, preparing for a long expedition.

"Good to see you, Ed. How can I help you?" Roger asked.

"I'm going to explore our new charter, just arrived from the king." This new charter was two hundred miles north, in what is now Maine, enabling Plymouth Colony to expand even north of where the Massachusetts Bay

Colony had settled, to further the fur trade. "I'll be taking the inland route up the Connecticut River and then traversing over to the Kennebec River. I hope to establish inland routes and set up trading posts, always upriver from the Dutch. I'll want to plan on about a month of travel to and from, and some time to trade," said Edward.

"Would you like Algonquian-style cakes? That is the most effective food; they last several weeks," said Roger.

"Just what I was hoping for. I'd also like your advice on what goods I should take to trade with the natives on the way, aside from wampum. Do you know what they most need?" asked Edward.

"I don't know that they'd need anything. Last time I was with them, English clothing was very popular. I can't explain that, but that's what they wanted," said Roger. "Were the Wampanoag like that when they introduced Tisquantum?"

"Tisquantum liked to wear English clothes around Europeans and Algonquian dress when he was with a tribe. His tribe was decimated by plague, and, as far as I could tell, he was never really at home. He spent so much time in England, between the Catholic friars and the English shipbuilders, he may have been more English than Wampanoag. He always struggled to fit in wherever he was," Edward commented.

"So you really spoke only English to him?" asked Roger.

"Yes, and he never offered to speak his language with me. In fact, I would say that when he spoke to Massasoit, he was still struggling to communicate at times. He was young when he was taken the first time, and his family and local dialect are completely wiped out."

"Interesting. I find that Sachem Canonicus can communicate with Massachusetts Wampanoag, including Massasoit's braves, quite easily. They sound different, much as an Irishman sounds different from you and me, but he recognized the speech. Myself, I have more trouble," said Roger.

"That makes sense. We've been trading up north on the Kennebec now for six years. We really want to set up a permanent trading post, well north of the Dutch. I'm hoping to do that, and to settle some people on the Connecticut on the way back," said Edward.

"How many people will you take with you?" asked Roger.

"There will be about ten men in all. If they can settle and make permanent structures and survive the winter, then we can add families at planting time," Edward replied.

"I suppose you will supply the men, and you'll need enough food for their winter," said Roger.

"Which is lighter to carry, food or wampum?" asked Edward.

"I would not count on wampum to buy food. You never know what changes in population or shortages you may hit. We will send bare rations for the winter for ten and hope you can supplement with fishing and trade," proposed Roger.

"Sounds right. Let's do it," Edward concluded. With that he turned to see what other goods he might make use of on this trip.

"I heard you are thinking of running for governor next year?" asked Roger.

"We'll see how this new exploration turns out. Will you support me if I do?" asked Edward.

"You would make a just and fair governor," said Roger. "I'd be honored to support you."

A few hours later a young adult entered. This time the conversation was in Algonquian.

"Good morning to you, Meiksah, and who is this young brave man with you?" asked Roger, nodding to the seven-year-old boy with Meiksah.

"This is Canonchet, Miantonomoh's son. His father is my cousin. This young man will hunt with me this winter. His father would like him to learn some English. Can I leave him some hours with you?" asked Meiksah.

Roger was delighted but did not show it. He looked the boy over and said, "If Canonchet will show me what he knows, I will show him what I know." Miantonomoh wanted Canonchet to have routine experience with the English to show him they were not all as dishonorable as Yotan made them out to be.

Roger continued, "Meiksah, I would like to have a stock of traveling cakes for my store, the kind that last for months. I would like two thousand of these. What could I trade you in return for this?"

Meiksah pondered. "My father, Canonicus, is in a dispute with the Wampanoag. They have become violent. We need knives and axes. Can you teach Canonchet how to use this axe?"

"I can do this," said Roger.

Meiksah nodded. "I will supply the food you request."

Canonchet stayed, as requested. He and Roger spent time on vocabulary and basic conversation skills, and when they exhausted the boy's language-learning patience, Roger showed him an ax and how to fell a tree and make it suitable for building. He had a feeling the boy would be showing many others. They discussed how to clean and sharpen, and he gave the boy a place to practice out in the back. Meiksah returned for him in the late afternoon.

Roger asked, "May I accompany you back to your camp? That way we can discuss when I can pick up my order after you've had a chance to negotiate with the squaws."

"Certainly." The three took off, Roger asking Meiksah and Canonchet to name plants and trees in the woods as they went.

When they reached the tribe, Roger stayed for some time, observing Narragansett life and learning as he watched the tribe members talk. They let him stay and share food and a smoke with him. After a while they went on as if he was not there. These were the times he appreciated most.

Thomas Agnell was trustworthy enough and fully capable of running the trading post. Often Roger left for days to observe, with Canonchet as his young guide. In this way he became so familiar to the Narragansett that he was treated as they would treat any brave from a neighboring tribe, except that he made it clear he already had a wife in Plymouth and was just visiting, not angling to stay.

Inside Canonchet's family, Roger found structure. As they neared the tribe, he saw communities of women caring for children and tending to agriculture. Upon arriving, he learned of men out hunting and fishing and involved in negotiations with respect to territory. At the campfire that night, he learned about the Algonquian concept of a creator, and if he understood correctly, they believed their ancestors were delivered to this land from the far west on the back of a turtle. He found a relationship much like marriage, with Miantonomoh and his children protecting his wife, the children's mother, to the point that they would not even share her name with him.

The most impressive thing Roger witnessed was the governing structure of the Algonquian. He learned that each knew his territory, and, should others from a different territory hunt in a sachem's territory, it was proper to pay tribute with a gift of some of the meat or ceremonial sacred objects. He learned that the leaders of a tribe must serve the people well, or the people could leave for another tribe. All the tribes were actually interconnected peoples and distant kin. It was not unusual for the lower-status or less-respected men to travel and earn respect in a different tribe and to take a wife and set up an additional family. Local sachems were subordinate to regional sachem, and the regional sachems gathered together in a council to make the most important decisions and settle disputes.

Each night at the campfire there were stories from young braves, stories told over and over again until newcomers and children could repeat them.

The oral history of this people was vast, and it reminded Roger that the Old Testament was once oral history. One night he heard a story about people who were called upon to steward the land, and he was reminded of Adam and Eve.

On other evenings he heard stories that featured a repeating archetype of a brother and sister sending children to travel to, and become the elites of, new nations. First there was the story of a brother and sister leaving home and getting blown west in a storm, landing on shores far south and west, with a soft, yellow, fleshy fruit for food but no rootstock. The fruit had no seeds, so without the rootstock they could not plant. The story recounted how they used their horticultural skills to develop new plants from the wild plants they encountered, first for the rope to make fishing nets and then for food. Their children were strong and wealthy and made high-status matches in surrounding tribes and became rulers managing vast civil engineering projects, like sets of stairs that crossed the mountains. Eventually the yellow fruit became a distant, mythical memory.

Another night there were another brother and sister who married on the high plains where corn was developed from grasses. Their children were also sent out to make high-status matches with new tribes to form new peoples.

The Algonquian also had marked class divisions. To Roger's observant eye, the leaders were physically different from the average commoner.

By the time Roger returned to Plymouth, he respected Algonquian culture more deeply than ever. These Algonquian peoples were already producing more furs and wampum than at any other time in their remembered history. Otherwise they were little changed from their ancestors during the previous centuries, and they were the closest thing to a self-governing people Roger would see in his entire life. He watched and observed. He was amused when they wanted English clothes from him, as their own were so much more effective, both in the winter and in the heat of summer. He saw them watching him as closely as he was watching them. They traded knowledge and tools and friendship.

All this structure disturbed Roger, for he knew, as a European, that the English, French, Dutch, and Spanish all treated this land as un-owned and un-peopled and therefore available to be claimed. Roger took these concerns to his own leaders, the governors of the colonies.

The leaders of Plymouth, led by William Bradford, didn't know what to do with these concerns. All their power and sense of order in how to govern was derived from the king's patent, which Roger's claims seemed to call into question. Roger never explicitly called into question the king's power, but that power was predicated upon the king granting rights to occupy a land that was previously a vacuum, devoid of human civilization. Roger's observations made very clear that the land was occupied and civilized. Thus, uncomfortably, it no longer seemed to be a vacuum. As the leaders of the English colonies were at heart politicians and investors, they were completely uninterested in facing off with King Charles over an issue that would make their own governing power and profits weaker.

William Bradford asked Roger to put his concerns in writing, so the leadership could think about them further. In part, they were looking for a way to bury the issue. That night, Roger labored to write out a letter to the Plymouth council that was convincing. In response, the leaders began to obtain deeds from the Algonquian for territory. That didn't work very well, however, as the Algonquian viewed territory as occupied by season, and, while they granted the right to use the land, they were not granting anything like ownership. Often they granted use to multiple Europeans, which seemed devious to the English.

In Plymouth itself, Roger was daily among the people that had been followers of Leiden's John Robinson. These colonists were part of the Scrooby congregation of Pilgrims arriving in 1621 on the *Mayflower*. Such close proximity, and yet there was no communication about HH. Johannes de Cerf and John Robinson had both been dead since 1625. Both the Anabaptist confession and the Robinson response were gathering dust in attics in Leiden. In Plymouth there were more immediate needs to attend to—food, civil order, and relationships with the Algonquian.

CHAPTER 18

Axmouth, AD 1632

Jane Whalley Hooke loved to stand or sit on her horse on top of the cliffs at the edge of the meadow overlooking the sea. Sometimes in the daytime she gazed down at the cliffs, watching for birds and following them by sight to their nests. In the evening and by the moonlight she loved to watch the sea. Her sharp, crystalline eyes pierced the distance, watching for ships. Often she saw Massachusetts- or Providence- or Plymouth-bound ships set sail; in the full moon she also sometimes saw Dunkirkers.

It felt good to be back in England. William was serving as vicar at Axmouth in Devon. The younger Jane had never thought she'd be happy coming back from the New World, but the East Indies had not been the new world she'd imagined. There was ocean, but no meadows. There were breezes—warm, muggy, and buggy—but no cool, refreshing breezes. There were diseases for plants, animals, and men. England had bad years, but there were good years in between. 1629 to 1632 seemed like a long run of disease and habitat destruction. She longed for the productiveness of Otes.

Marney was back in England briefly, hoping to escape the wrath of Boston after his last adventure. He planned his schedule to include sailing out by the cliffs of Devon on nights with a good moon, hoping to see the billowing silhouette of the woman of the town of Axmouth. He thought she was the most beautiful sight he'd ever seen. He wasn't quite sure whether she was human or angel. Since his successful raid in New England, he stalked about, watching for the next big outgoing group of ships laden with winter supplies. The colonies were growing stronger now, and most of the ships now were laden with people. Marney held out for one with few passengers and valuable goods, but he was losing hope of a large plunder. He was also thinking of starting over in New Amsterdam. He had been a mercenary naval captain for the French once, and he was considering what it would take to fit into the Dutch militia.

When he was in the Indie's, Jane's husband William was minister to people that didn't want a demanding minister. In Axmouth he was back in a familiar culture and he enjoyed these families, the mothers with babies, the youth struggling to become adults, and the adults struggling to eke out a living. Most loved the Lord, and he was happy to serve them. The practicalities of his sizable and isolated parish and his genteel nature meant he was quite happy to conform. He was an upstanding Puritan, reading his Bible every day, doing his private prayers, and believing in the conversion of the heart. In front of his congregation, he conformed in ceremony. He hoped that would be enough for Bishop Laud. Given his and his wife's connection to Otes, he knew he had all the wrong friends, from Laud's perspective. He heard of their fates and wondered, and continued diligently but quietly to serve his parish.

In their joy at the return, neither Jane nor William anticipated the full scope of the venom with which the bishop was enforcing conformity. William Hooke had always been an upstanding Puritan preacher. Eventually he felt he was the last Puritan left standing in England, and that, if he did not leave, he would soon be found and cut out. He hoped he was in a quiet enough corner that the bishop would not be paying attention. For a few years, he was successful at being unnoticed and unremarkable. There were bigger fish to fry.

Jane and William especially looked forward to making some time to visit Otes, but the day never seemed to come. Sometimes Elizabeth Masham forwarded her letters from the Winthrops, and those were favorite moments. Martha Winthrop, Elizabeth Masham, and Jane Whalley Hooke could all read, which was rare. The women loved to gather to have letters read to them while sewing and to talk about the letters by the fire after tea. Soon Jane had friends in Devon to whom she could read the letters that Elizabeth forwarded. Elizabeth rarely got a return letter, but she understood and did not stop writing.

Off the Coast of Massachusetts, AD 1632

By fall, Marney was back in the New World. He hoped Boston had forgotten him. He was tempted north by the more lucrative English trade, since the Dutch were in decline in New England. If the looting business was poor enough, he had a commission in the Dutch army as a backup job for the winter.

The English, on the other hand, were building larger ships and engaging in ever more complex industrial ventures.

Marney was lurking off the coast of Massachusetts and had his eye on a vessel that might have valuable ironworks forging equipment. He was waiting for nightfall to pounce.

John Mason was being paid by the owner of the *Charles* to watch for Marney, who had not been forgotten and who had made a resourceful enemy. The ship was loaded with metal—that much was true. Most of it was weaponry meant to sink a pirate ship. That wasn't the word around town, though. They'd advertised the vessel as carrying ironworks supply equipment, and John Mason had seen to it that the lucrative nature of the load was well known in town. John Mason calmly stood ready for an attack, with guns loaded and waiting. Twelve hours prior a possible pirate ship had been spotted, and if engagement was planned, he suspected it would come after dark.

After nightfall, Marney approached. He was taken by surprise by the viciousness of the counterattack. His boat was sinking within thirty minutes of his approach. Most of his crew was wiped clean off the deck, and an orderly surrender at gun- and sword-point followed. With his ship sinking, surrender seemed like a better option than drowning. Within a few hours of his surrender, Marney was focused on how he could get out of the situation. In the end he used his Dutch army status. There was an English soldier in Dutch hands, and an exchange of prisoners was arranged. Mason was satisfied. The pirate was nothing without his boat, and the loot they confiscated from the sinking boat more than paid for the capture. He had no desire to have the expense of keeping prisoners.

He told Marney he owed him one and would let him know when and how he could repay.

In truth, John Mason was already repaid. He was a hero in Boston, and the sinking of Marney's vessel launched his career.

When the story was recounted to John Winthrop the Younger, he smiled. Someday, he planned to have a ship full of ironworks supplies. Now there would be one less pirate who could steal it.

Southwest of Plymouth, AD 1632

The Narragansett Steward rulers had controlled Block Island with the Niantic for a generation. The Pequot were growing very strong since the plague, however, taking traditionally Wampanoag and Massachusetts territory. The Pequot remained allied with the western Niantic on Block Island. Canonicus realized that, given the fur and wampum trade routes, it was time to reclaim this strategic land from the Pequot.

With Oonue running a camouflaged wampum factory on Block Island, they did not fear the Pequot on Block Island so much as being ambushed during transport to land. It was becoming critical that the Narragansett control land and sea between their winter and summer camps all the way to the most effective beach access to Block Island. The Pequot were strong in that territory, and Miantonomoh and Canonicus gathered the forces of the larger confederation of Algonquians to assist in the attack.

The battle was Algonquian in style—a massive show of force by Canonicus against the surprised Pequot, followed by the seizure of the territory by the side recognized as more powerful. When the Pequot saw that they would not be able to prevail, they quickly surrendered and paid homage, leaving behind some of their young women to work the fields in the newly Narragansett territory. They gave Canonicus wampum to show their respect and to secure the peace. The battle was concluded with no deaths. This was the traditional Algonquian way.

Canonicus had the responsibility from this day forward for these Pequot women who had been left behind and pledged to have them marry into his tribe, according to tradition. This was a very difficult concept for any of the English to understand and respect, even though they had similar traditions. In England, royal families intermarried for political gain. In an enormously popular ceremony, King James's daughter Elizabeth was married to Count Palatine of Bohemia. It was an arranged match, the two parties having only met once before their marriage, but the couple grew to be deeply and famously in love. Stories of this couple were told across Europe and New England, but nothing about the dirt-filled smoke holes where Narragansett ruling women lived evoked images of royalty to the English.

It was a fine morning, and Roger was about to climb into his canoe when he noticed Narragansett approaching in the distance. First came advance scouts, and Roger conversed with one and learned that a large party was coming to talk with him. He hurried back to the house and asked Mary to prepare a feast for the visitors.

The next arrivals were young warriors. Roger learned from them that his guests would include Canonicus. He headed in to change into his finest clothing and prepared the property for a more formal gathering. Although Roger had watched Canonicus many times in his native setting, this would be their first visit in Roger's territory, and Roger wondered what occasion had prompted such a visit.

The parties feasted through the afternoon, exchanging pleasantries. The Algonquians brought provisions, and Mary, Roger's servant Thomas, and the braves served the food. The joint production was a lavish affair. Finally Canonicus revealed the reason for the visit. He spoke directly to Roger: "A Pequot wife entrusted to me personally was foraging in the forest when an Englishman abducted her. I object to this uncivilized behavior and request that, to maintain your own honor and the honor of your people, you find her and redeem her to me. Can you take on this assignment?"

Roger groaned inwardly. An Englishman. Who? Where? On what ground would he claim her back? Was she still alive? He answered carefully: "I have not heard of this, but I will do everything in my power to redeem her. What more can you and your people tell me of the specific circumstances? Did you trail them to a specific location?"

Indeed, they had.

Roger set off shortly with a group of young Narragansett who led him to a large farm far from town. To his chagrin, he recognized the place as Richard Church's homestead. Bravely he set off and knocked on the door. Richard, a carpenter by trade, was fetched from his shop and returned to the house to speak with Roger.

"How can I help you?" asked Richard.

"I'm on a mission to keep the peace," Roger began. "Do you have in your possession a squaw you've recently acquired or come by?"

"As a matter of fact, my boys Joseph and Benjamin were out hunting when they came upon a squaw who begged for mercy and wanted to escape from her captors. We offered her the position of maid in our household, and she is working for me here," answered Richard.

Roger expected a story like this one, and he did not doubt that this was what had been reported to Richard. He did not want to start a disturbance, and he did not want to argue the situation. So he asked, "How much will you sell her for?"

After some negotiation, they came to a price, which Roger promptly paid. He considered it an investment in his relationship with Canonicus, and he departed with the woman, returning her in good condition to Canonicus. He was relieved that the woman was in good shape, as he had feared for her life and her health.

Canonicus, with the Pequot under control, were emboldened to consolidate power further. The Wampanoag were weakened from smallpox, and he reasoned it in his best interest to strike while strong.

Under threat from Canonicus, Massasoit, sachem of the Wampanoag, needed to increase his resources to ward off Canonicus's men. One evening as Roger was building a stone wall near the edge of his property, a Wampanoag brave approached. He asked if Roger would accompany him back to the tribe's camp for trade negotiations. Roger was happy to go. At the Wampanoag camp that night, Roger had a private meeting with Massasoit.

"As you know, my land is intertwined with that of Canonicus," noted Massasoit. "He threatens my village, Sowam. I need resources to defend Sowam and offer you in return the use of the land at the head of Narragansett Bay. This arrangement will help us both. My remaining land will be easier to defend, and I will have the resources to drive back the Narragansett. You will have a southern territory from which to trade and hunt and conduct your English business."

Roger agreed. He supplied metal axes, knives, and spades in volume. Roger stayed with Massasoit several more days to conclude the arrangement and then set off with the Wampanoag for a tour of his investment. By the end of the journey, Massasoit claimed that he considered Roger an adopted son. Massasoit maintained deep and strong connections to both the Boston and Plymouth communities. Unaware of the depth of the relationship Roger Williams was developing with Wampanoag rivals among the Narragansett, he sought to add Roger as one of his Plymouth connections.

Massasoit was successful that year in defending Sowam from the Narragansett tribes. Canonicus and Massasoit faced off Algonquian-style and reached agreements with no visible casualties. Without the two sachems realizing it, however, a Narragansett brave was infected with smallpox. For the rest of the year the western Narragansett struggled with smallpox. Fortunately, Canonicus and his immediate family escaped the outbreak, remaining healthy.

Roger wanted to explore his new acquisition, and he decided to go on an extended hunting and fishing expedition. John the Younger accompanied him to Narragansett Bay, and they explored and fished. John was particularly impressed with the geography of the land. He pointed out to Roger where a port should be built, along with a protected town, with access from multiple directions. Together they found old Algonquian campgrounds—large ones. They realized this must be a major meeting place for multiple tribes, with a rich history, given the variety of artifacts they were discovering.

John the Younger questioned Massasoit's motives, "So this sachem took weapons from you, and promised you land he could not have controlled for very long given these artifacts. Did he give you land that other Algonquian will shortly claim from you?"

Roger frowned. "I don't know," he admitted. "However, Canonicus did not dispute my ownership when I spoke of it to him afterward. He did ask me for use of the land for summer negotiations. I was excited that I would have a front row seat at Algonquian tribal negotiations occurring on this land, and immediately agreed."

"So now you have an open invitation to the meetings of the regional sachems?" asked John the Younger. "That could be more valuable to the English than the land itself."

"That is what I think. I was more interested in language and custom, but I agree that it could be valuable to the colonies as well."

John the Younger said to Roger, "You settle the south, and I'll take the north. We'll see whose acquisition is more productive." They laughed. It was all dreams at this point.

Plymouth, AD 1633

Roger did not return home until July. In August of 1633 everything changed when the Williams's first daughter arrived, named Mary after her mother. It was a difficult birth, with no midwife. Mary was in essence her own midwife, with Roger's untrained hands doing her bidding. Neither of them had anticipated the travail a baby could cause in this wilderness—and the loss of Mary's farm labor meant Roger and his servant Thomas were on their own. Mary began to long to be in town to raise her child.

"Roger, I'm not sure how much longer I can stand it here in the wilderness. With this baby, I'm not getting sleep. There's no one to help, no friends and relatives to support me here. Can't you find a nice safe position in town somewhere from which to teach and to trade?" said Mary after one exasperating day.

Late that night, pacing with the baby to allow Mary some rest, Roger considered. After the baby quieted and finally slept on his chest, he penned a letter to his good friend Sam Skelton in Salem.

Soon enough, they planned a move to Salem, to a fine house in town. On reflection, he had mixed feelings about his southerly land acquisition. On the surface there was no reason for it. It was two days' travel south of Plymouth. It seemed impractical now, if he was going to move north.

They left Thomas behind, running the trading post in Plymouth. It was a lucrative business, and Roger was not willing to give up his ties to the area. There were four more years in Thomas's indenture, and Roger decided to wait and see what the future would hold before selling out his stake in Plymouth.

Boston, AD 1633

The baby kicked inside her belly, and Martha was thrilled. She had waited so long for this child—a full three years. Now it seemed like a real person in there kicking, one she couldn't wait to meet. She wanted to tell John the Younger, but he'd left with twelve other men to start a new settlement in Agawam, several hours north. At least he had stayed until after their anniversary had passed in February. She smiled. That wasn't why he'd waited; he'd waited for the ice to melt and for spring to come.

Since May he'd been faithfully returning once a month to attend court as assistant, and she wanted to enjoy every minute of each visit. She hoped to follow John north. First though, he needed to create a homestead for them in the new settlement. She worried he was so completely focused on building his businesses that he would not take the time. She wanted to move in time to plant for 1634. Sometimes her worries made the visits tense. Every time John felt tension he seemed to disappear until his next visit. The more she tried to be at ease the tension seemed to increase. She couldn't hide her feelings from John. She had never been able to hide her feelings from John.

Looking out to sea, she saw a ship approaching the harbor from an odd direction, and she felt vaguely uneasy. The *Griffin* approached the harbor at Boston September 5. Two days earlier, a passenger had drowned while casting a line for a mackerel, bringing to four the total number of lost passengers during this journey. The mackerel is a twenty-inch fish, and it surely didn't seem to be worth a life. The crew shook their heads over the stupid things passengers do, and the passengers were a little shocked that they could lose one so easily, having come so far.

They'd stopped at Lovells Island to bury the passenger who had drowned. With three ministers aboard, and the general excitement of landfall, it was a more ostentatious affair than burials at sea. As a result, Captain John Gallop had taken the time to explore the channels near the island and develop a new if risky route into the Boston harbor to the inside of the island. The *Griffin* successfully navigated the route at low tide. The crew heaved a collective sigh of relief upon success, and the route was called Griffin's Gap in their honor. Captain John Gallop, with the help of a wealthy passenger, organized a feast for the upper echelon of passengers and invited John Winthrop Senior aboard for the honors.

After dinner the stories began. John Gallop started them off by mentioning that they hadn't expected three ministers on the boat. John Hall picked up the story.

"Yes," Hall declared, "my servant crew is interesting. I've brought your settlers cotton for their clothing, hookers for their fishing, and stones for their building." Everyone at the table laughed. He was referring to Reverend John Cotton, Thomas Hooker, and Samuel Stone and their families.

"They all boarded at Downs in Kent as my servants," continued Hall. As a widower with four children, I needed the extra servants. I was hoping that the searchers did not count too closely and compare the numbers to my last census. Fortunately Downs is a small port, and security was lax compared to larger ports. We had another close call at the Isle of Wight. Fortunately my "servants" were still in character and serving. The pursuers came on board, but frankly their hearts were not in the search. We dared not let the 'servants' out of character till we'd been many days on the ocean. By then we had some worship to make up, and so they've each been preaching: Cotton in the morning, Hooker in the afternoon, and Stone in the evening."

John Winthrop Senior asked, "And John, what brought you to masquerade as a servant?"

Cotton answered, "Bishop Laud requested an audience. I feared if I complied, it would have resulted in my imprisonment. At first I lay low, endangering one friend after another as they hid me, not daring to let Sarah visit for fear of being watched. After much prayer, we decided that God was calling us to an act of faith to give up the luxuries of England forever for a land that would preserve our futures in service to the Lord. I considered Holland, but I'll let Hooker tell that story."

Hooker picked up the tale. "We'd been in Holland several years, but we were not happy there. We found the church there to be all form and no substance. I wrote to John Cotton as much and that we were planning to immigrate to the Bay Colonies from Holland. I made one last trip to England to arrange my affairs. While there I visited Sam Stone. As we were smoking in his garden, a pounding came at the door. Sam answered while I hid, and they were looking for me! Sam covered for me, saying he'd seen me not an hour earlier at the market, and they left. All plans were put aside, and both Sam and I joined John in hiding. They put a watch on all ports, for all three of us. That's when we sought Mr. Hall's help and got passage as his servants from Downs."

John Winthrop Senior sat back. "You've had quite the passage, in only eight weeks. The *Bird* also arrived today, and she was twelve weeks at sea." He looked directly at Captain John Gallop and said, "Well done."

What they did not know now but would learn within two months, was that the escape had happened just in time. For in August while John Cotton was at sea, Bishop Laud became the archbishop of Canterbury, a position second in authority only to the king of England.

The gathering in the New World of the Essex ministers who debated the future of the church on their travels to Sepringham was now complete. However, the debates that had been easy philosophy in a carriage outside London now intensified and were acted out in life as social experiments in how to constitute both church and world. The men sensed an opportunity to get the structure right in a way that the world had not yet seen. They threw their passions and their careers into the experiment.

The following Sunday John Cotton preached a sermon he would never have dared preach in England. He proclaimed that the authority of the Church came from the body of Christ as represented by the congregation, and not from the king. He accepted the position as teacher in Boston only after having the congregation formally elect him. He would at first seem a moderate among the Massachusetts Bay Company ministers. He was no separatist, and would fight the separatists with every weapon. He was honored to represent the established church. Yet he also advocated forgiveness upon repentance.

John Cotton was a serious listener and thinker as well as a good speaker. The rides from Sepringham did seem to change one of his positions for the remainder of his earthly life. In the new world he consistently supported complete forgiveness upon heartfelt repentance. However, this seed of compassion became in him an oak tree of persecution as he passionately pursued with every spiritual and physical weapon all those he deemed in need of repentance, until they would recant, repent and rejoin the fold. He transformed in one ocean passage from dissident in England to pursuer of dissidents in New England.

The following week John Winthrop the Younger arrived in Boston for court, and he visited Martha.

"Put your hand right here …" Martha showed him where on her belly. After a minute, she asked, "Did you feel the kick?"

"Yes! What a wonder, this little life hidden away inside you," said John the Younger. "You know this will be my last trip down to Boston, as my assistant duties are complete. By not traveling so much, I hope to finish our house sooner. Maybe you can find someone to stay with further north in the meantime?"

Martha's eyes were wide, for she hadn't been looking forward to a long separation. "The Lord will make a way," was all she said. They embraced. After some moments she changed the subject. "What was your last case in court? Anything interesting?"

"Oh, yes," said John the Younger with a laugh. "There's no shortage of interesting characters here. Sometimes I think King Charles has dumped them all in New England on purpose. Today we grappled with a pirate, Captain John Stone. One of my fellow assistants gave grand speeches against him, allowing how he'd gone drinking in public and taken Bancroft's wife to bed. But they couldn't prove a thing, and the grand jury let him off of the adultery business. For his lewdness and drinking, they fined him £100, but you watch, he'll skip town in his trusty pinnace, and we'll never see that. He is too clever for our court system to deal with. At least we ordered him away from here. He needs to go back to Virginia where he's from. Let them deal with him."

On October 26, 1633, Thomas Hooker was chosen as the pastor of a small Puritan and Pilgrim congregation at Newton in the Massachusetts Bay Colony (now Cambridge), and Sam Stone became the teacher. While there, Hooker questioned the form of government being used by the Massachusetts Bay Colony, believing that all citizens should choose their magistrates. The vote in Massachusetts Bay Company was restricted to freemen, who had to be elected church members. He also firmly believed that the citizens should set the limits on what a government can or cannot do.

If Hooker was out on a limb, Roger Williams was out on a longer limb. Roger's letter to the elders at Plymouth was circulated more widely than at first, and it was read by his old debate protagonists from Essex. In their usual critical spirit, these new leaders found errors of judgment they wanted corrected and censured. They found that the letter blasphemed against King James because it stated that he had erroneously claimed via the patent to be the first godly authority to discover the lands to which he granted patent. Roger's letter also claimed that the patent erroneously called Europe Christendom when Christendom was the invisible Church throughout the world. Roger claimed no human could see for certain whether another is a heartfelt follower of Christ. Finally the letter made derogatory references to King Charles. For fear of having the Plymouth governing powers questioned in England for allowing such error, a review of Roger's letter to Plymouth was scheduled in the operating court for the colonies. Roger was asked to prepare an explanation, which he did. More careful now, he was purposefully vague in his response, avoiding threat to the colony, and claiming the original letter was intended to be private. His court appearance was scheduled for the next January.

CHAPTER 19

Mouth of the Connecticut River, AD 1633

Captain John Stone was traveling toward Virginia and saw an opportunity to do some trading with the Algonquian on his way south. Banished from Massachusetts, he was planning to stay south once he got there. Coming upon a Pequot village, he stopped. He and his men started by engaging in trade but ended drunk and violent, attacking and raping Pequot women.

In anger the Pequot braves took revenge by murdering him and six of his men and stealing his pinnace. The pinnace became the prize possession of the Pequot sachem, Puttaquappuinckquame, and he knew he must have a good explanation for his actions. He immediately set off to find Tatobem. Tatobem, however, was dead—murdered by the Dutch in a trade deal that went sour.

The most likely candidate to take over Tatobem's power was his son Sassacus, though he had competition. Sassacus and Puttaquappuinckquame conferred in council.

Sassacus explained that Puttaquappuinckquame's timing was good.

"In truth we owe revenge for the death of Tatobem, but we cannot afford to alienate the Dutch further. We know that most of our people cannot distinguish a Dutch marauder from an English marauder, as they are all white men and intruders. Your murder of this pirate can be advertised broadly as our retribution. The Dutch will continue to trade with us, and we will continue to threaten possible retribution over the murder of Tatobem to keep them pleasing us. In return, you will owe me tribute for the rest of your life."

Puttaquappuinckquame agreed immediately. He was a minor sachem, little more than the head of a family. There were many like him. This event would increase his stature in the tribe. He had a fast, top-rate pinnace as a visible reward, and he would be known as the avenger of Tatobem. "I will be loyal to you and your family for life."

Sassacus smiled. With a visible prize like this pinnace, the other sachems were likely to admire Puttaquappuinckquame and visit him. When they did, they would learn that he was with Sassacus. Many would follow.

There was just one problem, Sassacus thought. *What about the English? Would they find out what had occurred and avenge Stone as one of their own?*

Salem, AD 1633

That fall and early winter Roger had several seemingly casual but far from cordial "visitors." The first was John Winthrop Senior.

"Roger, I've read your letter many times now, and I will say privately that you have been blunt with the truth. I've no issue with treating the Algonquian peoples honorably, and I think you know that."

"I've never accused you of doing otherwise, John. That letter was meant to convince the Plymouth establishment to do the same."

"There is a problem, though. You know I've put several people threatening the established order of our colony on a boat back to England. The Brown brothers are back in England right now, and they are threatening the patent. They want to contest Plymouth's right to compel a worship service that does not use the common prayer book."

"Those men belong in England, where they can use the common prayer book as they please. Of course if you tolerated them using the common prayer book without the drama, you'd not have these issues. Yet, I see that the issue has grown beyond tolerance to an actual threat to our civil peace if the patent is jeopardized. They are little more than villains!" exclaimed Roger.

"You know I don't personally care what form of worship people choose, and I would not get excited about a prayer book being used or not. I've supported the Browns in the past. But they threaten the patent. I can't govern without the rule of law here, you know that much. The patent is what gives us authority to have the rule of law. What would you replace it with? Sachems' rule? I don't think so. I need you to disown this position and to respect that the patent is all we have right now. Be practical, Roger."

"I see. I'd not have the English learn the sachem's ways. That would surely be too severe. I can keep my views private. I won't change my views, but I can keep them quiet. For, after all, we are commanded in <u>Matthew 10</u> to be as shrewd as wolves and as simple as doves when dealing with the world."

"In truth, we are all doing that," Winthrop commented. "I'm glad you understand."

The next visit was from Thomas and Suzanne Hooker. While Suzanne and Mary retired to the kitchen, Thomas sat by the fire with Roger.

"Roger, I'm not sure you understand the full scope of the misery in England these days. Even before Laud was made archbishop, he forced us out of the country. When I returned to England just to arrange my affairs, he had me hunted down to Sam Stone's house as if I were a criminal. Now, as archbishop, Laud technically oversees the group that writes the rules that govern these colonies. He is far away. Yet he wants to reach his arms across the sea to control us. We must be careful not to offend in any way they can see across the water. We need him to believe that his ends are better served by focusing elsewhere."

Roger laughed. "The Archbishop of Canterbury loves his luxuries. I cannot imagine him for a minute chopping wood or scrounging a living from the wild land, can you?"

"In truth, no. But I couldn't have imagined it of John Cotton either, at least not before he had malaria and lost his first wife. Here he is, nearly fifty, newly remarried with a new baby. Laud has no mercy if he could chase such a man from his home into the wilderness of the New World. That, more than anything else, must make you feel the danger. Do you want to count on the wilderness to protect you? Laud will find men to do his bidding, if he is motivated," replied Hooker.

"I can assure you that I can be practical in these matters, as shrewd as a wolf and as simple as a dove. The letter was meant to be private. I never meant to endanger my good friend Winthrop, and, having been chased out of England myself, I surely do not mean to be of any help getting Laud to pursue us here," answered Roger.

The final visit was from Sam Stone.

"How's the missus?" asked Roger.

"Back to her melancholy ways," reported Sam. "I'd hoped the New World would revive her spirits and keep her busy, but she is as sad as ever."

"How did you find a perpetually morose wife with a name like Hope?" teased Roger.

"Forgive my optimism, but even in her sadness she can be exquisitely beautiful. It is just one more thing to keep me motivated to stay busy out of the house. Speaking of which, I'm busying myself today to give you a tongue-lashing over this letter you've written threatening the king's authority and calling him names. What were you thinking? Would you have us all in chains? We're afraid that's what will happen should we fail to censure you thoroughly. If we are lenient, the king himself will hear of it, and he will think that we agree with you. We'll lose the patent."

"I understand. I'm going to repent thoroughly and very publicly at court to spare everyone fear and misery. Others have been before you, and as I've explained to them, the letter was meant to be private and has been taken out of context."

Watertown, AD 1633

Bess Fones Winthrop Feake had everyone down for the Sunday after Christmas. Roger and Mary arrived from Salem with four-month-old baby Mary with them. They had been in Salem a month now, freshly moved from Plymouth. Martha and John were expecting a baby any day now, and Martha rode in from Boston, where she'd been staying with her in-laws, since John was still in Agawam. The Feake household was warm and celebratory, with two-year-old Martha Johanna and two-month-old Elizabeth, whom Bess said must be called Liz, never Bess! Bess invited Captain John Underhill and Captain Patrick to make sure her husband would actually stay for the whole evening. Captain Underhill and Captain Patrick had Dutch wives whom they left at home with John's mother.

This was not a Christmas celebration—there were too many Puritans in the house for that—Puritans disapproved of Christmas. They believed that Sabbath was the only sanctioned holiday in the Bible. The Anglicans elected a King of Misrule, who caused mischief throughout Christmas Day, and any behavior remotely resembling revelry or feasting on December 25 was against the law in the Massachusetts Bay Colony as a reaction against this tradition.

The afternoon feast consisted of roast venison, roasted corn, mashed and rebaked butternut squash, and fresh bread with butter. Most were too ravenous to talk during dinner. Martha Winthrop knew that the men would soon leave for their own conversation, so she used the meal to compare notes with Roger Williams.

"How is it that the Algonquian I've seen all have such wonderful teeth, and no swelling of any kind, yet they have no lemons or other fruits in winter?" asked Martha.

"They seem to chew on the needles of the white pine constantly while in the woods, and they recommend it for health of the mouth. They also eat the roots of the native wild water lily. Have you tasted it? It tastes more like a fruit than a potato. You can find that root most of the year as long as you know where to get through the ice," said Roger.

"No evergreen but white pine?" asked Martha.

"My friends prefer the white pine. I've seen them chew on spruce and fir when they are not around pine. They chew those needles like some Europeans chew tobacco. It seems to have a much better effect. Pregnant women especially seem to love the spruce," answered Roger.

"They don't seem to lose nearly as many babies as we do," noted Martha.

"I'm not sure why," said Roger. "I do see the women making all sorts of concoctions for women only, and I don't know what's in many of them or their specific purpose. Perhaps you should come spend time with the women in their camp."

"I would so love to do just that," said Martha.

"I'll have to see what can be arranged," said Roger.

When dinner was finished and appetites sated, the young mothers and their babies moved into the living area just off the kitchen. The men moved to the parlor.

"How do you like being in Salem now?" asked Bess of Mary.

"I love it. People think I'm crazy for moving so soon after the baby came, but I am so happy we did. Roger is so rarely around, and now I'm much closer to friends. Our house is so much larger—a very nice cottage at the edge of town. It was well worth the trouble of the move. We were able to time it perfectly so that I got the harvest out of our garden in Plymouth before we left. I've provisions for the winter stored up and time to plan my garden in Salem."

"And through all this you are feeding your own baby I see? How do you like it?" Martha asked Mary.

"I wouldn't have it any other way. It creates such a close connection between us, and I feel my baby is safe. So many babies expire while out to wet nurse," answered Mary.

"How long will you keep it so?" asked Martha.

"I intend to feed her for two years if I can. With food so scarce, she'll always be well nourished that way.

"I plan to nurse, but hear it can be painful," said Martha Winthrop. "It is so different from what we've always done back home.

"The pain will quickly pass," noted Bess. "I had to feed Martha Johanna myself, as we wanted to be confident of a food supply for her on the boat. I enjoyed it, and I'm starting Liz that way as well. Now that we're better off, I'm not at all sure I want to keep it up for two years, though. When Martha got teeth, it was easier to feed her adult food."

"I wonder how long the Algonquian feed their children?" asked Martha.

"It looks to be at least a year," said Mary. "They keep them swathed for a year, and they surely milk feed them that long, but it could be longer. My grandparents swaddled my mother and father, but I could not imagine keeping Mary swathed for that long. My brothers were walking before one year."

While the women talked of how to raise their children, the men focused on the Algonquian situations around them.

Robert Feake challenged Roger, saying, "I hear that John Eliot has taken in a Mohegan boy as a servant and is using him to learn the language and translate the Bible. He has the boy dressing like an English, acting English, and showing him how to say everything in Algonquian. What do you think of that approach?"

Roger was thoughtful. "He usually takes in boys from the Massachusetts tribe, so a Mohegan is a surprise. Their leader, Uncas, must be trying to accelerate Mohegan English language skills. Maybe he intends to ally with the English against the Pequot? In any case, John Eliot may learn how to talk about English ways in Algonquian much faster than I. He may even learn to speak the Bible in Algonquian more quickly than I. However, I predict that I will know more of Algonquian ways, and how to talk about Algonquian ways, with my approach. Watching them, learning what they find sacred or practical or frightening helps me understand what they really mean, no matter what they are talking about."

"Yes, I should think your approach might teach you something of the delicacies of where care must be taken in negotiations," said Robert Feake.

"Yet his approach may be more fruitful in a Bible translation, and in teaching the Algonquian the Bible stories," noted Roger. "Although to really get the Algonquian to feel the stories, it would seem we'd need to connect to their ways, as Paul did with the Greeks in Athens."

"I'll admit I haven't worried about either of those things," inserted Captain John Underhill. "I'm too busy working on finding Pequot and shooting them."

"Yes, we need that too," said Robert Feake. "I'm convinced, as is Winthrop Senior, that if we can weaken the Pequot, we thereby cripple the Dutch. Of course, you grew up in the Netherlands, and your wife is Dutch. Are you sure you are with us in this war with the Pequot?" Robert teased John.

John Underhill didn't see the humor. "I can surely speak Dutch, but I'm an Englishman through and through. My father was an English soldier, as am I. I know where my bread is getting buttered. I'll use the Dutch when we need to, but these Pequot pests need to be eradicated. I've seen them kill Algonquians and Europeans alike in cold blood for no reason," thundered Captain John.

"I'll vouch for Captain John right now," Captain Dan Patrick said entering the conversation midstream. "We've trained together and fought Pequot together."

"And you've Dutch wives together, but you are Englishmen," said Robert Feake in a more serious tone. "I'll vouch for both of you. These Pequot are a fierce nation. We may need the help of the Dutch from time to time, especially where our territories overlap. I think we need to watch for ways to turn the Dutch and Pequot against each other. Maybe you can help us with that," said Robert to Captain Underhill.

Later, Roger and Martha were outside sharing a private conversation. "I hear you already made a quite a splash with Father at your first meeting of the Bay Colony ministers," said Martha.

"It is good to work with Reverend Sam Skelton again—a man of fine character, true to his calling. However, that organization of conspiring magistrates and ministers should not exist. Your father-in-law says they mean no harm, but that is the gathering that the Bay Colonies used to pressure the church at Salem not to hire me two years back. Here we have the government in the New World imposing on the churches already, despite all John Cotton's sermons on congregational rule. This tendency must be fought back wherever it occurs. The government is not competent to run the Church. Christ in his body—the people—must run the Church," answered Roger.

"I see I stepped on a hot potato. If it doesn't work out here, maybe you'd like to join us in Agawam. I'm going soon to join John the Younger there, and he's going to form a city of the best engineers. We'll specialize in ironworks, water drainage, and other construction techniques. We'll gather all the best minds from Europe and gain a technological edge we can sell to the world," said Martha.

"Hmm … I'm meant to evangelize the Algonquian peoples. I think my path lies elsewhere somehow, but you never know. I'll keep it mind," answered Roger.

"In the meantime, Mary thinks I should come back with her to Salem till the baby comes. What would you think of that?"

"I'd be overjoyed to have you stay, Martha. Mary can use the help," Roger replied. He remembered Mary's loneliness in Plymouth after the first baby and wanted it to be different this time. Martha was an accomplished healer and would be valuable to have in the house. "By all means, stay!

You'll be that much closer to Agawam as well. We can stop in Boston and pick up some things and all return together."

"Thanks so much. I hope John the Younger can come down from time to time to visit, since Salem will be so much closer to him."

"In the meantime we can endeavor to have you meet the Algonquian squaws who manage the forests around our land."

Salem, AD 1633

Martha loved Mary's tidy new house, a roomy space that showed her intention of having many children. They chatted, Martha held baby Mary the Younger, and Mary cleaned. Then Martha's chatting stopped; labor pains had begun. Mary helped Martha to the bedroom and helped her give birth to a little girl many hours later. Bess had already used up the name Martha, so it would not be Martha the Younger. Martha decided to wait to name the baby until she could see her husband.

Saugus, AD 1633

When smallpox hit the first woman, one who had been working in town, Weekan made a decision to take Aunun and head for the woods for an extended hunting expedition. Most of the men were with the English now anyway, and neither Weekan nor Aunan was ready to take a wife with him, so their betrotheds were left behind with the tribe to survive as they could. Because Jole's tribe largely escaped the 1616 outbreak by being either under siege from the Abenaki or part of an inland tribe at that time, they were pummeled in 1633, losing over 80 percent of their remaining population. Jole's sons James and John were listed among the dead. Only one of Jole's sons, George, remained living, and he lived in Agawam and worked at the harbor.

Jole, her daughter Abigail, and her granddaughter Ale survived, and wampum production eventually resumed. Aunan's intended wife was lost to the disease.

In late fall, just as cold was setting in, Weekan and Aunun returned, knowing that smallpox always disappeared as the winter season set in. There wasn't much to come back to.

"I have no desire to go live with the English, and there is nothing left for us here. All the other braves are following the sachem into town," complained Aunan to Weekan.

"It's true. The only people left in the village are the old people. All the good women are working in town as servants, and the wampum factory can barely sustain itself. This place is an empty town. Our uncles and cousins would never respect us again if we went to live in town, so we must not."

"Let's go home. There's no reason to stay."

"Jole won't let Ale go."

"Don't ask her. Let's just take her and go. Who can they send after us—Sachem George? He's fat, and he'll have to be at work the next morning. He'll never find us."

"I can't do that." Weekan was thinking as a future sachem, knowing Miantonomoh expected him to make this clan grow and prosper and join forces with his own. They let the subject drop for now.

CHAPTER 20

Boston, January, AD 1634

Court convened in January.

Roger dutifully trekked down to Boston and provided a full recantation of the patent issues in writing and in person, as promised. He offered as a sign of his full submission that the magistrates could choose to burn his letter, or any part of it. The matter was discussed by the council, which arrived at two conclusions: first, some of the statements were vaguely construed and were not as evil as first thought, and second, in light of Roger's recantation, they could pass over the rest if Roger would take an oath of allegiance to the king. He did so, and the matter was closed. Unofficially, however, Roger Williams, far from having the respect of his fellow ministers, was being watched, and John Winthrop Senior made sure he knew it.

While in Boston, his stature in the community officially restored, Roger dined with the Winthrop family and was happy to be bringing them the news of Martha's baby girl. Margaret, John Winthrop Senior's third wife, was now mother of nine children with John, six of whom had survived to date. She had not given birth since her crossing to New England. Both John Winthrop Senior and Margaret were overjoyed to hear of his first grandchild and his first descendant born in New England.

Back in Salem, Roger taught about the separation between the first table and the second table of the Ten Commandments. The first-table commandments were the ones that relate to man's relationship with God. Thou shall have no other gods before me, though shall make no graven images, thou shall not take the name of the Lord in vain, and thou shall keep the Sabbath. Puritans included the honor of father and mother in the first table, as it relates to God's establishment of authority in the family first, then in the church. The church was considered as father to the people, so the fifth commandment fit into the first table.

The remaining commandments were part of the second table and were about keeping a civil society at peace. You shall not murder, you shall not commit adultery, you shall not steal, you shall not bear false witness against your neighbor, and you shall not covet were all second table or civil issues.

Puritans recognized all Ten Commandments. Many in the colonies believed they were building the New Jerusalem in New England. Others believed they were laboring for the visible Kingdom of God on earth. The ministers were specifically seeking to purify the church from errors they'd experienced in England, and before that from Rome. They intended to set up a government that would ensure that society and the church stayed pure. Where Roger diverged from the beliefs of his colleagues was in his belief that no human authority was competent to rule over the church. He was not seeking a system that would produce a competent ruler to run the church. He was seeking to remove the church and the first-table issues from the civil ruler's jurisdiction altogether.

Roger derived this concept from his reading of scripture. His fundamental point was that for any civil authority to impose a state church was tantamount to spiritual rape of a people, given that not all men are among the elect meant to follow Christ. If the government is Christian, then unregenerate men are forced into worship, a stench to God (Isaiah 66:1–6). If the government is not Christian, then Christian consciences will be raped (Psalm 50:16–17). There is no way to win. Song of Solomon 5:2–8 is viewed as an analogy for Christ and the Church and describes the horror of spiritual rape. So the civil government must limit itself to seeking the peace of the city, as in Jeremiah 29:7.

Roger's colleagues John Cotton, Sam Stone, and Thomas Hooker also derived their point of view from scripture. They quoted Romans 13:1 to prove that all governments are given authority by God and are to be obeyed. Since they were Christian governors, they would remand disciplinary matters to the church first, as indicated in Matthew 18:15. Finally, they would banish anyone they found not to follow Christ, as in 2 Timothy 3:1–5.

The flaw, Roger pointed out frequently in his sermons, was that mere mortals suffer from the noetic effects of the fall in the Garden of Eden, which include prejudice, faulty perspective, intellectual fatigue, inconsistency, failure to draw the right conclusions from information, and miscommunication. Roger had spent more time in the courts of England than any of these other men. He'd seen and heard first hand all these noetic effects impacting real-life decisions.

He knew from experience that even good men cannot tell perfectly which hearts are following Christ and which are not, per Matthew 13:24–29. In this parable men are compared to wheat and to a common weed that looks just like young wheat called a tare. When tares are young, a farmer knows he will not be able to tell the difference between young plants, and when they are older, the roots of the good and the bad plants are all tangled up, and he will kill both by attempting to pull the tare. Tares are therefore left until harvest and then burned with the chaff. Roger viewed this harvest as judgment, a time of God's harvest of men. Men who had never been farmers, like John Cotton, thought they could have earthly harvests as well, to implement justice, though imperfect, during earthly life per 1 Peter 2:13, so that evil would not spread. Roger believed that Cotton had missed the point. A tare is not just any weed; a tare is a form of evil that looks just like good early on, but ultimately it will be so far along in its evil ways that the consequence of killing it off is that both good and evil people are punished.

The difference between Holy Spirit inspired correction to human error and a rebellion of heretics was hard for a good and godly king like King James to discern, and much more difficult for King Charles. Roger reminded his Salem faithful often of the number of times England had switched between Catholic and Anglican monarchs, each time forcing a switch in religion, regardless of men's consciences. That couldn't be right. Roger would remove first-table crimes from civil jurisdiction and remand them to the church's discipline, if the person was a church member. He would not force people to attend any church. And if they were in church and were disciplined, he would limit the weapons used against them to spiritual weapons. When the Bible refers to the sword of Christ, it is talking about the sword of his mouth. The sword of his mouth is his word in scripture, and his followers' testimony.

The Boston ministers really had no answer to Roger's points except that in the short term, they didn't seem practical. In the short term, they had royalists to eliminate. They had children to discipline. They had sinners to lead to repentance. How do you achieve discipline if the civil authorities can't physically compel church attendance and good moral behavior?

Roger Williams just couldn't let it go, not even to be practical and avoid the criticism of his colleagues. It was the legacy of HH. He knew he had to keep the long view and stay true.

There was an uneasy truce for now. The nights were long and cold in winter in New England. Roger got up and wrote by candlelight most of these nights, and his thoughts matured as he wrote notes that someday would be transformed into *Queries of Highest Consideration*.

Lincolnshire, England, January, AD 1634

Montegu Bertie, now Lord Willoughby, lived at Grimsthorpe Castle in Lincolnshire and continued to spend summers in Orleans. He and his father rose in favor with King Charles, as they served him loyally in military and political capacities. Montegu was appointed to a series of titles that gave him increasing influence. Some of these positions, including High Steward of Boston, and Steward, Warden, and Chief Ranger of Waltham Forrest, were administrative, and he found them dull. His father assured him that they were but necessary steps in a promising career, and he dutifully discharged them.

His favorite appointment was as one of the Gentlemen of the Bedchamber. In this position he had unprecedented and near-private access to the king. He ate meals with him and provided companionship, while performing many more menial tasks.

Montegu's pastimes continued to be exercising cavalry maneuvers with his local troops and other outdoor adventures. Less publicly, he maintained his Uncle Perri's old printing press connections in France and continued printing himself. As technology improved, he modernized his press in the dungeon of his Orleans estate, and he had the power to produce pamphlets and even a book, with no one ever being the wiser. Montegu didn't use his power for anything but page-long pamphlets for now, but he enjoyed tinkering with techniques and papers and learning how to bind in his spare time. Uncle Perri might be an old drunk, but he had more interesting liaisons than Montegu's father. In every way, Montegu was keeping his nose down and clean in England, but always with an eye to his adventuring friends who might yet have something to say. Among those friends he counted Roger Williams, beyond the seas.

Salem, February, AD 1634

Roger returned home to the two babies in his house. He quickly resolved to travel to renew ties with the Algonquians as soon as the weather broke for spring, and the streams were navigable.

Martha stayed several more weeks to recover, and finally the ground did thaw enough to begin to turn soil. Mary wanted to dig her garden before the spring growth entrenched roots and made the job much harder. Martha tended the babies while Mary dug.

"Did you hear of the fire that burned the house that Craddock owns in the night?" asked Mary. The idea of her home burning in the night terrified her more than the wildlife. "I mean, I know he has enemies, given that he has written in support of revoking the Bay Colony patent, but burn his house? Roger says it was an accident. He's got a crew of fisherman in there, and they fell asleep with the oven going, and the fire caught the thatch in the roof."

"Anyone's thatch carelessly trimmed could catch fire," noted Martha.

"Do you believe that? Perhaps. They were lucky the tailor next door had a large order due and was up all night finishing it. No lives were lost. The whole thing still looks suspicious to me. Most people here were fleeing Bishop Laud when they left, yet Craddock and his buddies want to report to him that we don't use the common prayer book and get him to replace the Bay Colony leadership with a royal governor. Yes, he's lucky the tailor was up, all right. I'm not sure the fishermen were asleep, though. I do know I climbed up and inspected our thatch near the oven myself after hearing of it. We can't afford such a fire."

"I heard from the folks who came in on the *William and Jane* last spring that old Thomas Morton and Philip Ratcliff are up to no good now that they are back to England. They went to the king with a petition against the colonies. I'd say we are fortunate that Matthew Craddock hasn't chosen to come to New England, but we also can't afford him as our liaison in England. It must keep my father-in-law awake at night. We'd be as bad as England if Craddock got his way. But I'd not burn his house!"

"Yes, for what did we endure that crossing if Laud decides to pursue us here?" chimed in Mary.

"Oh, I'd do that again," said Martha. "It has been quite the adventure. All the new plants and medicine lore I've learned from the Algonquians, not to mention building a new world. Yes, I'd come anyway, if it were to do all over again. Speaking of medicine, did you hear of Hall's return? I had to tend to him and his two companions, as they were quite weak coming from the cold. They'd been gone over two months in midwinter and counting on trading with native people for food. But the Algonquians are having such a time of it with smallpox now, they would not trade with the English."

"Oh Martha, you can't take such risks. You've got two to think of. What if they'd had smallpox?" exclaimed Mary.

"They had no such symptoms, Mary. Believe me; I watched for them. They were just malnourished and weak and frostbitten at the edges. Nothing a few Algonquian remedies didn't take care of," answered Martha.

"And believe me; we'd know by now, since the incubation period has passed. I'm safe."

These were happy days that passed quickly. In March, when travel was a little easier, John the Younger did show up in Salem for a visit. He was pleased to meet his daughter, but he was brimming with excitement over developments in Agawam.

"We've launched our first ship full of seafood off to England. They were able to sell out at their first stop in Ipswich. Our fish were frozen below deck and did not have to be salted. Just think, exporting seafood to England from Agawam. We can do this every winter and get rich!" exclaimed John the Younger. "We've got excellent clamming beds and abundant fresh and saltwater catch in the area, not at all far from where the port is being built. We can use the prevailing winds in winter for a cold, rapid passage back to England, if we time it right. We've got species not even thought of back home that will sell as delicacies."

"That's great, John," Martha commented. "Just don't try naming the baby Ipswich! Have you a home built yet for the baby and me?"

"Almost," said John the Younger honestly. "We wanted to get the port open before we focused too much on permanent housing for families. You'll be able to come up before the end of spring, I promise. I'll have a nice little home ready for you and a garden dug. You just have to bring the seeds for what you wish to grow," he said with a smile. Then he looked mischievous. "What, you mean you don't want to call her Ippy? Too bad she's not a boy. We could have called him Mackerel—Mack for short."

"No way," said Martha. "I'm sorry I waited for you to name her."

"I'm joking, you know," said John more tenderly. "How about we name her Anne after your mom, my aunt?"

"Oh John, your dad tried twice with your mom to name a little girl Anne, and neither lived more than a year. Then Margaret tried, and Anne died at sea. Do you think this is the one who is meant to be Anne?"

"In truth, no one can know. It would be by the grace of God. But it would seem we must keep trying, don't you think? Anne is such a special name in our family. In her younger years our grandmother Anne must have been a lot like you. She knew several languages and read and wrote beautifully. So few women do."

"Anne it is," said Martha. "But I don't believe in name reuse, so this is the only Anne I intend to name. I get that point of view from another Ann, Ann Helwys Williams, Sydrach's wife. Do you remember how she didn't like reusing names, because each baby is a child of God, and she wants to pray with each one, even if deceased."

By May Martha was ready to walk with the baby swaddled Algonquian-style. She had seen Algonquian do this over and over, and despite English women's protestations that she was too frail, she wanted to be at Agawam and felt fine to travel. She talked her father-in-law into the excursion, and he set out May 3 from Boston and picked her up in Salem.

Mary remained happy in Salem, with the Throckmorton family as neighbors. Rebecca had a large circle of friends because of her house church for the women in town, and she introduced Mary, who quickly became popular.

Trail to Agawam, May, AD 1634

John Winthrop Senior was a soft touch for babies—more than most men. He didn't mind the slower pace and frequent breaks. The five-hour walk turned into an eight-hour walk, but he didn't mind. It was spring, and there was much to see.

Besides, he needed a break from the politics of the day. For years, he'd kept the charter under lock and key, showing it to no one. That was its best protection, given how many in England would have liked to revoke it. This year, however, his magistrates demanded to see it. Upon reading it, they'd discovered that the entire General Court—not just the small group that Winthrop preferred—had the power to pass laws. His loss of power and influence over the elders still smarted. The General Court was being morphed into a representative institution, and Winthrop did not approve of this development.

Baby Anne seemed to enjoy the scenery as well, and much of the trip was spent in the timeless art of meeting baby needs … a feeding, a burp, fresh swaddling, walking and watching, and napping.

With the baby asleep on Martha's chest in her sling, they walked a little faster.

Martha asked, "What do you think will happen now with Laud an archbishop and the petition against the colonies over the common prayer book use?"

"We'll go slowly, one step at a time. They could send a Royal Governor and dismantle all we've put in place. It would be within their right. But I think they know he'd have little support here. Let's hope they've got enough troubles at home to keep the soldiers busy, and they don't want to pick a fight. We're much stronger now, less reliant on England. So that means they've no way to punish us but to send men to do their bidding. So far it seems they'd rather send every nonconformist and miscreant they can find. King Charles is not stupid. He knows the mettle of the men who wrote that complaint. He can't rely on them. I hope he'll ignore it."

"What if he doesn't?"

"We've discussed some measures to collect ourselves and protect our cohesive ability to govern. We eliminated the old voluntary residency oath and have appointed a committee to produce a new one by next year. One step at time. It doesn't help to think too far ahead. There are too many shadows to chase, and there is plenty to be done right here. If John the Younger can build up Agawam to what he dreams of, we'll have a major port from which to export seafood to England. Let's focus on building a strong economic set of communities, and the rest will follow."

While at Agawam, John Winthrop Senior looked over his son's handiwork and pronounced it good. There was no formal minister in the town, so they had the senior Winthrop speak on Sunday. Then he set off to return to Boston.

Martha was overjoyed to start turning Agawam into a home. John the Younger was off attending to engineering projects to drain water from the wetlands and to build millworks to harness water energy or engineer irrigation for the fields. He envisioned vast hayfields in what were then salt marches. He was also considering transforming the marshes into a salt works, in order to produce salt as an export. Martha spent time foraging and learning the region. In the woods she would sometimes watch Algonquian women as they gathered and tended the land, copying their foraging and slowly building relationships with them. She especially enjoyed harvesting clams on the seashore with them.

Less enjoyable were the swamps. They seemed to be full of biting bugs, and you could suddenly come across bogs with uncertain footing. Algonquian women seemed to have a secret way through, for she lost them quickly every time she tried to follow them.

After a few weeks, she and the baby fell ill. When the illness returned after abating for a day, she recognized their illness as a dangerous fever, though it was not smallpox, as there was no rash. It grew worse, and the baby had seizures. Kicking herself for not being more careful in this new, wet land full of biting bugs, yet also not knowing where she got infected, she isolated herself and the baby from town in order to attempt recovery without further infection. She did not succeed. One night the baby didn't wake, and now Martha was not only sick; she was grief-stricken.

A few days later the fever was still raging in Martha. Slowly she sank into a gray fog—the most frightening thing she had ever faced. Yet, even with the baby gone, she felt she was not facing it alone. Snippets of Psalm 23 ran through her head: "Yea, though I walk through the valley of death, I will fear no evil for the Lord will be with me" and the Psalm 42 refrain: "Why are you cast down, oh my soul? Why do you groan within me? Wait for God, whom I shall praise again, my savior and my God." She ensured that her last conscious thoughts were praising the Lord, for the good times she recalled and the good things he had granted her in her life, and she waited for him. And finally, at a tender twenty-two years of age, he came, and she was in this world no more.

John the Younger wished that Martha hadn't forbidden him to visit for thirty days, lest he fall ill as well. But John was not ill, except with worry. After the danger was past, he hiked out to her isolation ward, as he thought of it. He found the two bodies and was sickened. He threw up and then he buried his wife and daughter. He stayed there a month, partly to ensure that he wasn't infected with something that would infect the town, but mostly because he was devastated and could not bear to leave, for this was his last contact with his family, and he was half-hoping he'd be taken as well. It seemed that all his dreams had been shattered at once. He knew that others had faced such loss, yet his own seemed more tragic, for Martha was irreplaceably special. He was sure that his daughter also would have been, should she have lived.

Still, after a few weeks he realized that his own father would have heard that he had gone missing. The slow walk back to Boston was the most miserable walk he had ever taken. Arriving home in Boston, he told his father that he never intended to go back to Agawam and that he could not go on.

John Winthrop Senior took charge.

"I need you to attend the October court, as you always do, in the role of assistant. After that, I've obtained passage for you on the next ship to England, son. You will cry your eyes out en route and be miserable the whole time. But when you arrive, you must carry on. You will carry on for the family, and for your own dear departed mother. Henry and Forth are both gone. You are the only son your mother and I have created that yet survives, and the whole colony relies on all our families producing well-mannered children. Go and find a new young wife who can bear you many children. I don't care that you think you can never be happy again. You are here for God's plan, and you must be thankful for all that we do still have. And you are ordered to carry on."

215

"When you arrive at Barnstaple, I've planned some visits to men considering New England investments. When your business is complete, go to the widow's shop in Lavenham, with this letter of introduction from the widow Onge. It carries family news, I'm sure, but she assures me she has eligible nieces and family friends. If you don't like them, find another. I'll expect you back within two years, expecting a child, I hope."

A few minutes later he was gentler. "My great-grandfather Adam started in Lavenham as a clothier. He turned out well enough. Perhaps it will be a place for you to find a new beginning as well."

Maybe so, John thought, *but it was not until Great-Grandfather died that his wife Jane's choice of second husband got your grandfather the apprenticeship in London that enabled him to become one of the three wealthiest men in England.* John the Younger would be fortunate if he could find a second spouse who could do as well by his future children.

Winthrop Senior's stern manner had no visible effect on John the Younger at that moment. But John the Younger complied and boarded for England, and his father's voice would echo in him as he walked off the ship two months later.

A few days later, with some coaching from Winthrop Senior, the remaining settlers in Agawam incorporated their town as Ipswich. Keeping the tradition of focusing on thanks for what remained, they named it after the town in Sussex, England, where they had been successful in trading seafood for goods. The town had been kind to the new settlers in becoming a first valued trading partner. Ipswich moved on.

Salem, August, AD 1634

Roger Williams came home late one evening.

"The Reverend Sam Skelton is dead. Always reticent in life, his departure was equally reticent. The burial will be tomorrow," said Roger.

"He will join his wife in heaven. Fortunately his eldest daughter is grown. I guess she'll have to take the children. How old could he have been?" lamented Mary.

"In his late forties, at the most. He was Cotton's chaplain once, back in England. I wonder if John will come up to Salem for the service. He was so disappointed in Sam when the Salem church decided to be a separated people, after he'd recommended him for the post."

"That was long ago," Mary pointed out.

The service was quick and small, and Cotton, now teacher at the big First Church in Boston, did not attend. Skelton's position as teacher was offered to Roger, and he accepted.

The Boston churches did not approve the process by which Roger was selected, meaning they did not approve that they were not consulted. Nor did they approve the selection of Roger Williams as teacher. There was a pending application from some Salem businessmen to annex and develop land in Marbleneck. The application was put on hold.

That the magistrates in Boston would put an administrative hold on a lucrative business opportunity for Salem because of a personnel decision in the Salem church incensed the elders of the Salem church. Ezekiel Holyman drafted a letter signed by all the elders of the Salem church to the churches in the Bay area. The men expected their letter, written in good faith, to be read in the churches to its members. The letter requested that the magistrates, who were church members, be reprimanded for their shady activities.

The letter wasn't read at all. The silence was deafening.

Ezekiel drafted a second letter, and again the Salem elders signed. That letter wasn't read out loud, either.

Boston, September, AD 1634

On September 18, 1634, Anne Hutchinson, her husband Will, and eight of their children stepped off the *Griffin* onto New England soil. It was a cool, clear, crisp, sunny fall day. For Anne, it was a dream come true. The family had been working tirelessly on this project since they heard late last year that John Cotton had surfaced in New England. They'd feared for their favorite minister's safety. In addition Will Hutchinson, a well-to-do merchant, saw opportunity in the New World, and it was a more stable business environment than ever before.

The Cottons invited them in for a welcoming supper. Sarah Cotton asked Anne, "This doesn't seem like enough children. Where have you hidden the rest?"

"My sister Katharine kept Francis, Katherine, and William. Katherine and William are toddlers, and I've heard too many stories of little ones overboard. I brought Suzanna, as she's a nursing baby and easy to control. Francis is in school and wants to complete another year in England. Besides, he'll need to help with the little ones."

"Does Katherine want to come to New England also, then?"

"Oh yes, we hope that in another year, maybe two, she'll be able to do so."

"Where are you hoping to settle?" John asked Will.

"I'd like to be in the center of the Boston region, for business reasons. Anne wants to be nearer your church than we were in England. After traveling so far, we'd like to make sure we don't again set up for a long weekly ride to get to church," Will said with a smile.

"I can set you up with some connections here for land and resources in Boston," offered John.

"That would be most appreciated," answered Will.

Another feast took place in Reverend John Eliot's house in Roxbury. Reverend Symmes and Reverend John Lothrop's families, also on the *Griffin*, were the honored guests. The children were completely fascinated by the Algonquian children in English servant garb tending to the table. No conversation with them was possible, for John Eliot used these children to learn the Algonquian language and, as a result, not much English was spoken in the house.

After dinner the Reverend Symmes commented that never before had he been questioned so resolutely by a mere woman as he had after preaching on the *Griffin*. Anne Hutchinson had often been in attendance at his sermons, and she had made it a point several times during the crossing to seek him out after the sermon and to dispute theological points from his sermon. She did not find Reverend Symmes to be inspiring, or even correct, in his emphasis on rules and moral contact. In her view, he'd failed to inspire his listener's hearts to Christ. Reverend Symmes mentioned Anne's unorthodoxy now at the table and professed to be happy to be leaving her behind in Boston to her beloved John Cotton's church, while he would be headed west to Charlton.

Reverend Lothrop was silent. He was overjoyed to be in a land where earnest worship and individual reading of scripture were encouraged. He was relieved to be in a land far from the Star Chamber politics that had imprisoned him, and where debate and discussion were possible. Anne had never complained after his sermons, so he was somewhat amused, wondering whether there were legitimate errors in the Reverend Symmes's teaching or whether she'd just slept through his own sermons. In any case, he soon headed south for a settlement close to Plymouth. John Eliot saw no reason to take Symmes's concerns to Cotton, and the evening passed in pleasant fellowship. The discussion was for now forgotten.

CHAPTER 21

London, February, AD 1634

It was a cold, sunless February morning. It was Alice Pemberton Williams's birthday, and she did not feel well. At the age of seventy, she figured she had a right not to feel well, and she ordered Katherine to cancel the dinner they'd planned. It was on her mind lately to update her will, and now that she was seventy, she decided to get it done that day. She had a new grandbaby in New England whom she had never seen and whom she wanted to protect. Sydrach owned the business left behind by James and had grown it substantially. She figured his family would be fine. Her mind was on the others, including her godchildren, her maidservant, and the women she'd mentored who would still need help. She called in Katherine's husband, John Davies, still her clerk, and dictated to him her wishes for her estate. She decided that Robert should have the rental properties. It was about time he owned something. She figured that he'd have the time to be the executor of all the rest, more than any of the others. When she was done, she swore John Davies to secrecy and had him lock the will away.

It was six months later that Alice died peacefully in her sleep. It was Sydrach, the eldest, successful business owner and family man, who had the composure to write to Roger with the news. His wife, Ann, and his sister, Katherine, made the arrangements for her burial.

As the weeks went by and Robert saw what was involved in collecting rent, cleaning, and a hundred other activities involved in running his mother's properties, he realized that it would be quite a challenge to pay expenses and come up with the tidy sums his mother had promised to the people in her will. He began to be late with payments. He had no wish to be a landlord. In fact, it had been Katherine who had always helped

Alice with the inn. What had his mother been thinking? He began to plot his way out by asking Katherine to take over the properties. He gave one building to a new owner without getting the proper permission to change the use of the feoff, a matter that would cause trouble between him and the rest of the family later. He asked Sydrach to imagine a way for him to extend the family business to New England. If that didn't work, maybe he'd teach.

Neals, AD 1634

Sir Edward Coke was enjoying his retirement from politics immensely. In the mornings he rode his horses; in the afternoons he could be found fishing or hunting or reading, and many evenings he visited his grandchildren. He watched with amusement as Parliament remained recessed. King Charles, unable to raise funds, chose to reign autocratically but austerely.

One summer morning Sir Edward's horse shied at a bird flying up out of a bush near a bog. The horse reared up and Coke, unbalanced for once, made the mistake of pulling back on the reins, which unbalanced the horse further. The two-thousand-pound animal fell backward, and Coke just managed to get his feet out of the stirrups and push partway clear of the main impact. His legs were hit hard and tangled between the horse, the saddle, and the ground. The horse, unhurt but frightened, rolled over and got up and ran back to the barn. Fortunately, since Coke's feet were clear of the stirrups, he was not dragged with the horse. When the stable hand found the horse unmanned, he tracked back to where Coke was lying. Alive and feisty, though clearly injured, Coke was happy for the help back to the house.

After a few weeks, Coke realized that he was not getting better as fast as he'd thought he would. Everyone seemed to want him to go for medical treatment. Coke had long observed that medical treatments at his age didn't help anyone who wouldn't get well anyway. He resisted. Besides, he was eighty-two, and he didn't want to spend his last days in treatment torture. Sure enough, on the fine morning of September 3, he dozed off in his chair in the sun by the window and did not awaken.

Salem, November, AD 1634

When he received Sydrach's letter in November, Roger Williams grieved his mother's passing. He knew it was time now to become the person he had been born to become. In a way he'd been waiting to receive his parents' remaining wealth, now distributed to him and his brothers as a lifelong stipend. It would make him financially independent of others. As early as his unsuccessful application for Jane's hand, he'd mentioned in his letter that someday he would inherit this asset. Here in New England, the small stipend went a long way to assuring prosperity for his budding family, even as he acted on his convictions at a new level. Roger could afford the risk, or so he thought.

Roger had another blow to deal with. The same ship that brought the news of his mother's death brought the news of Sir Edward Coke's passing.

Roger spent time in prayer and burned much midnight oil at his writing desk. The more he reflected on all he'd learned, the more the situation with the Algonquian bothered him. His childish dreams of bringing them all to a pure Christianity were crashing on the shores of a real people, with real feelings and traditions. First, he found the existing earthly church so far from pure Christianity that he hesitated to bring any new child of Christ from a different culture near it. Second, it irritated him that Europeans called the Algonquians heathen. Heathen were all the people outside the Jewish and Christian faith, not just naked Indians. Algonquians who followed Christ would not be heathen, even if they did not choose to follow European custom. Third, it angered him that Europe was called Christendom. He believed that there were many unregenerate souls in Europe. He feared that this included most Catholics and Anglicans, due to the laws and traditions that encouraged false worship. The true church was made of the followers of Jesus. These followers were invisible on earth, as no man can see inside another's heart. Thus the true Christendom, as far as Roger was concerned, was an invisible church of believers.

To date during his late nights, he'd mostly written practical letters attending to business at hand. Sometimes he imagined being back at court and wrote notes about what he'd like to say to the powers that be.

He'd also begun to take copious notes on the Algonquian languages he'd encountered in order to help him transliterate them and decipher their grammar and meaning. He'd also occasionally scribbled brief poems to help him remember Algonquian culture and scriptural messages that he'd like to convey. Now he started something different. He wrote a full essay intended for English eyes and ears, laying out his thinking on Algonquian souls, called "Christenings Make Not Christians."

Near the end of this essay he documented a refined understanding of what God was calling him to do as his own mission. Instead of seeking to baptize a continent of Indians, as the Spanish had attempted to do, forcing false worship or worse, he knew it was right to invite people to be true followers of Jesus. That is what the Great Commission had intended, as opposed to forcing people to become Christian, with European rituals.

Roger believed further that he was being asked to spend his energies toward reforming how the Great Commission was executed and creating a new infrastructure for society that could ensure that people in the future would share the benefits of following Christ. From this time forward, he would share Jesus's story with the Algonquians, but he felt no compulsion to get them into an English-style church. The Great Commission could not be fully successful until the New Jerusalem of Revelations—to him, a spiritual Jerusalem of the true church—was constructed. And like many other Puritans, Roger felt God calling him to start building that New Jerusalem in New England. In that New Jerusalem, Algonquian customs would be as at home as English customs.

Roger's respect for the Algonquian led him to believe that God might have planted physical archetypes for Christ in cultures beyond the Hebrew culture. If that was so, a man would be able to follow Christ without learning Hebrew or English. In Christian scripture Paul teaches that Christ came not to abolish Hebrew law but to complete it. Roger wondered if Christ might complete not only Hebrew law but also other God-given authority systems, directly. If so, the Algonquian people did not need to learn a Hebrew moral code, for they would fail to meet their own moral standards as fallen sinners like other men and could accept Christ's grace and forgiveness directly.

While Roger was wrapped up in preparing his teaching each week and in his nighttime writing, he was not involved in politics at all. So it was with surprise that he heard of the "Endicott incident," as town folks were already referring to it. John Throckmorton knew his friend Roger could be distracted and self-absorbed at times, so he paid a special visit to Roger's house to make sure he'd heard about the incident before he taught on Sunday.

"Roger, have you heard what John Endicott has done now?" John Throckmorton began.

"No, tell me."

"He took a royal insignia and cut the cross out of the flag. He says the cross is a sign of loyalty to the papacy. They say he'll be charged with treason."

"Well, I can't say he's wrong, in that St. George and St. Andrew were Catholic. But that red cross was to combine the red cross of St. George with the shape of the white cross of St. Andrew, showing that Scotland and England were one nation. King James was hardly inspired by the pope when he did that. Surely they know King James was an Anglican and not a Catholic? I knew King James, and, while he was no Puritan, he was no papist, either."

"I suspect that details like that were lost on Endicott when he acted. Some in town have banded behind him."

"Hmmmm, I'm not sure that's wise. We know how delicate the patent situation is. This is one we may want to sidestep. While I was in Boston last week, John Winthrop Senior showed me a letter that came in on the *Griffin*. Laud is now head of a new commission. The letter said that 'The Commission for Regulating Plantations has the power to oversee the Massachusetts Bay Colony, call in its patent, make its laws, remove and punish its (elected) governors, hear and determine all causes, and inflict all punishments, including death itself,'" said Roger.

"That sounds dire. What will Winthrop do about that?"

"He'll say it was delivered as personal mail and carries no weight, and he will ignore it. They'll have to send people to enforce it, and John Winthrop Senior does not believe Charles has the funds for that. He's counting on it being a low priority. Meantime, he surely won't want to give anyone the motivation to go and raise the funds or make the Massachusetts Bay Colony a high priority. How can we help defuse this matter?"

"I'm not sure. I heard on the street that they thought Endicott surely would have consulted you before committing such a brazen act. So you will catch some of the blame," said John.

"So, do you think I should teach against it publicly, then?" mused Roger. "On what basis? I think I'll ask them to be as shrewd as wolves in pursuing matters of conscience, not rebellious fools angering the forces against us. Yes, that's it."

"You'd better. I've heard that the authorities in the Boston and surrounding churches were already angry with Salem for inviting you to teach. Now, with this incident, they are likely to blame you. Thing is, most freemen I've spoken to agree with Endicott. So it will be interesting to see what they do to keep the peace—they are caught between fear of Laud and the passions of the freemen here. They need the freemen, as it's those same men out drilling with Endicott and Underhill every morning. They say it's to defend against the Dutch and the French, but we all suspect that it's to be ready for any vessel from England that tries to eliminate our patent and take over governing."

"It's those same men who will be in church when I teach. We must strive for loyalty and trueness to conscience, while discouraging them from supporting dramatic public unsanctioned violent acts—not to mention historically inaccurate ones."

"Just be careful, Roger. The freemen's request for land at Marbleneck is still hitting all kinds of administrative delay over the Boston elite's unhappiness with Salem. You are already blamed. The businessmen of our town won't put up with that for long. Don't make it worse."

"Yes, that's the bane of Salem. Blamed by Boston for being a separated people and making selections true to our convictions, and unwilling to live with ourselves if we don't. Endicott's been living on that sword edge for many more years than I."

Boston Area, December, AD 1634

There was another minister who was gaining respect for the Algonquian ways—John Eliot. As minister in Roxbury, near Boston, and with Mohegan in his household, he watched the native tensions escalate more closely than most. His servants spilled to him the long history of conflict in the region.

The Mohegans and the Pequot each wanted to be *the* channel for trade, not one among many. The Dutch preferred to trade with all the tribes in the region. The Pequot used all manner of violent and underhanded schemes to stay central to the fur trade. To hear the Mohegan tell the story, the Pequot had dishonored their ancestors and double-crossed their friends in remaining friendly with the Dutch.

Eliot was hearing Uncas's version of the story.

In November of 1634, Sassacus sent messengers to the Massachusetts Bay Colony with gifts. The Pequot were tiring of war on all fronts. The Dutch had murdered his father Tatobem. While he still needed the fur trade, he was beginning to distrust the Dutch and needed new allies. Before smallpox, the Pequot often dominated the Narragansett peoples. Now the Pequot were negotiating tentative, lukewarm peace agreements with the Narragansett, where the Narragansett had the upper hand. Feeling increasingly isolated, Sassacus tried to develop an alliance with the English. The English were dubious at first. They asked the messengers to explain the Stone incident. John Stone may have been a pirate, but he was still English. The messengers claimed that all but two of Stone's murderers had since died of smallpox and that they could deliver both of them.

As soon as the Pequot departed, the Narragansett showed up to object. After delicate negotiations, with the English acting as arbitrator, the Pequot agreed to deliver a wampum payoff to the English, who would deliver it to the Narragansett for allowing an English-Pequot alliance. If the Pequot succeeded in allying with the English, Uncas and the Mohegan would lose power. Eliot heard every half-true story of the violence of the Pequot that Uncas could tell his braves.

Eliot preached in Roxbury that the magistrates made agreements of peace with the Pequot, a very violent tribe, without consulting the people. He foresaw nothing but trouble stemming from this and detected a potential double-cross situation. He believed that the people should be consulted before such agreements were finalized.

Eliot came to the attention of the Massachusetts Bay court because he publicly rebuked the authorities in November of 1634. Eliot's hearing was scheduled for 1635.

As the days led up to court, John Eliot received private visitations, among them John Winthrop Senior himself. After exchanging pleasantries, they got to the business at hand.

"How may I help you, Mr. Winthrop?"

"I want you to recant your positions in court. You are a valued minister in Roxbury, and I don't want to have to participate in your censure. I do believe you've overstepped your ministerial authority in calling into question decisions of the Massachusetts Bay Colony. I want you to understand how dangerous that is, given what is going on behind the scenes." He went on to explain the threats to the patent and reminded Eliot of his own flight from England as known assistant to Thomas Hooker.

"I see. I am willing to do as you say, but can you explain to me here in private why our government is befriending violent murderers of Englishmen and other Algonquian tribes? I believe the people should be consulted before you take such a position."

"This is not a democracy. The people do not have the knowledge or the authority to govern. That said, consider who exactly they've murdered. I sat through John Stone's trials for adultery and piracy. He's a clever fellow and has always managed to squeeze out of any verdict. All we could do was banish him and let him return home to the Virginia colony whence he came, though I wanted to return him to England in chains. We did write to the governor of the colony, but of course he never made it home to face justice. I have no doubt from other interviews that he was stealing Pequot women and raping them during the nights before he was murdered."

"The murder of John Stone is not the only violent incident attributed to the Pequot. My household tells me of other stories of abduction and torture, Algonquian on Algonquian. How can we be allied with them?"

"We are not allied solely with them. We will use the Pequot for what they can offer us. I can promise you we'll also stay friendly to their enemies in the Narragansett and Mohegan. In fact we are attempting to broker a peace treaty between the groups of Algonquian. It is complicated, and I don't expect you to follow every move. We've got an agreement that the Pequot will give us use of Connecticut lands, that they'll deliver us the two remaining murderers, and we've already received great volumes of wampum. What I need is for you to encourage the people to trust their government and to follow edicts that we issue."

"I can do that. We'll see if they deliver on their promise."

The two murderers were never delivered.

Off the Irish Coast, December, AD 1634

John the Younger attended the Boston court in October 1634, just as planned. He then set sail for England in late fall, in a ship set up for cold winds and rough seas. That fit John the Younger's mood perfectly. Accompanying John was the Reverend John Wilson, of the First Church in Boston. Sometimes John wondered whether his father had arranged Wilson as chaperone, but Reverend Wilson denied it, as he had always planned this return to attend some lingering family business.

The seas were so rough and the weather so foul that the original destination of Barnstable, England, seemed more and more remote. The ship felt small and weak to John, very unlike the *Lyon* of his first crossing. His melancholy mood evaporated, replaced by fear, as he sensed actual danger in the twenty-foot waves buffeting the boat. He had no control, no way of defending himself. He felt utterly helpless. It seemed that the ship could break apart at any moment, and John turned his thoughts to God. As he had been trained to do all his life, he began to count his blessings and give thanks. His skin grew cold, yet he sweated, and he shivered more inside than out as each wave hit. Eventually they were countless, and it seemed that he'd entered an eternity of terror, one that must be fought without end. He imagined that this might be what Martha would have grappled with as each wave of fever hit. He disciplined his mind to give thanks for Martha and to praise the Lord. Eventually he was numb, in a world far removed from the present situation, and he was comforted.

The first view of land after the storm was not England, but a remote segment of Ireland. Another storm was incoming, however, and there was no passage to landfall visible. The boat weathered the next storm, sustaining damage to her sails, and eventually, after more delays, she limped into Galloway for repairs.

John the Younger had suffered enough at sea. He arranged for a horse and set off for Dublin by land. He spent a few days in Dublin getting his bearings back by making connections with other men of his station. One of those connections, Sir John Clotworthy, invited John the Younger up to his estate in up north in Antrim. Sir John was a solid Puritan, unhappy with the religious environment under King Charles and Bishop Laud. He was hosting a long-planned meeting of men considering a move to New England. For him, John the Younger was a great find. John the Younger provided many stories and encouragement to the gathering. This group of men provided John even more connections, and John traveled on to Scotland and through the north of England, following up and promoting New England with Clotworthy and Winthrop connections. Finally he headed by sloop to Ipswich on his way to Lavenham.

The Reverend Wilson, having fewer resources, stayed with the boat. He waited for the repairs, and it was January by the time he was back at sea. There were more storms, and, during a particularly horrible one, the Reverend Wilson watched in horror as other boats in the distance sank. On the evening of January 14, 1635, he suddenly felt the warmth of God's arms around him, out of nowhere it seemed. His fear left him. Eventually the seas calmed, and he did make landfall.

CHAPTER 22

Boston Area, January, AD 1635

The bitter cold of a January morning did not dissuade anyone from traveling to Boston. The ministers, the governor, and the magistrates were all present in the meeting hall. Every man of privilege was present. The topic that drew them was a promise to discuss the stand of the Massachusetts Bay Colonies should England send out forces to implement the revocation of the patent and the institution of a royal governor.

Endicott started them off. "We can't afford the Laud commission's persecution here. All that we've built here is at stake. Rumor is they are turning back ships now on the theory that they might find Puritans aboard, given their failure to find key men last year before their emigration. Ships full of royalists and artillery will replace the sixteen ships of people that think like us. There's word from a boatyard in England that war ships are under construction, bound for Boston, larger than any ship we've yet seen."

Cotton responded, "Governments are put in place by the authority of God. On what grounds would we object to revocation of the charter? The Lord gives, the Lord takes away. The king gave the patent; he surely has the right to take it away."

An uncomfortable silence followed Cotton's speech. No one here was ready to advocate for the people's right to choose. Democracy was not the ideal in their minds. At the same time, they weren't ready to let Laud chase them out of New England.

Governor Dudley proposed pragmatism. "What if we accept the royal government and appear to acquiesce? We will continue to live as we live, however, and not give up anything we've established—not property, not worship format, not one aspect of the New Jerusalem we've put in place. We'll offer to be peaceable and make them show their hand. They'll be badly outnumbered, with no clear military target to shoot at if we appear to acquiesce."

Many speeches later, Dudley's approach was adopted as their strategy. Most were dreading the arrival of ships to the harbor, with deep misgivings about what England might send to them.

One further matter was agreed. The men with a right to vote for governor of the colony were all freemen—male church members with no debt. Increasingly, residents were not all church members, as the Puritan church sought to restrict membership to like-minded men. The church's exclusivity might have successfully kept royalist Anglicans out of government, but it meant that they could live in town as spies and neighbors to Puritan families. To prevent a visible royalist opposition living in the colony, a new oath of loyalty was discussed as a possible requirement for residency, and this oath did not declare loyalty to the king but rather to the Massachusetts Bay Colony's administrators and laws. A similar oath had been voluntary in the past, but it was now proposed that they make it mandatory. Two refusals to take the oath would mean banishment. The wording of the oath was debated, and the matter was put on the calendar for a final vote in March.

The January court was one of the most contentious ever. John Eliot originally attended this court to apologize for his public statements, a routine matter that was completed in minutes. His repentance was accepted and his name cleared. However, as he'd watched the disputations on other topics he became aghast and was instrumental in lobbying for such behavior to be contained.

These men were fundamentally agreed in purpose—building a purer church and society, the New Jerusalem. They were agreed on how to go about it: they all shared the Puritan belief in men reading scripture themselves. As Christian men committed individually and together operating as a cohesive unit, they became the Body of Christ. Through the Body of Christ the church would be purified and the New Jerusalem government enabled. With Reverend John Eliot's urging and his own humble penitence for public exhortations against colony decisions, the men felt an urgent need for penance and thanksgiving, and a public day of humiliation was declared that Lord's Day, from sunset January 13 through January 14. After all, with their good Reverend Wilson out on the seas traveling toward England, they could ill afford to be punished by the Lord for their bad behavior. They were vulnerable, and they knew it.

On the appointed Day of Humiliation, all the ministers spoke to their flocks. Cotton spoke of the creation in Israel of cities of refuge, from <u>Numbers 35:13</u>, about setting up places of refuge for those who had committed crimes like accidental murder or manslaughter, so that the family of the victim would not have to meet or take revenge against the killer in the street. He took this to a whole new symbolic level and compared those who would follow the king's orders in persecuting Puritans in New England to accidental murderers, saying that they should be banished from the colony to prevent Puritans from having to meet them in the street. In other words, they should not be killed but rather sent away. This sermon set up the theology of banishing anyone who could not be counted on to be loyal to the colony because they were misguided in their loyalty to another God-given authority, the king.

John Eliot spoke passionately from <u>Lamentations 3:39</u>. "The public dissent in January was sinful. Scripture dictates dissent must be private, and if not resolved, it must be a church matter, and finally, if still not resolved, a court matter. No dispute between church members should ever reach the court if society is working well. God's authority rests on the church as in a family. A father's authority is final. So, too, is the elder's authority over the members of the church."

He went on, "When we participate in public bitter debate, we sin. Lamentations calls to mind that we must not complain when the Lord punishes us for our sins. In this wilderness home, there are many opportunities for fatal episodes at sea and on land. So far this year, four were lost at sea. Others froze to death. Yet some punished were spared ... one was lost for twenty-one days in the snow and survived, and two others were lost for six days and found by Nipmuc returned to health. Who knows what calamity will be next, given our sin."

Would a warship arrive with a royal governor? Minds wondered, but the question was not asked out loud. The very fact of their continuing lives was a great blessing. Who of them could complain? All humbly gave thanks.

Roger Williams's teaching in Salem on the public day of humiliation was different. He decided that this was the time of reflection when he must speak out from Isaiah 66:1–6. He spoke of how men in the Anglican and Catholic Churches were not Christians just because they'd been christened. He said that anyone not following Jesus in his heart was heathen and that many non-church-members in New England were heathen, as most Algonquian men were yet heathen. He said that all these men were heathen and thus must not be forced into false worship—i.e., forced into participating in worship that they did believe earnestly in their hearts. To cause false worship would be a profanity to God, worse than the stench of unclean food—e.g., the blood of pigs—offered to the Lord. It would be a complete abomination, worse than the worship of idols. Roger then went on to say that compulsory church attendance, forced contributions to the church (taxes to support the church), and oaths in the Lord's name all constituted false worship. Each of these was common practice in the colony. No heathen resident should be forced to take an oath. This flew in the face of recently passed laws and was tantamount to public dissent from the rulings of the colony authorities. Yet Roger Williams was persuasive. Many Salem residents understood his arguments and supported him. They would work to defend these concepts in the law. Unfortunately, they would sin in that they would do it in public, not in private.

Each church member heard at most one of these sermons. Each sermon was persuasive. The men of Boston began to banish people more frequently, both for being suspected royalist/Laud sympathizers and for any other public dissent from the laws of the colony. Serious dissent from the colony's laws that was also dissent from the laws of England, however, could still be punished with a passage in irons to the courts of England. The men of Roxbury counseled private versus public dissent successfully with their nearby Boston peers, and the court become more a place to document agreements than a place for fights and debate.

The men of Salem sought to change the rules being approved by the magistrates. Unfortunately for them, they didn't seem to get the message about private dispute and public unity, and they expected to debate at court.

John Winthrop counted the Day of Humiliation a success when, months later, he learned from Reverend Wilson of the overwhelming peace he had experienced in the storm on January 14.

England, March, AD 1635

John the Younger set out on a fine, blustery day to walk to a trading partner in Ipswich. The walk felt good, his grief receding with each stop. He found himself thinking of the future and ready to make decisions. The first decision was to reconfirm he would not go back to Agawam and resume life there. Therefore, he would not need to visit his trading partners in Ipswich. That was freeing thought. He would start somewhere new. *I could walk to Lavenham right now*, he thought. *It's only six hours away. As good as walking feels right now, six hours will make me a new man.* He set out for Lavenham. Second, after an hour's pondering, he decided to return to New England. All his engineering dreams remained in tact. Third, he would find a woman as expeditiously as possible and get back to his life quickly. He wasn't going to spend much time renewing connections in London unless it was with women who might qualify to be his wife.

Inactivity had made him soft, and stress had made him gain weight. That wasn't the silhouette he wanted to project while looking for the mother of his future children. By the time he got to Lavenham his feet hurt. The trip back to London would have to be in a carriage.

He got a room for the night and cleaned up, trimming his moustache to a new style that he would keep for the rest of his life. The next morning he explored the town, ending up at Onge's shop.

Staffing the shop was Elizabeth Read, the widow Onge's niece. She was calmly studying her scriptures when John the Younger peeked in, for, unlike the widow Onge, she was a devout Puritan. The store was neat and clean, boding well for her housekeeping skills. She was a sparkling twenty years old, eight years younger than John. John decided that life was looking up. He introduced himself. "I'm John Winthrop the Younger, fresh off the boat from Boston. The widow Onge asked me to call on her shop and bring her a report. I've this letter of introduction."

"Oh my, this is a complete surprise. The widow Onge's daughter Marie just left for Boston in April. I've been missing her so. Do you suppose the letter has news of her?"

"Perhaps. I don't know. I didn't read it. Why don't you read it now?"

Elizabeth opened the letter and read it to herself. John noted that she could certainly read rapidly and easily, for she was not struggling.

"It says that Aunt Frances has done really well in New England, with land at Watertown, a very large house with plenty of room, and a shop there that makes this one seem small. It says every day there is more culture and refinement in New England, and that I should think of closing up and selling the shop here and joining them, as Marie misses me horribly. Ohhh. I do miss her so." At the next section, Elizabeth blushed. "It says I should consider accompanying you back to Boston!"

Their eyes met, and John the Younger smiled for the first time in months. Father and the widow Onge didn't miss a trick. "Well, yes, I rather hope you will. First, I'd like to know if you'd accompany me to London to visit some friends this weekend. I hate to show up alone. They are family men."

"The shop is usually open on Saturday."

"Haven't you any staff that can watch it for you?"

"I suppose … I've never left her all alone … I'd have to teach her a few last things … but let me check and get back to you."

"I'll return tomorrow and hope that things have been arranged. Good day."

With that, he left. He wondered how he would spend the rest of the day. He hired a carriage and driver for Saturday and wrote a quick note to Sydrach to let him know he was coming and dispatched it that day by personal carrier. John the Younger could make things happen.

The next morning he again visited the shop. Elizabeth was there, smartly dressed, with another young woman whom she was busily training. John smiled.

On Saturday the two headed out to London, to Sydrach's house. They had many hours to get acquainted on the way.

Sydrach and Robert greeted John the Younger when he and Elizabeth arrived. The old trading partners were quickly trading business notes and dreams. Elizabeth headed inside with Ann. She'd been dreading this moment, as she did not know these people. As soon as she realized that she and Ann shared strong Puritan convictions and deep scriptural knowledge, the two become fast friends.

Sydrach's son James was keen to hear all the stories from the New World, and John the Younger did not disappoint. He spoke of fishing and his dreams of establishing ironworks, and how they were building deep-water ports. Robert was listening in, thinking of the trading opportunities for Sydrach's business. He'd been dreaming of joining Roger in the New World, and this visit made that dream feel like it could become real.

In the kitchen Elizabeth Read met ten-year-old Anna Grace and six-year-old Elizabeth Williams. She dreamed of her own children as she helped the girls cook a feast for the families. Anna Grace latched onto her and told her of her dreams for America.

Their discussion turned to religion, and Ann explained that she had continued her mother-in-law's tradition of house church ever since her death. They found that they both had rebel ministers in the family: Ann's

237

father, Thomas Helwys, and Elizabeth's stepfather, the Reverend Hugh Peter. Ann invited Elizabeth to attend with her at her next visit.

Late in the evening, Sydrach was sitting with John the Younger, and the room was quiet and comfortable. He worked up his courage to ask about Martha. "John, what happened with you and Martha? It's hard seeing you without her. You were such a pair."

John told Sydrach the story.

"I'm so sorry. You are one strong individual to be back in the game so soon," Sydrach said with a smile. "I'm not sure I could do that if something happened to Ann."

"I didn't want to. My father ordered me to do it. And he was right. He said to take two months of dreadful grieving and then to march on like a soldier and create a new life. If something happens to Ann, since you have no living father, you'll need to use my father's advice for yourself. It was delivered with a good kick in the rear that I sorely needed. Don't forget it," lectured John. He was mostly still lecturing himself, Sydrach could tell.

A wonderful time having been had by all, the exhausted Elizabeth was deposited back in Lavenham just in time to open shop Monday morning. All she really knew was that she hoped John the Younger would stay in Lavenham long enough to ask her on another adventure.

John planned to look around first, but in his heart he already felt a tugging to return to Onge's shop and Elizabeth.

Boston Area, March, AD 1635

The Hutchinsons finished construction on the largest house on Shawmut Peninsula in the Boston area. Their sheep grazed on an island the Hutchinson's owned in its entirety. They also had a country estate of ten acres, ten miles to the south. Will was set up as a merchant in the area, and Anne was again a midwife using herbal remedies combined with spiritual counseling. She soon had a large network of women friends loyal to her teaching.

After Anne Hutchinson moved into her new house she began entertaining. She renewed the tradition of the English house church for the women, inviting women to join her on the Lord's Day between church services. The women quilted, embroidered or sewed while discussing the sermon. Many of the women who attended could not read the scripture for themselves, or write. The format of the meeting was a Bible study where each verse of scripture was read and pondered and then the sermon discussed. At home in the Boston church, Anne's love of John Cotton's teaching and her familiarity with his theology of heartfelt conversion made her certain that she would easily be able to summarize and defend his positions eloquently.

The next Boston general court was in March. A dispute occurred again among the men debating the Endicott affair. A great deal of support was expressed for the actual act of changing the royal insignia to something other than the cross, yet there was a strong contingent that wanted Endicott censured in some way. Having been through the Day of Humiliation, however, and not wanting to repeat an acrimonious spirit, they tabled the matter for three weeks, to pursue it further in private. Civility had been introduced to court.

Boston Area, April, AD 1635

By April agreements had been brokered in private. John Endicott, however, was not privy to them. His core issue was respected, and the royal insignia was changed to red and white with no cross. For a moment it seemed like victory. Then Endicott was formally censured by being prevented from holding any public office for a year, for having committed a very public, irresponsible, and incendiary action that exceeded his calling, and for not having sought the court's advice in advance. For while Puritans all believed in individual study and worship, they also believed that, individually, no one had any authority. According to scripture, all authority came from a body of Christian men, where two or three at a minimum were gathered. No one had authority to act alone. Endicott was shocked and chastened.

The residency oath was finalized at this April court and made mandatory. Roger's exhortations seemed not to recognize the political threat, and to the administrators he seemed confused. Cotton privately offered to speak with him, and no further public action was taken at the time.

The residency oath was not acceptable to Roger at all. To him, it was inconsistent with the entire spirit of the New Jerusalem they meant to create. He welcomed debate on it. Many freemen were convinced of his views.

However, those who were not persuaded included John Cotton, Richard Mather, John Eliot, and the pragmatic John Winthrop, who was choreographing the gentle dance of avoiding King Charles. Their answers come from the God-given authority of a government, as in a family. A Christian man may correct his unregenerate wife. So too can magistrates require of unregenerate subjects whatever they need to govern.

England, April, AD 1635

John the Younger and Elizabeth were together in London, as they had been routinely now as often as they could schedule it. John the Younger was staying with his childhood friend Edward Howes. Elizabeth stayed with Ann Helwys Williams and attended house church with her at every opportunity.

"I'd like to meet your parents," said John. He wanted to ask permission to marry her, but he wasn't going to say that out loud yet.

"My father's dead. His brother's dead, and so his nearest kin would be his sister, and that's the widow Onge. I guess you'd have to go back to New England to talk to her," said Elizabeth with a smile in her eyes.

"And your mother?" asked John.

"That's not much easier. She remarried. Her husband was a lecturer at St. Sepulchre, but he was a Puritan, and Laud chased him to Holland. He is a minister in Rotterdam now. Do you want to take a trip to Holland?" she asked. She knew they wouldn't need to do that. She was secretly helping her mother plan disguises for them so they could get through customs and onto a ship headed for New England, scheduled to leave in August. She couldn't say that to John, though.

"Hmmm. I've arranged some key connections in the upcoming months. I'm not sure when we should arrange for that."

"I don't think it's a good idea, anyway. I'm perfectly capable of making my own plans." She hoped he could accept this for now without too much question.

John and Edward talked about it late that night, and John came to his decision.

The next evening, Edward expertly arranged an elegant meal for the two of them and then claimed he had business elsewhere. After they had eaten, just as Elizabeth was expecting dessert, John kneeled and asked her to marry him.

She said, "Yes."

Elizabeth was still afraid to jeopardize her stepfather's plans. She knew there was near royalty involved, along with her father, and she felt she had no right to divulge anything. Yet she must say something.

"John, there are things I cannot tell you until we reach the open seas out of England. I need you to respect that. Can you?" asked Elizabeth, feeling more afraid than she'd ever been. She didn't want to hurt this relationship.

"Well, if I must," said John with a frown. He'd rather hoped that she would trust him.

"What I will say is it would be very nice if we could travel on the *Abigail*. Do you think it could be arranged?"

John's eyes transitioned from frustration to understanding. Someone she loved was on that ship. Her mother and stepfather? He wouldn't ask. "We'll find a way onto that ship."

John the Younger was twenty-seven, and Elizabeth was nineteen, according to their applications for passage on the *Abigail*.

When John and Elizabeth announced their engagement to the Williams clan, Anna Grace was so excited she couldn't stand still. She paced, while the others dutifully congratulated the couple, and built up her courage. Finally she got a chance to take Elizabeth off to the side and ask what was on her mind.

"You are really going to get to go beyond the seas, and this year!" she started.

Elizabeth's own happiness was uncontainable. "That's the plan!"

"You know that's what I want to do, too, more than anything," Anna Grace continued earnestly.

Elizabeth nodded to encourage her.

"I really think you'll need a personal maid, don't you? Someone you can really trust, someone just like me," she finished triumphantly, immediately wondering whether she'd said too much.

Elizabeth was listening.

"Won't you please take me with you?"

Elizabeth was completely surprised. Anna Grace was all that Robert had, and Ann was like a mother to her. What would they think of this? On reflection, though, she knew that it was common for young women to hire themselves out as indentured servants to better-off relatives. Robert had been Anna Grace's single dad for a long time. Elizabeth told Anna Grace that she would think about it, in that way adults have that probably means no.

Anna Grace walked away, a little disappointed, but not for long. Anna Grace never stayed sad for long, and soon she was pestering John the Younger about his plans when he returned to New England.

Ann encouraged Elizabeth to approach Robert. Ann knew that Robert still wanted to emigrate and just hadn't mustered the courage or the funds. Maybe this was the Lord's way of creating a path for him.

When Elizabeth finally approached Robert, it was Elizabeth who was surprised.

"Let her go. I will hope to follow her. I'm jealous and wish I was on the boat myself, but I'm not ready yet," proclaimed Robert. "If the paperwork can be arranged, let her go."

John the Younger was a master at getting paperwork approved, and soon Anna Grace was an excited ten-year-old setting out for the New World as Elizabeth's personal maid.

Many people had final conversations with Anna Grace that were full of instructions.

In John the Younger's presence, her father, Robert, told her, "Anna Grace, you be our eyes in the New World. You must learn to write well, and I'll be expecting letters from you to your Aunt Ann and me constantly."

"That's a capital idea," said John. In fact I've a list of women asking for letters now that Martha isn't writing anymore. I can't bear to dump that on Elizabeth, as they were Martha's friends from youth. Anna Grace, perhaps you can take over her voice in the wilderness for them? It would mean so much to them."

"John, why don't you give the list to Ann, and she can take Anna Grace's letters and forward them to the other women. That way Anna

Grace can write one big letter and have postscripts for myself and Ann, and the big letter will go to everyone?" Robert didn't want to miss any news from his Anna Grace. This way they'd get it all.

"That's even better," agreed John the Younger.

"Anna Grace, you've got to scout out a place for us to live once I get there," Robert instructed her. "You'll have to report on all your travels. Meantime, let's get you practicing your writing."

Essex, England, May, AD 1635

Montegu Bertie enjoyed his shifts keeping the king company in the Audley End House. The job was a combination of servant duties and companionship. The king was lonely and had few close friends. He found it satisfying to pass his private time in the company of the Gentlemen of the Bedchamber, as it was one of his few opportunities to get information outside formal channels that was not carefully scripted.

"Essex was known as the hotbed of Puritanism. Laud tells me he's got it tamped down and under control. Do you think the common people will agree?" asked King Charles.

Montegu considered whether to tell the king what he knew Laud would want him to hear or the truth. He finally opted for the latter, a rare risk. "It is true that the exodus to New England is slowed and that sports are now legal on Sunday. The people enjoy the day of relaxation and sports, that's for sure. However, I would point out that you are losing taxes by slowing emigration. Men will still leave, just via another route through another country, if necessary, and you will be shorted the taxes. Additionally, when Laud cracks down on playwrights and public figures, it backfires. The crowds follow them to prison and cheer. For every man you send to prison you create a crowd that spawns a hundred new rebels. Anyone with lopped off ears is a hero to the common man. Forgive me, but it's the truth."

"I deeply appreciate your honesty, and you will be richly rewarded. What would you do if you were me?"

"You've already collected taxes on all the counties of England for maritime support. Tax every ship that enters from or leaves for New England. Then let the emigrations proceed. A Puritan in New England is not spawning new Puritans here. Approve patents in the New World to offset the Massachusetts Puritans. If you do, they will argue with each other and not at your expense."

"I've applications to leave the harbor. Laud has recommended I decline. We'll try an experiment and instead approve them even with known Puritans aboard, for a fee. Let's see where this leads. I think it would be appropriate to start with the *James*, as my father always did have a soft spot for the Puritan fellows. We'll just quietly stop searching so carefully and see what happens."

Puritan emigration picked up again after a year of near cessation, with the *James* and the *Abigail* departing the harbor in July. Many Puritans still went in disguise, as there was no public approval for their passage, but the searches were less and less thorough.

CHAPTER 23

Boston Area, June, AD 1635

It was a June's Lord's Day, and the women were gathering at Anne Hutchinson's house. The gathering had grown from a few women to nearly thirty. Bridget baked fresh bread, and the smell permeated the house with the warm, comforting smell that meant to all that there was fresh, warm food aplenty. Francis gathered the children upstairs in the spacious house for children's stories and play. Downstairs, the wood-framed house had arches enabling a large meeting space in the formal living room. Anne had personally designed the room to facilitate just such Bible studies. The women gathered. There was a cross breeze through the windows to keep the women cool as they talked and sewed. There was excitement in the air, more so than usual. The news coming with the ship that came into harbor that week was too good to have even hoped for, according to their men. This was their first chance to discuss it among themselves. They'd taken to discussing issues of the day as well as the Bible. The women found that it made them better able to carry on conversation with their men, and they found it satisfying to have more meaningful input, especially unified input, after discussions among themselves. The colony did not otherwise consult women in any formal way. The women were becoming an invisible political force.

Mary Dyer, Anne's close friend, started off the discussion. "So Fernando Gorges will not be the royal governor after all, bless his soul."

"Imagine his ship breaking apart in calm seas and sinking with all aboard. It is a sign from the Lord, directly," said another.

"Yes, it is God behind this New Jerusalem. If God is with us, who can be against us? Praise the Lord," said Sarah Cotton.

"Okay, let's get started. The scripture for the day is ..." Anne said, starting their formal study.

Boston Area, July, AD 1635

The complete failure of private discussions with Roger caused his matter to be considered by the July court. Again the court asked him to reconsider, lest he be punished, and the matter was scheduled for the September court. The charges against Roger Williams and followers were consolidated to four, and they were to be sentenced in September, should repentance not be forthcoming.

The court charged that Roger Williams disputed the right of a magistrate to:

1) administer punishment for violations of the First Table;
2) administer an oath to an unregenerate man;
3) pray with unregenerate people (even a woman or child);
4) give thanks after meals or after communion (versus before).

The ministers and magistrates were sent again to Roger Williams and to his followers, to attempt to teach him the error of his ways. Again they were welcomed, for Roger was confident that any Christian man building New Jerusalem would be persuaded. Roger was well loved.

As harsh as these men were, their honest purpose and expectation was a recantation, a returning to the fold. This was the ending they all expected. Many men had been in Roger's position, Endicott and Eliot among them. Every man with a reputation, a standing, and a future recants. They did not even consider that Roger might not recant.

England, July, AD 1635

It was a hectic week. John the Younger closed a deal with Lord Say and Lord Brook, who appointed him governor of an area at the mouth of the Connecticut River for one year. He had a new settlement to plan and resources to procure, and he wanted as many of them as possible loaded into the *Abigail*.

Just before boarding the ship, Elizabeth and John the Younger married in a small, private ceremony in London, with Edward Howes as best man and Ann Helwys Williams as best matron.

With fond farewells, they went straight from the wedding to board the *Abigail*. The *Abigail* already had passengers from foreign ports she'd been picking up since June, and she would stop one more time. Once they were safely aboard, there was a small, private dinner where John the Younger finally met Elizabeth's mother and her stepfather, the Reverend Hugh Peter. The Peters were on the run from Laud and were traveling in disguise, as members of the Freeman family, so there were many Freemans at the dinner as well.

The Lord Harry Vane the Younger, also traveling incognito, boarded the *Abigail*.

The first two weeks at sea were routine, though exciting to Anna Grace, as she watched the land recede and made the acquaintance of passengers. It seemed completely magical that, once they were on the high seas, a humbly dressed young man let on that he was a lord—the Lord Harry Vane. With his golden curls and a chubby, youthful face that had never known hunger, he was decidedly the most handsome man on the ship. It wasn't just Anna Grace who felt this way, but nearly everyone. His manner was royal and confident, but his smile made everyone feel they were a part of his plan for New England.

Then, a month into the trip, smallpox was discovered in the servants' quarters. Those with symptoms were quarantined, and a pall fell over the ship. Anna Grace approached John the Younger.

"My grandma always said I'm blessed to escape from plagues, because my mama died from it when I was a baby, and I didn't die. It seems that everybody is afraid of these sick people and has left them to die. My Grandma Alice never would have done that. She'd have been there caring for them, just like she did for me. My Aunt Ann would have been there too, since she believes all Christian women must serve the weak and sick, even at the cost of death. Won't you let me help them?"

"Your dad would never forgive me if anything happened to you, Anna Grace," John the Younger answered. "There are different kinds of plagues, and escape from one does not mean escape from all."

"Oh, but don't you see, if I don't help, it will ruin my very soul," exclaimed Anna Grace.

He talked it over with Elizabeth. "The European plague of 1625 that Anna Grace might have survived was the Black Death. The plague on the ship, however, appears to be smallpox. In truth, everyone on the ship has some exposure."

Elizabeth's view was simpler. "Anna Grace is called to this work. Christians through the centuries have tended to the sick when no one else would. If the Lord wants Anna Grace to live, she will live. But if you keep her from her calling, it will not give God glory."

John the Younger taught Anna Grace rudimentary nursing skills to care for those quarantined below. She became the bright, shining light singing to some as they met Jesus. For others she was a hard-rowing, determined soldier, pulling them back to shore. By the time the *Abigail*'s quarantine was over, she was a hero among the survivors.

John the Younger watched this whole process closely and saw that the girl had real talent. He began to teach her the most common treatments in Martha's book of medicines.

Salem, August AD 1635

Mary with her toddler daughter watched the rain pelt the house from the shed. The winds were picking up, and she'd been trying to get the last of the beans, beets, corn, and squash harvest in before it was blown to pieces or washed away. The potatoes she would leave, as they did not eat those greens, and tubers are protected below ground. This was no normal storm. The good news was that it was a very warm set of wet winds, so she and her daughter were pleasantly wet outside in the fields, which was more pleasant than if they had been dry, but inside a stuffy house.

Mary the Younger was walking now and more dangerous than ever. She was Mum's little helper, though she was doing more exploring and tasting than anything else.

Mary was seven months pregnant, and the baby was kicking often these days. It was uncomfortable to stand now, so she was doing a great deal of the picking on her hands and knees. That kept little Mary more engaged, so it worked well.

Her good friend Rebecca Throckmorton was also seven months pregnant. John was often out traveling. His boats went up and down the east coast, as far south as Virginia and as far north as Canada. He was safely south of the storm track, as far as she was aware. While he was not a captain or a sailor, as the business owner and master planner of the ship's trade, he often went on trips to arrange supplies and manage business deals. Rebecca had twins Patience and John, now almost eight years old, to help her. Often Mary borrowed one of them, but not today, because of the impending storm.

Roger was in town on business. She hoped he'd get home before things got too serious.

In another hour the winds had picked up even more, so that it was no longer easy to stay outside, as leaves were ripped off branches, and some branches began to fly. Mary and little Mary made their way back to the house, ensuring that everything loose was brought in or tied down.

Evening fell eventually, and with it came a drenched Roger. He reported that the stream level was rising dangerously, and there were fallen trees already in several spots. The storm was just beginning; there was far to go.

Hours later they heard a large crash. Now the wind was a constant scream, so the fact that they could hear the crash was ominous. They decided not to check on it till morning, when the weather was calmer. The couple read the psalms together and retired to listen to the howling wind. It was impossible to sleep, and they told stories of better times and hopes for the future. Roger talked openly for the first time of a contingency plan to start a trading post south of Plymouth on the Narragansett Bay, and broke it to Mary gently that she might be facing a wilderness lifestyle again someday. Mary hoped that the children would have a chance to get a little older first, and she said as much, but Roger wasn't quite sure he could make that happen for her. Maybe he would go, and she would remain at their current house for a time.

About two a.m. the winds calmed for a while. The couple peeked out, but it was very dark, and they could see nothing. Soon enough the winds were back, though they were not as strong as before. They were from the opposite direction, and anything that was braced for the earlier winds was vulnerable to these. There were more loud crashes.

Sunrise was invisible, though the world turned from black into a dim gray while the hurricane finished with them. The baby was up, so they ate and went about their indoor chores, waiting for the rain to let up.

When they could finally go outside later in the morning, they did not recognize their world, their street, or their fields. Neighbors were in the street, coming out one by one to survey the damage. One neighbor lost a roof, a tree had fallen on another one's house. Another's house, closer to the stream, had a foot of water inside. The Williamses counted themselves fortunate indeed. The fields were a thatch of tree branches and mud, with gullies full of drain-off still flowing, but they were safe, and the house was sound. They took in less fortunate neighbors, and Mary started an endless kettle of soup for anyone who was hungry. Sometimes groups of workers stopped to eat, and sometimes the folks whose own houses were under repair stopped to visit; the house was open to all.

It seemed that half the trees in New England had fallen. Every able-bodied man was out with an ax, trying to restore passage through town.

Neighbors helped to shore up damaged houses with emergency repairs. Roger was one of the fitter men of the community. By rowing, riding, and walking he always stayed physically fit, as had his mentor, Sir Edward Coke. Every ounce of that fitness was useful now. For the next several days he with other men tore into the downed trees like madmen. They worked from dawn until there was no longer light to see. If there was moonlight or starlight, they kept going, as there was no end to the work that needed to be done. Roger came home exhausted and left barely refreshed the next day. Slowly, the town was returning to a recognizable shape. And through it all, Roger maintained his teaching at the church in Salem three times a week. He earned the respect, love, and support of all.

Slowly the stories poured in. Men had been taken by rogue waves three times the size of a person while they stood and gazed at the sea. Families had been crushed in their houses. This was the worst storm New England had known since Salem was founded.

All felt there was evil afoot, and the Lord was punishing them. Different people had differing opinions about whether it was the magistrates or the populace, as led by Roger Williams's opinions, who were evil. The people noted, in whispers, that while Roger was out helping restore the town, other ministers were not physically assisting; they focused on calling for prayer services. The magistrates, in fear of the Lord, stopped administering the oath of residency, to ensure that they were not administering oaths to unregenerate people.

By the time emergency repair activity subsided, Roger had to turn and begin to restore his fields before winter froze the ground. When he finally had to go to court, he had a respiratory illness that had taken his voice.

With all the work to do to restore the town, the woods were left untouched for now, and they were all but impassable, with huge trees blocking the paths used by European and Algonquian alike for generations. Trees across streams made canoeing treacherous as well, and getting to court was a challenge.

The Sea, August, AD 1635

While the *Abigail* was carrying Hugh Peters, the *James* was carrying Thomas Shepard, Richard Mather, and their families out of England. All boarded without incident. While they had escaped Laud, they had not escaped natural disaster. While the *Abigail* was facing smallpox, the *James* was blown north, taking longer to cross, and was caught in the aftermath of the hurricane. The crew worked tirelessly, and yet the *James* headed directly for the shoals in the gulf of Maine. The wind and waves were treacherous, and the passengers feared for their lives. Then the sails split, and the crew lost control and was reduced to watching as the damaged ship was driven toward the rocky shore. The ministers prayed.

Just in time, the wind shifted. The ship was driven back out to sea. Lives were spared, and the hurricane passed on. The crew managed to repair the ship well enough to limp toward Boston harbor. The *James* made landfall while the *Abigail* was still quarantined offshore due to smallpox.

Thomas Shepard and Richard Mather entered New England by the grace of God and were immediately popular voices in the colony. Shepard took the church outside Boston in what is now Cambridge (then called Newtown), and Mather headed down to Dorchester to minister where the hurricane did the most damage as it made landfall. The town was in shambles, the people eating acorns for food, and Mather was immediately up to his elbows in practical pastoral ministry.

Thomas Shepard and Richard Mather immediately joined Thomas Weld in being the most conservative of Puritan voices. They believed that discipline was most important in the wilderness in order to maintain the rule of civilized law. They were not after repentance from violators. They were after elimination of the violator in order to preserve the remaining souls. Mather's early experience with the looting in Dorchester, which had nearly been destroyed, served to harden him to the plight of anyone endangering the town.

John Mason, still well known for his pirate capture, was chosen to organize the Dorchester civil recovery, and within a month order was restored. When Mather and Mason finished, they'd built a far more robust town than existed prior to the hurricane. They garnered financial support to fortify the Boston harbor, ensuring that Dorchester and other towns like it were better protected in future storms.

Boston Area, September, AD 1635

Eventually Roger's September court day arrived. His breathing was still rough, and his voice had not returned. The recantation that the Boston magistrates and ministers expected did not arrive at court, verbally or in writing.

Endicott and the elders of Salem, including Roger Williams, came to defend the letters written to the churches. Endicott raised a protest in defense of the letter. He was put in jail. He spent a few hours in the jailhouse, in deep shock, while the ministers worked on the elders outside. The Boston ministers told the Salem men that it was a sign from the Lord that Roger Williams couldn't speak and that they must recant or they would all face punishment.

When Endicott recanted under pressure, most of the people followed. They were allowed to leave, and the expectation was that the church would formally disown the letters. Only one man stood by Roger's side in public—John Throckmorton.

Everyone knew that hurricane recovery had to be the focus for now, and sentencing was rescheduled for October. The court adjourned after only two days, so they could return to more urgent, repair-related activity before winter set in. Endicott's recantation was a significant event. Roger Williams could see that the people would have to choose between him and Endicott. Each was a persuasive leader, and each was well loved. After this court session, Roger Williams, still unable to speak, wrote his church at Salem a letter. The church must choose. It could either have Roger Williams as teacher, separating from the churches in Boston, or it could follow Endicott, recant its earlier positions, and retreat into meek submission.

It was Roger's version of a resignation letter. He hoped but did not expect that it would move the church to galvanize around him and reject forever Endicott's recantation. The next Lord's Day, a heavy-hearted church voted by a bare majority not to separate from the other colony churches. Roger was teacher at Salem no more.

Boston Harbor, October, AD 1635

The *Abigail* pulled into the harbor on October 6 after her quarantine was complete. Not all who departed England landed in New England. The decks were scrubbed and the passengers examined by New England physicians on October 7.

Among the healthy were the returning Reverend John Wilson, minister of the First Church of Boston, and the winsome twenty-three-year-old bachelor Lord Henry Vane, who was already telling everyone to call him Harry. John Winthrop the Younger and John Winthrop's new wife, Elizabeth Read Winthrop, climbed down arm in arm. Elizabeth's party included her maidservant, Anna Grace Williams, and Elizabeth's mother and stepfather, Elizabeth Read Peter and Reverend Hugh Peter. The Onges and the Winthrops turned out in force to meet them.

John the Younger and Harry Vane were close friends after the twelve-week voyage. John Winthrop Senior met them at the harbor and invited them both to a coming-home feast. Roger Williams was in town for his upcoming appearance at court and was staying with the Winthrops and so joined them at dinner. John the Younger and Elizabeth planned to keep Anna Grace's identity a big surprise, in order to announce it in the morning.

John the Younger introduced Roger to Harry: "Harry, this is Roger, one of the best Algonquian speakers around, and one of the most outspoken Puritans in the colony. You two are the only two people I know who get excited talking about the invisible church and its implications."

Roger winced. John couldn't already know exactly how outspoken he'd become.

"Roger, meet the Lord Henry Vane, our most noble colony resident. You two can trade notes all night about what goes on in the Privy Council and the Star Chamber, and maybe you can give the young man some survival advice. He'll need it. He's already got his father worried."

Harry laughed, "My father. He would have me applying for all sorts of positions at court. He wanted me to apply to be a Gentleman of the Bedchamber so I could dine with the king and keep him company. I declined. He's dearly hoping I get the both the brashness and the Puritan out of my system before I return home. It won't happen."

John commiserated. He knew all about fathers and their expectations. "I used to feel the same way about my own father. But now that we're a little older, I usually follow his advice, and I'm happy to have him near."

The discussions went on deep into the night and revealed some key theological commonalities between Harry and Roger. Harry was strongly convinced that ministers were called from the population at large and that the whole notion of succession was a mistake. He agreed with Roger that the true church was invisible to man, though his reasoning was different from anything Roger had heard before.

Harry said, "The gospel of John says Jesus urged us to be one church. And the church clearly contains the departed elect, which we cannot see. We can pray with them, but we cannot see them. So therefore the one church has to be invisible, not visible."

Roger said, "I agree that no man can see the true church, that it is invisible. I think, though, that the stronger rationale is that men cannot see with any precision other men's hearts. Only the Lord can, and so only he can see his church. We are agreed in the main conclusion, though, that no civil magistrate is competent, then, to judge or rule over the church. Only Christ, who can see it."

By morning the three men were a knit team. The relationships would be tested but never severed. Each would accomplish more, given the support of the others, than would have been possible alone.

The next morning over breakfast, John the Younger introduced Elizabeth and Anna Grace to Roger. "Roger, look. I've gone off and married a woman in love with your sister-in-law's house church. She's actually spent more time with Sydrach and Ann than I have on this trip. You'll have to talk to her to catch up on your own family."

Elizabeth added, "Your nephew James and your niece Anna Grace all have dreams of joining us in the New World, as does your brother Robert. In fact, we loved Anna Grace so much, Robert let her come with us as my maid. And here she is!"

Anna Grace was in the kitchen waiting, and she made her dramatic entrance with a bowl of steaming porridge. Setting it on the table with her biggest smile ever, she ran to Roger.

"Uncle Roger, Uncle Roger! I can't believe I'm really here! You'd better pinch me to make sure we're not all dreaming."

Everyone laughed.

The Cotton family invited the Wilson family and the Peters family for an arrival dinner a few nights later. There the conversation was more sinister. Cotton said to Reverend Wilson, "We've been working all summer to get Roger Williams to recant his erroneous opinions. I've gone to him personally, as have others. He's in court in a few days, and no word of recantation has reached any of us. I fear we'll need to censure him."

The Reverend Wilson, never fond of Roger, said, "Reverend Hugh Peter is as orthodox a Puritan as I've met. Let's place him at Salem, and he'll have that church in shape in no time."

"The Lord has made clear his plans. He has already provided for Roger William's replacement. Praise to the Lord," said Cotton.

Boston Area, October, AD 1635

When the court session opened in October, there was still no recantation, written or verbal. Williams was offered another month of private consultations, given his recent sickness, but he refused. He asked to dispute that day. The Reverend Thomas Hooker was chosen as the most likely to succeed in convincing Roger to recant. Hooker stood up, knowing from the fire in Roger's eyes and the rounds he'd had in private with Roger, that Roger would not be swayed. He set out the right of the magistrates to govern, and indeed Roger answered with all his usual arguments. They could have gone on for hours, but there was no use. The disputation was closed as quickly as possible, and sentence was pronounced. No record was kept.

"It is ordered that Mr. Williams depart the jurisdiction within six weeks." Later that day, when Roger Williams made clear that he was still ill, the magistrates granted a delay till spring.

It was the twentieth banishment of the year and the second of the morning.

Roger was in shock. In his heart he hadn't believed they would dare banish him—not their own peer. *Now what?*

The magistrates were shocked themselves. They'd fully expected a recantation, and when it didn't come, they were backed into a corner, forced to make good on their word. Once proclaimed, they'd all stand behind it, at least publicly. The credibility of the Colony was at stake.

The ministers were especially angry. It was their failure, in that they were expected to teach Roger the error of his ways, and they'd failed utterly. In their anger, many, especially Shepard, became rigid and unrelenting in private, pushing for harsher sentences like execution or a return to England. They didn't want to live with their failure thrown in their face. They knew Roger better than to expect that he would be silent if not muzzled. They had already been embarrassed enough in front of their congregations when the magistrates ceased giving the residency oath, due to popular outcry.

Outside the courtroom, still stunned, Roger ran into the fellow who was banished before him the same day—a man similarly stunned. John Smith was the miller of Dorchester, the community reduced to rubble in the hurricane. This man was banished for his dangerous opinions as well, though neither the court nor the man divulged to the public what those opinions were. Roger introduced himself.

"I'm Roger. I see your name is John Smith?"

"Yes."

"John Smith the explorer was one of my heroes as a youth. Are you related to him?"

"I'm named for him. Dad claims to be his half-brother, but I think it's just wishful thinking. Who names two living children John Smith?"

"Have you read any of his books?"

"I really don't get to read much, except the Bible," said John. "I'd like to read, but there aren't many books in Dorchester."

"Do you have plans as to where you'll go now that you've been banished?"

"No, not at all. You have any ideas?"

"Yes, I will settle down on the Narragansett. I'd be proud to have John Smith's namesake as one of the founders of this settlement, and I know we'll need a miller. Did you know John Smith was almost hanged just before he was appointed to his role as trade negotiator for the settlement?"

"No!"

"It's true. Even though he didn't choose to publicize it, I've a friend whose uncle knew."

"What saved him?"

"One of the investors in the colony had named him leader in a sealed envelope, written before departure but read as they landed. Once that was read aloud, they didn't dare touch him. We are God's children, and his plan for us is under similar seal until the time is ripe. This is not the end. We, with God's help, will make it the beginning. Come with me to Salem and wait while we plan when and where to go," said Roger.

"I will. Thanks so much." There was new hope in John's eyes, a flicker of light.

Roger knew he'd need manpower, and he fully intended the new settlement to be a place that would not punish men for expressing their convictions, only for breaking civil peace. John Smith, chosen for his name, was in.

Anna Grace's first letter back to England brought the bad news. She felt the New World was worse than the old. She knew well the family stories of Aunt Ann's father, and of all the people who had left England because of Laud. But now it was happening to her uncle in the New World. Where on earth had they sent her? The Puritans had all jumped from the hot coals of England to the raw fire of the New World.

Anna Grace, ever the caregiver, was all over John the Younger as well.

"You've got to help him!" she'd cry. "Can't you make them change things, now that you are back?"

"No, my dear Anna Grace. Only Roger himself can do that. He could recant. For practical reasons, he could. Many have done it. I don't think he will, though. He's got support among the population, he's got support among the Algonquian, and he's got John Throckmorton, Harry Vane, and me to catch his back. Mostly, though, he's got his principles and believes he is on God's mission, and he's decided to make his stand here and now."

Chapter 24

Salem, October, AD 1635

Roger's attention was soon turned back toward home, as Mary gave birth to a daughter the same week that Rebecca Throckmorton had another baby girl. In the long tradition of giving thanks in hard times, they named the girls Freeborn and Freegift, respectively.

No longer teaching at the church, and unwilling to keep company with those who had voted him out, Roger returned to the family tradition of house church. He was still a popular teacher, especially among the women, and his house was soon full of twenty to thirty supporters every week.

After lessons, there was tea and bread and soup for all who stayed, and Roger began talking openly about his plans to open a trading post on the Narragansett Bay, where he already owned property purchased from the Wampanoag. The Throckmortons and about a dozen other families were ardent supporters. Roger Williams began selling property in Salem and mortgaging his house. He was putting aside cash and supplies he would need when he migrated south, and he was planning to leave in the spring.

The Reverend Hugh Peter was rapidly installed as the replacement teacher in Salem's church, and immediately focused on conforming the church to Boston's leadership. In order to please his peers in the Boston clergy, Hugh Peter asked each member of the Salem church to denounce Roger Williams. As a demonstration of thoroughness, the church was urged by their new teacher to excommunicate Roger Williams and John Throckmorton. After two formal admonitions, they complied.

Boston, November, AD 1635

The house church at Salem was beyond irritating to Reverend Hugh Peter, as he could not control it. It was more popular than his teaching, and he wanted Roger Williams gone. When he shared his needs with Boston, uproar ensued. Some demanded Williams's immediate execution, while others demanded that he be banished to England. Finally, Roger Williams was put back on the docket for the next court.

One by one, men from Salem made their way to Roger's house and asked whether they could join him. The first was William Harris, an attorney's clerk. Soon after, Joshua Verin arrived.

John Throckmorton knew he would be a welcome neighbor; he didn't have to request permission. Others came by and discussed possibilities but had not yet decided.

John the Younger was anxious to start his own colony south of Boston at the mouth of the Connecticut. His father wouldn't hear of him leaving, though, until Elizabeth was confirmed pregnant, so he organized an advance party of twenty men and sent them on ahead. He knew they'd have a slow trip, as they would have to clear roads en route. The men set off in November, and John the Younger hoped to join them by spring.

England, December, AD 1635

Upon receiving Anna Grace Williams's first letter, Ann Helwys Williams fell to her knees in prayer. Then she copied the letter with shaking hands, as she'd agreed with John the Younger, and sent it on to the women on his list, including Elizabeth Masham of Otes, and Jane Whalley of Axmouth, Devon.

Later she read it to her house church, many of whom reported it broadly to their own networks of relatives and friends. Soon the Puritan women of England were praying as one for the future of the freedom to read the scripture and worship as the scriptures alone dictated. They prayed for New Jerusalem, in New England or in England, wherever God would will it. It could not be that the New Jerusalem would be lost so soon to the likes of Laud.

One of the women praying was Agnes Woodbury of Somersetshire, England. Her husband was already in Salem. She'd married him on his trip home in 1628 and had gotten pregnant but had talked him into letting her stay a bit longer. With her mother and extended family all around, the "little longer" had day by day turned into seven years. John "the planter" Woodbury was now insisting that she join him in Salem. He'd advertised it to her as a civilized place, full of promise. His house was ready for their son. Then the hurricane hit, and now little Anna Grace Williams's letter made it sound worse than England, as far as oppression went. She knew she needed to go, as her husband John had already arranged passage for his brother William to escort them to Salem. She dared not disobey. She prayed urgently and passed the letter on so that her entire family prayed with her.

When the day came Agnes dutifully boarded the ship.

Boston, January, AD 1636

The January court was told there were over twenty men now planning to join Roger on the Narragansett come spring. Moderate men were in a vise. On one side were Reverend Hugh Peter and the Reverend John Wilson, who were demanding Roger's immediate execution, and on the other side was a faction led by John Winthrop Senior, who declared that further punishment would make them no better than their persecutors in England. Led by hard-nosed conservative Governor Dudley, the court eventually voted to send Roger to England to stand trial, and several days later the General Council chose to reprimand John Winthrop Senior for being too lenient with the disaffected. They issued a summons for Roger's arrest and expected him to travel down to Boston to submit honorably.

Watching and waiting was Harry Vane. He did not take sides publicly, intending to move both sides to his position someday.

Anne Hutchinson had been listening to the Reverend John Wilson preach for three months now. From the beginning she disagreed with his strong emphasis on morality and works as leading to salvation. She began criticizing him in her house meetings. Will pointed out to her that it was not Christian to criticize John Wilson behind his back to his parishioners, so she initiated private meetings with Wilson and reported on them to her house church. As the controversy grew, so did the size of Anne's house church.

Salem, January, AD 1636

It was the dead of winter, and the house was quite cold and dark till midmorning. Roger had been up most of the night walking a colicky baby, and he slept in, an unusual move. He'd had little sleep and little voice for weeks, and Mary was up tending the fire and preparing a gruel to revive him.

The magistrate from Boston arrived in Salem and knocked on the door of Roger's house. Mary answered.

"Roger Williams, please."

"Roger is ill. What can I do for you?" Mary asked calmly so as not to scare the children.

"Deliver this summons to him, please."

"Certainly."

"I need to see you do it."

"Come with me, then. She took the summons, and the man stood at the door while she went into the bedroom and handed Roger the summons. He did indeed look ill and did not speak.

The magistrate was satisfied. "I'm sorry, ma'am," he mumbled as he departed.

Mary and Roger opened the summons and reviewed it. It was dated January 11, only two days earlier.

"I'm not going to report," declared Roger.

"You'll be a fugitive." Mary was scared.

"I'll be a prisoner, and you'll soon be a widow if I report. That just isn't the ending I have in mind to this whole affair."

"What will we do?" She could feel her comfortable life slipping away.

"I'll go south as soon as the weather breaks. You can join me later. They won't dare do anything to you. Let's gather supplies now, and I'll be ready to leave at a moment's notice."

"What will you take?"

"Make me those cakes like the Algonquian carry. That's the best for travel. I'll dress as the Algonquian do in winter and head for their territory. I want the canoe. I know I can't use it in freshwater now, but it will be needed badly later. I'll repair that snowshoe-shaped sled I made last year so I can drag it. I've used it as shelter before and can do so again."

Mary actually laughed. "Did you forget about the hurricane? There's no dragging anything! You'll be in a thicket of downed trees from start to finish."

"Oh. Good point. Maybe we'll get snow." He was lost in thought, and Mary went out to start making corn cakes.

From then on, Roger suspected that they might come for him. He resolved to be ready. He remembered Johannes's father's story of soldiers on sticks covered with leather and animal fat, and he strove to make a pair. When first snow came, he experimented and slowly made nearly serviceable skis. He repaired the wide snow sled for his canoe as well and practiced pulling it on skis.

265

Boston to Salem and Back, January, AD 1636

When the Boston authorities realized that Roger had not responded to the summons, they were incensed. Captain Underhill was ordered by the governor to go and find him immediately. John Winthrop Senior mentioned the pursuit to John the Younger, shaking his head, commenting that Roger couldn't sense when to be practical. It was out of his hands now, beyond his ability to help.

Elizabeth was finally taken with morning sickness, and she had missed three periods. The women informed the men over dinner that she was pregnant. That night, agitated by the news in town of Underhill's pinnace being readied for departure up to Salem, and ecstatic about Elizabeth's news, John couldn't sleep. He stole softly to the stable, believing he was unwatched.

Anna Grace climbed quietly through her first-floor window and trailed after him. She watched as he saddled up his favorite horse. He rummaged about for quite some time among the trunks he'd brought on the *Abigail*, many of which had not yet been unpacked. Finally he seemed to find what he wanted—a small box. As hard as Anna Grace tried, she couldn't tell what was in the box. John left, and she climbed back in through the window and stole back to her room in the house. She dreamed up all kinds of stories as to what might be going on. Finally she decided that he must be leaving for Connecticut after his men. Maybe they needed that box.

John Winthrop the Younger took off in the dead of night and rode hard—letting off all the stress from the last few weeks—but not toward Connecticut. He arrived in Salem by daybreak.

Banging on the door without worrying about waking the babies, he roused Roger and Mary.

"Roger, it's urgent, let me in and can you get some coffee on?"

"We may yet have some of your Levant coffee. Let me have Mary get working on it. Man, there is a snowstorm brewing. What on earth are you doing here in Salem and at this hour? I thought you'd be in Connecticut by now. Your horse is hot. Go and walk him out, or he won't be able to move."

Roger pulled on warmer clothes, and went out to rejoin John.

"Now, what has brought you up here?" Roger asked as they walked the horse out of earshot of the house.

"They are sending Captain Underhill in a pinnace to arrest you and to deliver you in chains on the next boat departing for England. You are to go to England with a list of charges sure to land you in the Tower, and they really may take your life. I thought you'd want to know," said John the Younger, warm coffee now in hand.

"You are endangering yourself by coming here," replied Roger, a cup of traditional tea in his own hand.

"I told no one I was coming, and I must return," said John the Younger.

"Yes, get out now and take the back way out. You'll have to cross some trees, but that way you won't be seen. Thanks. I owe you my life now, good friend," said Roger.

"Where will you go?" John sensed that Roger had a plan, since he hadn't seemed surprised.

"South. Listen, do me a big favor. The proceeds from my house are with Woodbury, the planter. There will be a ship in at some point in the next two months with my mother's inheritance. I am going to need that currency. Can you have John Throckmorton bring it down to Narragansett Bay, or bring it yourself on your way to Saybrook, with any other supplies you can spare? I'll be there waiting on that land I got years back from the Wampanoag. You remember it, right?"

"Yes, we camped there once fishing, as I recall. I'll see what can be done. Listen, I've one more thing for you." With this, John the Younger pulled out a box.

"This was a gift to me from a trader in the Levant. It's heavy, but it's accurate. It's a dry compass. You'll need it in this storm."

John returned just as fast and never admitted to the trip, not even to his father. As far as he was aware, all that everyone but Elizabeth knew was that he had a hard morning ride. He told Elizabeth he went for a walk and fell asleep in the barn before his ride. Anna Grace frowned when Elizabeth repeated the story to her, but she said nothing.

Salem, January, AD 1636

Snow was falling by noon. Roger wondered for a minute whether John the Younger had gotten back safely, but then he turned to his own situation. He was about as packed up as he would ever be, and he had the canoe fitted on the sled. He was wearing moccasins for cold protection, and his clothing was loose-fitting wool covered with waterproof outer garments, Algonquian-style.

Wool Algonquian-style meant yards of cloth wrapped loosely for insulation, easily removable, given different levels of activity. Before the Europeans brought wool in, it would have been skins. The Narragansett rulers were technology opportunists and recognized immediately that wool was warm and light. They enjoyed their wool colored deeply, so Roger had been acquiring wool and having Mary dye it. It was clothing, and it was material for trade.

He had the skis but hadn't tied them on yet. On the left was a longer ski, while the right was a very short ski, more like a snowshoe, that he could use for pushing off. They were little more than leather-covered planks, though he'd curved up the front end of the longer ski. He covered each with fresh, tight skins, sacrificing a pair of leggings to do it. He asked Mary for her lard supply and greased them thoroughly.

He knew he couldn't row in the open salt water. Besides the danger of the cold waves, he'd be discovered on the way to Boston. Therefore he would be traveling inland to the area near what is now Worchester, deep into Nipmuc country. Then, when the weather broke, he would canoe down the Blackstone River to Narragansett Bay.

Another reason to travel inland, aside from the obvious fact that Captain Underhill was reported to be coming in a pinnace, and he was therefore somewhat limited as to what waterways he could use, was that he needed to get out of the hurricane's path of downed trees if he was to travel by land. Since the hurricane made landfall heading west at Dorchester and then turned north and swept up the coast, west was his best bet. He also knew that the Algonquian camps this time of year were all inland.

He and Mary had been praying for snow, so that he could slide out rather than trudge. The base of snow before this storm was only several inches in the woods, and he knew he'd need a whopper of a storm if he was to make good progress. Judging from the skies, God was ready to help him out.

Roger's expectation was that the biggest challenge would be keeping his direction, especially on cloudy days and nights, and John the Younger had just solved that problem for him. He'd heard of folks circling about lost in the snow for days and weeks, unable to find the direction home. He knew that he'd be visually challenged for some time. Even though the compass was heavy, it was a must. Because it was a must, it was good that he'd have the canoe in which to carry belongings, as the compass was bulky. Another bulky set of items he believed he must carry was yards and yards of wool cloth, as well as steel knives and axes that he hoped to trade with Algonquian. In the last few months he'd turned a great deal of hard currency into items he knew Algonquian would trade for. They were his primary hope.

Roger knew from experience that, as long as he was working and moving, he'd be fine. It was good to walk in the winter because it kept the circulation to the feet. Problems occurred when you stopped or got wet. He hoped not to stop until he found Algonquian, but that could be challenging.

By 3:00 p.m. six more inches of snow fell, and by nightfall there was over a foot. Roger decided to get one more night's sleep in the warmth of home, and early the next morning he kissed Mary and his daughters good-bye.

He bound the skis to his feet with leather. He looked more like a polar caveman than an Englishman. He'd been scouting in cold weather before; he knew what he would face. In some sense every life experience to date represented training for what he was about to undertake. His physical fitness, his knowledge of Algonquian clothing, the languages he spoke, his knowledge of the Dutch skis for travel in snow, the lay of the backcountry he'd been exploring for years—all this would help him now.

For a while, Mary sat beside the fire, forlorn and afraid. It was still snowing. She dreaded the next knock at the door. She hoped Roger was right that they would leave her alone when she could not deliver him.

The snowstorm was a record-breaker, and there were three feet in the woods when the storm broke for a time the next morning. Mary explored a bit while the children slept, noticing that almost all the downed trees were covered well, and there were no tracks out. *Good*, she thought. Then she realized that she had just walked in the direction she'd seen Roger go, and she had now left tracks that marked the spot. Panicking, she looked back at the house to see whether company had already arrived. All was quiet. She headed back to the house, donned a pair of Roger's boots, and tramped out in several more directions. Finally, with the children awake and crying, she rebuilt the fire and collapsed, exhausted. Then she saw that Roger had taken the entire winter store of lard. She shook her head in resignation and quietly gathered cream from the cow's milk and began to churn for butter.

It was a powdery snow, and the wind was still strong. She needn't have worried, as most of her tracks were gone in two hours. By evening the eye of the nor'easter had fully passed, and it was snowing again.

She told herself that this was no different from a hundred other times he'd left her alone, but in her heart she knew it was different. This time it felt like there were no friends she could confide in and many foes.

Boston, January, AD 1636

The pinnace stayed in the harbor for the duration of the storm, three days. Captain Underhill was in no particular hurry, since he did not imagine that his quarry had been alerted. Besides, he liked Roger. A soldier's soldier, he would execute his orders to the letter, but there was no need to endanger his troops. It was three days later when he sailed into Salem and disembarked.

There was a strong undercurrent of support in Salem for Roger Williams and against Hugh Peter. The church in Salem lost over a third of its regular attendees, especially the women, but now also the men. The house church continued unabated, much to Hugh Peter's frustration, again under the leadership of Rebecca Throckmorton.

Wilderness Week 1

The first day was magical. Snow was falling, and the wind was blowing. For this time of year it was not as cold as it could be, meaning well below freezing but not below ten degrees. It felt good to move. Glide was an overstatement, as there wasn't really much gliding with these skis and the weight Roger was pulling. The snow level was well above most of the tangle of downed trees, so he was walking on a smooth coat of snow that covered an otherwise impassable mess. The snow cover was a tremendous gift from God for which he was grateful. He felt that even if all Massachusetts was against him, God was with him.

Roger attempted to maintain a direct westerly direction—the northern route to the river. If it had been good weather and a summer trip on roads and trails with no weight, it would have taken about seventeen hours of walking and fifty miles to the river he planned to canoe once the weather was warm enough. With hurricane tree damage and snow and staying off the roads, he knew it would take longer. At least with the cold, he could cross the frozen streams without problems.

On the other hand, he soon noticed that he was drinking his water supply very quickly. All the water he was carrying was next to his body in leather skins. There were three reasons for this: to keep it warm and unfrozen, to keep it handy for drinking, and to provide one more windbreak in his attire.

About three miles in he hit a frozen freshwater brook. It was already near noon, so he now knew that he was traveling less than one mile per hour, for he knew the brook. He thus figured that it would be about a week to the river. That was fine, as long as no one found him. With greater difficulty than he'd imagined, he broke the ice on the brook and filled his water supply. He managed to get his arms wet in the process, and he worked up a sweat. This was his first big mistake. Wet was the enemy of the traveler in the cold. He knew he must shed the wet clothing and get going and stay going until he was dry. Wet clothing worn next to the skin would not dry; it would suck out heat and stay wet long enough to cause a perilous drop in body temperature. It would cause more issues than lack of clothing to a working person. Wet clothing off the person freezes hard first and then eventually dries, the water sublimating from ice to air. More lightly clothed now, he moved on.

Once again, as long as he was working and moving at a slow, steady rate, he was fine. As soon he tried to stop, whether to eat, to find water, or to rest, he grew cold. By midafternoon he found he was traveling uphill, or at least it seemed that way, more than he'd expected. He did a direction check with the compass and found he was off course, going north. Sighing, he headed back southwest and made sure to correct his course once again before dark. It was cloudy, so the dark came very early, and it was very dark. But Roger didn't want to stop. Stopping was cold.

Then he walked into a tree. Once he realized that it was so dark he could not see his hand in front of his face, he knew he could not go on. Then he tested one of the critical parts of his plan. He struggled with cold hands to undo his bindings in the dark. He crawled back to the sled, where his supplies were, under his upside-down canoe, with a space left just large enough for a curled-up Roger. He packed snow along the windward seams between the canoe and the sled and heaped snow over the canoe for insulation. He left the lee side open for ventilation and crawled into the structure—part igloo and part cave. It was cold. Really cold. He went back to work on narrowing the opening. He needed it to be small, but he could not eliminate it, as he would risk suffocation.

Snow is a good insulator. Water is a terrible insulator. To the degree that Roger's body heat melted water that reached him, he would freeze. The trick was to stay dry. There was no thought of building a fire in this dark wind. He hoped for sleep, but it was a long night. It didn't seem that he'd slept at all by morning.

As soon as there was any light, he was back at work again. His feet were numb. He had to start walking. He had to dig out his sled. This he was able to do. He had a harder time locating his skis, but the hardest part of all was reattaching the bindings with very cold hands and feet. Eventually he was moving. The morning was clear for a while, and he got a reliable reading of his direction with the compass. By afternoon the storm was back again, however, and his progress was very slow. He was not sure of his direction. He knew he was somewhere north and west of Saugus, over frozen water or swamp in the Saugus woods. Jole's tribe should have been there, but he did not find anyone. Jole's son was sachem in this area, but he knew that sachem was in town sleeping in an English bed. He wondered forlornly whether they were all in English beds. It was not his favorite tribe. He hoped to continue west and find Nipmuc.

The terrain was tricky here. He hit a hill that he knew was a waste to climb, as there was a trail at sea level. He didn't realize it, but, with the low visibility, he'd traveled in circles and gotten turned around. The only purpose of his walking that day was to generate heat and stay alive. He made less than a mile of forward progress, and the night was again dark, windy, and howling. This time he stopped before it was completely dark and hid under his snow igloo supported by the canoe. He got some sleep, regardless of the cold and discomfort.

The third day dawned clear but windy, and the temperature was dropping. He was very numb and realized that he must move if he was to live. He got his day mode going and walked on. Using his compass and the view of the hills, he stayed over the frozen lakes and crossed the Walden pond area, which was just another part of Saugus to him. He realized that to stay west he would need to climb a hill, and, using his compass, he managed to make some progress. While it was clear, and he could see, he hoped to make more progress. By the end of the day, his feet had blisters, and it was not comfortable to walk when his feet were not numb. When his feet were numb, he was too cold. No position was good. He debated whether he should stop at dark or try to keep going. With moonlight and starlight from above, and the bitterness of the cold, he decided he was safer if he was moving. Besides, it was too hard to get those binders off. Bleary now, and not quite rational, he moved on through the night.

He trudged through the next day without counting the hours and without taking in enough water. He was not hungry and did not eat. He was out of immediately accessible energy, including the type of energy required for his brain to operate well, and he was not thinking as clearly as before, but knew he must keep moving. At length he suspected that he was not coherent. This next night he stopped and made his cave again.

In the morning he saw the sores on his feet; the blisters had burst and were rubbed raw. He knew he must get water. His muscles had cramped overnight, a sure sign of dehydration. He suspected that he had a fever. He decided that his only objective that day was to get waters and supplies. He began to consider. If Englishmen had not discovered him yet, did that mean there was no longer a chase? He was pretty certain he was closer to Boston than Salem now, though west and likely north of Boston. In truth he was well north of his intended route.

He decided to rest and camp, rather than walk, for a few days. He had weeks until canoeing weather, and the thought of reattaching the skis over his blisters was a bit terrifying. Perhaps he could scout out Algonquian if he was still and watched the land. It took him most of the day just to find fresh water and return to his cave. He resolved to move his little cave to the water source the next day, if he could bear the pain.

With his water supply assured and his cave moved to a more protected spot and fortified, Roger's situation was stable. His camp was stationary for days, his clothes were dry, and he felt mentally restored, even if his feet were still full of sores. He counted out his cakes. He had started with a good five-week supply. He had fewer than four weeks left.

So far, his mind had been focused on his own survival. Now, camped out but unable to move comfortably, he began to ponder the situation in the colony. He reviewed over and over again how he had gotten to this spot and what it meant to him. He was not yet thinking deeply about what he would do next.

Salem, January, AD 1636

Captain Underhill hung out in town for a few hours before approaching Roger's house. As far as the men in town knew, Roger was home tending to a new baby with Mary and healing from his exhaustion-related illnesses.

Finally, he knocked on Roger's door.

It was the third morning since Roger had left. Mary had been expecting this knock every hour. She'd practiced what she would say and do a hundred times.

Calmly, she answered the door.

"Roger Williams, please."

"He's not here," Mary replied.

"I have authorization to search and detain." Captain Underhill produced his papers.

Her skin crawled. "Come in, then."

He and his men searched the house, the barn, and the outbuildings and surrounding woods for two hours. Roger was not to be found.

"How long has he been gone?" Captain Underhill knew when the summons was delivered. That was the outside time frame.

"A long time. I've a new baby, and one day blends into the next. I'm sorry." Mary was convincing in her bleariness. It was truth. There was no lie here, only an unstated truth. She knew exactly how long it had been since Roger had kissed her good-bye.

Captain Underhill retreated with his men, and they regrouped on the pinnace and discussed plans.

"Let's review. We have a man gone into hiding. Do you think he's in town somewhere?"

"Likely. No one could survive the cold of the woods for long. If he's not in town, he's frozen somewhere by now."

"Men have often survived over a week, sometimes on the order of a month, delirious in the snow," Captain Underhill reminded them. "We find them all the time."

"It's possible. Even if he is in town, nobody's talking."

One of the men asked point blank, "Are we obligated to pursue now?"

Captain Underhill said, "Go on, what is your alternative?"

"We know where he intends to be in spring. It will be a lot easier to ferret him out come spring down on Narragansett Bay."

"More pleasant, too," another chimed in.

Captain Underhill thought about it. There were two cases. Roger was hidden in town, or he had left town. If he left town overland, he could not get far quickly, given the destruction from the hurricane. If he was on the water, they would be best served to find him in their pinnace. He nodded and smiled slowly. "We'll head back and check every open waterway. If he's in his canoe, we'll catch him yet. We'll have the constable here watch for him. Do any of you want to volunteer to stay to assist in that? If we don't find him, we'll ask permission for an expedition to the Narragansett come spring. Now, any volunteers to stay in Salem?"

Two of the men were from Salem. This was a gift. They would be on duty at home. They were quick to volunteer.

The pinnace started a slow return trip, hugging the ice-line on the shore and examining all water flow escaping the land. In truth, there wasn't much. The water was iced over even where there was tidal flow, in an unusual, eerie quiet. This was an exceptionally cold winter; even the larger bays were frozen over, and the major rivers had been frozen since mid-November.

CHAPTER 25

Wilderness Weeks 2 and 3

The cold was deep and bitter, with a new covering of snow every few days. Some days Roger stayed in his cave doing calisthenics to get his blood flowing. His choices seemed bleak. Walk and rub his open wounds rawer still, or stay quiet and let his toes turn black. Staying still seemed the worse option of the two. He did not want to move his camp, though, and spent a few hours most days exploring, seeking out a new location for his camp, and trying to ascertain where he was.

After many days like this, beginning to be concerned that his food supplies were dwindling, and not finding any Algonquian company, he chose a new campsite and moved to it as efficiently as he could. He was pretty sure he was out of the area affected by the hurricane now. Still, he would have liked to make it to the river before the streams thawed and before he had to give up his skis and sled. He resolved to move camp every other day, spending the day in between scouting, scavenging, and hunting.

Available food sources, aside from his dwindling supply of cakes, included nuts, freshwater clams, water lily roots, and cattail roots. All the hibernating animals had beaten him to the best nuts long ago. When he found acorns, he had to have days where it was above freezing to soak them in water to reduce their toxicity. Clams were hard to find in frozen freshwater, and he was too far inland for tidal water clamming. It was a wet and muddy experience to search for them and right now the shoreline mud was hard as rock. Cattails and lily roots were also beneath frozen ground. The outlook was bleak until the weather warmed up. Mary's cakes were his main sustenance, with a few grubby acorns. The frozen grubs provided more nutrition than the acorns.

Having set himself a new routine, he managed to move about three or four miles every two days. His mistaken route north had cost him perhaps ten miles, making the total mileage about sixty. At the close of week three he was a little over halfway, with one week of food remaining. The cold had not given him a reprieve.

While he hadn't seen the Nipmuc, they had seen him. They hadn't decided what to do about him yet.

Boston, February, AD 1636

Captain Underhill was in Boston, reporting to the General Council.

"We searched Salem immediately after the storm and found no sign of Roger Williams. Roger's wife was with a toddler and a newborn. We searched the town and obtained no further information about his whereabouts. The hurricane damage was very severe, and all the men are having a tough time navigating even well-known trails in the woods. Finally, we stationed two men in Salem, and we returned hugging the shoreline in case he made his way by canoe. There was no sign of him in the water. It is our assessment that he could be dead or will turn up in Salem, or he could be found at the Narragansett in spring."

The General Council discussed its options. They decided to review the matter again come spring.

John Cotton took one more step. As teacher of Boston, he was the head teacher of all the churches. He'd known Roger a long time. Whether out of love or out of fury at Roger for heading down this erroneous path, he decided to make one more attempt at correction. He wrote Roger a letter.

He sent the letter up to Salem with the next available messenger and asked that they leave it with Mary. She would be the first to know how to reach him. John Cotton was betting that if Roger was alive, he was with friends, quite possibly Algonquian friends, beyond European reach, and one of his new friends would be in touch with Mary to assure her that he lived. At that point she would be able to forward his letter. He sealed the letter and smiled.

John Winthrop Senior quietly made a similar calculation. He wrote a note, and the same carrier had both letters.

Wilderness Week 4

Roger decided that his food situation was becoming dire. Heading out with an ax one morning, he searched out cattails and resolved to gather roots. This was easier said than done. Cattails live in wetlands, which were now frozen over. Even if he broke the ice with the ax, there was water underneath and then mud between a scavenger and a cattail root. Wetness was still the enemy of life. Puzzling about this as he examined a particularly large stand, he decided that the most effective way to get this done was by stripping off his shoes and skins, furiously scavenging for roots, and then dressing again before he froze to death. A fire would have been a nice way to warm up, but he'd been avoiding fire for three reasons. One, he couldn't afford to be found. Two, in such bitter cold, starting a fire was a major project, and keeping a fire going was also a major project. Three, any fire inside his shelter would threaten his canoe, and any fire outside his shelter would need another protective shelter. While Roger was pondering these thoughts, he spotted a brave in the woods edging closer and closer, watching him.

I must look strange to this fellow, with my ax poised over ice and my odd clothing. Roger began speaking calmly in every Algonquian dialect he knew, in turn. He knew that the dialects were close enough to be partially intelligible, even though Nipmuc was not yet one of his specialties.

His words were "Hello. I come as a friend. I am hungry and cold. I have items to trade for food and would like to find some people. I would really like to find some people." He made this speech into a mantra and repeated it.

The young man in the woods listened for some time and then turned and ran. Roger was betting that he was going to get company and would return. He stayed put and deferred stripping down to scavenge cattail roots for now. He laughed out loud when he realized how close the brave had come to discovering him naked, axing his way through ice.

While he waited, Roger thought about the little he did know of the Nipmuc. These were a private people, much devastated by disease over the last decade. He hoped that this tribe would be under the guidance of Canonicus, as he was the regional leader of the sachems for all tribes in alliance with the Narragansett. Roger did not know any of the local sachems, but they could be distantly related to the families he knew and able to get messages to them. He might be imagining too much, but he knew that if he was near the Blackstone River he'd been shooting for in his travels, it would lead him straight into Canonicus's homeland. On the other hand, if he had overshot his mark and was closer to the Connecticut River, the Nipmuc would more likely be aligned with the Pequot. Sachem allegiances were fluid and hard to track, varying as family ties and trading relationships were established.

Eventually Roger realized that he had been still way too long. There was no sign of anyone returning, and he headed back to camp, hungry and a little feverish. Eventually he thought of a scenario even worse than the brave being from a Pequot-allied tribe: he wondered whether the whole sighting was a hallucination.

Salem, February, AD 1636

Mary waited, and she was sick. It seemed that half the town was sick. At first she assumed it was just exhaustion, as Roger had claimed before he left. But the rumor in town was that the hurricane had dredged up old diseases that were now spreading through the towns. Combined with the challenge of the cold, many were falling ill. Maybe Roger was sicker than they knew when he left. She wished she'd hear a word from him—any word at all.

Sometimes she felt that her every move was being watched, though no one hostile ever spoke to her. Sometimes she thought she saw a constable off in the woods lurking about.

There had been no word from Roger. There were a dozen letters waiting to go with any messenger claiming to know how to get to Roger. One was from England, many were from friends in town, and three hailed from Boston. If she gave the letters to someone, it would have to be out of view of the soldiers. If she invited a stranger into the house, that would be a red flag as well. She pondered how she could ever effectively communicate with any messenger without having them followed back to Roger.

Finally, she decided on a plan. She gave the letters to Rebecca Throckmorton when she visited, and Rebecca concealed them under her heavy winter clothes when she departed. She planned to deliver them to loyal friend John Woodbury, since her husband was not home. If a messenger arrived, he would be directed to meet with Mr. Woodbury, and he would have to evade the watchers.

Then Rebecca's household fell ill, and she did not make it to Mr. Woodbury right away. Patience went down with fever first, and, as usual, was especially ill and weak, and seemed not to be able to recover. Then the baby and John got the illness as well. Rebecca was the last to fall ill.

In town, the Reverend Hugh Peter soon had the church in Salem appearing to conform to Boston's practices. Attendance was down, but he blamed the fevers.

The reality was different. The empty pews were growing, but not only because of the fever. Underneath the visible smiles, there was a backlash against the new leadership that was supporting Williams's banishment and the changes in the church. The Salem church had a long history of independence from Boston, which was being forcibly obliterated.

In Boston the power structure was divided, and the disputes among magistrates remained vitriolic. The backlash on the side of leniency included many friends of families with members who had been banished for "dangerous opinions." It seemed especially unexpected, given their status as a Puritan refugee colony, as if Laud were getting his way without even having a representative doing his bidding.

A younger generation including Weld, Mathers, and Shepard provided popular conservative leadership by promising to keep civil order and create prosperity, and Cotton and Peters receded in influence.

Wilderness Week 5

Roger decided to push on. Feverish and not quite rational, he picked up the pace and focused on making progress now.

The young man Roger sighted had not been a hallucination, and the young man recognized the Narragansett dialect Roger spoke. When he returned to his tribe, his sachem decided to send downriver to a neighboring tribe that traded routinely with Canonicus. Canonicus's nephew Yotaash happened to be in that town acting as a trading advisor and relationship ambassador to the Nipmuc, and he decided to come upriver and investigate. This took a few days. Meantime the Nipmuc tracked Roger from a distance. He seemed to be heading directly for their settlement, now at a faster pace.

Finally, after three days, Yotaash and the Nipmuc brave tracked Roger down. He was fewer than ten miles from the Nipmuc settlement near where two smaller streams met and formed the head of the Blackstone River.

Roger was weary and hungry and had no food. He dreamed of finding nuts, but what he took for nuts in the distance was a splatter of dirt on the snow from some animal encounter he couldn't quite identify. Then he saw the form of a man, but again he was not sure whether or not this was a shadow. He squinted, beginning to hope. Then he was almost sure it was a hallucination, as the figure was familiar.

Yotaash greeted him in the traditional style of a brave approaching another tribe. He called an Algonquian hello from the trees and stepped forward slowly. As he neared, he called another, louder, hello. He continued, expecting Roger to answer him.

Roger returned the greeting. Yotaash stepped from the trees, with his "hello" now a shout, and with food in hand. He'd been told this was a strange man who spoke Narragansett, but he was quite surprised to recognize Sachem Roger Williams. The Nipmuc had a reputation for feeding lost Englishmen and then retreating to leave them to find their homes on their own. Yotaash had been given food by the Nipmuc to offer to the Englishman, and that was what he was holding in his outstretched hand when he recognized Roger. Then the shouted hellos with an outstretched hand quickly changed into a bear hug.

Roger was not well. He did not even expect the man and the food to be real and was only reaching out halfheartedly when he was suddenly enveloped in warmth and realized for certain that he was not hallucinating. It was beyond his best hopes, meeting an Algonquian he knew almost as family. Yotaash, the Nipmuc brave, and Roger ate and drank together, and introductions were made. Yotaash translated for the Nipmuc brave, and Roger began, even in his deteriorated state, to add Nipmuc to his repertoire of Algonquian.

Yotaash and the Nipmuc brave took turns lugging the canoe, and they soon led Roger to a well-worn trail—one with no snow. Roger ditched his skis, and the group began to travel more quickly, making their way to camp.

In camp Roger was treated as royalty, at Yotaash's insistence. The Nipmuc were a series of small, extended-family "tribes" in the valleys of western Massachusetts. Like most tribes, they were interconnected by family ties with surrounding tribes and were not really a separate nation or people. They were more like threads in a blanket of communities across a landscape—a Nipmuc set of threads here, and Niantic there. The Nipmuc were apolitical. They saw ruling tribes come and go and were usually unwilling to be a warring people. For as long as their oral history remembered, they had always been under someone else's protection.

Currently the Narragansett and the Pequot were the only two families strong enough to rule other families, so each smaller Nipmuc family was allied with one of them, in a fluid way that changed over time.

Currently, most of the eight operating Nipmuc "tribes," each with its own sachem or family leader, were allied with the Narragansett, voluntarily submitting to their rule. The sachems voluntarily maintained a tribute-based relationship with the Narragansett sachems, and Yotaash was a Narragansett representative of that ruling family. It would be normal to expect to interconnect via a family relationship to cement the relationship. Each tribe put forward its high-status women.

Yotaash's intended travels were to visit each "tribe" of Nipmuc and then on to the Massachusetts tribes of Jole that his family was connected to or allied with. Each would owe tribute to the Narragansett, and he in turn would take back requests for support from each tribe to Meiksah and Canonicus. Yotaash was aiming to find his nephews Weekan and Aunan before he returned home. Until this moment, he had been in a hurry to get beyond the Nipmuc to the Massachusetts.

Yotaash's request was the Nipmuc's command. They wanted to please him. A feast was prepared, and a wigwam was assigned to Roger. A Nipmuc woman created potions for him to drink to restore his health, though what they actually did was to make him groggy. Roger's stomach was warm and full, and his feet were burning as the feeling returned to them. He fell asleep for two and a half days and then slipped in and out of lucidity for several more days. Yotaash examined the contents of the canoe, carried on his own business, watched the women work, and waited.

Salem, February, AD 1636

Rebecca Throckmorton had a fever. It was cold in the house, but she didn't move. The children's cries were muted, as if they had no energy left, either. She did keep nursing the baby, but that was about all she was capable of accomplishing that day.

Early the next day she felt that her fever was down a little and forced herself up. She built the fire and checked on the little ones.

Only Freegift was recovering well. Rebecca, Patience, and John were recovering slowly and were still confined inside with hacking coughs, loss of strength, and pale skin.

Rebecca decided not to resume house meetings until March. She longed for group prayer.

Wilderness Weeks 6 and 7

Roger was finally awake and lucid. The night was cold, but there was a fire. Braves, women, and children sat around the fire in concentric circles. This was a story-telling evening, and they first turned to Roger, as the new guy and the man with the lowest status, with some explaining to do. Yotaash acted as Roger's interpreter. Roger spoke Narragansett Algonquian and in truth could already put together simple sentences in Nipmuc. Speaking in Narragansett, he could improve his Nipmuc by listening to Yotaash translate. Roger put his story into the context of the fluid tribal relations these men understood—one that did not diminish his stature yet got his points across.

He began by explaining that all these Englishmen were sent from England on a mission to trade with the native peoples and bring to them the good news of a powerful God who loved them. There were multiple families of English, just as there were multiple tribes of Algonquian. The English desired to set up different forms of trade by region, and Roger was to resettle in the south to start a new settlement. Others would follow, but he was to be the first.

"Why was he sent off so poorly?" asked the sachem.

"As a test of my endurance and diplomatic skills," replied Roger. "To be sachem of this new settlement I must demonstrate my ability to survive with only Algonquian allies. I am at your mercy, with only a few goods to trade for your hospitality."

Young Nipmuc men were sent on hunting quests, so this story, while avoiding the harsh realities of disputes with England and inter-English controversy, stuck to a truth that made Englishmen sound honorable.

Yotaash translated the question of a young man in the audience, "How did Roger survive these weeks in the wilderness in the cold with no wigwam and no fire?"

Roger knew he'd been watched, so he stuck to activities that had been observed. He described his plan to canoe down to Narragansett Bay in spring, which influenced his decisions on what to bring and how he constructed his shelter. He described, with widespread approval in the crowd, bringing a month's supply of Algonquian grain cakes as his survival food. Finally he described avoiding stillness and wetness at all costs.

The next storyteller was a young Nipmuc brave. He told a story familiar to all his people, which was meant for the children and the newcomers.

"Long ago, before the age of corn, our people came in from the north and west, from regions of many lakes and seas. We fished and clammed and ate the wild onions and mushrooms. We made flour from the cattails. Our people have been here longer than other peoples. We do not defend our territory but are friendly with all who come. If another tribe wants to defend territory, that is fine with us; as long as they are respectful to us we will support them. We come in peace, and we feed all who come. We expect all who come to leave before we leave, and we care for them while they are here. We are the people of the ages. We came before, and we will stay after. We are the nameless, the ageless, and the ones in harmony with the lakes and streams. You are the temporary, the strong, the makers of alliances and bringers of new things. We will respect you and trade with you, but we will not tell you our names. We are beyond names."

There were more stories of hunts and hurricanes, and finally it was Yotaash's turn to tell the story of his people.

"I come from the great line of rulers from the south and west. About twenty generations ago our people brought the milpa to this region, vastly increasing the winter food supply. Our people intermingled with the people of the blue hills and eventually produced fit braves for vast kingdoms. My great-grandfather was the great sachem over the blue hills area and many other areas. So many people paid tribute to him that he had no peers in the land. When it came time to marry his son and daughter, there was no one around for an ally as powerful as his family without traveling more than a season. He decided to keep the kingdom whole and not to dilute it with intermarriage by marrying his son to his daughter. This tradition kept the qualities of Steward rulers flowing to our descendants. This marriage was fruitful and produced four sons and two daughters, all of whom are sachems to this day.

"Canonicus was one of those sons. He inherited from his father the role of grand sachem or home sachem over all these regions, and you all know his son Meiksah that lives just south of here and receives tribute for the Narragansett from your people. Mascus, Canonicus's younger brother, was a diplomat sachem until his death from plague in 1617. Since then Canonicus has treated all his nephews as additional sons. These nephews are my brothers and I. We are ambassadors for the Narragansett people.

"To this day we, the Steward ruler family, have ways with plants that we share with no other people. Our ancestors deep in time learned how to change plants to make better food. They started with fruits only found in the far west beyond the sea. Then, when their boats were blown across many waters, they lost access to their rootstocks and needed new plants to eat. That is what drove them to develop the corn from a wild grass— changing it from a grass in the woods to the lush ears you have today. They learned to plant with squash and beans, with a fish for feed so that the plants would be strong and vigorous. When I leave here, I will go to the tribe of my Aunt Jole, who married into the Massachusetts, who have been here many seasons, like the Nipmuc. We are able to defend, and we will respect your people. We drove back the Abenaki for the Massachusetts. We can keep the territory safe."

Yotaash chose to pass over other parts of Yotaash's extended family, as they didn't make his points as well. Uncle Wekeum's daughter married into the Pequot, and the Pequot were turning out to be an internally divisive, rather difficult bunch of folks. Canonicus and his allies' challenge was to keep the factions of Wekeum's family fighting each other and away from Narragansett territories. To this end, they supported Juanumo, brother of Meiksah's wife. Juanumo was a son of Canonicus's sister Oonue the Elder, who married a man descended from Wopiguard as well as from Niantic blood. On the one side, they opposed the purer Pequot side of Wopiguard's family from his Pequot wife, which included Sassacus. On the other side they opposed Wopiguard's half sister's son Uncus, split from the Pequot and now called Mohegan. The generation of Yotan, Meiksah, Miantonomoh, Juanumo, Yotaash, and Pessicus were both allies and rivals, but Canonicus taught them to be allies first. Uncas, Sassacus, and Juanumo were similarly related as family, but it would seem that Wopiguard's teaching was that they were to be rivals first.

Then there was Pessicus. Pessicus was by many years the youngest son of Mascus and had listened to the older boys talk about the west throughout his childhood. As soon as he was old enough, he trekked west. He intended to establish a relationship with the Mohawk to the north and west, but hadn't been heard from in two years. The story had no ending.

Yotaash stuck to good stories he could tell to win loyalty. He did not put the Nipmuc people to sleep.

After some warmer days, Yotaash offered to take a message back to Salem for Roger. He was ready to go find Jole, so part of his expedition this winter would be near Salem as a matter of course. After that he should be returning south. He might stop and see representatives in Salem and bring a return message. Not admitting that he might be a hunted man, Roger agreed. There was no way he could admit to being hunted without explaining intra-English disputes. Just as Yotaash was not sharing the inside story of the Narragansett family, Roger would not share the inside story of the disputing English. There was also no way he could write to his wife, Mary, and retain status. He instead wrote to John Throckmorton and told him the story he had given the Algonquian, asking him to convey the news that he was safe to Mary. Yotaash departed, traveling very light. He took the same Nipmuc brave with him for the first leg so that he would have more food than he could carry, and Roger instructed John

Throckmorton to resupply Yotaash. The snow was less formidable now, and Roger warned Yotaash of hurricane-downed trees in the area.

"I will be able to clamber over trees. I do not carry too much, unlike English," Yotaash answered.

Roger settled in with the Nipmuc and made himself useful to them in daily activities and in trade. He worked beside the young men at their hunting and their games. He worked beside the women at their cooking and their tapestries. He had his own wigwam, decorated with a combination of the wool cloth he'd brought and gifts from the Nipmuc hung beneath the walls of skin. The hearth was in the middle, and there was a bench to sleep on. It was a pleasant existence. Roger was not just working beside his new friends, he was also soaking up their language. From where he hoped to settle he would be able to trade with these families, so each interaction was a long-term investment in a trading relationship.

It should be a pleasant, downstream two-day canoe to Narragansett Bay once the water was high and clear of ice in spring. He had no desire to go on before wild onion season, however, and he hoped for Yotaash's return with messages from Salem.

CHAPTER 26

Salem, Late February to Early March, AD 1636

As soon as the cold abated, John Throckmorton's ship came up from the south. This was John's first trip home since the hurricane, and he was anxious to meet Freegift. He was also bringing up John Woodbury's wife Agnes, along with their son.

When he arrived, his mood quickly darkened. He learned that he'd been away far too long. His family looked sickly. Rebecca and Patience were especially weak. Roger had been banished, and Mary felt alone with little Mary and baby Freeborn.

Yotaash arrived in Salem during the night and knew enough from Roger's directions to find the Throckmorton home. Spooked by soldiers at the edge of the woods, he slipped by them quietly and did not stay to talk, as he was uncomfortable near these English. He left a rudely crafted arrow (not one he'd taken the time to finish properly) embedded in the wooden door with Roger's letter attached and departed even more rapidly than he'd arrived. He had no urgent need of resupply from the English, and he moved out to find Jole. She was living in the woods with the old medicine man of her tribe, even though her sachem sons were in town. He headed straight to Jole. He would do his business in the Algonquian way.

John Throckmorton heard a noise and opened the door carefully to look about but saw no one. He went back inside. Even in the morning, the family was internally focused, and he didn't see the arrow until nearly noon. By then Yotaash was many miles gone and would not be taking any return messages with him.

John read Roger's letter with some excitement. Roger was safe; he was alive. He wanted John to arrange supplies to build first temporary homes and then real ones down on the Narragansett in spring. He asked John to visit Thomas Agnell in Plymouth and have him plan a move to the mouth of the Seekonk in spring. John knew Mr. Woodbury was holding the proceeds from the sale of Roger's house for him, awaiting a plan. So John had the resources to arrange all this, and the ships with which to do it. He just didn't want to leave Rebecca behind again, at least not for long. He started to make plans.

The first plan was to get the good news over to Mary. Rebecca, energized for the first time in weeks, wanted to go with him to see Mary.

"We need to get the letters to Roger," pointed out Mary. "Can you write one out that I will dictate so he'll have one from me as well?"

"Surely, but the brave who left this message is long gone. It will be quite the tracking exercise to find Roger. I know just the fellow to send, though—Richard Waterman. He's the best hunter among us, and he'll track him down."

"Will he want company? There've been fellows come by offering to join him if only I would divulge where he is. I think some were paid by the constable to find out where he is, but some had good reasons. That fellow from Dorchester who was banished the same day as Roger is still down at the inn, and I'm pretty sure you can count on him. No one else wants him, and he was planning on accompanying Roger come spring, before this mess with being chased out."

"I'll find him," John promised.

Relief overcame Mary. She felt a weight lifted. They were talking about plans that they wanted to implement miles south, making the future seem near at hand. Realistically, though, they knew they needed to harvest crops in Salem one more year before the women would be able to join the men down south.

Later, John headed down to the Ship's Tavern, one of the two inns in town. The owner pointed him to John Smith, who was sitting in a corner looking glum.

"I'm John Throckmorton," he began.

"John Smith."

"Roger William's wife suggested I find you."

At this his countenance brightened considerably. "Has there been any word?"

"Maybe. I'm putting together a party to go search for him and accompany him down to Narragansett Bay if they find him. Are you interested?"

"Interested? That's what I've been waiting for! Roger gave me permission to join him the day we were both banished, but we thought we'd leave in spring. I'm from Dorchester, and my wife Alice is upstairs with my children. I came up here to make a plan with him and then he disappeared. I knew if I went home we'd never reconnect, and we have nowhere else to go. So I'm really glad to see you here."

"So you'll be alone, then, on this trip?" asked John Throckmorton.

"Actually, I've a young man indentured to me to learn to be a miller. I was hoping to take him too. He's strong, and he owes me service. I can't very well just send him back to his father. It would be a waste."

"What's his name, and where is he now?"

"Francis Weekes, son of George Weekes of Dorchester. He's upstairs with my wife and two children. We all came down. There's so much hurricane damage in Dorchester, and there's no food there."

"Can you go get him? I've another man due to arrive in moments, and we'll all want to talk."

John Smith went up to fetch Francis, and John Throckmorton settled in to wait for Richard Waterman.

Moments later, Richard entered the tavern with his tomboy daughter Mehitable, twelve years old. Richard was a weathered and muscled man, clearly more comfortable outdoors. His daughter looked to be following in his footsteps, becoming a woman of the wild.

"Welcome, have a seat," said John Throckmorton. "Thanks for coming down on short notice. I need your help."

Richard was the best tracker in these parts—at least the best English tracker. He was a hunter, and his daughter had been hunting with him since before she could carry the gun properly.

Just then John Smith returned with Francis Weekes in tow. They all settled in after introductions.

John looked each man over. "We've heard from Roger, and he's alive. The messenger bringing the news is gone, likely Narragansett or Nipmuc, I couldn't tell. Roger's note says he'll be awaiting word from us with the Nipmuc at the head of the Blackstone River. He clearly thought we'd meet the messenger, as he asked me to resupply him, but the man left the note on an arrow in the door and fled the territory."

"I know where that is," said Richard. "It's about fifty miles from here. We can find Roger if he's still there."

"He says he'll stay, as he's given me instructions and wants word back on my plans. Here's my proposal. My wife and children are ill. I'm just back from Virginia myself, and I don't want to leave again soon. What I propose is that the four of you trek out to meet Roger and have him review the letters I am sending with you. Then one or two of you return. Richard, I'm thinking that's you. We mostly need you as guide and support."

The men nodded, and he went on.

"It's still pretty cold. You'll have to tell these others how you want them dressed, Richard. I think you should start out soon, as the going will get much tougher as the land begins to thaw. It's a lot of wetlands between here and there."

"In fact, we need to go now," said Richard. "The ground will be significantly thawed in another two weeks, maybe a little longer, given the cold winter."

John was pleased that all the men seemed to be going along with this proposal without much challenge. The planning turned to details. Richard kept emphasizing that he would want them traveling light, with no supplies.

John Smith looked worried. "I don't plan to come back. How will I get my things if I travel light like you suggest? Shall I have my wife and children travel with us in midwinter?"

John Throckmorton said, "That's where I come in. I'm going to wait another week or so and then make a run to Plymouth. There I'll be conveying instructions to Roger's lad, Thomas Agnell, who he expects to join us eventually with his entire trading post of supply. When Thomas is ready, I'll hope to make a first supply run up the mouth of the Blackstone, and I expect to find you all there waiting for me. I will not stay, as I want to get back home. Later, once supplies we'll order from Plymouth arrive, I'll make a much larger supply run in and hope to move to the new settlement myself. So, you can tell your wife and children to gather your things, and I'll take them all for you. Anything you can't carry per Richard's instructions will come with me."

"Let's get to it. The weather is only going to grow warmer from here," commented Richard. "I'd like to leave early in the morning."

John Smith's and Francis's eyes went wide. "We better get to work," said John. "Alice will be really surprised."

On the walk back to the house, Mehitable was excited. "Father, can I go on with them? I'd like to help build the new settlement. I don't want to return with you. I'd rather go on."

"We'll see," said Richard, thinking that Mehitable was only twelve years old and a girl. On the other hand, many daughters were apprenticed out before this age. Richard mulled it over. He would like to move to Roger's colony himself if things worked out. If a savvy businessperson like John Throckmorton was behind it, and Roger set up a place truly free to worship in peace, Richard would want to be a part of it. "Let's see how these men behave."

There was one more man on Roger's list. Apparently he'd told William Harris he could join the party. John Throckmorton stopped by his house on the way home. He didn't really know Harris that well, but the young man was a poor attorney's clerk, a much less physically fit person than the others.

"William, we've heard from Roger. Some men are going on a rapid trek out to where he is, and they hope to accompany him down the Blackstone to the Narragansett. I will meet them on the Bay in a couple of weeks. I understand you are a part of the team Roger has put together, and I'm thinking to take you with me on the supply boat."

"I want to go with the men walking out," insisted William after a time. "I want to be in the first party that does the site selections and lays out the plans. I'm sure he'll need more hands."

"Let's go find Richard Waterman, then, and discuss this plan with him." John was thinking that the expedition was getting too large, but he'd let Richard decide.

The men walked to Richard's house, and, on the way, John stopped to retrieve the letters for Roger. William was a clerk, and this reminded John of his duty to get the letters carried out with the men. Then, for the second time that evening, John Throckmorton knocked at the Waterman residence.

Richard answered, and they quickly decided that William Harris was going with the men. Richard was relieved, as now his daughter Mehitable wouldn't be the slowest. This would help balance the group.

John offered the letters to Richard, but Richard turned to William. "William, you can be our official letter carrier. Make sure you bring supplies for return messages. I'm not going to stay long enough, and Roger will surely want to reply to these. There are far too many for me to remember a response!"

Early the next morning before the sun was up, while the ice was the hardest it would be all day, the men were packed and bundled, and Richard got them moving out. The constable was sleeping peacefully. No one was sure whether or not he was really watching for Roger anymore, but they didn't want to take any chances.

Once out on the trail, Richard Waterman found an opportunity to talk to William Harris alone. He and Mehitable had been traveling at about the same speed, and even though both were having a much harder time than the others, they'd provided encouragement for each other.

"William, I like your persevering attitude. You seem like the natural leader here so far."

William was surprised. "Thanks."

"Mehitable is begging to stay with the group when I return to Salem. Roger has a lad from Plymouth who will be joining him, and John has brought his lad Francis. Mehitable's as good a hunter as any lad, and a hard worker. She can cook in the wild, and it seems like the party could use a woman's support. You'd have to watch out for her. Do you want to take on Mehitable as your servant until I get down there?"

"I can sure use some help in the hunting and ways of the wild department." He thought for a bit. He really hadn't planned too far ahead, and now, faced with this long trek, he realized he was in over his head in the wilderness. Mehitable had been with her father in the woods for years.

She could be a big help. "This would be of great benefit to me, actually. I'd be happy to take her on."

"It's settled, then."

They walked on in silence.

Rebecca's next house church was the largest ever. Not only the usual women, but many of their men, attended. Attending for the first time were Mr. John Woodbury, with his wife, Agnes, who was new to Salem. John was one of the original settlers, and his presence gave the meeting a weight and authority it would not otherwise have had. Agnes brought the news of little Anna Grace Williams's letter read at the house church in Somersetshire, at Axmouth, over much of Essex and much of London. Women all over England were praying for Roger Williams and for the towns of Salem and Boston to rise above the ways of Bishop Laud.

The women and men of Salem were cheered. Mr. Woodbury mentioned the letter in general terms to Reverend Hugh Peters. He in turn mentioned it to his wife, Elizabeth, who mentioned it to her daughter Elizabeth, who discussed it with her father-in-law, John Winthrop Senior. John Winthrop Senior was impressed enough that he wrote in his diary of the women of Salem going so far as to be in communion with the churches of England. The Boston and Salem ministers, led by Hugh Peters, were determined to bring the women of Salem under control.

Wilderness Week 8

Richard Waterman found the head of the Blackstone River and yelled an English "hello" across to the Nipmuc village. Roger, among others, heard the English voice and headed out to greet the newcomers, wary lest it be the constable. He was relieved to see his friend Richard Waterman in the distance. The rest were farther back.

"Richard, what brings you here?" asked Roger. "I was expecting Yotaash, the brave we sent. Is the constable behind you?"

"No, I surely hope not, though there are stragglers behind me who wish to join your trek. John Throckmorton asked me to come. We've been walking for two days given their pace. John did not believe the others would find their way without a guide. I'm going back in the morning, now that I've found you in good shape just where you said you'd be. Thanks for that. How are you?"

"Much better now. I should have thought to have you guide me here," said Roger with a laugh. "You've made much shorter work of it. My toes are still black, but my fever is down, and I'm feeling well. How did you find crossing with all the trees down? I left when the snow was higher."

"That is why I brought an ax. Many we could hop over, but some of them I cut a notch in. I forced everyone to travel extremely light so they could clamber over them. You'll find them hungry and weary. It'll be much shorter back for me without them," said Richard.

It was two hours before the last man straggled in, in exactly the condition Waterman predicted: starving and bone-weary. On a more serious inspection, aside from blisters and scratches, they were all healthy and whole and would recover just fine.

Roger and the Nipmuc women had used the time well, and there was a feast ready for the men and Mehitable as soon as all had arrived.

After the evening meal, Roger settled in to examine his letters. Since Richard wanted to leave early in the morning, it would be a late night for Roger, responding to his correspondence.

First he read the note Mary had dictated to John, with John's postscript. He was heartened to hear that Mary and the children were well, especially given the news about Rebecca and John's twins being weak and ill. He hoped that Mary and his children would remain well until he could see them again. It seemed that that might be a long time.

Then he moved on to John Winthrop Senior's note. John was encouraging, saying that he would plan to have peaceable relations, if it were up to him, should Roger settle on the Narragansett. John Winthrop had always been like an uncle to Roger, if not a father, and this was a huge burden lifted. John Winthrop Senior was not always in power, but he was always influential. Roger and John Winthrop Senior had similar backgrounds, both having started with meager resources and both having relied on other, wealthier, men for grooming and placement. Just as Sir Edward Coke had mentored Roger, Henry Rich had mentored John Winthrop Senior. The difference was that Henry Rich was still alive, and in fact had just arranged for a grant of land to John the Younger in Connecticut. Roger valued John Winthrop Senior's friendship.

The next letters were from people in Salem, and some were from the people who were with him now. They'd written and given their letters to Mary, not imagining they'd be in the same trek out as the letters. Nearly to a one, people from Salem thanked him for the tremendous help after the hurricane and professed surprise at his need to depart. He felt loved and missed. At least he didn't need to answer the ones from people who were present. John Smith reminded him that he was waiting on Roger and needed to go with him by spring because of his own banishment. William Harris reminded him that he had promised his wife and son that they could come. Roger looked up. Richard Waterman was sound asleep already, but William Harris was still tossing and turning.

"William, what of your wife and son, and John Smith's family?"

"We've left them in the good care of John Throckmorton, who promises to make several trips down with free passage for our families."

"I see." Roger could not imagine that they'd be ready for families very soon. He hoped that John took his time, and, in fact, he hoped to talk John out of that plan for a while. He thought about how he might say this is in a letter, and finally what he said was just that conditions would be rough at first, and women and children should take their time in arriving. He hoped it was enough.

There were letters from Joshua Verin, rope maker, and John Greene, a doctor from Boston, who were both excited to come as soon as possible.

Each had his issues with Puritan authorities. There were letters of support, offering assistance and allegiance should the settlement be successful. There was one from William Arnold, an interpreter who might be useful to Roger in his new role relying on Algonquian trade; another one was from Roger Mowry, a tavern owner in town. Finally there was a letter from John Francis that sounded on the surface like the others. Roger had never known John to be a friend, and he did know that Francis was a lieutenant for the Massachusetts Bay Colony. He wouldn't answer that letter, for they would use whatever he said against him.

The final Salem letter was from Mr. Woodbury, a good friend and fellow planter. He too thanked Roger for helping the town after the hurricane. He mentioned that he'd finally brought back his wife and that she'd already had news of his predicament in England and that her house church was praying for him. Now that was an eye-opener. Mary and Roger didn't even know this Agnes, of Somersetshire. How did that even happen? It warmed his heart, and then he thought, *Does it mean Laud knows as well?* He shuddered.

The next letter was actually from England, from his sister-in-law Ann Helwys Williams. It appeared that Anna Grace had written her already and that she was heartbroken over his situation and was praying for him. She had gotten his mother's old house church network to pray as well. The Baptist churches, as well as the Dutch Reformed church, were also praying for him. Ann knew someone who knew every good Christian in England, Roger realized. That must be how Agnes learned of him. It overwhelmed him: with that many prayers from the truly faithful, he was lifted high, high, high. With God's wind behind him, how could he fail? A tear came out of the corner of his eye. He looked up, and all were safely asleep. *How do you even answer a letter like that one?* He answered it on his knees, praying to God, in thanks.

There were two letters more from Boston. The first was from his new friend Harry Vane. Harry offered condolences and friendship. He noted that the atmosphere in Boston was worse than ever and that soon they would be after other leaders if things were not brought under control. As a hotheaded young man new to the scene, and likely a short-timer at that,

Harry figured he had nothing to lose except his father's respect, which he said he had already lost. He said he was going to step in and ask them to man up. He sent Roger for comment the draft set of "Civility Rules for Magistrates" he planned to impose in case they were useful to Roger as he formed his new settlement.

The rules were:

1. There should be strict discipline in both civil and military matters. Discipline was critical, given the curses on men's minds after the fall of man in Genesis 3, but it was even more critical in a vast wilderness where the veneer of civilization was especially thin.

2. The magistrates should ripen their consultations beforehand, that their vote in public might represent the voice of God to the people. Government was always put in place by God and was intended to speak with God-given authority.

3. In meetings out of court, the magistrates must not discuss business in the presence of outsiders.

4. Magistrates must end trivial matters quickly and choose weighty matters for deliberation to honor their station.

5. When differences between magistrates did occur, they must:

    a. not touch each other in confrontation, but use only words;
    b. use a respectful tone of voice and speak in modesty;
    c. propound the difference in public by way of a question;
    d. defer the matter to another time, if possible;
    e. after public sentencing, honor the sentence, dropping differences without further distaste;
    f. visit each other privately and frequently so that they will naturally be tender to each other;
    g. honor the governor in all matters;
    h. support under-officers, their own and others;
    i. punish contempt of court severely, as a deterrent.

Roger smiled. He wished he could watch that. If the Privy Council obeyed those rules, England would be a more civilized country. He hoped Harry would be safe. He also realized that, if Harry was successful, he would be bound to support Roger's banishment publicly until it was rescinded. Roger sighed. It was just unbelievable that he had actually been formally banished. These were his friends.

The final letter, the one on the bottom, was from John Cotton. Did Mary do that, or John Throckmorton, or William Harris, who had carried the letters. He was betting on John Throckmorton, and he wondered whether John had spit on it too. Dear old John Cotton! What would he say? When Roger opened the letter, he saw immediately that the tone was different from that of all the others. Cotton said that it was Roger's own fault if he was dead or suffering. He said Roger deserved it and that he should have repented. It just stopped Roger cold, and he was paralyzed in thought and movement. *How could he? Had he never suffered? Where was his compassion?* Roger's toes hurt and his head ached, and he was tired. He wouldn't answer John Cotton directly. *The man was on the run from Laud; had fled England himself; he must know what fleeing in harsh circumstances felt like? Had Laud written Cotton such a letter upon hearing that he was teacher of the church in Boston?* he wondered.

Roger thought about John Cotton for a long time. *The man had always been a wimp, getting others to read in his church from the Common Prayer Book, even though he believed it was wrong. He always kept up appearances and seemed not to understand the importance of guidance by principle. Even though the man was unwelcome England, he had never endured true physical hardship. He has never been in the wilderness. Possibly he really doesn't know.*

Could the ministers of New England be so callous? So evil? It stopped Roger's heart. All remaining human-to-human relationship with them seemed dead at this moment.

He thought on. *I know first hand that John Cotton is not mean-hearted. More likely he is simply convinced that he is right and I am wrong. He expects his letter somehow to turn me back, even at this hour. If that is the case, he is at least honest and faithful and has convinced himself his behavior is the best way* to love me as one of Christ's. Unbelievably callous, and a handmaiden for the devil, but honest. Cotton is misguided, and he is the one that needs correction.* He decided how to answer John Cotton, how to convince him. He pulled out the note to John Throckmorton and added another note on top.

> *John,*
>
> *I need your help. I need you to find a paper I've hidden these many years, to copy it, and to forward the copy on to John Cotton. You can forward it anonymously.*
>
> *The paper is hidden inside the head post on my side of the bed. You will have to take the bed apart and open a compartment that does not appear to open at first to find it.*
>
> *The paper is a translation of a letter I once received from a man in prison. I received it a few sentences at a time on old milk cans, written invisibly. This paper is the coherent whole of it.*
>
> *It is my prayer that John Cotton will come to realize how wrong, and how unscriptural, his behavior is.*
>
> *Mary can help you find where it is, but she does not read well, so make sure you've got the right letter. It's against persecution for cause of conscience.*
>
> *With all compassion, give my love to Mrs. Throckmorton, the twins, and the baby.*
>
> *Roger*

Roger continued to think about his letters and the responses and did not sleep much that night. By morning he was focused on making his new home a settlement set up for those persecuted for their thoughts, and keeping government to maintaining a strong civil peace. With good business instincts, people like John Throckmorton could make the new settlement more successful than the old. He would follow his Savior and find twelve good men. He looked around him. William Harris and John

Smith were not his first choices, but they might do. He needed to recruit. The man he wanted to join him was Richard Waterman, and maybe he could be talked into joining them later. He thought through the letters. Roger Mowry was a good man, but he was not as sure of Joshua Verin. He would hope to recruit William Arnold, who also spoke Algonquian, as much of their dealings would need to be with the Narragansett. That was six, not counting their lads and families, and it was just the first night. He'd continue his recruiting in the morning. The more he wrestled with it, the more he was convinced that he had been preparing all his life for this moment to arrive.

The whole struggle in the court and in the wilderness were most painful developments, like Mary, mother of Jesus, giving birth in a manger. It was a time of growth, when God's purpose was not fully visible.

When Richard Waterman slipped out at dawn, Roger was sound asleep.

CHAPTER 27

Saugus, March, AD 1636

Yotaash found his eighteen-year-old nephew Weekan overjoyed to see him. He was ready to be married to Ale, his betrothed, and now he would have a respected authority from his tribe to witness the event.

He found Aunan in poorer spirits. Aunan wanted to return to the Narragansett to find his bride, and he didn't want to come back to the Massachusetts afterward.

Yotaash had news of his own for everyone that changed everyone's plans. At the campfire with Jole, Webcoit, Weekan, Ale, and Aunan present, he laid out his case.

"The Pequot and Mohegan have become murderers and thieves. When Mohegan Sachem Uncas passed through our land, he brought tribute for his hunting, as he should have, and was friendly to our faces. But in the woods he took two of our women given us from the Pequot and raped them, and when they dared to fight returning to his camp with him, he killed them as a deterrent to other women who might resist. He was not honorable. Miantonomoh and Canonicus asked me to come and get all your able braves, as he will need a show of force by summer to get them back under control. Our strategy has long been to let them fight each other, but now we need to teach them respect for the honor of the Narragansett."

"That is a very serious offense. What has provoked this action, and are you certain it was not English who did this to your women?" asked Webcoit.

"Uncas has taken many captive women. Our women resisted. Our women have honor. He killed them. Uncas is not an honorable Algonquian. He's been claiming to have a right to rule over all the Pequot as well as the Mohegan, and using every maneuver against Sassacus, now that Tatobem is gone. He does not fight Algonquian style but rather adopts the worst of the English ways. He seeks exclusive partnerships with the English, to counter Sassacus's Dutch ties, but he seeks out the dishonorable killing English, not the peaceable English. " By this he meant that Uncas was choosing soldiers with violent track records, not the hunters and traders who worked peaceably with the Algonquian.

"I see. Is there more?" asked Jole.

"Some of the Nipmuc have talked of switching allegiance to the Pequot down by the Bay. I have just been on a tour to all the Nipmuc clans to assure our protection. We need to keep the Nipmuc to the north under our wing. We will likely have to protect them."

"Finally, Pessicus has been seeking trade with the Mohawk. An honorable alliance with the Mohawk would shore up our western front. Pessicus has delivered one load of wampum to them already."

"That is a tall order," said Jole. "Nanepashement could never accomplish anything lasting with the Mohawk. Be careful. They can be as treacherous as any Pequot. You have my blessing to take any braves you need for this effort, but you cannot take the ones with formal jobs in town. The English would not approve of this."

"We do not want our actions visible to the English at this point anyway," replied Yotaash.

Jole turned to Ale. "Do you want to travel with these braves and then stay with Oonue until it is time to return?"

Jole was steps ahead of everyone. She knew she could count on Ale to return, whereas the others were all imports into her clan. If they did not return, she was looking at the end of her clan as a population separable from the English. She knew this, but she would not admit it to any of these men. She also believed this was the route most likely to be successful in having Ale produce children in the near term.

For her part, Ale was excited to go. It was unusual for a young woman to travel out of her horticultural region. She looked forward to seeing Oonue again.

As the group headed south, Yotaash took Weekan aside and told him the real reason underlying his trip. Their Uncle Wekeum, the older brother of their father Mascus and of Canonicus, lay deathly ill. Canonicus had requested that the family members gather, in anticipation of examining them for fitness to lead, and of assigning new responsibilities. The issue with the Pequot and the Nipmuc was very real, and it would be used to test character as part of the family rites that would soon occur.

Wilderness Week 9

A big rainstorm broke the ice in the Blackstone two days after Waterman departed.

Now that he had company, Roger was less comfortable living with the Nipmucs. His companions knew no Algonquian and were not respectful of Algonquian culture. He wanted to move out.

They hired braves to bring enough canoes to carry the parties to the mouth of the Blackstone in one group and set off. They travelled from the land of the pigeon Nipmucs, as the Narragansett had named the people they were with now, to the land of the people called the Pass-through-Nipmucs downstream. Roger was told that the northern Nipmucs had gotten their name because they reproduced so rapidly. He wondered whether it was also because they were easy targets, sitting like pigeons, with no defense against the stronger tribes around.

The Pass-through-Nipmucs got their name because they held the territory surrounding the major rivers that wound toward the vast meeting grounds of the intertribal councils at Narragansett Bay. As a result, they collected tribute—usually choice pieces of meat or other wealth—from all who passed through. They were the toll collectors of the Algonquian "highway."

The trip took longer than two days because they stopped to hunt. Since they were in another tribe's territory, it was customary to visit and pay out part of the game as tribute to the home tribe, and that lengthened the trip even more. It was just becoming spring, and small quarry were awake and feeding. There was grass for the deer in the meadows. Fresh game and wild onions were starting to appear.

Roger selected a site just south of the nearest Nipmuc clan's region in an area once owned by the Wampanoag—the region he'd purchased from Massasoit four years back. He should have no issue with Algonquian in occupying this territory. From an English perspective, the land was undeveloped but technically inside the Plymouth portion of the patent from the king.

Upon arrival, Roger set the men and lads to work, clearing fields and constructing makeshift shelters. Spring was coming. That meant rain, and it meant planting.

Boston, March, AD 1636

Thomas Shepard was the first minister in good standing to question the extremely popular John Cotton. If Harry Vane was the new younger voice in politics, Thomas Shepard was the new voice among the ministers. Listening to Harry Vane's now famous rules for the magistrates and ministers, Shepard first questioned Cotton in a private letter.

Cotton's ministry focused on the grace of God, on undeserving sinners being forgiven. Shepard believed that Cotton was too lax about the required works of the people—the outward signs of salvation that should be seen as fruit from any legitimate saint. Cotton would let all sinners into the church to hear and repent, to experience God's grace, and acknowledged that even the elect fall and must continually receive forgiveness, or grace.

Shepard wanted to demand that the elect bear immediate and continual fruit or be cast out of the church.

When Cotton did not respond to Shepard, the sermons down in Cambridge became pointed barbs at Cotton, critiquing his sermons. The critiques began to have support in the community, and Cotton found himself on the defensive.

If Roger Williams would attack Cotton for enabling persecution, Thomas Shepard would attack Cotton for not persecuting enough ruffians.

Puritans were viciously attacking Puritans, no Laud required. King Charles would be smiling. As complaints made their way back to England, he didn't necessarily help to resolve them. He actively thwarted proposals by Laud to spend more money to control the colonies, taking the tack that the religious dissenters would weaken each other. In all cases, he continued to maximize trade profits and thereby mercantile tonnage and poundage taxes.

Salem, March, AD 1636

Richard Waterman was quick in his return, since, in order to travel light, given the fallen trees, he did not even stop to hunt. He successfully delivered the return letters to John Throckmorton and made a report.

"Roger looked good, for all his reported challenges. He claims to have been sick and starving till the Nipmuc took him in, out of food and out of sanity. The man dragged his canoe all that way, replete with goods to trade. He did ask me to keep his route and his condition private, so you and I need not spread it far. He doesn't want the Nipmuc bothered with yet more company."

"How did he react to the men you took?" asked John.

"I don't think those were his first choice of friends, frankly. On the other hand, he was starved for company, and they will do him good. I'm sure what he really wants to see is your pinnace rounding the entrance to the bay and bringing him supplies and decent lads to help him create a settlement. It's great country down there. If he's successful, perhaps I'll join him in a couple of years."

John read his own letter and made his way to Mary.

"Roger's well, and I've got a letter to read you, Mary," he said with a big hug for her. This was the news she'd been waiting to hear, and she was weak with relief. "He's already giving me assignments! The first is here in the house, a matter of extracting papers from a bedpost."

"Oh, my. I've never seen him put papers in the bedpost. Are you sure?"

"Yes, let's go look."

After spending several minutes dismantling the bed, they found what he was looking for.

Mary was clearly surprised. "He must have packed those away back in England before we were married!" she exclaimed.

"Possibly. I really don't know. He asked me to copy them and send them off and return the originals to their hiding spot. Do you mind if I copy it now and then we'll put your house back together before I go?"

"That's fine. Let me get you a bowl of stew while you wait."

"That would be wonderful, Mary. Thanks."

John copied the papers and reconstructed the bed, thinking about the next steps in their paths. "Mary, I'm going to head on down to Plymouth in a day or so and then over to the Seekonk/Blackstone area to find Roger. Do you want to come with me? Others will be taking the ride down and plan to stay."

"Oh no, John. I'll wait. I'd rather be up here near Rebecca with the babies so young. Roger told me to wait until he was well established. He told me to plant up here this year. Their crops may not be all we'd want down there this year. You'll make more trips, won't you?"

"Yes, it seems I've a new stop on my way to and from Virginia now, at the mouth of the Blackstone. Don't worry. There will always be a place for anything you need."

"What will happen next? Do you know?" asked Mary.

"I'm about to run him a load of supplies, and he's asked me to pick up Thomas Agnell in Plymouth and to bring Joshua Winsor along. Roger's even given me a letter for Winslow at Plymouth, so there are no surprises. He seems to count him as a friend. We'll see. Against my better judgment, I'm going to bring John Smith's wife and children as well. John made me promise, as they've nowhere else to go. Finally Joshua Verin and his wife Jane plan to come. It is likely to be a lot of physical labor, so it is wise of you to wait," answered John Throckmorton.

"I think I'd better, although I'll miss Joshua's labors here. I'll stay for now, as I want to plant here as we planned."

Two days later John's pinnace set sail and made good time to Plymouth.

Wilderness Week 12

The men continued to dig and wrestle with the land. The days were long, the work wearying, and the sleeping conditions were little better than camping on the ground. The weather was in the forties often now, but storms could still be bitter cold. Game was plentiful, and fish was abundant. It was a good country. The first priority was to get a food supply started, so until crops were in, there would not be a focus on building a town.

The sun was out, and the field Roger had planned was so large it seemed that the labor would never end. It was so warm that sweat was pouring from his brow as he struggled to dig out particularly tenacious tree roots. Always using her hunting skills, Mehitable silently popped out of the trees and was by Roger's side before he was aware of her.

"There's a small ship. Come and see."

Roger happily dropped his ax, and the man and the girl headed down toward the mouth of the river. Half an hour later, they could see it in the distance, and he immediately recognized one of the Winthrop vessels, the *Blessing*.

Roger and Mehitable started waving and shouting, even though the pinnace was surely still too far off for them to be seen or heard. The men onboard were watching the shoreline through scopes, and after a while the ship was heading straight toward them.

A rowboat was lowered, and John Winthrop the Younger and another man rowed to the shore.

"Roger, you are looking great for a city boy who just spent the winter in the wild." John the Younger was elated to have found Roger so easily.

The two men hugged.

"You are our very first visitor," Roger said, beaming. "We've actually been here at the Blackstone's mouth just over a week, so we are lucky you didn't beat us to the Bay."

"Don't worry. We'd have kept at it until we found you, dead or alive, or an Algonquian who knew of you. I'm on my way down to Connecticut to join the settlement I'm supposed to be running. I'm really glad to have to found you so soon, as otherwise I might have gone on and come back to search later," he admitted.

"How's that settlement going for you?" asked Roger.

"It is contested land. A couple years back, Father informed the Dutch guy in charge of their fort, Jacob Van Curler, that the English king had given us patent, but Father says they said right to his face that they won't give an inch." The truth was that Winthrop was strategically trying to outmaneuver the Dutch for Algonquian wampum trade, in order to drive away the Dutch out over time. "Now we're constructing a bigger, better fort, and we've got Lion Gardiner to defend it. I know Father is looking forward to your good relationships with the Algonquian here so that between us we'll force out these Dutch for good."

"The rulers of these tribes outdo Machiavelli for intrigue. Choosing our allies is the most critical decision. Just remember, the guys who approach us first may be the weakest tribes, hoping for strategic help. I was approached first by Massasoit, and I learned the hard way that he is in charge of very little," advised Roger.

"It would seem to me the Dutch would be seeking out the Narragansett now that they've ruined it with the Pequot in that Tatobem mess. We'll need to be better friends to them than the Dutch, and I can't do that from Connecticut," said John the Younger. "My job is to befriend the Pequot, while Mason befriends the Mohegan."

"The Dutch were seeking out the Narragansett even before the Tatobem mess, from what I understand. The whole reason the Dutch killed Tatobem in cold blood was that he'd executed a Narragansett delegation seeking Dutch trade. The Narragansett don't fight that way, and they demanded that the Dutch punish this dishonorable way of proceeding," said Roger, repeating Yotaash's view of the situation. "It was the only way Canonicus would enable continued trade with any Dutch, they say. My view is that the Dutch got suckered into killing off the archrival of the Narragansett, the Pequot grand sachem. The Narragansett say he—Tatobem—was sachem over twenty-six other Pequot sachems. It's as if the Spanish conned the Dutch into executing King Charles. Who are the pawns, and who are the players? If we're not careful, they'll use us next. Canonicus has the last laugh, if he can use the Dutch to weaken the Pequot."

"Will the Pequot take retribution for Tatobem?" asked John the Younger.

"I haven't seen that. They still seem to pursue the Dutch, but also want to pursue English trade. They are known for their vengeance and their violence. The Pequot are stronger in numbers, but from what I've heard, the Narragansett strategy is to let them fight each other over who will succeed Tatobem and become weak in the process. The Narragansett here prefer to stay out of it, though they can't really. They are married into it already in several places, apparently. They're all stirred up, that's for certain," said Roger.

"The Narragansett elite are surely the better-looking people. The guys are even taller than the Nordic peoples, and their muscles ripple like those of the racehorses I've seen in the Levant. Martha said the women die less often in childbirth than our own women. They seem to live longer, grow taller, and look like a bigger, stronger human species than the rest of us. Did you notice?" John's scientific eye was intrigued.

"I've heard many a woman and man alike remark on how undeniably handsome they are, especially when you start to realize that their men commonly reach eighty and ninety years old. Other tribes have more scars of smallpox, perhaps from the earlier epidemics the Narragansett managed to avoid, but you're right about the height. I've heard around the campfire that the Narragansett elite many generations back brought the milpa. That's the way of planting corn, squash, and beans with fish, which so many tribes use now. Perhaps they were actually better fed for many generations?"

The truth was that the Narragansett elite descended from a small ruling class called the Inca, among other names, whose tradition was to join or create an elite, technologically advanced upper class that would eventually rule the local tribes. These elite Steward rulers took on a local name in each place yet always retained the culture of their ancestors. They were the people in the New World who originally came from the Polynesian Islands across the Pacific Ocean, rather than through the Siberian Strait. They invented the milpa among other advances and they spread over much of South America, the plains of Mexico, and southeastern North America. Lasting impacts included 1) the concept of voluntary, fluid pools of followers (rather than ones determined by genetics, violence, or territory)

315

ensuring leaders were competent and creating a robust balance of powers; 2) sophisticated counting methods that originated in South America and relied on knots in ropes or nets; 3) development of domesticated, food-producing species like corn, tomatoes, and potatoes. In fact, ancestors of these people domesticated the banana in the Old World, even before they came to South America; and 4) the concept of weaving metal into cloth for a strong, waterproof mesh.

Some technology was lost to this particular Narragansett group even as newer changes were adopted and integrated. Already the Narragansett were quick to adopt steel tools and wool cloth into their repertoire without ever allowing the strongest members of the ruling class to be ruled or assimilated into English culture. They would rule or die honorably. Their power depended on the quality of their rule, the superior technology they imported, and the loyalty of their subjects, not sheer inheritance or numbers of followers. They could not afford to engage in violence that was deadly to their followers. The weakness of the elite was intermarriage, as they sought to keep bloodlines pure even as they migrated and lost touch with kin. Their bloodline was also their key strength. As master horticulturalists and species developers, they knew it. They needed fresh blood for robustness, yet they wanted to retain bloodlines for transmission of their superior physique and prowess. New leaders were selected with visible traits of the ancient elite, as well as extreme competence, not birth sequence. Roger and John could watch this in action, but without knowledge of genes or of human history on the New World continent, they could not fully understand what they were seeing.

"Yes, Lion's got his hands full. Pequot, Mohegan, and Dutch. I don't think I'll be bringing the family down while the situation is this tense. Little Anna Grace wanted to come in the worst way. Tried to blackmail me, your niece did. Appears she saw me leaving and digging out the compass and thought I was up to no good."

"What did you tell her?" Roger knew that John the Younger didn't want anyone knowing about his visit.

"The truth. She's your niece. I swore her to secrecy, though, on pain of return to England. She wouldn't agree until I promised something in return. She's a tough negotiator that one," said John the Younger.

"What did you promise?" asked Roger, frowning.

"To convert her apprenticeship from being Elizabeth's maid to being a doctor's assistant, and soon. I actually think it's a brilliant idea. I haven't told Elizabeth about our deal, so don't tell Mary. I've found I can trust Anna Grace with anything, and she doesn't tell anyone, not even Elizabeth. She's really progressing in learning Martha's remedies, though I have to translate them to English from code so she can read them. Elizabeth isn't too fond of her cleaning skills, so she will be happy as long as I provide a replacement," finished John the Younger.

Roger turned, hoping he was out of Mehitable's earshot, and said, "I hope you're not teaching Anna Grace the secret code?"

"Out of respect for you, I'm not. She's smart enough, though. It's tempting."

"I did want to thank you for the compass. It came in handy in helping me get to the Blackstone. It was still a long trek, but at least I only went in circles when I could not see. May I return it now?" asked Roger.

"Yes, that would be wonderful. Throckmorton has most of your money for supplies, but I'll give what I brought, along with some sheep as gifts for your new settlement. Let's get unloaded and upriver, and I'll take the compass on the way out," said John the Younger.

"Sounds like a fine plan." Roger turned to Mehitable and realized that he'd neglected to introduce his unusual companion. "By the way, this is Mehitable Waterman, Richard's daughter. She's our hunter and has been has been keeping us well fed. Richard's left her to be William Harris's servant, and her job is to teach Harris some wilderness coping skills."

The two men had a hearty laugh. The reverse roles of master and servant were funny enough, but then there was the sheer hopelessness of teaching frail William Harris survival skills. More likely, Mehitable would just keep William Harris, and the rest of them, fed.

John the Younger turned to the man who accompanied him in the rowboat. "This is John Greene, surgeon. He hails from Boston, since crossing the water last year."

Roger reached out a hand and said, "Glad to meet you. I got your letter."

"Likewise. But I'm not from Boston anymore. I'm freshly banished. I spoke out for tolerance within the Boston church one too many times, and they couldn't tolerate me," said John.

"You qualify for my settlement, then. You will fit right in." Roger wanted to have a surgeon join the team. "Will you stay, or are you set on Connecticut?"

"Judging from the conversation, it will be more peaceable here. I'll need to bring my family soon, and while I may travel to a battlefield to triage wounds, I don't want my family anywhere near that."

"It's fine with me if he stays," said John the Younger. "We'll know where to bring our wounded, and we'll know where to find him."

"It's settled, then. You are no longer just our first visitors. Dr. John Greene is promoted to our first settler since coming downriver," said Roger.

"Do you happen to need an assistant?" John the Younger asked Dr. Greene.

"I may now, I just may," answered Greene with a smile.

"How many do you have here?" asked John the Younger, gathering now that Roger, William, and Mehitable were not alone. "By my count the Greene family is the fourth: we've got the Smiths, the Harrises, my own, and now the Greenes. Each family has a lad working as well, or one on the way. I hope to add the Watermans and Throckmortons to my list, if they are willing. I will be looking for twelve fine families in all, following the footsteps of Christ as we plant this kingdom where he, and only he, will be head of the Church." Roger said this smiling at Mehitable, as they'd already discussed Roger's hopes of recruiting Mehitable's family to follow.

John the Younger stood back, in awe. "And I thought my dreams were big. I just want to gather engineers to create a vast ironworks comparable to none. You want to rebuild how men put together society."

"What God will do, I cannot know. I can only hope to serve him where he has planted me in his providence. We are called to rekindle his true church."

After John the Younger was gone, Mehitable walked with Roger back to the field, deep in thought. When they reached the field, she stood around as if she wanted to say something but didn't quite know what to say.

Roger eventually looked up and asked, "What are you puzzling about?" He expected that she had seen some novel tracks in the woods, for she was a keen observer and often noticed things that others missed.

"What is God's providence?" she asked. "Is that word in the Bible?"

"The word *providence* isn't exactly in the Bible. The Bible does say in many places that God provides. God's providence is how God works with his creation. He created the laws, but his active providence is required to keep them working—to keep the very essence of our bodies alive. He has a plan for each of us, a plan that will help us prosper and build his kingdom if we work with him. He opens the womb that gives us birth, he gives us breath in the morning, and he calls us home when we die."

"We worked hard to get here. So who got us here—us or God's providence?"

"Both. God uses his creation to accomplish his plans. Even the miracles are his work, using his laws, which we cannot see—if you look carefully, what you see is that they usually speed up or strengthen some process he has designed in the natural world. He never breaks his own rules. Our work is required to accomplish his providence."

"What if we don't?"

"Then he will call another to accomplish his ends. It is always our choice. Yet his plans will not be thwarted."

"So you think God wanted your toes to get frostbitten in this cold wilderness? God wanted you to suffer miserably for trying to cooperate with his providence?" asked Mehitable.

"I think he must have a much bigger plan, and therefore my suffering must have a purpose—a lesson he needs me to learn or a change in place he needs me to make. It will all work out for his glory. You will see," answered Roger.

"What do you think God was trying to do, then?"

Roger paused. That was the question he'd been asking himself. His words started flowing before he really knew where they would end.

"We can trust that God's providence placed you and me meticulously, according to His plan for us. He must need me to have personal friends in the Narragansett ruling family. Listening to their stories, we know they hail from an ancient civilization. I feel now that we are not just to carry the Gospel to them, but that this people must also know something we need to learn. Their leaders, even though from a ruling family, are not like our European rulers. Each brave is free to choose which leader to follow. Just as each man is free to cooperate with or fight against God's providence. Maybe he wants us to learn how they govern."

He went on.

"If I look further back, God has given me training in ways my family, my teachers, my church could not have planned, all of which I'll need now."

"Like what exactly?" Mehitable was fascinated now.

"For example, I was born at a time when there was a revival of reading the scriptures. For a thousand years the Church hid the scriptures behind a closed altar and in a foreign tongue that few could understand. My mother's house church was part of a revolution that rekindles the original power of Christianity by recognizing that God calls to individuals directly through his unadulterated Words in the Bible. Scripture conveys the authority of God and teaches us directly how God wants us to cooperate with him in building his kingdom. Scripture says the Holy Spirit dwells within each Christian, and when those indwelt persons join together to form a Church, the spirit is the most powerful of all. The authority of God doesn't come from a pope or a king; it comes from the Spirit arising from gathered Christians reading scripture."

Mehitable nodded, and Roger went on.

"While I was still home, I learned a shorthand code from the Dutch that enabled me to get an apprenticeship to the one of the brightest legal minds in our nation. I was able to attend court and learn how the English govern. That man spent his whole life shrewdly but persistently establishing the rule of law. His signature accomplishment was something called the Petition of Right, which lays out the principles of the rights of the people to be ruled by just laws, not just the whims of a king. My mother could not have planned that; only God could have planned for me to have both of those training experiences. And in England even now, King Charles isn't enamored of the Petition, and all England is still suffering from his unhappiness, yet here I am on this blank canvas with a need to create a government."

"If that's so, he must have big expectations of you. How will you ever meet them?" asked Mehitable.

Roger agreed, and one piece of him wanted to say, "I'm scared too, and I don't know!" But he didn't, because he certainly didn't want to look weak in front of a girl.

Instead he said, "God provides the tools each in its time. He had the Dutch teacher at school teach me about skis in a place that had no snow.

He provided Algonquian and you to provide for our food, when all Boston would have had me starve. The man who just left and his poor deceased wife are two of the best engineering scientific minds I've ever known. Now Anna Grace is learning Martha's ways from her extensive notes as John the Younger translates them for her, so that Martha's gifts are not lost. I've watched John puzzle out designs and build them, only to fail and try again. John the Younger always claims he is never tired until he's tried and improved a design at least ten times. God must want me to be like that. God provides, in an awesome, unpredictable, powerful way that we can only see in hindsight. God always provides for his people who are cooperating on his plans."

"What kinds of things does John try?"

"I think he is on try number eight or so with his windmill design. He thinks we can get more power to draw well water, run our mills and port lifts from the wind, as well as from fire and water. He's got novel approaches to building shipping harbors, and, as you heard, he is planning his first attempt at an ironworks. John and Martha were two of the most detailed observers of facts and methods I have ever seen. John studied Francis Bacon's experimental approach and will likely put his principles into practice more carefully than old Bacon ever could have. In the same way, I must study the Algonquian and learn what to copy from them, as I study every good gift of learning God puts in my path."

Mehitable worked beside Roger silently for a while.

"I feel we should call our new settlement Providence," she finally concluded.

"Maybe so," said Roger with a smile.

"I'd really like to meet Anna Grace someday," she added wistfully. It would be nice to meet another woman who thought about something besides babies all the time.

Will Roger's approach work? she wondered.

322

When John the Younger wrote about it back to Elizabeth on the boat that night, he certainly thought it was dubious. So far, Roger had attracted to himself the destitute and banished in Harris and Greene, the hungry miller from Dorchester, and some lads. And there were more where those came from, each making their way to Roger Williams.

John the Younger was more generous than his father. His father called the new settlement the latrine of New England.

CHAPTER 28

Plymouth, March, AD 1636

Ed Winslow was examining Roger's note to him. John Throckmorton waited patiently, letting the man think through his answers.

This was a crucial moment, as Roger was on Plymouth territory. While Plymouth was not under the Massachusetts Bay Colony directly, they were allies and cooperated closely on many fronts. Ed's history and background led him to want to support Roger. He had come to the New World from the church in Leiden. He'd empathized with Johannes during the dispute with John Robinson, and privately encouraged him.

Ed Winslow's years in the New World had left him hard and practical. He needed the Massachusetts Bay Colony. He'd seen how Salem was treated just for hiring Roger Williams without asking permission first. He had no intention of being in direct violation of Massachusetts Bay Colony decisions and edicts.

He'd read the letter three times. Eventually he came to a decision and penned a response that he handed to John Throckmorton. John was on his way without much discussion, but John could see the trouble brewing in Ed's eyes, and his heart sank. *What now?* he wondered. He would wait for Roger to tell him the contents of Ed's letter.

It took John an hour to get to the old trading post site where Agnell still kept shop.

"Good day, Thomas. How's business?" The two traded often. Thomas brought in Algonquian goods for the New World and in return supplied them with English goods from Throckmorton's ships.

"Business is booming. Wait till you see what I've got for you." The two men looked over a set of fine furs and the milled logs Thomas had prepared from trees that had been downed near Dorchester. "How are you?"

John Throckmorton shared his and Roger's fates. Then he turned to the real reason for his visit.

"Thomas, Roger wants you to pack up and move the shop—all of it—down to where he's making a new settlement. He promises it will be at least as lucrative as this site, and he says when you are free in a year he'll make you a leader and landowner in the new settlement."

"That's big news. It will take some time," said Agnell.

"I know. I plan to relocate my base as well, you know. My debts will be paid about the same time as your indenture ends. We'll become freemen together. We'll build bigger business than ever before. Let's move and get you packed before the men of Plymouth recognize their loss. Can you get Algonquian help to load, so that we don't alert everyone to the extent of your departure?" asked Throckmorton.

"Yes, I believe I can. Let me work on it," answered Agnell.

Wilderness Week 13

Within a week of John the Younger's visit, John Throckmorton arrived, as promised. The fields were dug, and planting was nearly complete, and the men were at first overjoyed to see Throckmorton arrive with milled lumber and other desperately needed supplies. John Smith was very happy to be reunited with his wife, Alice, though it would be challenging to accommodate her and the two children, five-year-old John Jr. and four-year-old Elizabeth. Joshua Verin and his wife, Jane, along with Thomas Agnell and a couple of other lads they'd recruited while loading the boat were exploring the scene.

Then Roger read the letter from Winslow. He sat down and read it again.

Then he gathered the small community together.

"Ed Winslow intends to be our friend," he began. "However, he cannot support us on land within the boundary of the Plymouth Colony. We must move."

There were audible groans and exclamations. The men who had been there were bone-weary from digging out fields they'd just planted, and they were incredulous that they were being asked to abandon them.

Roger let the implications sink in before going on.

"We are not in any hurry. He asks us to relocate in an orderly manner and then he intends to be our ally and to work peaceably with us."

"As a result, we will not unload the boat today. Instead, John Throckmorton and I will be leaving for some days to scout the territory and to negotiate with the Narragansett. For this means we must move off the land I've purchased and must acquire new land." To himself he added, *It's a good thing John the Younger brought me some of the proceeds from my house sale. Otherwise how would I accomplish this? God provides.* He looked at Mehitable. They would find the place that God intended.

"Mehitable, will you accompany us?" Roger asked as he left the center of the group.

"Certainly, sir. I'd be honored."

John Throckmorton and Roger Williams scouted around the bay, aided by Mehitable's keen eye. They picked several spots and then Roger had John drop Mehitable and him off near his smaller canoe, and they paddled up to seek out the advice of Canonicus.

Roger hadn't seen Canonicus in years. He only knew where to find him because Yotaash shared the family news that Canonicus was with his oldest brother Wekeum, who lay deathly ill. Roger had intended to pay respects soon, and now he must find Canonicus if he was to establish his settlement peacefully. He asked Mehitable to track some choice game, and within the hour she felled a young deer. They butchered it together and packed up the choicest parts to take for tribute to the sachem. The rest they packed away for their return.

Deep in Narragansett territory they found the family gathered. From a distance Roger shouted hello to the tribe in Yotaash's dialect, waiting until there was a response before coming within arrow shot. This was Mehitable's first organized experience with Algonquian in their towns. She'd been with her father when they had shadowy encounters in the woods, each watching closely and retreating before seeing very much. She'd been in towns where Algonquian were dressed as English servants. This was very different. This was a real town with Algonquian homes and families.

She was an immediate attraction at the event. Juanumo, Canonicus's nephew, noticed her right away and couldn't take his eyes off her. Roger was asked who this fine young woman was by more than one family member.

"Is she your wife?"

"No, she is my assistant."

"Is she your daughter?"

"No, she is a good friend's daughter."

Canonicus was pleased to see Roger and accepted the tribute while looking Mehitable over with an expert eye. He viewed it as auspicious that Roger would show up at this key family moment when his sons and nephews were competing. Canonicus was looking for a minor English sachem to make strong. As he listened to Roger's story of needing to move across the bay, he realized that he'd found a promising candidate.

As he watched Mehitable admire his men, he believed he'd found the other element that had eluded him. He needed high-status females for his men, in order to integrate cultures. It was completely foreign to Canonicus that Mehitable's own people would refuse to have her marry even a high-status Algonquian man. This would theoretically be so not because of his looks but because the man was not a Christian. In truth, though, it was pure prejudice against the foreign that made the Puritans look down on the Algonquian. Canonicus asked Meiksah's wife Matantuck who was also Juanumo's sister, to look out for the girl.

Juanumo was looking for a wife. His first wife had also been his niece. She bore him two daughters and then died in the most recent smallpox epidemic. Juanumo was the one of the highest-status men in the tribe, the eldest son of Canonicus's sister Oonue the Elder. He thought Mehitable could be beautiful someday—something he had never thought about any other Englishwoman he had ever seen. Tall and lithe, graceful from years of hunting, she was the picture of beauty by Algonquian standards, even if she looked like a tomboy to the Englishmen. She was young, though, and he needed a wife now. On the other hand, high-status wives took time to negotiate. His sister Oonue had already offered to add his daughters to her tribe of children in the meantime, if need be. He continued to watch Mehitable.

Mehitable thought Juanumo was the most handsome male she had ever encountered. She could not stop watching his every move, for she was fascinated. She wanted to learn everything about these people, and about him. Just as she had begged her father to allow her to stay with Roger in the Nipmuc camp, that night she asked Roger whether she could be allowed to stay with these people to learn their ways.

Roger had been busy with ceremonial rituals of respect, telling his story of the need to move, and of the possible sites. He was completely oblivious to the reasons for the interest in Mehitable's status. He was annoyed by her insistent questions this time and told her that she was obligated to serve Harris, as her father had arranged. She would return with him this time. Mehitable was a tracker. She also knew how to return at will. A bright girl, she spent the rest of the visit learning Narragansett Algonquian.

After a day together during which Matantuck watched Mehitable learn, admiring her attention to detail, she told Mehitable, "You will always be like a daughter to me. Come and visit us any time."

Canonicus adopted Roger and treated him like another of his nephews. He was sitting at a family council where no outsiders were invited. Even Massasoit, a more distant relation, was not present. Massasoit had been eliminated from the competition already—destined to remain a minor sachem in the overall region—and Canonicus was focused on remaining potential successors to his position. Roger watched the young men spar for power, and he negotiated his own situation. When he and Mehitable left camp, Roger had been granted a most choice section of Narragansett country. More, he had deepened a relationship with a family that would last a lifetime.

Wilderness Week 14

The land grant enabled the little settlement to move fewer than five miles by land. It was farther between the sites by canoe, as the Blackstone wandered a bit before reaching the Bay. They were moving across the Blackstone to its eastern side and then camped between the northern side of a stream feeding the Moshassuck River and the western side of the Woonasquanticket River. Each of these rivers was already tidal in this region, so the only drinkable water was from the stream. The new location was much closer to a deep finger of bay water reaching north, and farther from the quiet of Roger's favorite canoeing country. Seafood was abundant, but the fields needed to be farther from town.

The land grant reached upriver several miles and down as far as the shores of Aquidneck Island, but Roger chose to be close to the fields they'd planted so that the people could steward the fields for a one-year crop as well as spend their time building houses. The new fields would be targeted for the fall growing season. After all, Winslow said they didn't need to rush.

They were near the hill where the sometime allies and sometime squabbling Wampanoag and Narragansett met annually for games. There were established trails to the flat camping and to the choicest fishing spots. In truth, the reason Canonicus was so generous was that the land was only recently his, and fights over it were frequent. Having his ally, Roger, permanently stationed there would drive others away. Massasoit was not at all happy about this arrangement. He'd lost not only the land he sold to Roger originally, but his hopes of taking back this more valuable land. He complained to his English friends.

Ed Winslow got messages from the Massachusetts Bay Company, ordering him to force Roger farther on, based on the news from Massasoit to them. This time, Winslow ignored them, preferring to be a peaceable neighbor.

The men worked to get housing structures in place, as well as barns and a working mill.

Alice Smith watched her children and complained. She was a city girl, still traumatized from the hurricane in Dorchester, and this camp lifestyle was not her cup of tea. Mehitable could not stand her and spent most of her time in the woods and on the seashore. She'd already been up to see Matantuck twice, and her Algonquian was becoming passable. As far as the English knew, she was hunting. She always brought back great quantities of wonderful food.

Juanumo made a casual visit to observe the new settlement on his way to Block Island, where he would be taking on the role of temporary Narragansett sachem over the Eastern Niantic, where Miantonomoh once ruled. His daughters were with him, and he was taking his time before he put them with Oonue's children on Block Island. The eastern Niantic on the island and the mainland would now be paying tribute to him. He tracked down Mehitable and spent a lazy afternoon with her and his daughters, showing them all how to catch and prepare eels and lobster. They caught the silver belly eels with spears, the girls stirring them out of hiding places and Juanumo making the kill. They cleaned them and soaked them in fresh water to remove the poisonous blood. When the eels were safe to touch, they rubbed them down with leaves to remove the slime. Next they half-cooked them on the grill and hung them out to dry.

Juanumo explained that for them to be edible, they could steam them, salt them, or smoke them. Since Mehitable planned to feed hers to the camp right away, she steamed them with lobster, using leaves that Matantuck had taught her about to spice the mixture.

Mehitable's feast for the settlement that night was thanks to Juanumo's skill, but the English were none the wiser.

Miantonomoh was headed inland. He'd been promoted in the clan to Canonicus's emissary to the English, a position that put him in line for succession to grand sachem, possibly still behind two of Canonicus's sons. Juanumo was also in a career-building position. He did not expect to stay on Block Island, as it was technically Miantonomoh's land. Inland territory could eventually be Juanumo's, but for now Meiksah managed it, with Matantuck as squaw sachem Yotan, Meiksah, Weekan, and Aunun were spending time preparing for war. To most of the English, it appeared that Miantonomoh was sachem now and that Canonicus had disappeared.

At the end of week fourteen, the Smith family was the first to move into a real home. They all hoped Alice would stop complaining. Informally, they stopped calling their site camp and started calling it Providence.

CHAPTER 29

Boston, April/May, AD 1636

John Cotton received the anonymous letter via messenger. On reading it, he was pretty certain that Roger Williams was the sender. That told him that Roger was alive and well and deserved a response. His response was even more stringent than his original provocative letter; in part it was a defense against the pressure Cotton was feeling from the likes of Peter and Shepard. He sent the letter back the way it came.

Harry Vane's first visit to Anne Hutchinson's house church was something like a campaign stop. Men didn't attend these meetings, so his presence was odd. None of the women could vote for governor, so any influence would be exercised through their husbands. Likely, if he'd been married, he'd have sent his wife.

Harry Vane would someday inherit a Privy Council seat in England. As such he had the status of royalty in the women's eyes. His youthful good looks and smooth manner belied a clever mind that had already outmaneuvered every other politician in the colony. He'd been as good as his words, expressed to Roger, using Hugh Peter and other ministers to side with him in forcing the levels of discipline and civility to rise. The word from their husbands was that he was the man to bring people together and that he had been successful in forcing Dudley to be less severe and Winthrop to be more disciplined. In getting both these men labeled negatively, he'd brought each down a notch, making a pathway in which he hoped to rise. At this house church he was smiling and hugging, and he even kissed a baby. He didn't teach, he didn't advocate, and he also didn't hear anything in the least controversial. The meeting was an afternoon Bible study among women, most coming from having attended church in the morning. Anne's discussions were insightful and scripture-based.

The women invited him to return any time.

Two weeks later the magistrates chose him to be governor of the Massachusetts Bay Colony, to take office on May 25.

On May 30 Harry Vane took the reins, and he immediately ordered the colony to show unity on the Salem church distraction, a political payback for the support he'd received from Hugh Peter. The order was that all house churches in Salem must cease meeting at church time, and church members must show up at church the next Lord's Day and the Lord's Days following or be in jeopardy of excommunication. John Cotton was sent to Salem to preach the first sermon. His popularity was a real draw and filled the pews not only with Salem members but also with his faithful followers who were willing to travel. Hugh Peter's daughter, Elizabeth, now living with her in-laws in Boston and attending Anne's house meetings, arrived with Anne Hutchinson.

The pews were overflowing, the sun was shining, and greetings were warm. It buoyed the spirit to hear God's people singing in unison. People realized they'd missed this church. John Cotton chose to speak on Jeremiah 5:5.

"The yoke is what binds each individual ox to a team of oxen that will pull a cart. The ox is only effective as part a team; no individual can alone pull the cart. Similarly the church is a team. Our yoke as followers of Christ is obedience to the scriptures, which command the unity and fellowship of his church. This message is not just for the people of Israel, but all people of all ages."

Never mind that the Church of England was separated from the Church of Rome. Never mind that most of them had been chased out of the Anglican Church as well. These people were starting afresh; they were going to do it right this time. The irony wasn't lost on anyone. What would be different this time? Men were still fallen and their minds untrustworthy, given the noetic effects of the fall. Brows wrinkled, and faces reflected puzzlement. Was John Cotton turning into Bishop Laud?

John Cotton was a tremendously powerful preacher, and he could see he was losing his audience. He slowed up a little in his delivery and continued as a father to a child, sweetly and lovingly.

"God has given you leaders, and he has spoken to them. He knows they know his requirements, and he knows when they are following His commands. It is your duty to follow your leaders, all of whom have bathed in the cleansing waters of repentance, all of whom are standing before you as one ready to take up the yoke again and follow the Lord. If you do not yoke with us, hear what happens to the unrepentant."

He paraphrased what happened next in Jeremiah. His tone became crisp, and he spoke with power the next lines, which he hoped would hit home.

"Every single one who is going out from God's people is torn to pieces.

Every single one … is … torn … to pieces."

"God's peoples are ordered to go up on the wall and to destroy. Not to wound, not to be lenient, but to destroy the unrepentant. There will be no completion, no salvation; these branches will be turned aside, as they are not Jehovah's."

"They were never Jehovah's."

Immediately his voice turned sweet again. "Yet each of you is a little lamb Christ would search long and hard to find and bring back to the flock, the herd, the team, the Church. Christ accepts all those who repent and covers them with his grace. Show that you are his. Repent and return. Stay with your Church."

All were impacted by this sermon. It was masterfully delivered, and the church was full in the coming weeks. In the wilderness of New England, there was great safety in togetherness.

Harry Vane's masterstroke was yet to come. It was at Harry's suggestion that Elizabeth and Anne were invited to Hugh Peters's house so that his wife could host a special dinner for them, along with the notable women of Salem, including Rebecca Throckmorton. A women's dinner was an unusual move. Normally they'd be serving the men. This one was strategic. In preparation, Harry proposed a set of rules for successful house churches, and Hugh Peter reviewed them in order to make them a touch more conservative. Harry got Anne herself to buy in and agree to advocate them, and Hugh Peter asked his daughter to do the same. The rules were:

1. All people if they are physically able should attend the established church.
2. Bible studies should not be in place of church or at the same time as church.
3. Women should lead Bible studies for other women, with men invited only as observers to ensure doctrinal correctness.

The dinner was a success, and, under the pressure of her peers, Rebecca agreed to the rules. What choice did she really have? Harry Vane, Elizabeth Winthrop, and Anne Hutchinson made a powerful team, and they were friendly and persuasive. Rebecca wanted to be a member of this elite group of leading women. When Elizabeth asked her a huge favor, she agreed to it.

"I understand that your husband's ship is expected back to Salem any day now. Will he be heading south soon?" asked Elizabeth.

"I do hope so. You have more ears in Boston than I have here in Salem."

"I have an urgent need to reach John the Younger quickly. We think the baby is dropping already, and he was told it wouldn't be here until August. I so miss his company. He's so busy with the Saybrook settlement. I really want him to be here for the baby's birth. I've a letter. Would your husband perhaps be the fastest way to deliver it? I am sending word via every possible channel. He'll have to travel nearby to get to Virginia anyway, right?"

"I'll do my best. I'll let your father know when it's on its way. Yes, it means so much to have family close by for a birth."

"My mother is to return to Boston with me until the baby comes. Between her and the in-laws we should be fine, but it's not the same as having John here."

With the exception of Harry and the Winthrop men, even Roger's friends began to take a wait-and-see attitude, watching to see whether Roger would be torn apart and destroyed.

As for Harry, he was doing whatever it took to consolidate his power, and he had gotten a title even his father had to respect. Now he could begin to woo the magistrates to reason, he hoped. John Winthrop Senior was made deputy governor.

Providence, June, AD 1636

Structures were complete for all of the people, and most resembled a barn. New fields were outlined, and some were planted. Mehitable and the Narragansett women tended the old fields occasionally, gathering as they saw fit, but the others were focused on the new. There was common property, but no common structures were underway. Councils and worship services were held outdoors.

Roger gathered them together each Lord's Day morning for a service on the hill below his new home. In the afternoon he held a service on the same hill in Algonquian. Even if there was no speaker of Algonquian present, he practiced. Soon, however, there were many Narragansett in his household and in others' houses as servants. These daytime residents made his story-telling about the white man's God known. His Algonquian preaching was popular and welcomed, and soon his Algonquian gathering was larger than the English gathering.

On this Lord's Day, Roger's sermon, delivered outside, as always, dedicated the new settlement as Providence. God had been merciful and bountiful in his Providence, and for this they were all grateful. In their gratitude, they dedicated the church in Providence to be headed by Christ alone. No communion with any other church had been requested, and they would request none. No individual but Christ, who speaks through scripture, would have authority in this church. Many might be its preachers and teachers, but as individuals their words meant nothing unless two or three other Christians concurred. All matters would be decided by scripture, and the first decision in that light was that the sacraments of this church would be dictated by <u>Hebrews 6:2</u>. That meant a focus on repentance, faith in God, cleansing rites such as baptism, and the laying on of hands. Roger's mother, Alice, and Thomas Helwys would have been proud. Perhaps HH would have been hopeful.

The next day, Roger called the first town hall meeting. He laid out principles for the civil government, one of which was borrowed directly from Sir Harry Vane. The rest Roger believed to be fitting, as he interpreted scripture, for keeping a civil peace while preventing persecution for acts of conscience. The colonists all thought they resonated thoroughly with the principles. Yet not one really foresaw the practical implications. They were, however, committed to the noble experiment.

The civil principles were:

1. No government is qualified or authorized to mediate between man and God. Therefore, the civil government is limited to the second table of commandments, commandments dealing with the civil peace (e.g., do not steal).
2. Government is charged by God with keeping the civil peace and must exercise strict discipline in civil and military affairs.
3. False worship is an odious sin and will not be required, encouraged, or tolerated.
4. All spiritual truths are first typed out in the physical. The physical settlement will therefore endeavor in all its dealings to practice the prior three principles even when they cannot see or do not like where they appear to lead (e.g., they must allow Turks—should they show up—to worship freely).

5. Algonquian peoples are people worthy of receiving the gospel and justice and of being allowed to worship freely.

The greatest challenge of all was principle four—living out the physical details in a fallen world.

CHAPTER 30

Block Island, July, AD 1636

John Oldham and John Gallop watched each other's backs.

Gallop owned a twenty-ton fishing vessel he liked to operate out of Boston Harbor when he wasn't captaining other men's ships at sea. Gallop lived on his own island. His wife wouldn't follow him to the New World and remained in England. Gallop was alone and lonely while in New England but for his companionship with other traders. Today, he had a man and two young lads with him as his crew, and he intended to go from Connecticut to Long Island to trade. The wind shifted suddenly, and he was put off his route to the east, where he could see Block Island. He spied a small boat adrift in the distance and drew close to say hello. As he approached, he recognized John Oldham's boat.

Oldham's pinnace was covered with people. Gallop knew that Oldham normally had a crew of four lads—two English and two Narragansett. Today, however, there were natives all over the deck. He and the boys counted, and after a time they settled on there being fourteen different individuals visible, all native. Something was amiss.

Oldham's claim to fame was pulling a knife on the Plymouth Colony leader, Miles Standish, and getting himself banished. He'd had good reason. Plymouth authorities intercepted some letters he'd written to people in England complaining about them—letters carefully hidden in a man's shoes, or so he thought—and after that they'd been out to get him. It was self-defense against a very angry and out-of-control leader, but nevertheless he stood no chance, given his unpopularity. Before he left town, he'd been forced to run a gauntlet with pilgrims using the broad end of their muskets to beat him. Thereafter he kept to himself, living in his pinnace and trading with the Algonquian and amassing wealth. The Narragansett saw Oldham as a lucrative trade contact for Block Island, and they didn't want him trading with their chief rivals for Niantic loyalty, the Pequot.

The Pequot had about twenty families loyal to them on the western side of Block Island, and the Narragansett had about the same number loyal to them on the eastern side. The relationships were strained; the Pequot had been testy ever since Tatobem's death, and one of Canonicus's military objectives was to drive the Pequot away from the island. Canonicus offered Oldham Block Island "ownership" if he would agree not to trade with the Pequot. "Ownership" to Canonicus meant "use of," as long as Oldham's agreement with him was kept. Oldham agreed to the deal, and it was Juanumo's job to ensure that promises were kept.

John Oldham wasn't about to be ruled by any one Algonquian tribe. He took Block Island as offered but continued to trade with both Pequot and Narragansett. Juanumo's Pequot background enabled Juanumo to travel among the Western Niantic. He spoke the language and knew the Pequot braves. He was comfortable with his mother's Narragansett family and his father's Niantic-Pequot family. Both families were elite, and Juanumo, as a young man, was calculating his opportunities on both sides, knowing his unique value as the liaison, yet also knowing that political forces would drive him to choose.

From the entrance to a great salt lake that nearly divided the island in half, Juanumo lurked and watched Oldham trading with a Pequot boat at the north tip of the island. As a new, young member of the Narragansett ruling family assigned to the Niantic people, Juanumo needed a bold act to give people a reason to be loyal to him, to sway families away from other leaders and toward him. Killing clearly treacherous English would fit his need perfectly. The Niantic would understand that the same fate awaited them if they gave him tribute and then made trades against him. Canonicus would have to have respect for his abilities.

Juanumo chose a team of five Niantic family heads or sachems that had been known in the past to deal with the Pequot but were not admitting to doing so now. He had credibility with the sachems specifically because his own father had Pequot blood, yet he was accepted as Narragansett. The two highest-status sachems brought three men each, and each of the three others brought one of his clan for the attack. Juanumo would have two Narragansett with him, and in addition, he knew the two Narragansett working for Oldham and could expect them to be loyal once the raid started or face worse than death.

Juanumo's better-than-Machiavellian training showed through in these calculations. Canonicus and Miantonomoh and their close relatives and loyal followers in the eastern Niantic population were not included. He wanted them to be able to deny involvement. If the affair was a success, he would give western Niantic the credit, and they would be loyal to Juanumo. But they would also attract revenge, which he hoped to focus on the Pequot if he could. If the revenge occurred as he forecast, once again the Narragansett ruling class in the person of Juanumo would have gotten one strong enemy to weaken another strong enemy with only a small investment.

Juanumo waited patiently for the right timing. He wanted a daylight raid, with another English boat on the horizon. He wanted the event to be seen by the English. Today the wind was blowing back toward Block Island, making a good getaway opportunity if he used the wind after the raid. Heavy seas were also expected, but not until later in the day. They therefore planned for some of the sachems to return to Block Island before the torture ended. While he waited, Juanumo prepared. He contemplated every angle and performed ceremonial rites that would ensure his strength.

Juanumo spotted John Gallop's boat while it was still far off, early in the morning of July 20. He authorized execution of his raiding plan. With a large canoe full of men and covered with swords, pikes, and guns, they paddled out. They approached Oldham's pinnace in a friendly manner, as if for trade.

Oldham invited the Niantic/Pequot braves aboard as he had many times before. Once aboard, the men grabbed the boys as choreographed ahead of time and sliced Oldham's leg with a sword, knocking him to the deck with one move. Goods were loaded to the waiting canoe, and the boys were tied below with net so that they had to watch what happened to Oldham. With the exception of the braves assigned to make sure the English boys watched the torture, the rest, including Oldham's deck hands, were sent up on deck to see if the watching boat drew near, so that they could sound a warning. When all was in place, Juanumo and the other sachems boarded the boat.

Juanumo and two specially selected western Niantic sachems took over the torture. Since he was a traitor, Oldham's torture was ritually planned to last for days. An especially strong and healthy man could last around three days. Oldham feared this next ordeal. The sword gash in his leg was deep, but he hadn't really felt it when it happened. This next ritual was timed and designed to ensure that he anticipated pain, experienced unbearable pain, and suffered the after effects of blood loss and hopelessness. For a minute he couldn't help but watch and then the knife pierced his skin, and he was in agony. He hoped the storm would shorten his ordeal, and he prayed. He wished he'd been to the Watertown church where he belonged a little more often, and he prayed that his maker would forgive his absence, among other sins. After a while he was numb and mentally elsewhere, and the torturers knew just when to take a break to chant, and when they had his attention, they started in again.

Juanumo was performing his first Pequot torture ritual, a rite of honor. Juanumo did not look like a man with human feelings. He looked instead like a man in a trance, using trained, skilled movements as he would have to butcher an animal. The difference was that Oldham was not dead, and the movements were performed slowly, ceremonially. Juanumo had been at cutting off Oldham's hands for hours and they hung by just the bone. He decided it was time to switch the pain point, as Oldham was barely conscious, and they needed to wake him up.

In fact, Oldham was conscious—terrified and crying—though he was doing his best to look brave and to pray in front of the boys. The issue was no longer the braves in front of him; he'd worked his way through that. Now he was confronting his own death. He'd apologized for behaviors on his pinnace of which he knew God wouldn't approve, both silently and aloud, for the boys' sake. But the terror now was that he was very aware of a gray, rainy, cold fog that seemed to envelop him, and he was afraid that God was just a delusion, that he was apologizing to no one. If that were true, there was no one coming for him as he left the earth. In the next instant, he knew that his doubts were a sin, and he was afraid lest he lose the mental discipline to deny his doubts, give thanks for blessings, and ask forgiveness for his last sin. That was the terror. What would be his last thought? What if his last thought was fear that God does not exist, and then He did? Oldham was in a terrifying battle for his soul.

Juanumo stood back and had the western Niantic take over. Each was awarded the privilege of separating Oldham from one of his feet.

Before Oldham's feet were completely severed, the alarm was sounded. Immediately the western Niantic sachem, Audsah, with sword in hand cleaved Oldham's head.

Oldham heard the alarm in the distance from a place mentally far away. God was merciful. Oldham's last perception was of a flash of light, and he believed with all his heart that it was God coming to get him. His misery ended.

The nets were taken off the boys and thrown over Oldham's body, and Juanumo, the English boys, and the two Narragansett sachems loaded into the canoe and took off with the booty for shore. The western Niantic, including five sachems and all the men, were on the deck. Oldham's Narragansett, who knew how to operate the pinnace, were ordered below with swords for their own protection. Juanumo wanted to make sure the pinnace returned to shore.

John Gallop suspected that Oldham was dead. The pinnace was not responding to his hails, and the normal crew was not to be seen. Then he saw a canoe heading rapidly ashore. The natives who were on deck wielded guns, pikes, and swords. Gallop fired a shot across the bow, and

343

still there was no response. He had two pieces of artillery and two pistols, with only duck shot for ammunition. He shot what he had and grazed the deck, forcing the braves to run for cover behind equipment on deck on the far side of the pinnace. Gallop, having a much larger vessel, rammed the smaller one and nearly upset it. Six of the fourteen were knocked overboard and were drowned. Now, instead of fourteen visible and an unknown number below against four English, it was eight to four. Not good enough odds to board. Gallop backed his vessel away.

Gallop watched awhile from a distance, while instructing his crew to fit the anchor onto the side of the vessel like a battering ram's spear. When they were ready, they rammed Oldham's pinnace again, effectively nailing themselves to her. One of the lads shouted, "Why, she's only an inch thick! Will she fall apart?"

"We're going to find out."

They raked her decks, fore and aft, with duck shot, but there was nobody in sight to hit. Eventually they let themselves back off from her, as they were afraid of harming their own vessel. They lowered the rope to their anchor and stood off again to watch. Five natives surfaced to survey the damage, and they tried to detach themselves. The seas were getting rougher. The pinnace was unstable and groaning, and she listed suddenly. The natives were knocked off into the sea, though the English would later claim they jumped. Now it was three natives they could see versus four English. Time to board, very carefully. They drew in the anchor and got close again.

One native surrendered. They bound him and tossed him into the small hold. A second native then surrendered, and they bound him. Gallop, however, had seen this trick before. Two bound and kept together would untie each other. He could not leave them, but he had no more room in the hold, and he did not have the manpower to watch over them. He threw the second one, a sachem, into the sea.

As Gallop and his men explored the pinnace, they came across Oldham's Narragansett crew barricaded with swords in the cabin. They had a good defensive position, and Gallop decided not to challenge them. He knew they were the first Narragansett he'd seen, and he wondered whether or not they were enemy. At this point he also knew it was white man versus Indian, and he was not about to let them out.

Gallop found the still-warm body of Oldham, stark naked, skull cleft in two, and his arms and legs mutilated. Sickened for their friend, the four English put Mr. John Oldham into the sea with a prayer. The men returned to their own vessel.

Gallop next tried to tow Oldam's pinnace ashore. This proved impossible in the rough seas, and night was falling. So he took everything of value, including the sails, and released the pinnace to the sea. Eventually she floated up to the Narragansett shore with the two Narragansett still locked in the hold and the one bound Niantic sachem aboard. This was not the ending Juanumo had in mind, but it would do.

The men and the pinnace were captured by Miantonomoh's braves.

Juanumo waited for Gallop to leave and the weather to calm, and then he made rapidly for Miantonomoh. He left the two terrified English boys with his brother Wepitamock. He needed to perform some spin control.

Gallop, eyewitness to kidnap and murder, was equally rapidly making his way west to the English authorities at Fort Saybrook.

John Gallop pulled into Saybrook in his ship late on the twenty-first to find that John Throckmorton had been at Saybrook since early morning. John the Younger was already preparing to return to Boston, given his wife's letter, and when he heard about the murders, the trip became even more complex and urgent.

Throckmorton's ship was big enough to fit John's horse, and, given the urgent news, he agreed to turn back immediately and carry Winthrop to where Roger was encamped. From there, John planned to ride like the wind home for the baby, rapidly gather news from Boston on what to do about Oldham's killers, and then return to the fort.

Woods North of Providence, July, AD 1636

Canonicus, Miantonomoh, and Juanumo were caucusing alone, with no ears to listen, plotting a strategy.

"We need to get to Boston and make sure they understand it wasn't us," said Miantonomoh. "This could start a war!"

"We need to say to Boston we've done the retaliation on their behalf. So, therefore, Miantonomoh, you need to take a very large show of force to Block Island and retaliate. Take Audsah back with you and behead him in front of his people. Then use the canoes to load up the booty and return. Bring the captives, and our women and children, back here, so we are prepared for any strike that may occur. Leave the braves on the island, and dismantle the wampum factory. That way you can hide our braves from any English army and surprise them with force or wait for them to leave," ordered Canonicus.

"What will we do with you, Juanumo?" Canonicus looked at him for long time. He was proud of him and yet was concerned that he had brought awful tribulation on all their people. "There were English boys, along with the wampum? Did I hear that correctly? What have you done with them?"

"They are safe with Wepitamock."

"We can assume that Gallop has riled the English about these boys, yes?"

"Yes."

To Miantonomoh he said, "Make a big deal of rescuing them. Make us the heroes in their story upon their return."

"Now, Juanumo. You know that torture is not our way. It is your father's heritage, I know, but it is not our way. Here is what we will do. You will take the honor name that you have earned among the western Niantic and Pequot people. That will increase your status. But I want a promise from you that you will not repeat this tactic when you are in my service, not ever again. You must do something of value for the English to redeem your status among them and endear them to us. Do you understand?"

"Yes, sir."

"What will be your honor name?"

"Ninigret."

"So you are a warrior bringing death to your enemies." Yotan had shaped Ninigret's outlook. Until now, Ninigret had wanted no part of the English. Now, Canonicus was asking him to grow, to be a bigger man than Yotan. It was a big opportunity. Canonicus wondered whether Ninigret would be able to rise above hating enemies, to learn to manipulate enemy emotions as a weapon.

Miantonomoh was bristling, as any status gained by Ninigret was status he was losing. Especially if Ninigret began to endear himself to the English, Miantonomoh's role could decline. He decided to make sure that didn't happen. He would be the best advocate the English had ever had, and they would know it.

Miantonomoh said, "We should send the two Narragansett braves from Oldham's pinnace with one more brave to Winthrop to be the first to inform him of these events. If the boys are your messengers," he said, looking at Canonicus, "it will mean they cannot be killed without starting a fight with us. At the same time it will be a sign of our respect for them. We should do it now, even before I return."

Ninigret agreed reluctantly, as he did not trust the English. "If they do kill them, the third brave should return and report."

Miantonomoh headed to Block Island with seventeen canoes, Audsah, and two hundred braves.

Ninigret stayed until they left, making sure the braves were able to act as witnesses, having seen Miantonomoh's grand force heading to Block Island, and then he accompanied the braves heading up toward the English.

Providence, July, AD 1636

"You can't ride overland to Boston just now. The Pequot and Wampanoag are stirred up, and it's dangerous," exclaimed Roger. "The Pequots' issues are with the Narragansett over trade treachery, but the Wampanoags are unhappy with me for settling in land they hoped to take back from Canonicus someday." Roger and John the Younger were standing in front of Roger's newly constructed home atop the hill. There was much activity around them, and there were wigwams perched in his yard.

"Actually, some of the Pequot have issues with me. My brother Stephen and I have been pushing them toward agreements Vane wants us to make, and they don't seem to like us. They are an angry people, and they really hate that Eliot has Mohegan living with him right outside of Boston. It was a major sticking point. Do you have a faster way for me to get home? I've got to get the news up to Boston, and I've got to be there for the baby. Once I get there, the English will be riled up too. Perhaps the Narragansett would like to assist the English in our revenge," said John the Younger.

"That's quite possible. I'll work on that, if you like," Roger said with a sigh.

"Why so many wigwams here?" asked John, looking around.

"I've gotten a reputation as being able to help their children heal. I encourage them to come, and I preach to them on Sundays in Algonquian. They don't stay too long, but Mary will be coming as soon as her harvest in Salem is in, and she strongly prefers them to have wigwams to stay in so that they don't come into the house."

John took off, and just an hour later the three braves arrived, apparently alone. Roger interrogated them briefly, wrote Winthrop a letter translating what he'd heard, and sent them on their way. He noted to Winthrop that he was a little suspicious of the boys and that it seemed there were some Narragansett sachems involved, though not Canonicus or Miantonomoh. He also explained that because the boys had been sent as Canonicus's representatives, the English could scare them but must not harm them. Roger wanted to prevent Vane and Winthrop from making an honor error.

John the Younger hadn't gotten far when a group of Pequot braves succeeded in scaring his horse into dumping him, and he was captured. This was not a good situation, John realized. The young Pequot saw a chance to rival Puttaquappuinckquame's fame among the Pequot people by killing an English. The horse was a particularly valuable prize.

These were teenage braves, hotheaded, out to impress the other braves, and unaware of what the authorities in their tribe might wish. John was quickly bound, and the Pequot were sharpening their knives when Ninigret and the Narragansett braves came upon them.

Ninigret sensed an immediate opportunity. Here was an Englishman he could rescue. The man would owe him tribute for life, and he would have his repulsive English endearment. Canonicus would be satisfied. He and his braves backed off without being detected and prepared their weapons as they planned a battle strategy.

They waited, lurking in the shadows, till John the Younger had a chance to be thoroughly terrified but before he was actually harmed. They first picked off the Pequot brave on watch in the woods and then they rapidly and silently shot with their arrows the men around John the Younger. When they were all down, Ninigret stepped out of the woods. He untied John the Younger, and they made awkward introductions. Ninigret began to realize just how valuable a save he had made. His plan was working out better than he'd imagined.

John the Younger understood Ninigret to be indicating that he was Canonicus's nephew and had Pequot blood. He realized that this man could be a long-term asset to his Connecticut plantation. John the Younger also knew he would be tied to Ninigret for the rest of his life. He did not know that Ninigret was involved in the Oldham murder, and Ninigret had been careful to ensure that Oldham's braves never really saw him involved. John knew he would owe tribute of some form to Ninigret each year. Right now he was glad to promise it. The two shared a meal and decided to keep their relationship quiet. Ninigret was relieved to find this way to satisfy Canonicus, and he believed that a private relationship, in addition to Miantonomoh's more public role, could benefit everyone.

John Winthrop the Younger departed toward Boston. *The baby almost lost daddy today,* he thought. He shivered and galloped a little faster.

Ninigret disposed of the Pequot boys, as the Pequot must never know about this incident, or he would lose all his recently gained Pequot status. Of course they would know that the boys went missing, but they would never know the culprit or the circumstances. If he was masterful, perhaps the horse tracks would suggest to the Pequot trackers looking for the boys that it was an English who had caused trouble. As for John the Younger, all he would ever say, to English or to native, was that Ninigret saved his life once, and he would not say when. For now, Ninigret thoroughly cleaned up the evidence and tracked John home to ensure that he had arrived safely. John the Younger was the most valuable English to Ninigret now. John the Younger owed Ninigret, and Ninigret and his extended ruling class family would be motivated to support John the Younger for the rest of his life.

Providence, July, AD 1636

John the Younger arrived home on July 23, in the morning. His first stop was to find his father and Harry Vane and update them with Gallop's disturbing news and Roger's view of it.

Also nearing Boston, Ninigret stayed in the woods and sent the three braves into town. The three braves went to Winthrop first, while John the Younger was in the household. Without saying why John the Younger vouched for the braves character and encouraged his father not to only to not to make an honor error but to let them go back to their people. After conferring with the magistrates, Winthrop wrote Williams a letter to be dispatched via the braves. The letter said that they were sending the two braves that had been on the boat back out of respect for Canonicus but that they reserved the right to expect them back again as prisoners. Unstated was that, given the braves' role in saving John the Younger, the issue of their return would never be pursued.

Winthrop Senior's letter to Williams went on to say that they expected to hear of the revenge on the islanders and that Williams should take care lest he be on the wrong side of a war with the Massachusetts Bay Colony or caught in the crossfire. He wondered privately whether Roger would be destroyed, as Cotton had implied.

John the Younger's second move was to find Elizabeth. She was already in labor.

Elizabeth the Younger was born the next day. John decided to stay awhile. In truth, he'd had enough of Connecticut, and his commission was up in a few months. He had no desire to leave his daughter. The sheer drop into a normal family situation overwhelmed him, and it took time to relax into the rhythms of daily life in Boston.

For Anna Grace Williams, John's return was a relief and a joy. Her responsibilities as a lady's maid were routine, indoors, and dull. Her primary relief was that John Winthrop Senior was teaching her to ride and to shoot a bow and arrow, something he was also teaching his younger children. She alternated between life as a servant and life as the tomboy niece of John Winthrop's friend Roger.

When John the Younger came back, she was pulled to him like a magnet to iron. "I hear there's fighting down where you were. Won't they need nursing help down in Connecticut? You promised me a new apprenticeship as a nurse."

"It's no place for a lady."

"That's what you said on the ship. There is always a place for a lady who can help people heal."

On another day, she asked, "When will we get to move out of Boston? I thought I'd see the wilderness and meet natives, but all I see is the floor when I mop it."

"That's not fair. Father says you are quite the rider, so you must be getting out."

"Yes, I'm thankful for all he's done for me, truly I am. But I want to ride somewhere farther than just our garden. I know I can help people, not just this one baby and her mum in this house."

John the Younger started to think about returning to Ipswich. He attended court and watched the correspondence fly between his father and Roger Williams and wondered whether he should place Anna Grace near her uncle if he took Elizabeth north. Roger was likely to have casualties to attend to, and John had already seen Algonquian congregate for treatment on the hill that formed Roger's lawn. Roger never turned anyone away, considering himself and his plantation a refuge for all in need. Anna Grace could really help down there, and he did need to keep his promise to her if he was to retain her trust. He wrote to Dr. Greene, offering Anna Grace as an assistant.

Boston, August, AD 1636

Miantonomoh rescued the English boys and put on a show of treating them well, as requested. He personally transported them to Boston, where he returned them. There was nothing he could do, however, to erase the terror of their stories or reduce the trauma they would experience periodically for the rest of their lives. Miantonomoh had severed the head of Audsah, the sachem who actually murdered Oldham. He claimed that the rest of the Pequot had drowned and that Oldham's crew did not deserve to die. Much of what he had done was the Algonquian traditional way—much show, a ceremonial killing, and a lesson taught.

When the report of only one casualty in Miantonomoh's revenge spread, the colony freeman pressured Vane to do more to revenge the killing of the English. They didn't feel an adequate job had been done to deter future events. Endicott was dispatched as general with four captains and ninety volunteer men. One of the captains was Captain Underhill. His mission was to kill braves but spare women and children, first on Block Island and then among the Pequot. The latter was ostensibly in retaliation for Stone's murder. Massachusetts Bay Colony had seemingly forgotten all about his drunken piracy. For the outraged, it was English versus native.

Williams's next letter to Winthrop was painfully similar to the one Winthrop had received from Lion Gardiner, who was in charge of the fort at the Connecticut's mouth.

Williams's letter said that Endicott had made a complete mess. First he hit the wrong side of the island and burned down eastern Niantic people's homes. What was he thinking? Canonicus was considering declaring war against the English over their barbarous behavior.

Winthrop agreed that Endicott had made a mess. While over forty Niantic pummeled the troops with arrows as the pinnace approached shore, as soon as one English landed, the Niantic disappeared into the brush, never to be found. Two days of searching turned up nothing. The English settled for burning empty homes. The Niantic believed that the English were acting without honor, worse than the worst of the native tribes.

Lion Gardiner's letter wasn't much better. The Underhill force swooped up the Connecticut River, destroyed homes and stole children, and only killed thirteen braves. The Pequot were so angry about the thirteen braves that they were picking off English one by one as they hunted and fished. Gardiner forwarded the hands and feet of a fisherman he'd been sent. One man was burned alive, and another tortured with hot coals. The bravest man of all lived for three days after his hands and feet were severed. Even the Pequot reported respect for this "stout" man. Now Gardiner was sending out English hunting dogs—mastiffs—to sniff out snipers when anyone left the fort.

Vane wrote to Williams to ask him to figure out how to make peace. The English couldn't really afford a war with both the Narragansett and the Pequot simultaneously. They would do what it took to pacify one or the other.

Providence, August, AD 1636

John Winthrop Senior wrote a private letter. He'd repented to the magistrates for his previous leniency and was doing his best now to show his unity with the group. With the clear love and gentleness of a father questioning a son, he now asked Roger six questions. Asking questions of leaders with whom you have differences was now the preferred politically correct style, and on the surface Winthrop was just putting it into practice. In reality, he was deeply interested in the answers. He would have loved to restore Roger to the Massachusetts Bay's good graces. Roger had already shown that he was a real asset in Algonquian diplomacy, no matter how Endicott's mess worked out.

Roger was struggling to think through succinct responses to Winthrop's recent questions. Unlike Roger's sermons and speeches as civil administrator, these responses were written.

Roger's letter reads:

Sir, Worthy and Well Beloved,

I was abroad about the Pequot business when your letter arrived and did not receive it immediately.

I thankfully acknowledge your wisdom and gentleness in receiving so lovingly my late rude and foolish lines [with respect to the Colony's recent military endeavors]. You bear fools gladly because you are wise.

I am touched by the love and faithfulness in your letter and cannot but believe you would love me as a child of God even were I Turk, Jew, etc.

Your six queries are welcome, my love forbidding me to surmise that a Pharisee, Sadducee, Herodian or other intending me ill wrote them. Rather, I choose to believe that your love and pity framed them as a physician to the sick.

He that made us these souls and searches them, that made the ear and eye, that sees and hears all, he knows that I do not lie. In his presence I have sadly sequestered myself to his Holy Tribunal, to answer your interrogatories. Begging from his throne those seven fiery lamps and eyes, his Holy Spirit, to help the scrutiny, desirous to suspect myself above the old serpent himself, and remembering that he that trusteth in his own heart is a fool. <u>Proverbs 28.</u>

I ask that you take my answers seriously and give them double diligence, as double weights of the sanctuary implore us to do.

1. *What have you gained by your newfound practices?*

   I confess that if a man's system of counting is used, what I have gained is the loss of my friends, esteem, and ability to maintain my family. If I count by the method of his Excellency Jesus Christ my Lord, then I know I have gained the honor of one of his poor witnesses, though in sackcloth.
   To yourselves and others of God's people yet asleep, this witness in the Lord's season at your waking will be prosperous. The seed shown will arise to enable the greater purity of his kingdom on earth, through greater purity of the ordinances of the princes of the kings of the earth. To myself, through his rich grace, my tribulation has brought some consolation and more evidence of his Love. I sing Moses's song and that of the lambs, in that weak victory which by his help I have subdued the beast. <u>Revelations 15:2–3</u>.
   If you ask for numbers, my witnesses are but two. <u>Revelations 11</u> (I see yourself and myself agreeing in witnessing newfound practices.) Once proven physically, how many millions of Christians in heart will call on these truths?
   Gideon's army was 32,000, but cowardice returned 21,000. Ninety-seven hundred men were sent, and but 300 showed up to do the battle. It may irritate and exasperate if I compare your company to Gideon's, so I will stop.

2. *Is your spirit as even as it was seven years ago?*

I will not follow the fashion either in commending or condemning myself.

You and I stand at one dreadful tribunal. Yet what is past I desire to forget, and to press forward toward the mark for the price of the high calling of God in Christ. I accept that price may well be life itself, as it was for Christ.

As to the evenness of my spirit: toward the Lord, I hope—no, I long to know and do his Holy pleasure only, and to be ready not only to be banished, but to die in New England for the name of the Lord Jesus; toward yourselves, I have begged of the Lord an even spirit, and I hope ever shall maintain one. First, I pray to reverently esteem and tenderly respect the many hundreds of you. Second, to rejoice and to spend and be spent in your service according to my conscience for your welfares. Third, I rejoice to find the least swerving in judgment or practice as I experience the help of any, even the least of you. Last, I mourn daily, heavily, unceasingly, till the Lord look down from heaven and bring all his precious living stones into one New Jerusalem.

3. *Are you not grieved that you have grieved so many?*

    I say with Paul, I vehemently sorrow for the sorrow of any of Zion's daughters who must rejoice in her king. Yet I must grieve because so many of Zion's daughters see not and grieve not for their soul's defilements. So few bear John company in weeping after the unfolding of the seals. Only the weepers see and understand what the seals signify.

4. *Do you think the Lord has utterly forsaken us?*

    I answer that Jehovah will not forsake his people for his great namesake. 1 Samuel 12. That is, the fire of those whom he once loves is eternal, like himself. Far be it from me to question his eternal love toward you. Yet if you grant that you are as Abraham among the Chaldeans, Lot among the Sodomites, as Israel in Egypt or Babel, and that, under pain of their plagues and judgments, you were bound to leave them, then depart, fly out. I do not mean this physically but as an archetype. Leave the filthiness of their sins. I know assuredly that if it is proved that, though you came far, you never came out of the wilderness to

*this day, then you will be among the many thousands of God's people
that must read*

Psalm 74, 79, 80, 89
Lamentations
Daniel 11
Revelation 11, 12, 13

*Thus I beseech you, more seriously than ever, to abstract yourself
with a holy violence from the dung heap of this earth, the credit and
comfort of it, and to cry to heaven to remove the stumbling blocks.
Cry to remove the idols and sometimes the Lord will then give his
own answers.*

*Let me add, that amongst all the people of God, your case is the worst
by far. While others of God's people tenderly respect such as desire
to fear the Lord, your very judgment and conscience leads you to
smite and beat your fellow servants, to expel them from your coasts.
Therefore, though I know the elect will never be forsaken, yet God's
earthly judgments on Sodom, Egypt, etc. are the archetypes for the
judgment you will experience. It should drive you out of this world to
Christ, to the calling of being his elect on earth as witnesses.*

5. *From what Spirit, and to what end do you drive?*

    *Let the Father of Lights be pleased to search and be you also pleased by
    the scriptures to search. I hope you will find that I seek Jesus, who was
    nailed to the gallows, that I seek the lost Zion, that I witness patiently
    in sackcloth, and that I long for the bright appearance of the Lord Jesus
    to consume the man of sin within. I wish prosperity to you all, from
    governor to people, and mourn that you do not see your poverty, your
    nakedness. Yet I rejoice in the hopes that as the Lord through Paul
    told Apollo, within a few years (though I fear many tribulations) the
    way of the Lord Jesus, the first and most ancient path, shall be more
    plainly discovered by you and by me.*

6. *Would your former condition not have stood with a more gracious heart?*

This question really makes me wonder about you. You know the sins, all manner of sins a child of God may lie in. I need not set them out. Who knows how a gracious heart, before the Lord's awakening and calling, and drawing out, may lie in so many abominations. Do you not hope Bishop Laud has a gracious heart? Do you not think you had a gracious heart even with the poison hauberk [mail shirt] of banishment on your back? But while one judges the condition fair, other souls are driven by fears, doubts, and guilt into a willingness to experience broken bones and even death to right what they judge an unfair condition.

In closing, my heart's desire is abundant, and exceeds my pen. In my head and actions I am willing to be, as Paul says, "the least of the Lord's people". Ephesians 3:8.

Where I err, may Christ restore me. Where I stand in his will, may he use me to further his kingdom. No powers will prevail against him. I will ever mourn that I am no more yours, though I hope ever for restoral.

Roger Williams [2]

CHAPTER 31

Providence, September, AD 1636

The Pequot business referred to in Roger's letter was direct fallout from the Stone and Endicott attacks. The Pequot considered the English terrorists because they burned homes and murdered or enslaved women and children, contrary to longstanding Algonquian tradition. Their grand-sachem, Sassacus, believed that the English must be defeated once and for all, and to that end wanted to align with his tribe's distant relations and old rivals, the Narragansett. The Pequot nation and the Narragansett nation were roughly the same size, with each able to muster five thousand fighting men in an emergency, counting subsidiary tribes. Vane was counting on Roger Williams to keep that alliance from forming.

Pequot messengers approached Canonicus, and a conference was set up near Providence at the old meeting grounds. Canonicus was the host, with his sons Yotan and Meiksah. The sons of Mascus were gathered as well: Miantonomoh, Yotaash, Cojonoquant, and Pessicus. A meeting with Sassacus was a meeting with the prominent Pequot great-great-grandson of Wekeum, and if there was an alliance, it would be portrayed as a family alliance. As a result, his sister Oonue the Elder's sons Ninigret and Wepitamock were expected to attend as well. In a deliberate, in-your-face move, Canonicus would also have Roger Williams, adopted son, at the conference. It signified a level of trust for an English unheard of by the Pequot, and it immediately put them on the defensive. Canonicus purposefully arranged the conference to be one family line alliance versus another potential family line alliance, making it clear before a word was spoken that he saw opportunity in both directions.

Roger's invitation arrived by messenger just two days before he was expected. The weather was not good, with a cold rain and enough wind to form white caps in open water. He needed to row thirty miles to get to conference. He set out immediately.

Rowing steadily Roger found he had a cross wind most of the way. However on arrival to the bay he could not get his boat turned into the desired inlet. He struggled with tired muscles for some time before he figured out he could row in backwards. Canonicus smiled as he saw Roger rowing ashore backwards. Englishmen did seem backwards in many ways, though they were advanced in others. As the water grew shallow and the wave height declined, Roger was able to turn adeptly and come ashore properly. He arrived before the Pequot delegation and that was all that really mattered in order not to lose status and not to dishonor his host.

Roger made a point of acting on Winthrop Senior's behalf, keeping him up to date on the proceedings by sending out a messenger with a written update each day. He ensured that Winthrop understood his sacrifice in braving a storm in his canoe to reach the conference at the right moment. He did not set out on the return to Providence until the Pequot were well gone, three days in all. This also signified status—status above that of any of the Pequot. Ninigret and Wepitamock were treated with the same honor. The message was that, although they might have English or Pequot blood in them, they were Narragansett in allegiance.

Canonicus found some of the Pequots' arguments persuasive. These English were intruders and could not be trusted. They did not operate with honor. Yotan certainly agreed.

From Canonicus's perspective, however, the Pequot made two fundamental errors. First, they proposed a war with little honor—one of killing cows and burning homes. *If the complaint was that the English had no honor, would we have our own people act without honor?* he wondered. Second, the Pequot showed themselves to be untrustworthy and vicious in dealings with the Mohawk, Narragansett, and Mohegan. Canonicus did not want to be a tool to kill English, only to be subjected to Pequot rule. Canonicus didn't say any of this. He let the Pequot talk.

Then it was Roger William's turn to make the case for the English. When Roger tried to claim that the English were honorable, Canonicus interrupted to name ten instances where they had not been honorable in the least. Some could be explained, but most could not.

Roger's next point was much stronger. Even if a Pequot–Narragansett alliance killed off every Englishman in the colonies (something, he added, that would not be done merely by killing women and cows), more settlers would come from Europe. The new colonists would be even more desirous of revenge and therefore more treacherous.

Finally, Roger knew that crossing over the ocean was made possible by European technology that the Narragansett valued highly and hoped to adopt. Just by mentioning it in this context, he knew he was reminding them that no Pequot alliance could facilitate the adoption of European technology like an alliance directly with the English.

Canonicus was aware that the first New England–made ocean-going ship was under construction in Marblehead as they spoke, with laborers from Jole's tribe. In Canonicus's accounting, technology always won. If the Narragansett allied with the English, they could choose together who was allowed to settle and rule the Narragansett territories. The Narragansett would have technology the Pequot could never provide. If successful, the resulting people would, as in all prior ruling family migratory conquests, have many English traits, but they would also be loyal to competent Steward ruler leaders, and they would have the tendencies of Stewards to adopt technology for entrepreneurial purposes. It would be a world power second to none.

In the end, the ruling family went with technology sharing and allegiance to the strongest tribe: the English. At least Roger thought it did. He didn't dismiss the thought that perhaps there was also a secret alliance between cousins to which he was not privy and could never hope to be.

For the next several months, amidst harvest and hunt and other necessary preparations for winter, Roger took the time to keep track of his Algonquian friends. Miantonomoh was invited to hold court on his hill, and at times there were as many as sixty wigwams on Roger's property. He was busy writing daily notes to Vane and Winthrop about movements and negotiations. Some were personal, inquiring after the status of Pequot women captured and desired by Yotaash. The Narragansett and the Pequot leaders were rivals, and they were rapidly producing children with dual heritage, in the Algonquian way of pursuing balance.

Boston, June through December, AD 1636

John Winthrop Senior was carefully rebuilding his reputation and his following. Dissatisfied with being deputy governor, he hoped to run and win against Harry Vane in 1637. Toward that end his work behind the scenes aimed to repair his relationships with the new, more conservative ministers. Key allies were Thomas Shepard of Cambridge, Thomas Weld of Roxbury, Hugh Peters of Salem, John Eliot of Roxbury, and Richard Mather of Dorchester. Slowly, he associated Vane with the failed military maneuvers by Endicott against the Pequot and with Hutchinson's house church views.

A brother-in-law of Will Hutchinson arrived in New England June 1636 seeking refuge with his wealthy relatives. John Wheelwright was a minister who had been officially forced out of his church in England for taking money from the basket. He claimed it wasn't so and that he was chased away for his strong views about God's grace not requiring works. He taught that each man's individual soul was indwelt by the Holy Spirit and owed no submission to magistrates. These views were not consistent with the totality of scripture, and his views were on the fringe in New England—considered so even by Roger Williams.

The Boston Church admitted Wheelright the month of his arrival, and at first relations were cordial. Anne felt obligated to support him. With Will Hutchinson's economic success in the colony and Anne's large network of female supporters, they began a quiet campaign to get Wheelwright named to a paid position in the Boston church, preferably one to replace Wilson.

Wheelwright was an outspoken, controversial speaker. He attended Anne's house church regularly and, as a minister, he often spoke. He used the forum to critique the sermons and began to promote the extreme teaching that grace saves all people and that they need not obey any external church authority. Vane, Cotton, Hutchinson, and others in the network of supporters of Anne's house church got a reputation by association for supporting grace to the exclusion of works—in its most extreme form, a recognized heresy. Anne Hutchinson was known for charity work throughout the colony. She had visible good works, and John Cotton saw great irony in the fact that Wheelwright's views were coloring the younger ministers' opinions about Anne.

John Cotton soon found that it was his turn in the hot seat of controversy. The new crowd of Shepard, Peters, and Mather, with support from Eliot, spoke as one voice against him. They associated him with the unpopular Wheelwright, because Anne Hutchinson, his ardent, long-term supporter and fan, was the conduit through which Wheelwright was reaching a broad audience. The audience was in fact so large that in early 1637 it wouldn't fit in Anne's house anymore, and they began to meet in the local church.

In October John Cotton took the unusual step of setting up a meeting with the ministers and Anne to try to resolve the issues between them. In private, they grilled Anne about her views, and, when pressed, she did say that she had issues with the emphasis on good works by ministers like Shepard and Wilson. The ministers accused her of antinomianism—of saying that Christians need not follow the law. They also accused her of saying that Christians in their perfect union with the Holy Spirit need not try to avoid sin; that they can do whatever feels and seems right. Anne defended herself well. As a well-studied Bible reader, she could navigate between the apparent paradoxes in the Bible. She knew the theology of grace, meaning forgiveness for all who repent and that the consequence of accepting grace would be a desire to follow the law. While she did believe in revelation of the Spirit, she believed the Spirit would communicate most often through scripture. She had never advocated that the Holy Spirit would lead one to positions inconsistent with revealed authority in scripture. Nor had she ever advocated free love or other immoral acts associated with the other sects with which the Puritans tried to associate her. She was herself a godly family woman.

The matter was put to rest for a few weeks. Winthrop took advantage of the new popularity of Shepard and supported a proposal to move the vote for governor to the more conservative Cambridge, in hopes that fewer of Vane's supporters would vote.

Providence, November, AD 1636

Mary Williams and Rebecca Throckmorton were together with the children, their harvest in and all their belongings packed onto one of John's ships, headed for Providence. The ship stopped in Boston, and among the newcomers was Anna Grace Williams. She was also headed to Providence, with her much smaller parcel of belongings.

John Winthrop the Younger dropped Anna Grace off at the ship with a fond farewell and some last instructions about finding Dr. Greene. He found Mary and introduced them.

Mary hadn't seen Anna Grace since she was five. Now she was a beautiful teenager, poised and graceful. She was experienced at baby care, having served John the Younger's Elizabeth, and she was an immediate help with Freeborn and Freegift.

The arrival in Providence was a happy reunion. Roger had a house all prepared for Mary, and John had one for Rebecca right next door. The women were closer neighbors than in Salem, and Providence looked like a civilized, if small, town.

Mehitable watched Anna Grace disembark. Here, at last, was one of her kind. She could tell by the way Anna Grace walked that she was athletic. Upon further conversation, they found a common love of wilderness, Algonquian horticulture, and archery. Mehitable wanted Anna Grace to teach her to ride, and Anna Grace wanted Mehitable to teach her to fish. The two were immediately inseparable when not working, and it wasn't even ten days later that Mehitable took Anna Grace on her first visit to meet Matantuck.

Anna Grace was two years older than Mehitable. She was starting to develop a figure, and her golden curls made her appear girlish, in startling contrast to Mehitable's tomboy looks. Both girls were strong and athletic underneath, but Anna Grace got away with acting like a tomboy while being credited with ladylike manners. The English thought Mehitable would forever be a lone wolf.

At Matantuck's wigwam Oone's daughter Sochepo joined the two girls and soon they were off to hunt and fish together. Before long, the three girls had sworn to be best friends forever.

England, January, AD 1637

Robert Williams read John Winthrop the Younger's letter again. John allowed Anna Grace to move to Providence to become part of the nursing support in Providence, to bolster the healing mission there. She was living with Roger Williams and would work for Dr. Greene and would not be moving with John Winthrop the Younger. John was deciding between Ipswich and his salt works at Ryall-Side near Salem. The issue, he conceded, was that Elizabeth didn't like either one. She stayed continually with her in-laws in Boston, and there wasn't much use for Anna Grace there. He visited often enough to keep Elizabeth pregnant but spent most of his time traveling.

Anna Grace had several more years of service ahead, and so John sold her apprenticeship to Dr. Greene so she could train as a nurse instead of just having maid duties. She would be a nurse charged with learning and extending Martha's ministry of healing. John the Younger had completed the translations of Martha's remedy formulas, and Anna Grace was a clinical apprentice. John's use of the few remedies he kept prepared was in demand, and he wanted her to carry on the medical tradition while he focused on his businesses. By working for Dr. Greene, she'd get more traditional training as well. Anna Grace was also riding horses and was a decent shot with a bow, and the arrangement would be profitable for her future, profitable for John now, and would provide support for Roger Williams and Dr. Greene in Providence.

Anna Grace's father Robert had been saving faithfully for his own passage to New England, and he wanted to emigrate as soon as he'd found a wife. He'd taken the Winthrop approach, and courting had been a much higher priority in his life since Anna Grace's departure. He was currently considering a match with a woman named Liz. Ann had introduced Liz and Robert and had chaperoned their first activities together.

Privately, Sydrach told Ann and Robert that he was considering shutting down his business in England and moving to Italy. His plan was for Robert to take the retail side of the business to New England while he worked the supply end in Italy. Sydrach was waiting for Ann's next child to be born and for Robert to be ready to depart.

Liz was dining with Sydrach, Anne, Robert, and the children, as she often did. Ann had been feeling weak, with uncharacteristic morning sickness, and Liz often helped out with the children. Tonight the company had been good, the food delicious, and times happy. As the women were about to leave the table to reconvene in the kitchen, Robert stood and then dropped to one knee.

"Will you marry me?" he asked.

Liz was surprised. She'd resigned herself to his trade mission to New England and expected him to be leaving her behind. She hadn't been sure her humble background was good enough for this merchant family. Tears came to her eyes, and she murmured, "Yes!"

The couple decided not to marry in England, however. They wanted Roger Williams to preside and Anna Grace to be present. They would marry in New England. Arrangements were busily made, and passage was booked on the *Speedwell*, set to depart in April.

Boston, AD 1637

The pressure from the Pequot in Connecticut was a political nightmare for Vane, and the timing could not have been worse. He was faced with either appearing to take no action or committing the able-bodied men to war, knowing that mothers would lose husbands and sons. If he did nothing, the Pequot would continue to pick off Englishmen one by one, torturing and mutilating anyone caught alone. If he sent troops, he would have to face the likelihood that the Pequot would disappear in the bush, and his men would be picked off as they chased Pequot through the swamps. Either would be a disaster during an election. In the end he commissioned Underhill to fight with twenty men, timing their departure so that the election occurred before the casualty reports could arrive. Hooker in Hartford eventually agreed to send John Mason with forty men and talked Vane into sending Patrick with forty additional troops. One of the forty was Robert Feake, Elizabeth Fones Winthrop Feake's often absent husband.

John Mason was well respected as a military and civil project leader, having most recently built up Dorchester after the hurricane. He and Underhill decided not to wait for Patrick, but to use him in a second-wave assault.

The religious controversies deepened. Wheelwright gave a sermon saying that if division among them was required to preserve the Gospel, they must not back down but must defend the Gospel, whatever the consequences to the church. The other ministers said that his sermon purposefully incited mischief and immorality. Harry Vane believed strongly that, as followers of Christ, all Christians were teachers and that these appointed ministers had no special authority. Out of friendship to the Hutchinson family he tried to defend Wheelwright and his covenant of grace for a time, and he quickly realized it as political error.

Vane's support for Wheelright ended one Lord's Day. Wilson preached that day, and after the sermon, Hutchinson's followers visibly turned their backs or otherwise heckled Reverend Wilson when he prayed. Harry Vane did not approve and decided to take matters into his own hands to defuse the immediate situation. He reached out to Wilson to offer him the chaplain's position with Underhill's expedition. Wilson was relieved when the assignment as chaplain to the Pequot military expedition was offered to him, and he and Vane both hoped that Wheelwright would be banished before his return.

Between the religious controversies and the Pequot, Vane's honeymoon with the colony was over, and his support level was at an all-time low. Winthrop won the election for governor easily, and Harry Vane was not even returned as deputy. Harry Vane decided to return to England at the end of his term.

Now that John Wilson was the chaplain for the troops, Anne Hutchinson used her influence to have her followers refuse to volunteer for the militia. From that moment on, not only were the ministers sniping at her, the magistrates in charge of commissioning the military were also after her. Underhill was one of her followers, but her actions made it very difficult for him to recruit. Even he was frustrated with her. Vane's loss of power ensured she experienced the magistrate's wrath without his intervening diplomacy.

Vane's war approach of sending out men who did little, other than make the Algonquian angry, was most unpopular with Lion Gardiner. Gardiner remained accountable for protecting the safety of the settlers on the Connecticut River. Day in and day out he had to deal with Algonquian living around him. From his perspective, Vane was sending Underhill to fight with green recruits again. Gardiner's recent memories were of living with stealth attacks ever since Block Island, and Underhill was one of the captains he associated with that mess. He was so displeased with Underhill's approach that he kept his men at home, leaving Underhill and Mason to seek the Pequot on their own.

Winthrop Senior knew that Vane had long-term power coming to him, whatever the situation was in New England short-term. He tried to make amends. He invited Vane to dinner with Hugh Peter, and Vane not only declined but also very publicly convinced Hugh Peter, who was thinking of returning to England sometime in the future, to dine with him instead. Harry had already risen above the reach of petty Massachusetts Bay Colony politics.

It was a blustery spring Tuesday morning when Bess Fones Winthrop Feake made it down to visit the Winthrop household. Elizabeth, John the Younger's wife, was still living with her in-laws. Bess brought along Martha Johanna, who was just about to turn seven and Liz, who was four. Elizabeth the Younger was less than six months and was just learning to sit up. There was another baby on the way for both of the women, though John the Younger's Elizabeth was not yet showing.

"Have we got enough people here named Elizabeth?" asked Margaret with a laugh. She loved it when the grandchildren were over, no matter what their names. All of her surviving children were boys, and her grown stepdaughter Mary lived far away with no surviving children.

It was Bess who turned the talk to business. "Do you go to that Anne Hutchinson's house meetings? I hear they are very popular."

"I have been to them. They remind me of Ann Helwys Williams's house church back in England, and I really enjoyed those," said Elizabeth Winthrop.

"Those Hutchinsons have taken a real bite out of the trade at our stores in Watertown. They've got all the latest fabric coming out of London, and it's usually less expensive than what I can find. Her popularity makes everyone want to be in Will's store to hear the latest. She's got connections to Vane, who is practically royalty, and that brings in the customers too. Not to mention that, as a midwife, she knows every mother personally."

"But we're the Winthrop family, and John Winthrop Senior just beat Vane in the election. Won't that bring you nosey customer traffic?"

"Possibly. Maybe you should come run a house church for me!" said Bess. She was only partly kidding.

"Actually, that house church is getting controversial. The minister in Cambridge has been preaching against it. John Cotton just distanced himself from it now that Wheelwright has been teaching there. I think I will quit my own attendance, and perhaps I can influence a few others."

"Get them to come to Watertown to shop. We'll run a house church in my store if that will help."

"Let's not. Rebecca Throckmorton has my stepfather reading her the rules, and now Anne has a whole crowd after her. How about we just meet for tea, and you have some special cloth in from England for the ladies, and we'll get people traveling to see your store in no time."

The women were silent for a while, working at their sewing. Elizabeth felt she was at the edge of an idea but couldn't quite get it out. "When I was in London and while I was courting John, I stayed with Sydrach and Ann Williams. He was in the cloth import business, and he seemed to have connections all over the Levant, in Turkey and elsewhere. John the Younger seemed connected to it somehow, and they discussed it a lot. Have you thought of partnering with him?"

Bess was intrigued. "I've known those guys since I was a child! Elizabeth, that's a good idea. I didn't realize that Sydrach still had such connections."

"Sydrach's assistant Robert … didn't you hire his little girl? Where is she, anyway?"

"She's been sent to Providence. John the Younger and his father took a real liking to her, and she's apparently a gifted little nurse even if she is too insolent for my taste. He wanted her down where they could ship in casualties from Connecticut to Dr. Greene. She was spending more time riding and shooting and learning healing concoctions than she was cleaning for me. I got a maid who actually cleans in return. Her father Robert wants to come to New England, and I understand he's booked passage already to come in the spring. Oh, and he's going to marry yet another Elizabeth!" exclaimed Elizabeth.

"Now we know it's meant to be."

Bess couldn't help herself. "I know this lady Anne Hutchinson is popular, but it seems to me that they banished Roger Williams just for speaking his mind. Why isn't she banished, too? It's not fair."

The women's eyes met.

"I wish they'd stop banishing people for what they say at Bible studies. It makes me uncomfortable. It's too much like the persecution in England," said Elizabeth.

"It's just business." Bess was serious. For her it was just business. If Anne repented, she'd be allowed back anyway, hopefully with a couple years' profits given to other stores. "It's not like they'll hang her!"

The Winthrop women slowly worked their influence as a unified team. The Hutchinsons' popularity declined further.

Suddenly, Anne Hutchinson was caught between Wheelwright, who was family, and the authorities of Boston, led by the Winthrop family and a united front of ministers.

CHAPTER 32

Narragansett Bay, AD 1637

If Anne and Will Hutchinson were isolated English, in the Algonquian world Sassacus was equally isolated. The English were considered so dishonorable, killing women and children, that his people would not support him if he allied with them. Uncas had, on five different occasions, tried to take over Sassacus's role as rightful heir to lead the Pequot, and each time Sassacus defended himself in the Algonquian way, with a show of force that ended with Uncus apologizing in front of the other sachems. Each year, Sassacus grew a little older, and each year Uncus grew stronger and cleverer. Unfortunately he was also less honorable, in the Algonquian way of measuring honor. Sassacus was seventy-seven and as yet had no offspring with anywhere near the diplomatic or military skills of Miantonomoh, Ninigret, or Uncus. He had family ties to all three growing leaders. He could see the handwriting on the wall—that the twenty-six minor sachems beneath him, including his brother Mamoho, would eventually choose loyalty to one of the others or return to their Iroquois cousins, unless he could hold out enough years to let his younger children rise to power.

After Saybrook, Sassacus did not cooperate with any English. Even with the Narragansett's current allegiance to the English, he believed that the English would behave so dishonorably that the connection would be temporary. He was counting on that, waiting for it, training his sons to watch for it. His hopes still lay for the long term in a Narragansett alliance with Canonicus and his descendants.

Uncas bet on a different path, more like the one favored by Canonicus. He was betting that assimilation with the English was inevitable and that relationship with them was required. Uncas, however, was not a Steward ruler; he had no interest in horticulture or technology, and he had no intention of winning any popularity contest. He was a dictatorial ruler willing to kidnap to obtain numerous high-status wives. He was respected and feared, but no one liked him. He was a ruthless and power-hungry leader with a chip on his shoulder, in that he was certain he should have been in Sassacus's place, and he had learned much from the Puritan English about dictatorial power. The first lesson he'd learned was to choose powerful friends and serve them well, right up to the moment it became profitable to betray them, preferably in ways they could not even detect. He knew that nothing he said was questioned thoroughly, and he could get away with half truths sprinkled with a few outright lies. He told a trader on the Connecticut River via an interpreter that Sassacus was plotting to attack the English. Then he chose to appear to serve John Mason in planning the predictable English preemptive strike.

The English sailed and made a show of arriving, with Underhill recognizable on deck. Miantonomoh's son Weekan trotted off to warn Sassacus, just as soon as Miantonomoh saw Underhill. The English waited three days on board just offshore in the Narragansett Bay, first to let John Wilson pray with them at Sabbath, then two days for a storm to pass. Weekan returned with his message safely delivered before the English even got off their ships, and the Narragansett appeared to join the effort as allies, as they had promised to do.

On May 25 John Mason with John Underhill alongside came ashore with an assembled a force of eighty English soldiers. He had Uncas at his side with another eighty braves. He had a surgeon on board, a Dr. Pell, and Reverend John Wilson. He was trying to follow a battle plan that Miantonomoh had suggested to Roger Williams. Mason knew for sure that Roger Williams was no military commander. The map was so general as to be useless, and Mason requested a direct conference with Miantonomoh.

John Mason tried to avoid the mistakes Endicott made on Block Island. He knew there were plenty of swamps here as well. Miantonomoh's original plan was reviewed. The plan was to come in visibly from the sea, which they had done, then backtrack over land to Missituc and Weinshauks, putting an ambush between the Pequot forts and their safety in the swamps before attacking. At the conference, however, Miantonomoh pointed out quietly that they didn't have nearly enough men to execute this strategy. The English assumed that that meant he wanted to send his own men with them and go forward.

Miantonomoh knew that this English man killed women and children and burned homes to the ground. Sassacus would have a chance to evacuate and prepare so that valuable people who Miantonomoh hoped would soon be loyal to the Narragansett were not lost. Miantonomoh did give the militia free permission to travel through his lands, a necessary accommodation if they were to execute his strategy.

Mason and Underhill departed. Dr. Pell chose not to go with them, and stayed back, setting up a place to treat the wounded with his peer Dr. Greene from Providence. Patrick was on the way with additional troops, and the men hoped to use those men to reinforce their numbers and provide a fresh second wave of attack. The Narragansett braves declared they would set out later, as they were not as heavily loaded with gear as the English, who were wearing metal mail covered with leather to repel arrows, carrying gunpowder, and packing provisions. The hike took all day for English soldiers, and the men were exhausted when they camped that night on a rocky shore beside a lake in the valley below the target Pequot camp. In the morning they had to hike about an hour farther. The Narragansett caught up to them in the evening and camped in the woods. Yotan, Weekan, Aunan, and Cojonoquant were all present and watching closely. In the night there was a great noise of singing and carrying on from Pequot Missituc. Calls went back and forth between the woods and the fort, and yet the English thought they had some element of surprise. They assumed that such singing and calls were normal.

They were not normal. The peacetime occupants of Missituc were on Long Island or in the swamps by now, depending on their status. One hundred of Sassacus's finest braves were in the fort (out of a total force of a thousand), and they expected to die the next day. They were preparing to fight to the death. Sassacus had sent them to do harm to the English, to slow them while he continued to evacuate his hometown, Weinshauks.

Each of these hilltop towns was a circle of poles with over an acre of homes and gardens inside.

In Sassacus's and Miantonomoh's way of waging war, one or two braves should die before whoever was outmatched had the decency to back away. With Underhill involved, Miantonomoh had forewarned everyone that there was no decency to be expected. In the morning, as the English approached the fort and saw brush piled chest high and not a person moving, the Mohegan and Narragansett braves saw the ambush that would come from the braves inside. They melted back, waiting for the English to realize they could not win and to back away. The Algonquian would not normally have torched the place, knowing that, if they won, they would take it over. It was valuable loot.

The English didn't see it that way. They let loose a volley at the fort intended to impress with sudden force, and, while the smoke was still clearing and their guns were recovering, they swarmed the fort. Whenever the English fired one of these unified volleys, the Algonquian laughed. It meant they were vulnerable—unable to shoot—for a minute. The Pequot inside the fort made use of the holes they'd designed in the structure to let loose their own volley of arrows and then quickly retreat, using the wigwams for cover.

The English left half their men on the perimeter, one every twenty feet or so. Underhill took half, and Mason took half of the remaining men. Underhill encountered hand-to-hand combat conditions before he'd even cleared the brush to the entrance. Again the Pequot attacked quickly and then took cover. Between the arrows on entry and the tough fight now, nearly half of Underhill's men were wounded. Mason did not encounter resistance, and they yelled a prearranged signal to begin to torch the town. The fire smoked out the remaining braves, who fought their way to exits and took cover.

Most remaining Algonquian braves made it through the perimeter of Englishmen because there weren't enough English to prevent it. Miantonomoh's plan dictated an ambush between the fort and the swamp, but now the Narragansett and Mohegan contingent was backing away from the English, and there were not enough English left on the perimeter. There was no effective second tier anymore because the Algonquian, to a man, disapproved of the English actions and didn't stop any of the Pequot braves from escaping. Many a Narragansett had turned back, disgusted at the torching of homes. Weekan was the first back to camp, and he reported to Miantonomoh. It was as he expected. Miantonomoh called back his people and began rescuing Pequot and treating the wounded, out of sight of the English, who were preparing to treat their own casualties.

The English had their backs to a burning fort, and they had to leave the hilltop. They professed to be heading toward Weinshaucks. However, the Pequot braves in the woods with Uncus's secret cooperation herded the soldiers in the opposite direction, toward the sea, using their arrows as a cowboy would use a cutting horse. On the way the English passed some Niantic fishing villages and torched them. The western Niantic were loyal to the Pequot, paying tribute each year to them. Western Niantic anger that Sassacus had failed to protect them gained the Narragansett many Niantic followers this day. Aunun was still with the group, sickened and angry, as they torched and burned. At the second village he ran ahead in an attempt to warn the people. As the English entered one town, Aunun was taken down with friendly fire. This is how Miantonomoh and Oonue lost a son to English carelessness. The rest of the Narragansett dispersed into the woods and returned to Miantonomoh. Only Uncas was still with the English, appearing loyal to John Mason until the end.

Patrick saw the smoking fort from the Bay and headed in, looking to meet up. When he found Underhill, they argued about what should happen next. Mason stayed back. Now that he'd seen Underhill in action, he was tired of the venture and wanted to part from the group as soon as was practical. Underhill did not want Patrick to go in. Underhill professed there were wounded who needed evacuation, and he wanted to use the ship to retreat. Patrick very much wanted to climb the hill and continue fighting, as he had not yet seen action. The wounded were not that numerous, and, if Underhill's account were true, they should head to Weinshauks and finish the job. Patrick and Underhill had a shouting match in front of their men that seemed about to turn violent. Eventually

Underhill had his way, and his wounded were put on the ship and taken back to get medical help. Patrick and Feake would see no action that day.

Only two English were dead, and those were from friendly fire bullet wounds. The Pequot were sending a message. They weren't killing. The English meant to massacre a tribe. Neither side accomplished its objective.

About fifty Pequot died on May 26 at the fort, and fifty escaped to tell the tale. More died in the woods and lay uncounted. Algonquian honor would have seen one or two men killed, some others wounded. At fifty dead, it was a dishonorable massacre. Yet the English had wanted to massacre a thousand.

Miantonomoh advised the Pequot to embellish the numbers of their dead so that the English would not come after them. Thus the mystical victory at Mossituc, hence called the Battle of Mystic by the English, was invented. The English later claimed to have won the battle and to have massacred nearly the entire tribe—hundreds of men. Underhill's and Mason's actions showed that they knew better, for the next year was a year of terror, as they attempted to hunt down and exterminate survivors.

Sassacus held a war council with his sachems deep in the swamp. They decided not to return to Weinshauks but to abandon it. They agreed with Miantonomoh that the best way to avoid further battle was to play dead and pretend not to exist. The Pequot disappeared into the swamps, having themselves torched Weinshauks.

Uncas started the week with eighty loyal followers. By the end of the month, he could claim three hundred. The remaining braves were either with Ninigret or with Miantonomoh or on Long Island, depending on where their family ties assured they would be taken in.

In truth, neither Mason nor Underhill could tell which Algonquian belonged to which tribe. Uncas could, but he wasn't telling. He, like Miantonomoh, hoped that the survivors would be loyal to him. John Mason cooperated in this to some degree. When a population of Pequot was discovered in Quinnipiac, he divided them equally as spoils for Miantonomoh and Uncas, payment for services rendered.

From the English perspective, the Pequot as a tribe died this day. From most Pequots' perspective, each man chose to switch his allegiance from an old man, Sassacus, to one of the rising powers: Uncas, Miantonomoh, or Ninigret, with a few choosing Long Island or the Iroquois.

The big loser was Sassacus. He planned to seek refuge with the Iroquois among the Mohawk. He marched toward them, skirmishing with English farmers on the way. With his vast store of wampum and a few of his closest loyal supporters, he continued west.

To Sassacus's surprise, the Mohawk executed him and his oldest followers on sight, cutting off their heads. In this way, they died with honor in June of 1637. Sassacus's young followers were invited to stay with the Mohawk. When they got to camp a Mohawk brave at the campfire explained the battle.

"Canonicus's emissary Pessicus arrived years ago. Pessicus heard stories of our tribe in the west for many years and he decided very young to go west, believing the stories of his older cousin Meiksah. He brought great sums of wampum and served us loyally, taking a wife and raising children with our tribe. He asked we finish the battle with Sassacus, and send his head to the English so they would know the Pequot are defeated. The Pequot braves are welcome, just as Pessicus was welcome, if they will commit to serve the Mohawk and pay tribute for being allowed their freedom."

In the aftermath, John Underhill also lost. Robert Feake complained bitterly to his in-laws about being kept out of what sounded now like an amazing set of military actions, ones that might have been even more successful had they gone on to destroy the second fort. Underhill was a suspected Hutchinson supporter anyway. Underhill was put on military trial regarding why Patrick was not allowed to advance and was banished. He returned to England and printed his memoir. Of course, in his book he was a grand hero, and many of the enemy died in combat. He would not leave England until 1640.

Providence, AD 1637

Robert Williams arrived in Boston with his fiancée, Elizabeth. They visited Bess Feake in Watertown before heading to Providence. He'd brought the full range of his brother Sydrach's wares, at her instruction, and a strong business partnership was formed, creating a new delivery system for Sydrach's business.

In Providence, Roger Williams performed the civil ceremony allowing Robert and Elizabeth to wed. Anna Grace, Mehitable, and Patience were the bridesmaids. John Smith and John Throckmorton, with his son, John, were the best men.

Good records weren't kept in Providence yet, and there was never an official wedding certificate registered in any authoritative place, but everyone knew they were married, and it wasn't an issue.

Robert and Elizabeth resided with Roger and Mary until they were settled. Robert would not be a freeman for some time. His mother's will said that he would pay Katherine and Roger for twenty years from the rent, and he and Katherine had never been able to collect enough in rent to pay the full amount consistently. They eventually let Alice's friend Robert Barthropp run one of the buildings, but they did not get proper permission to change the use of the feoff. Roger knew all about these debts and listened patiently to Robert's woes. Roger knew far more about the legal system in England than Robert or Katherine's husband, John Davies. Eventually he offered a plan.

"Robert, you pay what you owe me from earnings here. We'll stop the meter from the time the building changed hands. Once you are clear of debt, I will give you the opportunity to be voted a freeman. If I ever return to England, we'll pursue the matter in chancery court. I will sue you and Barthropp for the proceeds due from Barthropp. It's possible we can even collect from Barthropp, but at least we'll get your name off the feoff, and you won't owe continuing taxes. Besides, you will be absent, thereby escaping any punishment."

Robert agreed.

Connecticut, AD 1637

Puttaquappuinckquame did not follow the doomed Sassacus toward the Mohawk, nor did he affiliate immediately with Uncas, Ninigret or Miantonomoh. Yotaash spotted the old Stone pinnace beached at a secluded river spot. He was gleeful at this great find, and took his time considering his next move.

Eventually Yotaash managed to get off a clear shot at Puttaquappuinckquame, away from the group. His shot killed Puttaquappuinckquame, and Yotaash took over command of his large, nearly seventy-person family, returning with them to Miantonomoh. Unlike other Pequot who voluntarily associated with Miantonomoh, these were captives who had not yet sworn loyalty to the Narragansett. Yotaash did not see the boy that ran off into the swamp before the family was imprisoned aboard the pinnace.

When English continued to die in stealthy attacks, Hartford dispatched Captain Israel Stoughton to assist Mason in the cleanup operation. Fresh and aggressive, with no ties to the Algonquian tribes, Stoughton was not as lenient in the treatment of captured people as Mason had been. He knew Hooker wanted the area made safe, and he did not want Pequot hunting down isolated men. He stopped at Miantonomoh's base and demanded that the Pequot prisoners be brought to him.

Miantonomoh was no fool. He appeared to cooperate.

The twenty-two men who were brought to Stoughton were all Pequot or Niantic, previously allied to Sassacus and not yet professing loyalty to Miantonomoh. Still, Miantonomoh recoiled as Stoughton killed them all on the spot. Stoughton and his men then picked the fairest and finest women for themselves as their servants and ordered the rest onto

Puttaquappuinckquame's pinnace to be shipped to Winthrop as the spoils of war.

Yotaash and Miantonomoh objected, mildly here in person, but more vociferously later through Williams. They said it was Uncas and his Mohegan continuing to kill the English, not the Narragansett, and that the pinnace was rightfully theirs. It was not returned. They reduced their request to the return of a particular high-status widow whom Miantonomoh wanted back, and this request was granted.

Stoughton's ship, with the retrieved Stone vessel in tow, arrived in Boston harbor in the rain, which was fitting for the evil about to ensue. Any remaining light dimmed for the City on the Hill this day as John Winthrop dealt with fifty-two miserable women and children inmates on this boat. He picked out a few to keep as servants and transferred the rest to the ship *Desire*. *Desire* had been decommissioned as a fishing vessel recently and would now be turned into a slave ship to carry prisoners to Barbados. Stoughton, with Winthrop's support, had done everything the Romans did to rebellious subjects, except one thing. He didn't salt their fields. Perhaps it was because the colonists were staying, not moving on to capture another region.

The *Desire* was the third ocean-going ship built in New England at the Marblehead shipyard, and by far the largest. The *Desire* copied the design of her namesake, the third ship to circumnavigate the globe under the master hand of Thomas Cavendish. John the Younger's dreams of honorable glory for her were dashed this day, as she was forevermore only remembered as the first American-built slave ship.

Indentured servitude had been a tradition in England and in the colonies, typically for a period of seven years in a person's youth, before he established a family. Servitude of apprenticeship, of Algonquian learning English ways, had been a noble tradition. Young family members of middle-class families served wealthier relatives. Emigrants served established families. There was no shame in being servant or master under these conditions.

What was being done now, however, was shameful. Every man, woman, and child involved knew it was shameful. These people were being pulled from their families and their land forever and put into servitude until death in a foreign land, as punishment for a war they had not chosen. It was being done solely to prevent the other Algonquian nations from allowing these people to return to life in another tribe undetected, because the European whites were afraid these people would someday seek revenge for the last shameful acts of Captain John Underhill and Captain Israel Stoughton, each acting on orders from colony governors Winthrop and Hooker.

The women and children were driven onto the boat and put in the hold like cattle. Captain William Pierce, proud captain of the *Lyon* and other vessels, record holder for the fastest (twenty-three-day) trans-Atlantic crossing, was given the task of transporting them to Barbados, where they would be sold or put to work on the old Winthrop plantation of Henry's, still in Elizabeth Fones Winthrop Feake's name. Captain William Pierce, the Feake family, and the *Desire* all lost the pure, sweet nature of any true follower of Christ. The sin of slavery, practiced by the mercantile crowd for profit, had been hidden away from the Puritans of New England until now.

The shadow of darkness infected New England like a disease, spreading from the West Indies. In Barbados, the *Desire* was unloaded, and the Algonquian slaves were traded for the African slaves already there. She returned filled with cotton, sweet potatoes, tobacco, and slaves. When she disembarked in Boston on the return, the African slaves were sold at the same auction as the tobacco. The slave trade in New England was born.

After a year of this back and forth, Roger Williams was completely disillusioned. He realized that, the more he knew of the Algonquian, the more layers of relationship, strategy, and deal making he could detect. He had no reason to believe he had detected them all, so he worked to assure that he only reported facts in his letters, restricting himself to being a faithful translator for both sides. Both sides engaged in machinations not taken from the father of lights but the father of lies.

Miantonomoh was completely disillusioned as well. He maintained civil relations with the English out of respect for his uncle, Canonicus.

The campfire stories at night revealed the bitterness and Miantonomoh's son Canonchet soaked it in readily. Periodically Miantonomoh or Ninigret paid the English tribute by cutting off the hands of an Algonquian who had murdered an Englishman. These were sent to Roger to forward on to Winthrop, and Roger wrote each time about it making him squeamish. Miantonomoh was biding his time. Captain Israel Stoughton did not cut down one brave to send a message. He murdered in cold blood twenty-two men, braves like his sons. Some were his sons' cousins. The memory of that evil would not be forgotten. The women would never forget that their cousins were massacred or sold.

For now, the terror in the night was from the Pequot. In time it would also be from the Narragansett.

CHAPTER 33

Narragansett Bay, AD 1637

Mascus, Sassacus, and Wekeum were dead. Canonicus was the last of the old-guard generation of leading men still alive. He felt weak and ill, from grief but also from age. He looked over the younger men in his tribe and saw the same thing Sassacus had seen a year before. His sons were not as strong or as skilled as his nephews. He did not want to end up like Sassacus, ejected by a nephew. He willingly handed over power to Miantonomoh and Ninigret, encouraging his sons to swear their loyalty to one of the two. He knew that both were more and more disgusted with the English alliance, and for good reason. Yet he felt they were giving Uncas a winning hand if they ceded the English as an ally to him. He spent his time in strategy and contemplation and attending to his illnesses. One strategy was to support divisions among the English. If Uncas was allied with Mason, Miantonomoh was allied with Williams. He hoped that Ninigret would be able to develop a strong relationship with John the Younger. It was a hard winter for him personally.

Yotan had long been shut down for communications external to the tribe, and Canonicus viewed him as dangerous for his anti-English views. Now Canonicus wondered whether Yotan hadn't been right all along. Yotan still had leadership roles in internal affairs, so he knew all the young braves well and had great influence on their thinking. He spent his time by the campfire many evenings, rallying support among his peers against the English. One like-minded cousin of his was Ninigret. Following in Pequot footsteps, Ninigret had been pestering the English one by one in Connecticut and Long Island. Ninigret, however, was more complex, able to hold diplomatic meetings with Englishmen representing the Narragansett or Niantic during the day and fostering raids for the Pequot among them at night.

The end of the year brought a happier transition for John Throckmorton and Thomas Agnell. Both were free of debt and indenture, free to pursue politics and business interests, to purchase land rights, and run their own businesses. Both decided to make Providence their long-term official place of residence, and Roger Williams was happy to have them.

Throckmorton was now a wealthy man. Not only had he been paying down debt, he'd been amassing savings. He began scoping out a plan to purchase land in Providence and also near New Amsterdam, Barbados, and the Jersey shore. Much of his time was spent trading between these areas, and he commenced procuring indentured servants of his own.

Robert Williams focused on importing cloth from Italy via Sydrach and supplying Bess and others. He used Throckmorton to reach as far south as Virginia in distribution, and that was as close as he got to Sydrach's original dream of sending him to Virginia.

Roger's time was spent governing the settlement, and Thomas Agnell moved on to become a landholder. Roger Williams assigned him, like every other settler who chose Providence, land from the grant of use given by Canonicus.

England, AD 1637

Ann Helwys Williams died in childbirth, leaving a bereaved Sydrach, fourteen-year-old son James, and nine-year-old daughter Elizabeth. Ann was well loved, and her July 10 funeral was a large one—larger even than Alice Pemberton's had been. The Williams clan, the Helwys clan, and house church members from all over London came to pay respects.

Katherine took in her brother's children for a time, and within months Sydrach took to heart John the Younger's advice and began scouting for a new wife with Katherine's support. By fall he thought he'd found her in Judith Brown, and they spent the winter considering each other. In April of 1638 they married. By May, when he met and fell in love with Ann Pinner, Sydrach realized that he'd made a horrible mistake.

The children despised Judith, magnifying Sydrach's disrespect for her. Her life was miserable, and her attitude made it worse. She complained, didn't complete the chores. Sydrach began beating her—at first a slap in the face, but then a hard kick below the ribs, each time a little more severely. Soon she suffered lasting harm from her injuries. By August 1638 she was dead of the resulting infections.

Anne Pinner had been a widow for over ten months, yet she was visibly pregnant in August of 1638. Sydrach quietly married her in October before the grass had even grown around Judith's grave. Out of this mess a son was born near the end of 1638, and he was named Roger after his banished uncle across the seas.

The couple departed for Italy before Roger was even baptized and lived there for the next seven years. The business in England was closed, and the assets not assigned to Robert in New England were sold.

Boston, AD 1637

John Wheelwright and Anne Hutchinson were scheduled to appear in court in November. Will Hutchinson saw the likely ending long before Anne and John saw it. From his perspective, Wheelwright's arrival had been a complete political disaster. Will was a businessman more comfortable running his business than in the political limelight, and he wanted to distance himself from any controversy that might reduce his sales. He started exploring connections north of Boston for his minister brother-in-law and south for himself.

John Cotton made his peace out of court, rejecting each error the ministers put forward, and pointedly saying he was surprised that any of his church would propound such errors. Just as he did in England, he did what it took to stay in power.

The case against John Wheelwright was fairly short, as he was not repentant about any of the eighty-two errors he was accused of, and he recriminated on the stand and was promptly banished. With a few of his followers, though no Hutchinson family among them, he headed north toward New Hampshire.

Anne's trial lasted for days. She knew her politics and her scripture and she didn't intend to give them grounds on which to punish her. She had never propounded her questions shared with the ministers in public, and she had never signed any controversial statements. Until Wheelwright came to town, she had been a visible promoter of John Cotton, and he'd been cleared.

John Winthrop Senior and Thomas Weld were her main accusers. Again and again she answered questions well and gave them no room. After a day the crowd was on her side, and many of the ministers thought she had made her case. Winthrop turned to his political bag of tricks. His position was that she had promoted divisiveness and not respected authority. Here he put her in a no-win position, and everyone could see it when she asked, "Which authority? Would you have me obey my fathers in my family or my fathers in the church? When they disagree, how can I be loyal to both, as much as I might want to?" Once again, she had turned the fault back to the men, to the divisive ministers, to the authorities. In the Puritan mind, to do so was disrespectful of God granted authority.

John Winthrop rested his case.

An even meaner-spirited questioner took over in the person of Thomas Dudley, former and most conservative of governors. His claim was fundamentally that she was close to the people who were banished and that made her a coconspirator. To this she had no effective answer. They were her family. He drove her into silence.

Then Dudley began a below-the-belt attack. He brought up her statements, made in private to the ministers and under pressure, in public. He accused her of slandering the ministers.

Her answer was that the comments were made in private and in a context he was not representing correctly. In a private audience she must give true answers and submit them to scrutiny. If she hadn't, she would have been deceitful.

Anne was pregnant, and it had been a long two days on the stand. She was spotting and in pain and furious with these men. She could see no end to the questioning; there were too many men. In fear of losing her baby, she changed her strategy in a heartbeat and ended the process of defense. She instead gave them what they wanted when she spoke her mind.

She accused the ministers and magistrates of being agents of Satan and not true followers of Christ. The magistrates of Boston were not an authority she had been asked by God to accept.

She was banished and told to leave by end of March, and she was put under house arrest to keep her from her admiring followers.

For four months, she was held in the home of her accuser Thomas Weld's brother, Joseph Weld, two miles from her home. The Weld home could not have been more uncomfortable, with every move watched. She saw little of her children, as it was winter, and travel was hard. She lost the baby, delivering what looked like transparent grapes, and this information was made public to make it seem like God's punishment on her. A church trial was scheduled for March 15, 1638.

Will Hutchinson was busy the entire period, lobbying his fellow merchants and investors. He promoted the view that political divisiveness and the willingness to create such severe punishments for theological disputes was unhealthy for business. They should leave Boston en masse and go elsewhere. William Coddington was a wealthy merchant that came on board early on. Coddington and Hutchinson together carried weight in the business community. A group of the businessmen convened in Coddington's home and they crafted a draft agreement or contract binding them together, much like a corporation. The group elected William Coddington as their leader. John Throckmorton caught wind of this plan and lobbied Roger to get these business people to come to Providence, as much capital would be moving with them. Roger convinced the group to settle near Providence and to abandon plans of moving to Long Island or further south. He assured them freedom of conscience and the ability to establish their own separate civil authority. Land was granted from the willing Narragansett, to include Aquidneck Island.

By the time of Anne's church trial, the men had moved south, and beautiful homes had been constructed, using vast labor crews that only the wealthy could put together. A large portion of Boston's capital base for business expansion had just moved to Aquidneck Island. The Dyer family was among those moving. Mary Dyer was Anne's closest friend.

Anne's best friend, her children, and her husband went to great lengths to prepare her new home, making it warm and inviting, and awaited word of her release.

Boston, AD 1638

The ministers visited Anne, much as they had Roger before her. Some, like Shepard, were there just to collect evidence against her.

On March 15, when the church trial commenced, Anne was interrogated for nine hours, and, at the end of it, they had only managed to discuss four of the eighty-two points of error the ministers had collected. At the end, Cotton provided the summary. He pointed out that Anne had done some good among them, pointing to the fruit of her midwifery and her extensive charity with the women. Yet he conceded that there was error. The trial was recessed for a week.

John Cotton did his best to close the wound. Anne was his ardent follower, respecting him still. Painfully they put together a document for her to read that both recanted the errors and apologized for her error in attitude. John had been through this process several times successfully, and there was hope.

The next week Anne in deep humility and with contrition read the statement aloud. Mary Dyer was in the audience and was visibly sickened.

Two of Anne's older children, Edward and Faith, watched aghast. Katherine watched as well, in horror, hardly recognizing her sister. This woman was a pale, sick-looking, malleable creature.

Yet it was not enough. Thomas Shepard accused her of deceit. He said she was none of Christ's.

If nothing she could say would be believed, there was nothing more John Cotton could do. He quickly cut his losses and pointed out that if allowed to continue, the errors would surely lead to moral breakdown and the end of marriage—even though none of those things had happened yet. The vote was against her, and she was excommunicated.

In the shocked silence after the vote, Mary Dyer stood up slowly, turned her back on them, and walked out, never to return to this church.

Within hours, Mary, Faith, Edward, and a few others began the six-day walk with Anne to the boats that would carry them to Anne's new island home. She hadn't seen her husband or her younger children in four months. The group stopped frequently for sustenance in hopes of improving Anne's condition and spirits before she arrived. After the six-day moving retreat, Anne was indeed revived and ready to tackle God's next assignment.

Each of the more than eighty followers would eventually choose to go north to New Hampshire with Wheelwright or south with the Coddington and Hutchinson families. Boston was no longer a welcoming place. The magistrates went so far as to require Anne's followers to turn over all guns, shot, and other weaponry—apparently afraid they would incite violence. Some chose to go south, as it was just too cold to think about walking north.

Within weeks, it was time for Mary Dyer to give birth. Anne was the midwife, as she had been for all of Mary's children. This child, however, was deformed beyond the point where it could survive. The rumor promoted in Boston circles was that Anne's evil caused Mary to give birth to a monster.

Providence, AD 1639

John Smith's mill was operating nonstop to fuel the expansion, and many of Roger's followers in Salem decided that Roger had not been torn apart, but rather built up by God's providence. For the last year they'd been moving down one by one. Hugh Peter accelerated their departure by excommunicating anyone who would not renounce Roger Williams. Ezekiel Holyman was one. Since he was assistant minister to Roger Williams back in Salem, he did not have a credible way to renounce Roger. He was quickly excommunicated and moved to Providence.

On arrival he expanded on Roger William's ideas. In fact, he went further than in the Salem days. He cornered Roger one morning to explain. "I'm a little taken aback, Roger. You've been here several years, and yet there is not one common building. Are you spurning the need to gather God's people and to teach all those who can understand?"

"Not at all. I'm just doing it in <u>Nehemiah's</u> best tradition, outdoors."

"Roger, the people are taking it differently. There is no organized church here. It looks like you don't think worship is important. I'm worried about the children, especially. How will they learn?"

Roger paused. "Truthfully I cannot put together a church. There is no unbanished person to provide succession. Succession has surely been broken in the past, but am I to break it further? God's got enough to repair, don't you think?"

"I've been studying this a great deal, and there is another way. <u>Hebrews 6:2</u> honors the laying on of hands on a par with eternal judgment and resurrection. Why?"

Ezekiel saw the question in Roger's eyes and went on. Roger always referred to that verse as defining the necessary attributes for a church. That didn't explain why.

"The church is the body of Christ. When the church as a body lays on hands, it is Christ's hands, succession from Christ himself. When the church as a body agrees that a person has chosen voluntarily to say that Jesus is Lord <u>Matthew 16:15–18</u>, he or she provides the succession directly from Christ, new every time. Belief is the rock, not Peter as a person."

"So you would have us lay on hands?"

"I would have us do as Philip did in <u>Acts 8:26–40</u>. I would baptize the believer. Then I would lay the hands on to provide clear succession."

"So do you want to? Right now, I mean? Let's do it. Let's try it and see where it leads." Roger was never one to leave things theoretical for long.

The two discussed it at length in town with their peers, and soon there were twelve men of like mind. Roger took the special number as a sign of God's providence. It was Roger's answered prayer from the wilderness. These were the twelve whom God had given in his providence: Roger Williams, Ezekiel Holyman, William Arnold, William Harris, Stuckley Westcot, Dr. John Green, Richard Waterman, Thomas James, Robert Cole, William Carpenter, Francis Weston, and Thomas Olney. The twelve in turn elected Ezekiel to perform the first baptism, and Roger volunteered to be baptized first.

Francis Weston's land contained the perfect setting. There were hills on three sides, and the fourth side was the Salt River. The waters were calm enough to stand in, and deep enough to immerse in. Ezekiel first immersed Roger. Roger then immersed Ezekiel and the other ten men. Then they all gathered in a circle around the newly baptized and put their twenty-four hands one over the other on the man's bowed head and prayed.

Twelve other people very quickly joined these twelve. Chad Brown was one of the second set of twelve. Arriving on the *Martin* in 1638, he was a part of the 1638 set of newcomers to Providence. He was well known for his arbitration of disputes, and he was the first official surveyor of the lands of Providence.

The church grew like wildfire, and the people were called Baptists.

Within months, Roger was troubled. He was acting as chief administrator of Providence and as the teacher in the new church, making him a civil and religious leader. The whole point of his colony had been to separate these roles. Roger needed to focus on the weaker civil structure. Without the church to control the civil order, a stronger civil authority was needed. Maintaining civil peace was turning into one nightmare after another. Roger resigned as pastor, and the people laid hands on Chad Brown to ordain him as preacher. Roger returned to his preaching in Algonquian on Sundays and did not continue to attend the Baptist church he had founded. He did not disown it, but he had other priorities.

Roger always maintained good relations with Chad Brown. They talked often, and Chad viewed himself as minister to Roger as long as he had no other. Other critics, with less clarity, accused Roger of leaving the church over succession issues. Roger did have succession issues. He believed the Catholic Church had unalterably broken succession from the person of Peter and the apostles and that Henry VIII had made it worse. He thought that all sects had that issue, and that the issue wouldn't be resolved until Christ came again. In the meantime he was less comfortable with organized sects with earthly power than he was with small, separated churches. He believed in local control from the body of Christ. He did not want to disrupt worship, which his many critics liked to do if he showed up in public. He was more comfortable on the banks of a river or the side of a hill preaching in Algonquian. That he never stopped doing as long as he was in New England.

This Lord's Day the hill was filled with Algonquian. Because Miantonomoh led an Algonquian council the day before on the same hill, many Algonquian families stayed to hear Roger preach. Last evening there had been many stories by the fire. One story in particular provoked Roger's current sermon.

"The storytellers teach of your ancestors, who came from the blue hills to the south. There was a brother married to a sister, and they were sent out with their children to Steward new lands."

The people nodded. This was the history of the Narragansett ruling family. They all knew it.

"I tell you this story is not new. It has happened over and over again throughout time. Our people have such a story. Our story is about Abram. He was married to his half-sister Sarai, the daughter of his father but not his mother. The creator blessed Abram, sent him out of his homeland, and told him he would be the father of many nations. He did not have any sons until he was an old man, yet he believed God, and it was credited to his righteousness. When he finally had a son, one day he was asked to sacrifice that son as a tribute to God, and he would have been willing to do it."

Tribute was also a very familiar concept to his audience. All who passed through the land and hunted paid tribute to the sachem. As God's children we are all passing through God's creation and owe Him tribute. Roger taught the creation story often, and the concept of tribute to God was natural to them now. The Algonquian especially loved to hear how Abram was renamed Abraham when God promised that he would father a nation. The taking of new names at major life milestones was an Algonquian tradition, and it made Abraham seem like one of them.

Roger continued to explain the story: "Abram was asked whether he would offer his son as sacrifice to God, whether his loyalty was total. Only when Abram had shown that he was ready to do this was the son rescued and Abram credited with righteousness. This offered sacrifice prefigured the sacrifice of the creator's son and his rising again, a sacrifice for their own wrongdoings. At the last moment, God sent an angel and rescued Isaac, providing a choice ram for the tribute."

Every week Roger found some way to go from traditions in the Algonquian population to the good news that they too could follow Jesus Christ. Often he focused on how, not long ago, Europeans were much as the Algonquian were now, and the Gospel was what made them successful as a civilization. Always adopters of new technology, the Narragansett rulers wanted to hear more.

Since Roger was not the civil administrator of the Algonquian, he saw no conflict in being civil magistrate in Providence and preacher to the Narragansett. It was his favorite calling, his most enjoyable service to God.

Being a civil magistrate was certainly not Roger's favorite activity. It seemed the number of ways to break the civil peace was infinite. He had already banished people. For example, his next-door neighbor Joshua beat his wife Jane brutally for going to the church meetings in Roger's yard on the Lord's Day. He tried to claim that it was due to his conscience that his family should not go to church. William Harris had the nerve to support Joshua. Mary was upset terribly, as the beating was severe, and it took her and Anna Grace many weeks to nurse Jane back to health.

Roger explained over and over that they were all as in a ship. On the ship can be Turks, Jews, inner lights (e.g., Hutchinson), and Christians. He would defend to the death their right to have and to publicly display and discuss their beliefs and convictions, including holding forth in prayer and other worship. That, however, did not change the fact that the ship must be steered, the decks cleaned, and the behavior between men peaceable. Somehow, the last sentence never quite seemed to get through to Harris.

Joshua Verin was accused of breaking the civil peace with his abusive punishment. English law, by which Providence justice was administered, stated that husbands were the rulers of the family, and they were permitted corporal punishment of their wives. They were not, however, permitted to cause significant physical injury by that corporal punishment. Joshua Verin was banished from the civil privilege of living in Providence. He decided to go back to Salem and to take his family with him.

Jane Verin was at the house for the last time before they planned to depart. Jane said, "I'm going to miss you and Anna Grace so much. I don't have any friends left in Salem."

"I'm concerned for your safety," responded Mary. "I wish you could stay here and let Joshua go to Salem. We could find you a position in someone's household, and you'd be safe."

"I can't do that. We're married, and I love him. I know he gets angry, but he has his good moments too. Besides, this is not New Amsterdam, where they hand out divorces like birthday presents. I would lose all standing in the community. Everyone would look down on me and on our son Phil. What would become of Phil?" There was resignation in her eyes.

"I'm going to ask Roger to have people we still know in Salem and the Massachusetts Bay look out for you. You must reach out too. I can't stand the thought of you being there with no support."

The Verin family returned to Salem. Mary was frustrated. It seemed that even though the civil community supported Jane and formally punished Joshua, it was Jane who was being punished the most, as she was being deprived of the small support network she did have. She approached Roger and asked him to do something for Jane. Roger was equally concerned for her welfare, and for her son Phil. He wrote to John Winthrop and Hugh Peter to ask their assistance in watching over Verin to keep him in line. He was concerned that when Joshua told the story it sounded as though everything was Jane's fault or Roger's and that the beating would be accepted as reasonable corporal punishment, when in fact it had gone far beyond that, even by seventeenth-century English law.

Within two years Jane Verin was dead, in questionable circumstances, though no one was ever prosecuted. Mary and Anna Grace become stalwart if quiet champions for divorce, using their powers of persuasion first and foremost with Roger Williams, their husband and uncle.

Aquidneck Island, AD 1639

Will Hutchinson did not believe that William Coddington should be judge of Portsmouth for life, and many agreed with him. He ran against Coddington and won an election, only to have Coddington take his money and his remaining followers to the other end of the island to found Newport. Newport was soon more successful than either Providence or Portsmouth.

When Coddington moved, John Clarke moved with him and started a Baptist church in Newport. The Newport church was founded only six weeks after the Providence church and was based on the same keys as the church in Providence: believers' baptism, practices and beliefs guided by Hebrews 6:2, and civil toleration of all consciences. The core of the person, his soul, must be free to choose Jesus as Lord or not. That was how Jesus himself worked in Matthew 16:15–18.

In addition, the Newport church quickly had a building, while the Providence church did not.

New Amsterdam, AD 1641

Governor Kieft of New Amsterdam was under pressure to make more business concessions. The West India Company was not profitable enough to continue its operations and was threatening to relocate its headquarters. In order execute his plan he needed alternate sources of government revenue. There was a Swedish settlement on the Connecticut River providing competition to New Amsterdam, and Kieft needed to keep business centered in his territory.

When he first came to the area, he thought he had purchased land from the Algonquian but later found that the Algonquians thought he'd just gotten permission to use it and that he'd given them tribute to represent the agreement. That gave him an idea: an annual tribute to the government of New Amsterdam from the Algonquians for their use of the land. He sent soldiers to collect tribute from the Staten Island and Long Island Algonquian—a violent, extorted form of taxation. The Algonquians were angered, though a little confused about the intertribal affairs of the English. In their anger, the Algonquians initially retaliated indiscriminately against Europeans who were easy to pick off.

Weckquaesgeek Algonquian, angry with Kieft, looked for a reachable target. The elderly Swedish trader Claes Swits thought his relations with the Algonquians were good. When braves came appearing to want to trade, he was murdered in cold blood. After that incident, things got worse in a tit-for-tat set of incidents culminating in the shooting death by an Algonquian of a foreman at a New Amsterdam factory.

As he lost control of the civil peace, Kieft's unpopularity grew, and he began adding military options to his plans. He hired Underhill, after hearing of his great victory at the Battle of Mystic.

CHAPTER 34

Aquidneck Island, AD 1641

Will Hutchinson was not popular as judge of Portsmouth. He was absorbed in his businesses and was not willing to spend enough time arbitrating civil disputes. Men soon longed for the order that Coddington brought and openly proposed combining the Portsmouth and the Newport governments.

In response, Anne declared there should be no magistrates at all over Christian people. Church authority should be enough to govern. In despair, Will Hutchinson grew inactive, and he soon became sick and died.

Anne mourned and moved on.

Roger Williams and Anne Hutchinson had never gotten along, and now Will's moderating voice was gone. Looking for a change in scenery and a place to make a fresh start, Anne was enticed by the opportunities that John Throckmorton offered in New Amsterdam. New Amsterdam was a very secular community compared to Aquidneck Island and could be counted on to leave them alone.

The business community near Providence and on Aquidneck campaigned to bring in the stronger civil authorities of the Massachusetts Bay to protect business. Throckmorton knew that if that ever happened, there would be religious persecution that they had no desire to endure. Soon John Throckmorton and thirty-five followers were moving to a tract of land granted to Throckmorton by Governor Kieft. This land was called Throggs Neck, and it was located in what is now the Bronx. A pregnant Rebecca, John, Patience, and Freegift said their good-byes for now to Mary Williams and the children.

Anne purchased rights to use of land from John Throckmorton, and nine members of the Hutchinson household followed, including her daughter Anne the younger and her daughter's new husband, William Collins. As the eldest male in the household, he became the operating head of the household. They lived quietly in some isolation, their house church unimpeded by magistrates.

John and Rebecca felt free to embrace their own inner lights and to spurn organized church. Soon they joined the Quaker sect.

While Anne Hutchinson's views were similar to those of the Quakers to some degree, she was not a Quaker, and when she heard about John's newfound opinions, she took him to task.

"Where did you become convinced of this Quakerism?"

"Trading in Barbados. I admire the freedom of religion in Barbados. The only issue the Quakers have there is that they will not join the military. In Barbados, as long as you pay your fine, you are excused from military service. Quakers just pay and are left alone."

"That doesn't explain why you would become Quaker!"

"The primary attraction of Quakerism for me is that it replaces the uncertainty of wondering if you are to be among God's elect. We know God loves everyone. Everyone will be saved in the end. Instead of continually feeling one must purge oneself of the natural propensity to sin, one is confident of the indwelling of the Holy Spirit. Since all have the spirit inside, all are lights. Human judgment and rationality replace the authority of scripture."

"The problem is that there is evil in the world. I have experienced it firsthand in Boston. It cannot be avoided, and it will not go away," responded Anne with some anger. "Only the understanding of our inherited sin can explain our temptation to evil. Grace saves us, yes, but as soon as you are saved, you should want to serve Christ, to reject all evil.

The burden you felt is the Holy Spirit in you telling where you need to improve."

"Quakerism rejects the burden of original sin and thus the need to continually purge oneself of sin."

"We believe God's authority is revealed in scripture, and scripture explains evil with sin."

"We do not accept scripture as having final authority. We have our rational human judgment to determine what is right in our time."

"Then explain how your rational judgment will overcome this world's inherent evil tendencies. What will be your guidepost? How will you know you are building God's kingdom and not serving the evil one?"

John fell silent. When one knows in one's heart that one's own profits are based on the promotion of evil, one doesn't really want to explore evil. John wanted to hide from the knowledge of evil, to keep the darkness south, and the light of his family in the north. He took comfort in Quakerism, as it did not call him to reach for higher ground. Slaves toiled on, sugar production was higher than ever, and profits were good.

Anne eventually continued softly, "When you lose scripture, you have lost your compass. The Holy Spirit uses scripture to guide our inner lights. You are lost. I will pray for you."

Connecticut River, AD 1643

Miantonomoh's rivalry with Uncas turned ugly. It all started when Mason divided the Pequot he had in custody equally between them. Miantonomoh was insulted, for his tribe was far larger than Uncas's was at that time. Uncas, however, played a more pivotal war role for Mason. The day Stoughton massacred men and Winthrop arranged the sale of women and children was when the real ugliness began. Since then Uncas had encouraged local slaves owned by English to escape and offered them protection. Within the year, he married six women, including the widow of Tatobem, to protect them and to elevate his status. As he grew more powerful, Uncas went after ex-Pequot land claimed by the Narragansett. He continued to recruit and in some cases kidnap relations of the Pequot he already had. In retaliation, some ex-Pequot braves attempted to assassinate Uncas right in his hometown of Shantok. Uncas was wounded in the shoulder but not killed. The braves were followed as they retreated, and they returned to the Narragansett. That angered Uncas, and he decided to up the ante.

Uncas now planned to attack people who were attacking him and his Mohegan-Pequot.

Sequassen was a family head, or minor sachem, once Pequot, now under the care of Ninigret and therefore also of Miantonomoh. Yotan was conferring with Ninigret and Sequassen on Miantonomoh's behalf around Sequassen's campfire. Sitting beside Ninigret was his servant Wequath, Canonicus's son by one of his Pequot wives. Wequath was a messenger runner, planning to run back to Miantonomoh as soon as agreements were concluded. Around both men were key braves. They were sharing food around the campfire, enjoying each other's company.

Out in the woods a group of Uncas's braves walked directly up to a sentry and politely requested passage. Pretending to be ex-Pequot seeking Narragansett protection, they gave up their axes but kept their knives hidden. They were allowed to pass into the inner circle.

What they planned, however, was a massacre.

With their knives and the element of surprise, they killed six men, including Yotan and Wequath, before the Mohegan escaped. Ninigret did manage to kill two Mohegan.

Wequath was no longer able to be a messenger bringing news. Ninigret sent his nephew Morrano, Meiksah's son. Others would follow the next day, bringing bodies home.

Roger Williams was visiting Canonicus to let him know that he would soon be leaving for a while when the young boy Morrano ran in with the news. He whispered into his grandfather's ear first. Canonicus went pale and turned away. Then the tribe was gathered and the news announced. An audible wail arose from the camp. Preparations were made, and Roger stayed longer than he had planned, as an adopted son of this tribe.

The next day Yotan was buried as a tribal elder, with Wequath beside him. When the tribe came to the area of the grave, they lay Yotan and Wequath by its mouth. All sat in a circle for several hours and lamented and howled, with tears from Canonicus, Weko, and just about every member of the tribe. Even the children were there in large numbers, and they exhibited great and heartfelt mourning. Then the men were placed in the grave, buried with their favorite belongings. The men's mats, their bowls, and their favorite skins of clothing were laid beside the grave, and no one would ever touch them again. Then the tribe proceeded back to their dwellings. Yotan and Weko's home was burned in solemn respect of the dead. Weko and her sons would go live with Meiksah and Matantuck for a time.

Miantonomoh took the responsibility for achieving revenge.

New Amsterdam, January, AD 1643

In response to the murders of Claes Swits and others, Governor Kieft decided that the Algonquian who did not pay tribute needed to be exterminated. When a group of Wequaesgeek and Tappan Algonquian sought shelter in New Amsterdam from their rivals the Mohicans, Dutch soldiers, Underhill among them, appeared to let them in. Then they murdered them, including the women and children, in the night. One hundred twenty-nine Dutch killed one hundred twenty Algonquians. The Algonquian people were seething with anger.

Meanwhile, Roger Williams set out for New Amsterdam, since he could not leave from Boston, on his way to England. On the way, he overheard the anger in Algonquian conversations in both the Dutch and Algonquian languages and changed course to Governor Kieft with an offer of help. Given the failures of Underhill's efforts to date, Governor Kieft was quick to accept Roger Williams's diplomatic assistance.

At Roger's gentle insistence, he brought the local Algonquian to understand that the Dutch were angry over missing tribute. They got together a large tribute as a peace offering. Wampum, hard English currency, and furs were brought in such sizable quantities that even Governor Kieft was impressed. He accepted the peace offering, and things seemed to settle down.

Would it last? Roger wondered. He needed to move on. His settlement would be threatened by the Massachusetts Bay Colony's actions if he did not.

He boarded the ship on time.

Off the Shore of New Amsterdam, March, AD 1643

The Pequot war launched Roger's career as diplomat between the Algonquians and the Europeans. The Hutchinson flight from Boston made the Narragansett Bay a lucrative trade center with ample resources. These first two major events in the life of Providence were easy for Roger to chart, in that his principles guided him clearly, and the decisions were obvious. In the first event, he was a faithful translator and negotiator, and, if his advice was not always heeded on either side, he knew that he was not a military man. Roger did not agree with Anne Hutchinson but he knew that God's true test was for him to tolerate from a position of power those with whom he could not agree.

The set of conflicts he now faced represented a more complicated test, and it was why Roger was sitting on a ship bound for England this sunny day of March 1643 when he had hoped to be planting fields. It was all about the land. It was also about constructing a strong civil peace.

Roger's experience with land ownership was under the feoff system in England, where the king held all property. The king granted patents to governors, often with the titles like lord. The governors dictated how land was granted to feoff owners. The feoff owners rented portions of the land to others or worked the land themselves. Only feoff owners free of debt, as opposed to renters or laborers, had the right to vote in matters affecting the town. To change the use of the feoff, the governor must approve.

In Canonicus's experience with land ownership, no person owned land. Tribes earned rights to a territory according to their strengths and stewardship of the land, and they could grant use of the land at will, usually in return for a promise. The promise might be tribute of choice portions of game killed on the land, or some other agreement the tribe might wish to make. If the promise was broken, the land could be reclaimed. If the tribe could no longer hold the land, another tribe could claim it. When significant rulers died in a weakening tribe like the Pequot, surrounding tribes often claimed new land or reclaimed land that was theirs in prior generations.

Roger's first attempt to construct a government blurred the lines that were clearly drawn in the minds of Providence's English settlers. The land was not his by patent from a king, but rather on a promise of use by Canonicus. To blur things further, he gave all the right to a vote, even though Canonicus's agreement was only with Roger. With the rights of landowners, the men started believing they were landowners and began to challenge Roger's right to govern. Soon several wealthy men made their own land-use agreements with Canonicus. William Arnold, William Coddington, and Samuel Gorton were among them.

William Arnold was a wealthy man who cared little how the government was set up or how religion was set up as long as he got his way. Roger knew they were playing him for a fool, and he intended to stop it. They'd used every trick in the book. First, William Harris claimed that Roger Williams sold him his allocated land permanently, rather than temporarily granting him use of a common stock. Then, when Roger wouldn't do his bidding, William Arnold sought the protection of the Massachusetts Bay Colony directly. There was no way Massachusetts Bay Colony would militarily or civilly protect Providence without also instituting all their rules forbidding worship other than in the form they approved. Roger had seen the debilitating effect on Boston of the loss of the wealthy, and he wasn't about to let Arnold walk away easily. He needed to appease Arnold while being true to his own principles. That meant getting strong civil government in place. The only way to do that and have as much authority as Massachusetts Bay was to seek a charter from the English king.

William Coddington ran his own civil government on Aquidneck, and meant to have his own charter naming him ruler for life, approving those running the church as well as civil government.

Finally there was Sam Gorton. In his first year in New England he was banished by Boston, Plymouth, and Newport. Gorton ran a public campaign to have Coddington removed from office as judge in Newport, and Gorton was removed instead by popular vote. In Providence he lasted longer. Gorton was a most attractive, charismatic man, strong and persuasive. However, it was his way or nothing. He only followed his own inner light, unable to control himself for the sake of civil peace. He could be violent and confrontational. Roger Williams never questioned the right of the government to enforce civil authority, but he also hadn't built the machinery with which to enforce it.

At first, it was William Arnold who was the most helpful in controlling Gorton. He convinced the town that the case was not about religious liberty; it was the civil state that Gorton failed to respect. Because of Arnold's eloquent opposition, when Gorton was nominated for freeman, he lost by a narrow vote, meaning that he had no official say in Providence decisions.

Then a riot, an actual physical fistfight, broke out during the enforcement of a judgment to collect a debt from a Gorton follower. Roger had been terrified that he would not be successful in establishing civil peace. In the end he did regain control, and the matter was resolved peacefully. With the help of Miantonomoh, Gorton was enabled to move to another piece of land called Shawomet, outside of Roger's original land grant from Canonicus. Roger thought that perhaps the conflict had been resolved, but Arnold would not let it die. He turned against Roger in again seeking the militia of Massachusetts to enforce the peace, and he was willing to use any means to get it. Roger could only think of one place to turn against the wealthy forces arraying against him: a written charter from England and an official patent from the king.

So here Roger Williams sat. *How can I convince England to grant a charter?* The enormity of the task humbled him, and he prayed for insight. Then he remembered, *If this is the Lord's work, even English civil war will not prevail against it.* He was comforted.

England was at war with herself. There was once again a Parliament, and it was Parliament versus the king. Roger had friends on both sides. Harry Vane was in Parliament. Montegu Bertie served the king.

Montegu, now Earl of Lindsey, was as always the loyal son and cavalry soldier. He had stayed on the battlefield to tend to his wounded father, only to have his father die in his arms. Shortly after, Montegu was captured by forces loyal to Parliament. He had been in prison since October 1642. If there was any doubt that this was really war, Montegu proved the point. Roger wondered whether he could get Vane to help him exchange Montegu in return for some other prisoner. He needed to find a way to play all the sides to his middle.

Roger Williams reviewed the situation in England, as it was reported to him in Providence, searching for his opening. He knew the Massachusetts Bay Colony position to be desperate. Aside from the demand to turn in the charter, a request that they'd been evading for years, they could not pay their taxes to England, as they simply didn't have the cash. They'd largely regressed to a barter system, often using wampum as money, for satisfying New World debt, but King Charles wanted English currency. The situation was so desperate that Hugh Peter and Thomas Weld were in England as fundraisers. Roger knew that they would be trying to take his land on William Arnold's behalf. If they did, religious persecution would ensue. He had to defend his sanctuary for those persecuted for conscience. Roger smiled. God really had blessed Providence and the surrounding towns. He had the wealthy merchants, and he had no patent on which to owe taxes. He remembered his lessons from Harry Vane on playing to all sides. He chalked up the need to get taxes on colonies reduced or eliminated as something he had in common with Hugh Peter.

As the Massachusetts Bay fell into a depression, and Puritans sitting in Parliament acquired power, many of the upper class in Boston decided to go home. To them, the important fight for the City on the Hill was now being waged in England. The honeymoon with New England was over in the face of sanctioned human slaughter, slavery, and vicious Puritan-on-Puritan banishments. There was nothing like the king as a common enemy to unite the Puritan people. Roger counted this again as a common point with Hugh Peter and Harry Vane. They all had hearts willing to fight for the right to read and live by scripture. He wanted to add his insights to that fight.

Roger's primary objective remained obtaining a charter or his entire fight against persecution would be moot. Parliament had a Committee on Foreign Plantations. He needed any charter approved there, and rumor had it that Hugh's companions had lobbied hard to get the committee to approve their alternate charter, which gave Massachusetts Bay control. Roger needed a creative approach.

One strategy was to link his charter to the work of the Westminster Assembly of Divines, as an experiment in toleration. They were chartered with determining how the English State Church would evolve. But that was just a pipe dream. They had abolished bishops to bring the structure closer to Scotland's Presbyterian system, but no one was thinking of toleration of multiple consciences or of separating the first table of commandments from the jurisdiction of civil rule. They were fighting to the death over which consciences to approve. Didn't they see the irony? Roger needed to write down the reasoning for toleration.

He turned to his notes. He'd brought all his notes from the last decade with him. He had notes on native language and culture. He had HH's letter and Cotton's vitriolic response. He knew what to do. Hugh Peter and John Cotton were published as saying they'd only converted one native, as the Algonquian people were too uncivilized. That was clearly not the reason. What Roger needed to do was to tell the story. He needed to make the English public love the natives' souls as much as Christ did. Personal testimony would act as a weapon for Christ. This was scriptural. Real testimony was right up there with reading the word of God and martyrdom. Roger was relieved that he had been asked by God to provide testimony and not martyrdom like HH, at least not today.

He would unleash HH's martyrdom and Cotton's response to it as the second weapon. He would make HH's life and death count.

Finally he must unleash the Gospel of Christ, the Blood of the Lamb and its relation to their own souls. He must write out and preach the scriptural basis for toleration. He must make people realize that the blood of the lamb meant that they must tolerate others in order to build the kingdom of God. For their own salvation, if they were to be forgiven, they must forgive. Matthew 6:14.

Testimony, martyrdom, and the blood of the lamb were the keys to his strategy. If he could do this, he would have released all the spiritual weapons of Revelations 12:11. The peace of the Lord was upon him.

His task clear now, he began to write.

The passage to England was calm—excellent weather for Roger's writing activities. By the time Roger landed, he had completed his first objective, in *A Key into the Language of America*. He presented Algonquian language by life function and provided a set of verses in each chapter, explaining how the Algonquian culture worked, and where it was inferior and superior to English culture. He often pointed out where the Algonquian had applied the common grace of scripture, though he was also honest about where they failed.

CHAPTER 35

Shores of Narragansett Bay, August, AD 1643

Sochepo and Oonue were struggling mightily to get a small English coat of mail onto Miantonomoh's large, muscled body. He was grumbling. The mail was heavy, and he could not imagine how the English could stand to wear these for long-distance travel. He was already hot. The mail was a gift from the Englishman Sam Gorton, and Miantonomoh felt honor-bound to wear it.

Things had fallen apart ever since Roger Williams left for England. As far as Miantonomoh knew, he was in good standing with the English. He had even signed an official treaty at Hartford—a gesture of good will. He was not sure what the English thought it meant, but neither were the English sure what he thought it meant. It was a question of building good will.

The error he made was simple.

It was common knowledge that Massachusetts Bay and Connecticut both had aspirations to the land that Roger Williams was fighting to keep, even among the Algonquian. Powerful English merchants like William Arnold had called in their comrades from Boston to threaten people who followed the likes of Sam Gorton, and he was arrested and put in hard labor for a time. So it might have appeared that Miantonomoh had no excuse for his error. Gorton was soon released, however, as he was gathering new followers in the prison, and Massachusetts Bay feared English retribution if they treated him too harshly. It appeared that there was a truce, from the Narragansett viewpoint. Roger had long been a trusted middleman between Winthrop and Miantonomoh, and Roger had habitually covered over the divisions between the English. It was not clear to Miantonomoh that Williams and Winthrop were hardly speaking anymore, nor was it clear exactly how many communities Gorton had been expelled from to date. With Roger gone, Sam Gorton, with his charismatic presence, seemed like Miantonomoh's only English friend. The problem, for a European or an Algonquian, was that, with Sam Gorton for a friend, you got more trouble than help.

Seemingly working to restore his Algonquian honor, Uncas invited Miantonomoh to a traditional Algonquian confrontation to allow him to attempt to avenge the deaths of Canonicus's sons. If Miantonomoh showed up at Uncas's council seat, they would fight man to man.

Miantonomoh was eager for such a traditional confrontation. He gathered the Niantic, the Narragansett, and the other small tribes that loyalty could deliver and headed off to Cochegan Rock. In fact, he tried to gather help more broadly, but the Mohawk and Long Island Algonquian were uninterested in helping Miantonomoh get so powerful that he could eventually threaten them.

Uncas held all his tribal councils at Cochegan Rock. This rock was the largest glacial boulder in New England, and it stood six times the height of a man. Such an invitation implied they would show each other their strength, usually killing no more than one or two and then backing off to make crucial tribal agreements that would create peace and dictate territorial boundaries for a generation. This was how it had been done for centuries.

Miantonomoh marched a thousand braves toward Cochegan Rock. He was disgusted with the mail armor and was thinking of taking it off when suddenly arrows were flying. This was not the plan. Now it was Miantonomoh's turn to be angry.

Uncas had been planning ambush all along. He never intended to fight by Algonquian traditions. Thirty Narragansett fell in the first volley. The leaders of the volley had personally assigned targets. Among the thirty targets was Yotaash. Miantonomoh's life was only preserved by his coat of mail. He called a retreat, and the men sprinted away, happy to flee a death trap. Miantonomoh, in his mail, could only limp away. He felt that he should be honorably dead and that he was but a miserable speck of part-English rubbish like Uncas for wearing this armor of mail.

The ambush divided the Narragansett men. The back of the group was able to flee toward home. The leaders and the elite of the tribe at the front were walled off from the rest by continuing volleys of arrows, and they were forced to retreat east. Those who did not go down into the volley were now on the run. Miantonomoh was well behind this front group, but he was also angling east and not toward the safety of his people.

The leaders in the group reached the Yantic. The Yantic was a wild river, too broad to jump, but the Narragansett who were fleeing tried and failed and fell many feet into rushing, rock-strewn rapids. They were dead before their bodies reached the quiet pond below.

The Mohegans captured Miantonomoh and dragged him back to Uncas controlled Shantok. He was held prisoner there, though he begged to die the honorable death his elite status demanded.

Oonue was shaken. She wanted to help her husband. She dragged out of the vaults tremendous volumes of wampum and had braves visit Miantonomoh and make deliveries to him. They were able to improve his conditions slightly, but many times he asked to die properly at the hands of Uncus, his peer, and he was not allowed to.

Boston, September, AD 1643

Uncas wanted to preserve his appearance of being loyal to the English. Miantonomoh had his own English connections, and Uncas wanted English approval on the next step so that he didn't find himself targeted as an outlaw. With a little help from John Winthrop Senior, Uncas timed his request to the English exquisitely. He waited, with Miantonomoh as his prisoner, and presented his question at the next meeting of the commissioners of a new Puritan civic organization, the United Colonies of England.

Since May, Massachusetts Bay, Plymouth, Connecticut, and New Haven had all named delegates and agreed to articles for joint government. No settlement of banished persons was included, so Providence led by Williams, Newport and Portsmouth led by Coddington, and Pawtuxet led by Arnold were not included. Also excluded were New Hampshire area settlements like the one the Gorges brothers had founded beyond Pascataquack and Exeter, where Wheelwright had relocated.

In fact, the Massachusetts Bay and Connecticut decision makers were the same leaders of Connecticut and Boston who had so recently sent troops to make a show of being able to keep the peace in Providence, when the government of Providence wasn't doing enough, per the complaints of its wealthiest members. They hoped that this colony full of outlaws would soon be extinguished. A year ago it had been these United Colony decision makers who sent Hugh Peters and his companions to make that claim in England.

The one friend the Narragansett might have had in this set of colonies was John Winthrop the Younger. He, however, was linked to Ninigret, a leader who could gain followers with Miantonomoh gone. Besides, John the Younger was back in England again, raising money for his ironworks project. He'd been there over a year already, and Ninigret knew that because his annual tribute this year was very unusual. John the Younger arranged remotely for Ninigret to have his portrait painted, English-style.

Miantonomoh was an ally of Roger Williams. The United Colonies of England had a vested interest in seeing Uncas, friend of John Mason, ally of Hooker's Hartford settlement, as the major Algonquian leader. They could control Uncus. There was no trial. The United Colonies representatives conferred and agreed. Miantonomoh must die. However, they didn't want to do the deed. They instead asked that he be allowed to die at the hands of Uncas. They would then be able to say to Roger that they had granted Miantonomoh's own wish.

Uncas marched Miantonomoh to the spot where he had been captured and split his head with a hatchet. In the Algonquian value system, Miantonomoh's death was honorable.

An honorable death meant that his spirit would now remind his kin that he deserved honor, and his death must be avenged. There were now two Narragansett leaders to avenge. Canonicus did not want his leadership team distracted by internal contests to see who could avenge the dead, so he made his expectations clear. Ninigret was charged with achieving justice for the Narragansett. Meiksah and Pessicus were charged with the day-to-day operations and diplomacy, respectively. After the execution, Oonue decided that she would be called Wawaloam in public from that day forward. She intentionally chose a name that to the English sounded like crying. She felt that her tears were more numerous than the particles of soil on the earth, and she wanted them to know it.

While Ninigret contemplated revenge, he actually showed up in Salem to have his portrait painted, as arranged. The resulting portrait is one of the few surviving detailed and accurate images of the Narragansett.

Providence, September, AD 1643

Rebecca Throckmorton was finally visiting Mary Williams. Both of their husbands were away on business. The tables were turned, in that, for the first time, Mary had more children running about than Rebecca. That was partly because the fifteen-year-old twins had been left at home to take care of the house and animals, so that Rebecca could have an extended visit with Mary. Freegift and Freeborn were already eight years old and were inseparable. Now that they lived in New Amsterdam, John was home a little more often, and Rebecca was cradling a new baby, Deliverance, who was just over a year old. Both women looked very pregnant. Mary was due in December. Rebecca was not that far along, but she thought she was so big already because it was another set of twins. That was a scary thought, at her age, but she was comforted that Anne Hutchinson, who lived nearby her home in New Amsterdam, was the best midwife in the New World.

Of course, with the delivery of the malformed Dyer baby soon after her banishment, there were accusations that babies she touched would be scarred by the Devil. Rebecca didn't believe that for even a minute. She knew Anne and considered her the most inspiring Christian she'd ever met.

Mary had a five-year-old named Providence, who was dismayed that the older girls really wouldn't let her hang with them. She was stuck with her three-year-old sister, Mercy, two-year-old brother Daniel, and the grownups. After a while they got her to help with Rebecca's baby, and she was finally in a better mood.

The women had been long separated and lonely and couldn't do enough to catch up.

"Our town of Providence is so changed. Massachusetts keeps threatening to send in troops. I can't believe that our only hope lies in Sam Gorton," said Mary.

"Whoever put him in charge?" asked Rebecca.

"Well, we can't trust Arnold not to hand the territory to the United Colonies. Coddington's crowd refused. Most of the rest of the town are not political leaders, Roger said. At least Sam can energize the defense," explained Mary. "How many men do you know whom Massachusetts Bay released from prison out of fear that he was gaining followers? He is persuasive," said Mary.

"This territory is very different from New Amsterdam. It's interesting. Here, to everyone's consternation, we respect everyone's conscience and let them do whatever they want in their business. There, the business is tightly connected to the government, with all sorts of enticements to the businesses so they'll do the government's bidding, and no one even pays attention to religion. They hardly pay attention to whether you are Dutch or English. I mean, there is church, but it's mostly for show. Nobody takes it seriously. Roger would be up in arms about all the false worship there is in the little worship that does occur," answered Rebecca.

"It will be a miracle if this area still exists when Roger gets home," said Mary. She was scared, and it showed. "He seems to have such grand plans, but I'm afraid he'll take on the elite in London, and his hopes will be dashed by them, just like when he wanted to marry above his station."

"You mean Jane? You know she's been safely in New England now for nearly five years. You needn't worry about her. She has a house church, you know. I still keep in touch with Elizabeth Masham, and she keeps in touch with Jane."

"I can't imagine her digging in the dirt in New England," said Mary with disgust.

"I don't imagine she does. He's got a minister position, and she's got servants from Africa. John got some for them himself. I don't think she lifts a finger."

"Do you have servants?" Mary was curious.

"No, I don't want them. We're Quakers now, and we appreciate the simple. John keeps his business life very separate from us at home. The children are always asking him for stories, and he has some great adventures. I'm afraid they'll soon join him, and simple will be tossed to the wind. There is what we say, and then there is what John does."

"I don't see how such a separation can provide a good witness. I wouldn't want that for my children." At that moment Mary appreciated Roger Williams, husband and father. Roger had always put his life right where his heart was, in the hands of Christ, as his servant. It was a rare gift, for which she was thankful.

Rebecca would forever remember this as one of the happiest days of her life. For after today, though there would be small joys, the weight of tragedy would lie on her heart, and she would have a hard time finding the way back. She was about to learn that inner lights could die. True joy has to come from God, often catalyzed via God's revelations in scripture. For now, scripture did not have authority in her life. She would not find that outside source of joy until she found her way back to submission to scripture.

New Netherlands, September, AD 1643

The days were getting shorter now, and the men and boys at almost every home did the morning animal chores in complete darkness, often alone or in small numbers. At the Throckmorton home, fifteen-year-old John was outside with the cows early when a young Algonquian about his own age surprised him. The brave had his knife poised and was clearly nervous as he made his first kill. John never had a chance to warn Patience.

Two braves lurked about outside the house, sizing up the opposition inside. When they were certain it was only the girl, they pounced. She was dead before she understood that she was being murdered.

The braves moved on to the next house a mile away.

The Long Island Algonquian had long been resistant to the idea of a unified war against the English, fearful that the Narragansett would be their new rulers. Sassacus and then Miantonomoh attempted unsuccessfully to garner unified loyalty, giving gifts and asking for support, to no avail. The tide had shifted, and Long Island Algonquian had found alliances with Canonicus and Ninigret, with the Mohawk, and with smaller tribes that would be recruited. With great humility, Sachem Mayano convinced all to support this offensive attack. The English were oblivious, and the Dutch believed they had a peace agreement. Fifteen hundred braves were attacking in pairs and small groups, home by home.

At the Hutchinson house, there were many more people, and more braves were assigned. The Siwanoy had the lead, and Wampage was in command of the assault. Suzanna was nine years old when she watched her fifty-two-year-old mother die with Zuriel, age seven, in her arms. The braves by then had already stormed the outside, killing several servants and William Collins. Suzanna saw in the semidarkness that bodies were strewn about as she was dragged by her hair over a fence and taken away. William Collin's seventeen-year-old wife, Anne's daughter Anne the Younger, was killed, along with twenty-three-year-old Francis, fifteen-year-old Mary, and thirteen-year-old Katherine. The whole thing happened in just a few minutes. Suzanna was so traumatized she forgot to cry.

Suzanna was lucky to be a living white girl kidnapped by Algonquian forces. She was not raped, she was not sold into slavery, and she was not even scorned. She was given a new name, a new family, and allowed to heal in her own time. Anne Hutchinson's older children were also fortunate, as they lived north of the killing zone. Edward and Faith lived near Boston, and Bridget still lived on Aquidneck Island.

The occupants of over eight hundred homes were slaughtered by the time the English soldiers mustered their forces and had the Algonquian unified forces in retreat. As quickly as they could be gathered, Dutch and English soldiers responded. Captain Patrick was valiant on the scene, and Robert Feake was finally at the front of the action. Before the Algonquian were in full retreat, Captain Daniel Patrick was a bona fide military success. He found and killed Sachem Mayano and many more. Feake didn't know how many he killed or who they were. In his battle fury, he lost count.

New Amsterdam, December, AD 1643

Governor Kieft wanted the Algonquian responsible exterminated quickly.

In charge of the joint Dutch and English forces was Captain Dan Patrick. Robert Feake was by his side. Another soldier in his troops was Marney. Being fluent in Dutch and English, he was soon at Patrick's side serving as soldier and messenger.

Unfortunately it was cold, and the men were not really in excellent physical shape. No one seemed to know the area—there was no Uncas to guide the troops through the forest. There were many pauses where the men were not physically active. Metal in their mail shirts conducted body heat away from the men's core, and they were cold. Worse, once the sun set, it was a cloudy night. There were many streams and some rivers that could only be crossed by canoe. Most were tidal, and the same river might look utterly different in a few hours' time.

Eventually Captain Patrick had to admit that they were lost. It took all night, but they finally got their bearings, and in the morning they returned to New Amsterdam defeated, cold, and depressed. To the captain's credit, not one man was lost in the confusion, and there was no friendly fire.

Not one Algonquian had been encountered. The entire troop was defensive on the topic of how they got turned around and lost on Long Island, and no one wrote home or bragged about it.

The only real difference between Captain Patrick now and Captain Underhill at Mystic was that, upon his return, Patrick did tell the truth to his superiors.

It was a Lord's Day afternoon, January 2, 1644, and the soldiers were at a tavern in New Amsterdam getting ready for the next offensive. Captain Underhill would head a unit of fresh English soldiers, and Dutch General Montagne would lead the overall offensive. Captain Patrick was to be a part of the raid as well, with a force composed of English and Dutch.

The atmosphere at the tavern turned ugly when Marney shouted, "Captain Patrick told the enemy we were coming!"

Another Dutch soldier, Hans Fredrick, took up the taunt, "He's a liar and cheat. He led us around in circles the whole night."

Captain Patrick and his loyal followers were incensed. Patrick spit in Fredrick's face. Robert Feake struck the first blow at a random Dutch soldier. In the melee, someone pulled a pistol and shot Captain Patrick in the back. He died of his wounds in minutes, and the killer escaped. Hans Frederick tried to take credit, but Marney didn't believe him because Frederick and Patrick had faced each other the entire time. Marney had seen the whole thing.

Robert Feake was heartbroken. He continued on the raid with Captain Underhill, but it was a complete sham. They didn't find Algonquian. When they came to the abandoned Siwanoy town that the recently deceased Sachem Mayn Mayono had used as a winter encampment, they burned it.

There was not a soul inside. The Siwanoy had been gone since about forty-eight hours after the massacre, each to a new tribe. The melt-and-disappear maneuver was well motivated, as no one wanted to be sold into slavery.

When Underhill returned, he and his ilk boasted that between five hundred and seven hundred Algonquian died that day by jumping into their wigwams and burning with their homes. He claimed that the pile of bodies rivaled Cochegan Rock in size and was leveled so that no one could find it. He claimed that the Siwanoy were destroyed. The only claim that was truthful was that there was no longer anyone calling him or herself Siwanoy. They had all taken new tribal allegiances, many of them now Leni Lenape, Narragansett, Mohawk, or Mohican, depending on their family ties. Few became Mohegan. No one wanted to be friends with the English. There would be war, but not right then. It was time to hide and be friendly to the English, laughing that they could not tell one Algonquian from another.

When Robert Feake returned home, he told the truth to all who would listen. After all, bona fide war heroes could talk about failure as well as success, and Captain Patrick always learned from failures. Underhill dismissed him. No one believed Feake, and everyone believed Underhill. Underhill put it out that Feake had gone mad, and others were quickly willing to agree that something had been building for ten years. Underhill's fabrications prevailed, as they made the returning soldiers heroic.

Depressed and alone, without Daniel Patrick, who had been his best friend and constant companion, Robert Feake withdrew. Much later, Bess would eventually come to know it was Feake's story, and not Underhill's story, that contained truth. By then there would be no profit for her in making that realization public, and Bess was a businesswoman at heart. It was a private sorrow she would have to live with for the rest of her life.

CHAPTER 36

Toward Boston, AD 1644

When Roger arrived in London, he found Harry Vane about to depart for Scotland.

"I am counting on you to help me negotiate English politics. I've been out of touch far too long," lamented Roger.

"I will help. I've prepared a list of all the people you must lobby for support. However, the key is to go to an official meeting of the committee after all your lobbying and to get them all to sign at once, affixing the official seals. When that happens, the committee has approved and it will be submitted to the king. The king will sign anything that weakens Massachusetts Bay Colony, given their scandalous placement of control in New England and their refusal over the years to even submit copies to the crown."

"I need your advice daily though, as I encounter obstacles," Roger insisted.

"Send me letters, just as you did during the Pequot war. I will be sure to reply," dictated Harry. "I'll be back soon enough. Live in my quarters and write your books while you wait for my advice when you are unsure of next steps."

Roger wrote the three books just as he had planned, completing the third while in waiting for Harry's return. Yet God paved the path differently than either of them had imagined.

During his stay Roger watched the throne continue to weaken in the midst of a bloody Civil War. Two percent of the population of England, Ireland, and Scotland would give their lives in this war. That meant hundreds of thousands of lives. Genteel society was breaking down in face of the war. The fuel shortage during the winter made it Roger's coldest in England. Physically fit and unafraid of physical labor, he worked the winter for people, tirelessly gathering wood out in the country as he had once tirelessly helped people recover from a hurricane. He helped keep his sister Katherine's children and her poor tenants warm. He worked cutting wood nonstop except to jot down book ideas that he would take up in his customary late-night writing time. Life seemed at least as unstable in England as it was in the New World.

When Harry returned, only the innocent Key had been published. Roger's summary to Harry on the night of his return was simple, "In a fight, sometimes the other guy falls. In the case of Rhode Island, the Massachusetts Bay Colony's fall from grace was the behavior of Thomas Weld."

"You are calling it Rhode Island now?" asked Harry, surprised.

"Yes. It will be called the aisle of roses, the road to toleration. I've characterized it as a noble experiment that if successful should be copied across England and all her colonies," said Roger.

"Your dreams have grown big while I was away, what is the story?" Harry was curious now.

"Weld canvassed the committee over foreign plantations the whole year before I arrived, just as we thought. He was indeed proposing a charter that would have given Massachusetts Bay Colony control over Providence and the surrounding communities and that had no mention of the novel notion of toleration. Because of the insubordination of the Massachusetts Bay Colony in the matter of their patent, however, he had an uphill battle. He lobbied committee members one by one and got signatures as he went. He was missing one key signature entirely. When Weld tried to claim that he had had an alternative patent approved, there was an inspection, called by the man who knew he'd never signed. The seals associated with group approval were never obtained."

"Wow," was all Harry could think of to say. Weld was a Puritan minister. It made all Puritans look bad.

"The whole Parliament was extremely unhappy with the misuse of its hard-won authority. Now even those opposed to the king are unhappy with the Massachusetts Bay Colony. All sides in England are looking for patents to approve that would be sanctioned alternatives to Massachusetts Bay and the United Colonies. They want to put the upstart colony and its neighbors in their place. In truth, they would approve just about anyone credible with an alternative patent. I just happened to be the guy standing at the door with a patent at their next meeting, and I'm scheduled for a final approval vote after the review period ends," finished Roger.

"See. You have succeeded on your own, you did not need me," needled Harry.

"You are a gift from God. I could not have done what I did without your prepared list and without using your name to get access," answered Roger. "Our next target is to get toleration accepted in England. I want your help to write the forward to my book."

"Sure," said Harry. Roger went to get his papers.

Now that Roger appeared likely to succeed, Harry campaigned with him. Harry Vane was the most persuasive man alive, and he had the position of power to make good use of his persuasiveness. When Harry advocated, the listener thought he himself had come up with the idea before the end of the conversation. He was a patient listener and always had an insightful question. He and Roger became a tight-knit team. They appeared before the formal committee together and obtained all signatures and seals of approval. Soon enough, they had the signature of the king.

Authority in England was rapidly shifting. William Masham was in power now, and an ally in Parliament. Stephen Winthrop was in the military in England and was a key ally for soul liberty. The expectation was changed. Rhode Island was cast as an experiment, but the target was for a change toward toleration in England. Roger could tell that Harry Vane was just getting warmed up, but he also felt it was time to return home to Rhode Island.

John Milton introduced Roger to his printer, Gregory Dexter, though he was not the only printer Roger would use. Montegu Bertie had been part of a prisoner exchange and was free. He would never advocate for Roger in public but he was a personal, if private, supporter of toleration. He also wanted to keep Uncle Perri's dream alive, and he believed that if Roger was successful, England could be changed forever. This could be the last war fought with steel swords for concepts that should be fought over with words.

Roger planned his other two books and a pamphlet for publication after he was safely at sea. He reviewed Dexter's version while in England and corrected errata as footnotes so as not to delay publication. He then took a copy from the first printing and asked Montegu Bertie to have a second printing ready to go when the first ran out. Montegu transported his set to France while he was he was on official duty escorting Queen Henrietta Maria in her escape to France. Then he waited.

Roger climbed aboard a ship. It was hard to pull himself out of the intrigue in the lofty circles of Parliament. However, his project in Rhode Island was in dire peril, and he knew it. If he did not return and restore order, all would be for naught. His dreams for England hinged on finding a successful alternative form of government that could be successful in Rhode Island first. He knew there was much to learn. Roger Williams was on a return ship to the Boston from which he had been banished. He had two letters in his pocket that he believed would protect him. One letter was meant to guarantee his safe passage, and the other introduced the patent.

The books acted like time bombs. First came *Queries for the Highest Consideration*, written long ago, and now polished, with introductory letters practically dictated by Harry. The second was also released while Roger sailed toward New England. A full-length book on the scriptural reasons against persecution for causes of conscience, it included detail on how scriptures previously interpreted to condone persecution had been misinterpreted. *The Bloudy Tenent of Persecution for Cause of Conscience* led with the HH essay, exposed John Cotton's vitriolic comments as unsound teaching, and laid out a new theology of how the government and church could interact to achieve The Way. The book was a massive hit, right up until magistrates ordered it burned. Even the typeset was burned, and Dexter was put out of business.

Roger's final pamphlet was "Christenings Make Not Christians." He started by describing the humanity of the Algonquian people, building on his prior book. He pointed out that Europeans who have not personally committed to Christ as Lord are heathen. Algonquian people that have accepted Christ as Lord are not heathen, even when they utterly reject European culture. He went on to explain that Algonquian Christianity could not be full until civil toleration of Algonquian consciences made it possible for ministers to the Algonquian to explore with Algonquian converts what it means to accept Christ as Savior and worship in an Algonquian cultural context.

Six weeks after *The Bloudy Tenent of Persecution for Cause of Conscience* typeset was burned, Montegu Bertie smuggled the first copies of the second printing into England. Montegu Bertie's strength was his printing press in France. Books and pamphlets created on that press trickled into England. The English authorities could not snuff them out.

The burning was a marketing bonanza. The second edition was passed about in secret from one powerful person to the next and was very widely read. Montegu could not afford for his second typeset to be discovered, so there was no third edition. He just kept quietly printing the second edition and distributing it, ensuring that a growing river of copies flowed into England.

Some of the most significant moments were silent and unobserved on earth, though HH may have watched from heaven. Montegu Bertie, as Gentlemen of the Bedchamber, left a copy where King Charles's son, the future king, saw it and picked it up to read. Charles the Younger was fascinated by this book and months later Montegu smiled when he found the dog-eared copy under the boy's bed. The son became an ardent, if private supporter for toleration. Montegu hoped a day would come when Roger would return so he could tell him about it, as he dared not write about it.

If Roger's writing provoked men to conscience, his personal advocacy rarely won new direct converts. Roger could be personable and a good arbitrator, but he was never an effective verbal advocate for his own ideas. He believed them too strongly. A book could be put down much more easily than a conversation when his listeners needed a break.

Harry Vane, on the other hand, was an excellent advocate for Roger's ideas. When Roger left, Harry took over. Even Hugh Peter was eventually persuaded by Harry Vane to support toleration, and Hugh Peter evolved to be in favor of Roger's experiment in Rhode Island. As a sign of how much and how little things changed, bishops were eliminated by Parliament, Laud was in prison facing a death sentence, and Hugh Peter was living in Laud's old quarters. Peter wouldn't be returning to Boston. All hoped that the civil war would end, and peace would be coming to England. It hadn't yet, though, and it couldn't, because the people in power didn't understand that once you get power, putting your opposition on the death penalty list is not the stable path forward. Every action spawns an opposite reaction. Only toleration ends the conflict. Roger's book would work slowly, like a fogger spreading an unseen mist of slow-absorbing, long-acting medicine. It took time for the practical implications to become apparent, and to effect tolerant government systems.

The Boston Roger was returning through was a bitter, saddened place. The Boston economy was still wrecked, and if it was improving in the outer regions, the old money wasn't returning. Winthrop Senior was selling his property and downsizing, having donated a large part of his fortune to keep the Massachusetts Bay solvent. The United Colonies were as intolerant as ever, and they weren't too happy about what Roger Williams said about their beloved teacher, John Cotton, in his newly published book. The only welcome he got when he got off the ship September 17, 1644, was to be ushered out of town.

Not only had Weld been deceptive about his charter's approval status, William Arnold had proven that he wasn't honest, either. He physically altered the original land use agreement from Canonicus by cutting and pasting it to remove his own lands from Providence's control. He had been claiming that the forged document was the real one, and allowing Massachusetts Bay to Control his settlement. Both men's forgeries had been found out, and by rights Arnold and Weld should have been in some disgrace. They were wealthy, however, and Boston averted her eyes, hoping to attract investment. Roger decided that he should also forgive and move on from the conflict, hoping to retain his wealthiest residents.

Rhode Island had a royal patent. No one could stop Roger Williams now. He actually kept the patent on his person, not trusting it even to the bedpost.

In truth it was only the beginning. Rhode Island and Sam Gorton were in desperate shape. There would be more conflicts, and one of those conflicts would begin with Sam Gorton, who was even then on his way to England with his own desperate patent proposals. But for today, Roger was on top of the world. He walked out west to intersect with the route he had taken when his banishment was new. He hooked up with the old route at the Blackstone River west of Boston. He was like a soldier returning to the scene of a key battle. It was his touchstone, where he had found his calling. When fourteen large canoes full of cheering townspeople met him on the river, tears formed in his eyes. As he paddled home, he knew he was exactly where God intended him to be.

Heaven, the Future

A twenty-first-century American citizen conducted the following interview as Roger sat in line on Judgment Day.

1. Question: "Roger, what did you think of the nonsectarian prayers so often said at public events in the twenty-first century? Are they a testimony to your principles?"
   Answer: "Not at all! First of all, if the person does not earnestly communicate with God, he is participating in false worship. That

is a stink to God, and that is what I wanted most to prevent. It is more consistent to hear a heartfelt prayer from a Turk one day, a Jew the next, and a poem of devotion to the universe from an atheist the next. There must be a right to say a heartfelt and honest prayer to my Creator in my own turn."

2. Question: "Doesn't that force the listeners into false worship?" Answer: "No, not at all. Participation would force false worship. Being within hearing and observation distance is not worship."

3. Question: "What if it offends the listener?" Answer: "All persons need to be offended by some truth when they err, and we do all err. Truth from conscientious believers of all faiths shared will lead to communal truth. Even science has shown that communal truth is more accurate than individual truth. How could we share truth and learn without sharing and debating and testing our convictions? I spent my life fighting for the right to offend those who disagree, that we may both learn the truth."

4. With some consternation, "Okay, moving on." Question: "Did you think you were fighting for democracy when you said that a state should not be a nursing father to the church? Don't you think democracy is less fallen than a monarchy?" Answer: "I never fought for democracy. The freemen voted for governor even before I came, and that might be considered to be in the direction of democracy. However, that governor always received authority from a king. No matter how chosen, all authority in a civil state comes from God. All right to be ruled by law comes from God, not man. That is why a king or an elected head of government cannot take that right away. All men, elected or otherwise, are fallen, and no system on earth is infallible. The only thing that protects man is a balance of power between fallen entities, until Christ comes. Whenever there is only one power, greed corrupts. That is why elected officials are no less fallen, no less corrupt, than monarchs."

5. Question: "So that makes the church corrupt, since she is made of men?" Answer: "Clearly the church as a human organization on earth is corrupt. Yet the church is from God; she is the bride of

Christ. His elect will be restored at this judgment, and his church will be made perfect."

6. Question: "People say you are a seeker, spurning the organized church? Is that so?"

Answer: "No. My accusers call me all kinds of names. This was one of them. It is so frustrating to be remembered for the names my enemies tossed at me. My sons saw me at the river preaching every Lord's Day to the Algonquian. That is hardly individual worship. There were surely more than three most Lord's Days! However, in the sense that all people discern God's will most perfectly in groups of two or three, we all seek."

7. Question: "You didn't answer the question. Should there be an organized church in New England?"

Answer: "Many actually, and none controlled by the state. However, I have my doubts about creating new sects each week, and I do not pretend that its leaders can assume that the people in the church are all God's elect. I know all sects will be flawed. Christ clearly calls his people to gather to worship him, and the alternative to organized worship is the Quaker error of inner light. Men are supposed to correct one another, to prevent error, but with the sword of Christ's word, not one of metal."

8. Question: "Did you really think the Algonquian people were the tribe of Dan?"

Answer: "I had incomplete information then, and even then it was a stretch to play for the sympathy of the English crowds. I admit it. In fact I can see now that they were the descendants of the daughters of Cain, the abused ones who escaped Nod in great peril to settle with the children of Seth, and whose descendant married Noah's son Japheth. They became Japheth's coastal people. That's why their horticultural talents were matriarchal in descent, always, and required continual backcrossing for the genes of their leadership to be expressed. Who could have known that in my day? Even in the twentieth century they did not know. They were all confused by assuming that carbon isotope ratios were constant over time and were unable to see the past accurately. They were caught between literal counting of spans of time explicitly mentioned in the Bible and the near eternity that incorrect carbon dating suggests."

9. Question: "But surely there were unregenerate Algonquian persons when you preached in Algonquian?"

Answer: "Yes, all there voluntarily. All churches contain unregenerate men anyway. It is not ours to say who is chosen, who is elect. There is no problem with honest observers at worship. What is odious to God is if they are forced to participate in worship. Ridiculing observers would be different. That would be sin, and I would have ejected the heckler. No Algonquian ever ridiculed at our worship. They were intensely respectful."

10. Question: "Why did you leave the Baptist church?"

Answer: "As a civil administrator, it was inappropriate for me to lead my civil subjects in worship. There were other ministers who could do that. I did not want to hinder the sect."

11. Question: "But you didn't attend church, either?"

Answer: "Again, I attended church on the banks of a river with the Algonquian. I was always a controversial figure among the English. I did not want to disrupt worship. I did ask forgiveness for my lack of attendance when I recanted to be restored to the church near the end of my life, and I'm sure we'll be addressing my reliance on Christ's grace for the forgiveness of that sin here when I reach the front of the line."

12. Question: "Do you believe individuals have human rights?"

Answer: "As Christ's servant, I have no rights. Look at what he allowed to be done to him. If the civil authority recognizes human rights in order to keep the peace, then, to the degree that exercising those rights does not cause me to sin, I have civil rights."

13. Question: "What defines sin?"

Answer: "Scripture defines sin."

14. Question: "Who most influenced you? You are said in the twenty-first century to have quoted Bacon and Coke, so their work is credited with having influenced your thinking most."

Answer: "Did the creditors actually read the whole letter in which I mention Bacon? I quote him when he accuses anyone lacking tolerance to be pursuing his own ends versus Christ's. If you want the truth, it was Harry Vane who had me add the Bacon quote. We were name-dropping, trying to build support from all factions. The quote comes after I quoted the king of Bohemia on the topic, as that king was far ahead of England. Nobody mentions that when they try to claim that my ideas are original. In that letter, the quote comes after I quote scripture four times. Your century seems blind to the authority of scripture. My thought is derived first from scripture. It is laughable that someone thinks my proposal for Rhode Island as an experiment comes from Bacon, as it comes directly from Paul in <u>1 Thessalonians 5:21–22</u>: Try all things. Keep what is right. My ideas are not new. I was one of the first to try them out and make them work. I am but the least servant of Christ."

15. Question: "Speaking of scripture, you are aware that your method of interpretation is controversial, right? I'm referring to your characterizing the Old Testament as a set of stories that are physical archetypes for lessons that repeat over time in all cultures, as well as the physical preparation for the spiritual lessons of Christ?"

    Answer: "I see that. I am in good company, as Augustine used the same methods. This method reaches God's meaning more quickly in my opinion than that of those who would nitpick every number and detail and force a literalness that was never claimed. Literalists are more questionable than I. We watched Augustine's trial yesterday. There was much sin that Christ had to cover for him, but his search for archetype was not among them."

16. Question: "Do you support gay marriage?"

    Answer: "First, all marriage in the colonies was civil, not religious. It is a grace God gives all groups, not just his elect. If a civil authority grants pagans the right to marry, and that includes homosexuals, it could be respected. As Christ's follower, however, I could never have a same-sex partner without sinning. Of course I could never get through a day as a heterosexual without sinning either; it is just a different set of sins. We are all fallen. As a Christian magistrate I would have to consider pagan toleration and their civil flourishing in setting the law. However, once any magistrate executes a marriage civilly, especially any marriage with the possibility of children, things change. No matter how those children are conceived, they must be protected and encouraged and the children helped by the civil peace and support to thrive. I would add that my friend John Milton wrote a treatise on divorce worth reviewing. The same comments in the New Testament apply to divorce and homosexuality, so the treatise may be more relevant than it may first appear. In his view the purpose of marriage is comfort and refreshment against the perils of a solitary life. In God's perfect plan he created man and woman as complementary creatures able to supply this comfort and refreshment. All men and all women are fallen, even in our genes and natural attractions. We cannot escape those consequences. We can only look toward the ideal and move on."

"It will be interesting to see what happens to Milton. Look! He's at the head of the line for judgment. Let's watch!"

Acknowledgments

Thanks to Pastor George Hancock-Stefan and Lindsey Stefan Wood for their insights and research assistance.

Thanks to Mrs. Schofield for her study of genealogy, which started this project, and to all the others like her who have contributed genealogical research that is recorded now for all to see. I footnoted each helpful website as a reference to the List of Characters in Appendix 3. Thanks to the rest of my family for their patience.

Thanks to Google for digitizing and making searchable so many old books, a key research tool in understanding the historical context for the fictional characters in this book.

Thanks to Paul Boyd, now departed, who verbally boxed me about the ears for believing other people's opinions. He repeatedly sent me back to original sources to check for facts. When the facts didn't fit, the story has been changed from the truth.

Thanks to Hilary H., who edited the manuscript with care, and to Dawn Dove who provided additional critical perspective.

Thank you also to the many who over the years came to work with me in corporate America—you who shared your own search for the American dream. You spent so much of your personal and family resources getting to and staying in this country. Where did that dream come from, and why is it so resilient? With brave, failed attempts at democracy littering our modern world, democracy and individual freedoms cannot be the only ingredients. What have we modern people left out of the recipe? Will we lose our dream if we do not rekindle those missing ingredients? For here is what a tester knows: if you cannot replicate the behavior, you do not yet understand the root cause. The success of the Rhode Island experiment did replicate. First Charles II put the wording verbatim into the charters for additional colonies, e.g., New Jersey. Eventually similar wording was copied into the constitutions of the British Empire in order to keep them from revolting (as we had).

Thanks to the Algonquian descendant who named the stone bridge "valley" in their ancestor's native language from Rhode Island. The stone bridge near Middletown, New Jersey, was built a couple of hundred years after the Narragansett/Natick tribes were said to be "extinct." Yet the bridge is named with an Algonquian word, and not the language of the Algonquian from New Jersey, but rather a tribe from the land now called Rhode Island. To touch that bridge is to know that, like the Siwanoy who vanished before them, that tribe is likely not extinct. It has vanished into our own American tribe. The genes and the core culture have been transmitted into our own. Other Algonquian ingredients are also in our American recipe: their ideas did not come from England's Coke or Bacon. Christian scripture taught that we should try all plans and keep what is right. Roger Williams adapted a number of powerful elements from the culture of the Algonquian ruling class: loyal voluntary followers who select inspiring leaders; multiple powers, each keeping the others humble; and the rapid adoption of new ideas from anywhere.

APPENDIX 1

These are excerpts paraphrased from Roger Williams's books, as they may have been spoken. Roger Williams interspersed scripture with his statements, and he would have expected the reader to have had the scripture memorized so that they could picture the story in scripture much as a photograph accompanying the text. The hyperlinks in the digital version of the book will help modern readers quickly figure out the complete picture that would have been painted for a Puritan listener.

Selected Excerpts from Roger Williams's Writings

In Hard Times: *Spero Meliora*

There is a time when God though sought will not be found. <u>Proverbs 1</u>
There is a time when prayer and fasting comes too late. <u>Jeremiah 14</u>
There is God's answer to those who seek with a stumbling block. <u>Ezekiel 13</u>
There is a time God's answer is NO to our proud refusal of his will. <u>Jeremiah 42</u>
Love bids us hope for better things.
God promises that when God is sought with the whole heart, even from captivity, He will be found. <u>Jeremiah 27</u>
God comforts against all fears those that seek Jesus that was crucified. <u>Mark 16</u>

Williams, Roger. *The Complete Writing of Roger Williams*, Volume 1, ed. Samuel L. Caldwell, *"Letter to the Impartial Reader,"* p. 32 (Paris, Arkansas: The Baptist Standard Bearer Inc., reprinted in 2005, originally printed in 1867), p. 316.

Forced worship

An unbelieving soul being dead in sin
Being changed from one forced worship to another
Like a dead man shifted into several changes of apparel
Hebrews 11 (esp. 11:6)

Whatsoever such unregenerate unbeliever does
Acts of worship or religion
It is but sin
Romans 14 (esp. 14:23: "Whatsoever is not from faith is sin")

Preaching sin
Praying sin
Breaking of bread at Lord's supper
Sin

Yea as odious an oblation as swine's blood
Breaking a dog's neck
Killing of a man
Isaiah 66 (Isa. 66:1–6, 23–24)

Faith it is that gift which proceeds alone from the Father of Lights.
James 1:17

Till He please to make his light Arise and open eyes of blind sinners
Their souls shall lie fast asleep
(and the faster asleep if a sword of steel compels them to hypocrite's worship)

In the dungeons of spiritual darkness and Satan slavery

Williams, Roger. *The Complete Writing of Roger Williams*, Volume 3, ed. Samuel L. Caldwell, "*The Bloudy* Tenant," (Paris, Arkansas: The Baptist Standard Bearer Inc., reprinted in 2005, originally printed in 1867), p. 138. [Williams erroneously attributed verses to Phil 1:29 when they are from text that correlates to James 1:17]

Toleration

Sufferance of evil is not for its own sake but for the sake of Good
For God's own glory he suffers [i.e., permits or endures] the Vessels of
Wrath
Romans 9

Though He be of pure eyes and he can behold no iniquity
Yet his pure eyes
patiently and quietly
behold and permit
all the idolatry and prophanity
all thefts and rapes
all the whoredom and abominations
all the murders and poisonings
yet for his glory's sake he is patient and long permits.
For his people's sake
The next good in his Son
He is oftentimes pleased to permit and suffer the wicked to enjoy a longer
reprieve
He gave Paul all the lives that were in the ship
Acts 27

He would have granted Sodom a longer permission had there been 10
righteous
Genesis 19

Had he found some to stand in the gap he would have spared others
Jeremiah 5

He gave Jezebel a time or space
Revelations 2

For his Glory sake he permitted longer great sinners, who afterward have
perished in their season
Ahab, Ninevites, Amorites and more

Deuteronomy 24

It pleased the Lord to permit
the many evils against his own honorable ordinance of Marriage in the
world to suffer that sin of many wives of Abraham, Jacob, David, Solomon
with an expression that seems to give approbation
2 Samuel 12

Though we find Him sometimes dispensing with his law
We never find him denying Himself
Or uttering a falsehood
Therefore it crosseth not an absolute rule
To permit and tolerate
Toleration will not hinder our being Holy as He is Holy in all manner of
conservation
Even the permission of the souls and consciences of all men in the world
God suffers men like fishes to devour each other
Habakkuk 1

The wicked to flourish
Jeremiah 12

Sends the tyrants of the world to destroy the Nations and plunder them
of their riches
Isaiah 10

Two sorts of commands
Moses gave positive rules both spiritual and civil
He also gave some not positive but permissive for the common good
(e.g. Bills of Divorcement)
So the Lord Jesus expoundeth on it
Matthew 6, 7, 8

Moses for the hardness of your hearts suffered or permitted, a toleration

Williams, Roger. *The Complete Writing of Roger Williams*, Volume 3, ed. Samuel L. Caldwell, *"The Bloudy* Tenant,*"* (Paris, Arkansas: The Baptist Standard Bearer Inc., reprinted in 2005, originally printed in 1867), p. 166.

Overcoming Evil

God's people are all over-comers
When they fight with God's weapons
In God's cause and worship
Revelation 2, 3

Seven times it is recorded
To him that **overcommeth** in Ephesus
To him that **overcommeth** in Sardis
And so on ...

God's servants **overcame**
The Dragon or the Devil in the Roman Emperors
By three weapons
The blood of the Lamb
The word of their testimony. And
The not loving of their lives unto death.
Revelation 12

Williams, Roger. *The Complete Writing of Roger Williams*, Volume 3, ed. Samuel L. Caldwell, *"The Bloudy Tenant,"* (Paris, Arkansas: The Baptist Standard Bearer Inc., reprinted in 2005, originally printed in 1867), p. 190.

Wrestlers with God

Children of God in all ages
Under the protection of the Gospel

Who are therefore Abraham's true seed
The circumcised in heart
Newborn wrestlers with God,

the Antitype of Israel
Galatians 3 and 6

These are the only holy nation
A kingly priesthood And a Holy Nation
1 Peter 2:9

Wonderfully redeemed from the Egypt of this world
Titus 2:14

Brought through the Red Sea of baptism
1 Corinthians 10

Through the wilderness of afflictions of the people
Deuteronomy 8, Ezekiel 20
Into the kingdom of Heaven begun below
Even into that Christian land of promise
Where flow the everlasting streams and rivers of milk and honey.

Williams, Roger. *The Complete Writing of Roger Williams*, Volume 3, ed. Samuel L. Caldwell, "*The Bloudy Tenant,*" (Paris, Arkansas: The Baptist Standard Bearer Inc., reprinted in 2005, originally printed in 1867), pp. 327-328.

The Law

In whose hearts of flesh he writes his laws
Jeremiah 31:33, Hebrews 8, Hebrews 10

Williams, Roger. *The Complete Writing of Roger Williams*, Volume 3, ed. Samuel L. Caldwell, "*The Bloudy Tenant,*" (Paris, Arkansas: The Baptist Standard Bearer Inc., reprinted in 2005, originally printed in 1867), p. 358.

Debt

'Tis a universal disease and folly in men to desire to enter into not only
necessary but unnecessary and tormenting debts, contrary to the command
of the only wise God. Owe no thing to any man, but that you love each
other.

Romans 13:8

I have heard ingenious Indians say

In debts, they could not sleep.

How far worse are such English then,

Who love in debts to keep?

If debts of pounds cause restless nights

In trade with man and man

How hard is that heart that millions owes

To God, and yet sleep can?

Debts paid, sleep's sweet, sins paid, death's sweet,

Death's night then turned to light

Who dies in sin's unpaid, that soul

His light is eternal night.

Williams, Roger. *The Complete Writing of Roger Williams*, Volume 1, ed.
Samuel L. Caldwell, *"A Key into the Language of America,"* (Paris, Arkansas:
The Baptist Standard Bearer Inc., reprinted in 2005, originally printed in
1867), p. 188.

Sustenance

There is a blessing on endeavor, even to the wildest Indians, even the
sluggard rots not what he took in hunting, but the substance of the diligent
(either in earthly or heavenly affairs), is precious.

Proverbs 24:30–34

Great pains in hunting take the Indians wild,

　And with great effort the English same,

Both take in woods and forest thick,

To get their precious game

Pleasure and profit, Honour false,
The world's great trinity
Drive all men through all ways, all times,
All weathers wet and dry

Pleasure and profits, Honour sweet
    Eternal, sure and true

Laid up with God, with equal pains

Who seeks, who doth pursue

Williams, Roger. *The Complete Writing of Roger Williams*, Volume 1, ed. Samuel L. Caldwell, *"A Key into the Language of America,"* (Paris, Arkansas: The Baptist Standard Bearer Inc., reprinted in 2005, originally printed in 1867), p. 193.

Outcry from the Heart for Mercy

Jehovah will not forsake his people for his great name's sake. ... Yet mournfully read
Psalm 74, 79, 80, 89
Lamentations
Daniel 11
Revelations 11, 12, 13
I beseech you do this more seriously than ever

Abstract yourself with holy violence from the dung heap of this earth
The credit and comfort of it
Cry to Heaven to remove the stumbling blocks
Such idols
Sometime the Lord will give his own wrestlers with Him and answer.

Williams, Roger. *The Complete Writing of Roger Williams*, Volume 6, ed. Samuel L. Caldwell, "Letter to John Winthrop, October 24, likely in 1636" (Paris, Arkansas: The Baptist Standard Bearer Inc., reprinted in 2005, originally printed in 1867), p. 10.

Appendix 2: Algonquian Family Trees

Figure 1:
<u>Algonquian Narragansett</u>

Below is an image from the Prezi showing the relationships of the Algonquian Narragansett in this story and their key relationships to other tribes. http://prezi.com/o16_wvx2hlpf/?utm_campaign=share&utm_medium=copy

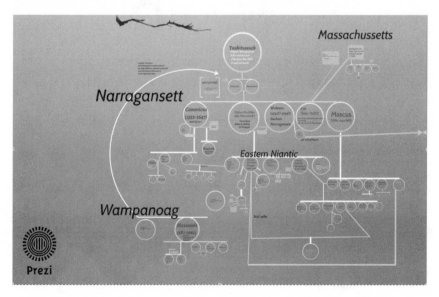

Figure 2:
<u>Algonquian Narragansett</u>–Pequot Relations

Below is an image from the Prezi showing the relationships of the Pequot in this story and their key relationships to other tribes.

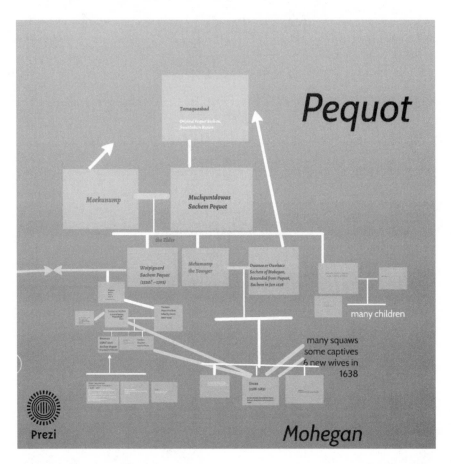

Figure 3:
Origins of Narragansett Ruling Class

Below is an image from a Prezi showing the hypothesized horticultural history of the Steward rulers.

http://prezi.com/yvrdggsgj8zp/?utm_campaign=share&utm_medium=copy

APPENDIX 3: LIST OF CHARACTERS

➤ Marney **Adrianson** (~1578–~1650). Flemish Dunkirker pirate turned soldier for the Dutch, for at least Kieft's War.

➤ Thomas **Agnell** (circa 1616–1694). A cousin of Roger Williams, he crossed the Atlantic as Roger's indentured servant and served for seven years. He was later one of the leaders of Providence, Rhode Island.

➤ Joan **Altham** (1617 or earlier –1638). Called Jug, she was the first daughter of Elizabeth Barrington by her first husband, Sir James Altham. Sir Altham was a judge, and he died in 1617.

➤ Bishop Lancelot **Andrewes** (1655-1626). Bishop who oversaw the translation of the King James Bible.

➤ Lady **Arabella** (circa 1585–1630). The most elite passenger in the great migration as daughter of the 3rd Earl of Lincoln, an investor in the Massachusetts Bay Company and a victim of the swamp fevers in Salem, she lived in New England less than six months.

➤ William **Arnold** (1587–1676). Wealthy landholder, trader, and translator English/Algonquian. One of the thirteen original Providence settlers, and one of the first dozen who formed the Baptist church. Banished from Massachusetts Bay's town of Hingham, likely for fraud. Author of doctored version of the land grant from the Narragansett for Rhode Island lands.

➤ **Augustine** (AD 354–430). An early Christian theologian. Augustine was the originator of the "City of God" metaphor for the church. He was in fact the first to interpret physical stories in the Bible as a metaphor for spiritual truths. He would not have said that the physical stories did not happen, but he did believe that their importance is in the spiritual truth represented. When his Puritans enemies complained of Roger Williams's way of interpreting the Bible, they were hypocritical in that he got it straight from Augustine, whom they quote freely on other topics.

➢ Sir Francis **Bacon** (1561–1626). Rival to Sir Edward Coke. Lost his first love when she married Sir Edward Coke. Parried for positions in government with him and traded accusations of malpractice with him. Never a wealthy man, he left office disgraced and in debt. A deep thinker, he developed the modern scientific method of making hypothesis and testing for truth with measured data. He caught pneumonia while stuffing fowl with snow for an experiment and died.

➢ **Bar-Jesus** (~30BC– AD 30). Magician in Pathos.

➢ Mary **Barnard Williams** (1609–1676). Daughter of Sir Richard Barnard of Nottinghamshire, a widower who did not remarry. Her father was a Puritan separatist minister and author of the "Isle o Man." He taught her to read but not to write. She was the homemaker for her four brothers and her father, and when they were grown she was servant to the Jug, Lady Elizabeth Masham's daughter from a former marriage. She married Roger Williams in 1629 and bore him six healthy children. She died in the year of the burning of Providence.

➢ Sir Francis **Barrington** (~1570–1628). English politician and lawyer.

➢ Lady Joan Cromwell **Barrington** (1589–1641). Married Sir Francis Barrington in 1573. Daughter of Henry Cromwell.

➢ Sir Robert **Barrington** (? – ?). Son of Sir Francis Barrington.

➢ Sir Thomas **Barrington** (? –1644). First son of Sir Francis Barrington.

➢ Montegu **Bertie** (1608–1666). Second Earl of Lindsey once his father, Robert, died in battle, Lord Willoughby before that. Brief stint at Cambridge in 1623 followed by being House of Commons (lower house of Parliament) member 1624–1626, commissioner to Parliament consistently urging reconciliation, soldier in English Civil War. He appeared loyal to King Charles until the king's beheading, yet he was not himself punished. He maintained a private retirement after the execution.

➢ Peregrine **Bertie** (Uncle Perri) (~1584– ~1633). Younger brother of Robert Bertie, Uncle of Montegu Bertie. With his brother, purchased John Smith's apprenticeship from Mr. Sendall.

➢ Robert **Bertie** (1583–1642). First Earl of Lindsey once his father died, Lord Willoughby until then. Montegu Bertie's father. Engineer of a large swamp drainage project in England that was completed in 1638. Loyal cavalry soldier for the King.

➤ The kings of **Bohemia** declared religious freedom in 1436, and it lasted until Emperor Mathias II, a Hapsburg Catholic, started restricting rights of Protestants in 1618. There was a revolt and a thirty-year war ending in Hapsburg victory and intolerant Catholic rule.

➤ John and Samuel **Brown** (~1583–1662). John and Samuel Brown were well-to-do men who did not approve of the new order of worship in the church in Plymouth. They set up a separate service using the common prayer book. In the first incident of persecution in New England, John Endicott led a group of men who banished them to England. In England they complained through the courts, causing several years of English attention and review of the Plymouth and Massachusetts Bay Patents.

➤ William **Bradford** (1590–1657). A member of John Robinson's Scrooby congregation from his youth, he became a surviving leader of the Plymouth Colony. He was the second, fifth, seventh, ninth and eleventh governor of the Plymouth Colony.

➤ Thomas **Cavendish** (1560–1592). Circumnavigated the globe with three ships, one of which was the original 120-ton *Desire* that he had commissioned.

➤ Robert **Carr** (1587–1645). Favorite of King James until the king replaced him with George Villiers. He was replaced after being accused of the 1613 poisoning of his administrative support, Thomas Overbury. Overbury opposed his match to Frances Howard. Carr first had an affair with Frances Howard while she was married. Then, once her former marriage was declared null in 1613, he married her. Under pressure from Coke and Bacon for justice, four people, including Gervase Helwys, were accused of being agents and hanged for the poisoning of Overbury. Robert Carr and Frances Howard were not among them. Carr might have been innocent, but Howard was almost certainly guilty.

➤ **Canonicus** (1552–1647). Grand sachem Narragansett and Steward ruler. [3]

➤ **Canonchet** (~1625–1676). Son of Miantonomoh was southern Narragansett sachem after Canonicus passed in 1647 at age twenty-two. At age fifty-one, he led Native American troops during the Great

Swamp Fight and King Philip's War, where he was captured and killed after refusing to make peace with the English.

➤ Abraham de **Cerf** [4](?–?). Schoolmaster at Austin Friars and father of Johannes de Cerf.

➤ Johannes de **Cerf** [5] (1601–1625). Son of schoolmaster Abraham de Cerf, at Austin Friars. Attended Leiden with Austin Friar's support 1617–1624. He was declared unfit for ministry at the end of his scholarship.[6] Died in plague year 1625. Roger William's closest friend.

➤ King **Charles I** (1600–1649). Son of King James, he ascended the throne in 1625. He married a Catholic, Henrietta Maria of France. His arguments with Parliament caused him to be short of funds in his military efforts to support the Thirty Years War. He changed the Anglican Church to be more like the Catholic Church and allowed the bishops a free hand in persecuting dissent.

➤ Richard **Church** (1608–1668). A carpenter in Plymouth and then Charleston and Hingam. He purchased an investment share in the ironworks in Taunton. He married Elizabeth Warren in 1637, and they had ten children, among them Benjamin and Joseph.

➤ John **Clarke** (1609–1676). Baptist minister in Newport, the second American Baptist church and the first Baptist Church to have a building.

➤ William **Clobbery** (?–?). Business partner of Sydrach Williams in 1625. Shipped merchandise to Virginia.

➤ William **Coddington** (1601–1678). A businessman, his initial capital was inherited. He was one of the original investors in the Massachusetts Bay Company. He sailed with the Winthrop fleet and became very prosperous in Boston. He married in England, but his wife died the first winter. He returned to England for another wife twice in his life. Coddington put together the Aquidneck compact, a set of agreements all settlers signed that governed the island. He was elected judge, the island's term for its highest elected official. The compact guaranteed religious freedom. Coddington fought the inclusion of Aquidneck in the Rhode Island patent and obtained his own patent with Harry Vane's help. When he tried to make his independent island a member of the United Colonies, putting religious freedom at jeopardy, his constituents disapproved, and he was not reelected. His successors then chose to allow inclusion in the territory of Rhode Island. Coddington became a Quaker in the 1660s, possibly to express his authoritative disapproval of the United Colonies in hanging Quakers.

➢ **Cojonoquant** (1605–1675). Youngest son of Mascus. Roger Williams commented that he always seemed to be drunk. Father of three sons.

➢ Sir Edward **Coke** (1552–1634). London lawyer promoted to posts including attorney general and chief justice and then demoted to Court of the King's Bench. He spent nine months in Newgate and recovered his court positions within three years. His most lasting contribution was the Petition of Right.

➢ Samuel **Collier** (1595–1610). Apprenticed as a page to John Smith at the time of the expedition to found Jamestown. John traded his apprenticeship to the Powhatan Algonquian, who killed him.

➢ William **Collins** (circa 1620–1643). Husband of Anne Hutchinson's daughter Anne the Younger at the time of their death.

➢ Myles **Coverdale** (1448–1569). Printed the first Bible in English to be printed on a printing press. Not a language scholar, he relied on five other interpreters who worked from Latin and German texts. After Tynsdale's death, he continued work to achieve improved translations from Hebrew and Greek. He was an editor of the Great Bible. His work was not requested or approved and often burned, until 1540, when King Henry VIII ordered that a Coverdale Bible created in 1535 be available in every English parish. This Bible was the English Bible that Roger Williams memorized in his youth. When later in life John Cotton and Roger Williams quoted the Bible with chapter and verse markings, they may have been using the popular Geneva Bible from 1560 first used by exiles while Catholics ruled England. Coverdale was a major contributor to the Geneva Bible, and it is largely Tynsdale-era work. The King James Bible, which incorporates improved Greek and Hebrew scholarship and removes non-scripture-based anti-Catholic margin notes was first produced in 1611. The King James Bible was not as popular as the Geneva Bible for many years after its creation, even though the Geneva Bible was a major influence on its text. The Puritan Bible in the 1630s and 1640s was the commonly used Geneva Bible.

➢ Balthazar de **Cordes** (circa 1555–circa 1608). Dunkirker pirate born in the Netherlands. He fought King Philip II's Spanish forces to win Danish independence and then terrorized Dutch shipping lanes in the Mediterranean and the spice routes from South America to Europe for three years from somewhere off the coast of Chile. He died in prison in the East Indies, arrested after having occupied the town of Castro, Chile. At the time, his fleet had five ships.

➢ Matthew **Craddock** (?–1641). Governor of Massachusetts Bay Colony while in England. While he never went to New England, he owned property and businesses there. He was a major figure in the tobacco trade. He was caught between a colony that would not produce the patent and a king asking him to produce it, and he wrote in favor of revoking the patent at one point. Accused of criminal acts, he was unable to act on behalf of the colony.

➢ Jacob van **Curler** (?–?). Ran the House of Hope Dutch trading post on the Fresh River in Connecticut.

➢ King **David** (1040–970 BC). A Biblical king with a strong indwelling of the spirit of the Lord. 1 Samuel 16:13.

➢ John **Davies** (circa 1590–circa 1660). Married Katherine Williams as her second husband in 1630, by trade a clerk.

➢ Katherine Williams **Davies** (1606 –?). Sister of Roger Williams. There was another sister named Catherine, born 1601, died approximately 1603.

➢ Gregory **Dexter** (1610–1700). Printer for John Milton and Roger Williams, pressured into emigration to Providence in circa 1647. Upon his arrival, he married Alice Smith, the daughter of John and Alice Smith, original members of Providence.

➢ Thomas **Dudley** (1576–1653). Governor of the Massachusetts Bay Company in 1634–1635, 1640–1641, 1645–1646, 1650–1651.

➢ John **Eliot** (1604–1690). An assistant to Thomas Hooker in England who migrated on the *Lyon* in 1631. He spent his life evangelizing the Algonquian, focusing at first on the Massachusetts and Mohegan, having more success with the Massachusetts. He translated the Bible into Algonquian, and his translation was the first Bible printed in America. Roger Williams called his translation inspired and believed it to be a miracle. Eliot organized the Christianized natives into praying towns that Anglicized the occupants and helped them practice their faith. When the Algonquian were under great pressure, these towns became another tribal home into which they could disappear. Eliot married Hannah Mumford, who bore him six children.

➢ John **Endicott** (1601–1665). Governor, soldier, and planter. He was the first, tenth, thirteenth, fifteenth and seventeenth governor for the Massachusetts Bay Colony, serving one-year terms each time. He supported a separated church from the English Anglican Church and the Roman Catholic Church but did not support churches separated from the approval and authority of the colony's civil government. In his singular act of civil protest, he cut the cross out of the English flag because it symbolized the Catholic papacy. Initially supportive of Roger Williams, he withdrew his support when he was requested to repent and joined the colony authorities in banishing and persecuting colonists for conscience. He persecuted Quakers to the death. As a soldier, he regularly trained the militia of the colony. He led the disastrous attack on Block Island. As a planter, he cultivated orchards. He had a son who died in New England by a wife deceased in England and two sons by his wife in New England.

➢ Robert **Feake** (1602–1662). Had militia service under Captain Daniel Patrick. Married Elizabeth Fones Winthrop after Henry Winthrop's demise. The three of them bought land in Connecticut that is now Greenwich. After Captain Patrick was murdered, he became unstable and left for England. His return to Massachusetts was not well understood, but he appeared to have been on public assistance from Watertown at the end of his life.

➢ John (Johnny) **Felton** (1595–1628). Disgruntled soldier who assassinated the Duke of Buckingham and was caught and hung for the crime.

➢ Thomas **Fones** (1573–1629). Husband of the sister of John Winthrop Senior, Anne Winthrop. He was an apothecary—much like a combination of pharmacist and doctor of internal medicine. His house in London was his shop. Anne died in 1619, and he would remarry and have more children. His estate was left to his son Samuel and his second wife, leaving his older daughters, Elizabeth and Martha, in need of their inheritance from their mother, Anne, which was in John

Winthrop's control. Elizabeth married John Winthrop's son Harry, and Martha married John Winthrop the Younger.

➤ **Freeman** family.[7] There were Freemans aboard the *Abigail*, and Reverend Hugh Peter and his wife, Elizabeth Read, Winthrop's mother, boarded the *Abigail* in disguise. Which names were really the Peters is not known. There were Freemans of the right age to make the disguise plausible.

➤ Lion **Gardiner** (1599–1663). In charge of the fort at the mouth of the Connecticut River.

➤ Sir Gerard **Gilbert** (1587–1670). Sat in the House of Commons as a member of Parliament multiple times and was the husband of Lady Joan Barrington's daughter Mary. Supported Parliament in the Civil War.

➤ Saxo **Grammaticus** (1150–1220). Danish historian and author of the first history of Denmark.

➤ John **Greene** (1594–1658). Surgeon and one of the first settlers in Providence. Banished from Boston.

➤ **HH** (~1590–~1616). Close prisoner at Newgate in 1609. See Hendric **Hoste**.

➤ William **Hallett** (1616–1706). May have gone back and forth between England and New England multiple times as apprentice in merchant ventures, accounting for the confusion about the date of his arrival in New England.

➤ William **Harris** (1610–1681). One of the first settlers of Providence, and one of the first twelve members of the Baptist Church in Providence

➤ Gervase **Helwys** (1651–1615). Cousin to Thomas Helwys, knighted by King James in 1603, appointed Lieutenant of the Tower of London 1613, found guilty of Thomas Overbury's 1613 murder and executed in 1615.

➤ Joan Ashmore **Helwys** (circa 1575–circa 1630). Wife of Thomas Helwys since 1595 and mother of his seven children. Was a leader in the early separatist women's church. Joan was arrested before Thomas and would not take an oath submitting to law before God. She served three months, and her fate after that is unknown.

➤ Thomas **Helwys** (1575–1616). Founder of the English Baptist church with John Smythe, home used for separatist Puritan worship, fled to

Amsterdam and then returned to be arrested after his wife was taken. Author of "A Short Declaration of the Mistery of Inequity."

➤ King **Herod** (74 BC--0 BC). Roman client king in Judea where the birth of Jesus occurred. God had angels announce the birth to shepherds in the field and not to Herod. <u>Matthew 2</u>

➤ Reverend Francis **Higginson** (1588–1630). Led an expedition of six ships to join Endicott's colony in 1629. He did not publicly divulge his separatist convictions until after his departing speech, where the bishop was listening. He and Sam Skelton took over the existing church in Salem, which had no trained minister. He died of fever in his first winter in New England.

➤ William **Hooke** (1600–1677). Minister at Axmouth, minister at Taunton from 1640, as teacher paired to minister John Davenport from 1645. Married Jane Whalley. He stayed in New England two years past his wife's return and returned when their son graduated from Harvard in 1656. Chaplain to Oliver Cromwell, he lived underground in London when the monarchy was restored. Hooke hosted the underground meetings of John Winthrop the Younger in the 1660s. One of many authors of the Savoy Declaration, a 1658 revision of the Westminister Confession of Faith that affirmed the autonomy of local churches.

➤ Hendric **Hoste**. Fictional son of fictional mother, Orrelia, and a factual father—a frequent financial support of the poor house at Austin Friars, named Dietrick Hoste.[8] Surviving siblings were Theodoras and Mary Hoste as of 1652. The character is based on factual HH, who was close prisoner at Newgate in 1609. Attributed as author of "Scriptures and Reasons, Against Persecution in cause of Conscience," printed first as a portion of the Anabaptist Manifesto of 1620 and reprinted in 1643 as part of Roger Williams's "The Bloudy Tenant of Persecution for Cause of Conscience, discussed." The death of HH in prison is not completely certain. If he survived and was released with other prisoners in 1616, as was Sir Walter Raleigh, he could have been Hendrick von Hoeus[9] of Crooked Lane, in Candlestick Ward, instead of being a Hoste. In this case he gave $1 to the Austin Friars in 1621 and lived quietly after that.

➢ Orrelia Van Meteeren **Hoste**. Fictional sister of Emanuel Van Meteren, mother of Hendric Hoste.

➢ Edward **Howes** (?–?). Alchemist and childhood friend of John Winthrop the Younger. They corresponded frequently as adults, and John Winthrop the Younger stayed with him in 1635 for a time. Alchemists never did turn other metals into gold, but they did pioneer the extraction of iron from ore.

➢ Anne **Hutchinson** (1591–1643). A godly woman leader, banished by Boston and massacred by Siwanoy Algonquian.

➢ Suzanna **Hutchinson** (1633–1713). Daughter of Anne Hutchinson. Kidnapped by the Siwanoy for three years and then returned to the family.

➢ Will **Hutchinson** (1586–1641). Wealthy mercantile husband of Anne Hutchinson.

➢ King **James** (1566–1625). He ascended to the throne of Scotland in 1567 and then to the joint throne of England and Ireland in 1603. While his mother, Queen Mary, was Catholic, King James was Protestant. He commissioned the King James Bible.

➢ **Jole** (circa 1565–1650). Fictional name for historical Old Squaw Sachem of the Massachusetts, related to Canonicus, and Nanapashemet's widow. Her surviving son worked in the harbor but ended up sold into slavery in the Caribbean, though he was rescued and brought back a broken man. She also had a surviving daughter.

➢ William **Knight** (circa 1602–circa 1625). Student at Cambridge until he was imprisoned for claiming that the king could be lawfully resisted if he was unlawful.

➢ William **Laud**, Archbishop of Canterbury from 1628 (1573–1645). Influential in the courts of King James and King Charles as bishop and then archbishop. Among other titles, he was one of sixteen on the Commission for Foreign Plantations,[10] a body with the power to make laws and give orders to the English colonies. Only five of the sixteen were needed to make a quorum. By 1640 the king's power was diminished enough that Laud was arrested. He was executed in 1645.

➢ Bartholomew **Legate** (1575–1612). Did not believe that God the Father, Jesus the Son, and the Holy Spirit formed one God in three persons. As head of the Anglican Church, King James had him burned at the stake after learning that he had not prayed in the previous seven years.

➤ **Luke** (AD 0–10–AD 74). Medical doctor and author of the gospel Luke and Acts. A disciple of Christ.

➤ **Lynn** (1598–1615). Fictional middle-class English girl. Apprenticed as house servant to the Howards—an upper-class family —at the age of fifteen. By seventeen she was pregnant by the lord of the house (of the Howard family) and was released from service as a result. Became a prostitute, quickly became diseased, and died of smallpox in December 1615. Gervase Helwys was a client.

➤ **Niccolò Machiavelli** (1469–1527). Author of *The Prince*, a book about the political realities of gaining power when one isn't born to it.

➤ Sir William **Martin** (circa 1585–circa 1650). Staunch Anglican merchant, neighbor of the Mashams. Critical of Roger Williams in writing.

➤ **Mascus** (1556--1617) Narragansett Algonquian Sachem and Miantonomoh's father.

➤ Elizabeth Barrington **Masham** (?–after 1656). Eldest daughter of Sir Francis Barrington.

➤ Sir William **Masham** (1592–1644). Second husband of Elizabeth Barrington. Fatherless at fourteen but inherited a great estate. Mentored by Francis Barrington, who had similar Puritan separatist religious views. When Barrington's daughter was widowed, Masham married her.

➤ **Massasoit** (1581–1661). Sachem of the Wampanoag Algonquian, and the first to sell land holdings to Roger Williams.

➤ **Matantuck** (1597--1660). (Magnus as a child, Quaiapen after Meiksah's death.) Meiksah's wife, sister of Juanumo, also called Ninigret. After Meiksah's death she was known as the Quaiapen, meaning "Old Queen Sachem."

➤ **Matoaka** (1595–1617). Born Matoax, called Amonute prior to her imprisonment in 1613, and christened Rebecca upon her conversion to Christianity, nicknamed Pocohontas. Daughter of Sachem Powhatan, first husband Kocoum. Played a role as sachem's daughter in a ritual to signify that John Smith was reborn as part of the tribe, which the English confused as her saving his life. Kidnapped in 1613 and held for ransom, converted to Christianity while imprisoned. Married John Rolfe on April 15, 1614, had son, Thomas Rolfe, January 30, 1615. Died while on her first visit to England. First known successful intermarriage of a Steward ruler class woman to the English.

➤ Sachem Mayn **Mayano** (?-?). Siwanoy Algonquian sachem orchestrating the 1643 massacre at New Amsterdam, killed in the retreat.

➤ Emanuel Van **Meteren** (1535–1612). Son of Jacob Van Meteren, consul representing Dutch merchants in London, postmaster, historian, and author who in 1599 published: *Belgische ofte Nederlandsche Historie van onzen Tijden. Excommunicated on paper from Austin Friars 1561.* [11]

➤ Jacob Van **Meteren** (1519–?). Knight, financier, and printer. Bible translator, possibly working closely with Myles Coverdale in secret.

➤ Orrelia van **Meteren** (circa 1520–after 1543). Daughter of William Ortelius, sister of Flemish cartographer Abraham Ortelius, wife of Jacob Van Meteren, mother of Emanuel Van Meteren and fictional Orrelia van Meteren Hoste.

➤ **Miantonomoh** (1600–1643). Narangassett sachem. Nephew of Canonicus, inherited leadership position from Canonicus, was killed by Pequot Uncas with English court's blessing, and Canonicus was reinstated.

➤ **Meiksah** (1685–1657). Canonicus's younger son. Alive in 1647, when he signed a document with Pessicus. [12]

➤ John **Milton** (1608–1674). Poet, served Oliver Cromwell, and was the nephew of Lady Joan Barrington. He went to Christ's College, Cambridge, alongside Roger for at least a year. Tutored Roger in Hebrew and supposedly learned some Dutch.

➤ Lord Viscount **Montague** (1574–1629). Grandson of the Viscount who was on Queen Mary's Privy Council. Inherited the position at age eighteen in 1592. Catholic and yet loyal to King James and King Charles. He was a supporter of the first King Charles's marriage to the French Catholic Henrietta Maria. He spent a year in prison after the gunpowder assassination attempt on King James by Catholic conspirators, even though there was no evidence that he was an accomplice. Privy Council records document that he was given permission to travel abroad in 1617 with his daughter and a servant. He authored "A Booke of Orders and Rules" about household operation.[13]

- Roger **Mowry** (1610–1665). Owner of the inn called the Mowry Tavern in Salem, removed from Salem to Providence.
- Thomas **Morton** (1590–1647). Tried to force an alternate service at Plymouth using the Book of Common Prayer. His Anglican plantation was called Merrymount.
- Bishop Richard **Neile** (1562–1640). A bishop on the High Commission under King James deciding the fate of those accused of religious heresy.
- **Ninigret** (1610–1677). Called Juanumo in the early years of adulthood, Narragansett with Pequot and Niantic blood, sachem, nephew of Canonicus, cousin of Miantonomoh.[14]
- Frances Read **Onge** (1583–1638). The Widow Onge emigrated on the *Lyon* with two of her thirteen children, arriving February 1631. Settled in Watertown as a merchant and brought over several more children.
- **Openchancanough** (1554–1646). Tribal leader in the Powhatan Confederacy in Virginia and Maryland. He was a brother of Chief Powhatan, a powerful warrior and charismatic leader.
- Abraham **Ortelius** (1527–1598). Flemish cartographer, nephew to Jacobus Van Meteren, who returned from religious exile in England to care for him when his father died. Brother to Orrelia Ortelius.
- Thomas **Overbury** (1581–1613). In service to King James. Friend and advisor of Robert Carr, the court favorite. Poet, publishing a poem called "A Wife" while attempting to dissuade Carr from marrying Frances Howard. King James offered Overbury a post as ambassador to serve in Russia, which he refused, preferring to stay in Carr's company. Imprisoned for his refusal in April 2013. Murdered in September 1613.
- Count **Palatine** of Bohemia (1596–1632). Also known as Frederick V, was a Protestant king of Bohemia for a year and four days. Installed after the revolt against recent Catholic Hapsburg intolerant rule, he lost militarily in a battle that started the Thirty Year War. He had a popular arranged marriage to King James I's daughter, Elizabeth Stuart.
- David **Pareus** (1548–1622). German Reformed Protestant theologian. He advocated subjects holding rulers accountable for their actions. King James ordered every copy of his book burned in 1622.
- William **Parke** (1607–1685). Son of Richard Parke, who was a friend of John Winthrop Senior, brother of Thomas Parke, who precedes him

to Boston by a year. Married Martha Holgrave, daughter of Salem settler John Holgrave. Neighbor to the Throckmortons in England. Settled in Roxbury.

➤ Captain Daniel **Patrick** (1600–1644). Colonial soldier and commanding officer of Robert Feake. He aided in the retreat at the Battle of Mystic and killed Sachem Mayn Mayano defending New Amsterdam from the Siwanoy during the massacre that killed Anne Hutchinson. After an attempted retribution for the massacre, he got lost and failed to find the target. He was shot in the back in a tavern brawl.

➤ **Paul** (AD 0–10–AD 60–70). Born Saul, a persecutor of Christians until his conversion on the road to Damascus. He experienced blinding light during his conversion encounter with Christ and had vision problems ever after. After his conversion, Paul continued making tents as a profession while spending his life as an itinerant missionary to the non-Jewish population. He was the author of many books of the New Testament.

➤ Dr. **Pell** (circa 1625–after 1656). Surgeon that Captain Underhill brought to the battle of Mystic.

➤ **Pessicus** (1624–1676). Miantonomoh's younger brother. [15]

➤ Hugh **Peter** (1598–1660). Stepfather of Elizabeth Read Winthrop. Salem minister who replaced Roger Williams. Removed to England to raise funds for the Massachusetts Bay Colony in its distress, but once there, allied with Vane, eventually promoted toleration, played a major role in the English Civil War disputes, and never returned to New England. Executed when the monarchy was restored.

➤ Captain William **Pierce** (1582–1651). Captain of the *Lyon* during Roger Williams's and many other crossings. Held the records for fastest crossing of the Atlantic during the 1600s, and for most trips across the sea. Captain of slave ship *Desire*. Married Jane Eales and had three children. His daughter was the second wife of John Rolfe of Jamestown. Killed by the Spanish in West Indies.

➤ **Puttaquappuinckquame** (?–1937). The Pequot sachem with Stone's pinnace after Stone was murdered. Puttaquappuinckquame did not join another tribe but rather hid his people in the swamp after the Battle at Mystic, but he was discovered and killed by Narragansett

Yotaash. The English put his men to death, took his wives and other beautiful women for wives, mistresses, or servants and the rest were the first Algonquian sold into slavery in the Barbados en masse after he was killed. The American-built ship *Desire* transported them, and William Pierce was the captain.

> John **Pym** (1584–1643). Lawyer and member of Parliament. One of five people King Charles tried to arrest when he sparked the English Civil War.

> John **Radcliffe** (1549–1609). Captain of the *Discovery*, one of the three ships on the Virginia Colony Expedition. Councilor of Jamestown, and the second president of the colony. He was tortured while bound by Algonquian women, a sign that he likely raped someone. He was burned at the stake.

> Philip **Ratliff** (circa 1600—circa 1650). Tried to force an alternate service at Plymouth using the Book of Common Prayer.

> Sir Walter **Raleigh** (1554–1618). Spent the 1580s attempting a colony at Roanoke, Virginia; it failed. In 1594 he explored Venezuela seeking gold. He was found guilty of a plot against King James and imprisoned in 1603. He was remembered and sent on expedition in 1616. Upon his return he was executed, having not been successful with his orders.

> Watt **Raleigh** (?–1617). Sir Walter Raleigh's son. Accompanied his sick father to the New World. Left father at base camp in Trinidad. Killed in battle with Indians upon landing in Venezuela.

> First Baron Richard **Rich** (1496–1567). Father of the wealthy Rich family.

> Henry **Rich** (1590–1649). Great-grandson of First Baron Richard Rich, mentor to John Winthrop Senior. A royalist in the English Civil War.

> Lord Nathaniel **Rich** (1585–1636). Wealthy merchant and adventurer. Investor in Providence Company, Virginia Company, and more.

> John **Robinson** (1576–1625). Puritan minister who removed to Holland. The Helwys/Smyth congregation in Holland began as a child church of Robinson's congregation but was disowned. Half of Robinson's congregation later became the Higginson congregation at Plymouth. Robinson stayed behind, intending to travel later. He was a full Congregationalist, disowning church hierarchy but reinforcing

church body discipline. He authored the vehement response to the Anabaptist confession, disowning believer's baptism and toleration. Delaying baptism undermined the church's authority over people while they were in their most tender need of disciplined instruction. He was against toleration of consciences because it undermined church discipline by enabling heresy to spread widely without any on earth having the authority to exterminate it.

➤ John **Rolfe** (1585–1622). Departed England on the *Sea Venture*, whose caulking was not waterproof. She was crashed deliberately in Barbados to allow for more survivors than in a sinking, and survivors spent ten months in Barbados. He lost his first wife and child in Barbados. With prisoner-servant Matoaka, he developed a new strain of tobacco that became popular for its high nicotine content and wonderful aroma, and he married her in 1614. Tobacco became the cash crop of Virginia that made the colony profitable. His son with Matoaka was named Thomas. His third wife was Jane Pierce, daughter of Captain William Pierce, and they had a child. He died after Algonquian attacked his plantation and burned it to the ground.

➤ Miriam Beijrens **Ruytinck** (circa 1580—–circa 1623). Married 1602 to Simon Ruytinck. Collector of milk cans at Newgate.

➤ Reverend Symon **Ruytinck** (1565?–1623). Minister at Austin Friar from 1601–1621. Sons Simeon (age seventeen in 1621; last scholarship in 1623) and Johannes (age seventeen in 1628; last scholarship in 1630) received scholarships from Austin Friars.

➤ Sergius **Paulus** (~0–~ AD 60). Converted from being a disciple of Bar-Jesus to a disciple of Jesus.

➤ **Sassacus** (1580-1637) Pequot grand-sachem.

➤ Reverend Samuel **Skelton** (1584–1634). John Endicott recruited Sam Skelton to come with him to New England and pastor the church in Salem. That church became independent or fully separated from the Anglican Church in 1630, a year after his arrival, in order to have a single church in Salem that pilgrims from the Higginson expedition and Puritans from the Great Migration could join. He married his wife Suzanna in England, and she bore him ten children, five of whom survived childhood.

➢ Thomas **Shepard** (1605–1649). Conservative Puritan Congregationalist minister and peer of John Cotton and Richard Mather.

➢ Alice **Smith** (circa 1605–1650). The banished John Smith's wife. First woman with children in Providence.

➢ John **Smith** (1580–1631). Adventurer, soldier, author. Member of St. Sepulchre; soldier captured and sold as a slave to the Turks, from whom he escaped; early leader in Jamestown; mapmaker of New England and Chesapeake Bay. No known descendants.

➢ John **Smith** (1595–1649). His father claimed to be the half-brother of the adventurer John Smith. John was the miller in Dorchester before he was banished on the same day as Roger Williams. He was one of the first residents of Providence.

➢ Reverend Ralph **Smith** (1589–1661). Minister in Plymouth from 1629, when he arrived on the *Lyon's Whelp* with his wife, child, and servants, until 1636 when he was persuaded to release the ministry to John Reynor. Smith defended Plymouth's separateness, to the chagrin of the Massachusetts Bay ministers. Smith was made freeman in 1633. He knew Sam Groton for a decade before coming to Plymouth, as they came from the same town. Reverend Smith's wife was tired of the strictness of the Puritan religion and found Sam Gorton's company from back home far more entertaining. Reverend Smith drove Sam Gorton out of Plymouth as a result. For several years after leaving the Plymouth ministry, he preached at Jeffrey's Creek near Salem. He was from time to time at Ipswich as well. He married a second wife, Mary, the widow of Richard Masterson, in 1648. He died a farmer in 1661.

➢ John **Smythe** (1570–1612). Minister in Holland. First to self-baptize, initiating believer's baptism with Thomas Helwys. Later reconsidered, desiring succession, and urged his flock to join Mennonite church.

➢ King **Solomon** (970–931 BC). God granted Solomon special wisdom. <u>1 Kings 3</u>.

➢ Henry **Spelman** (1595–1623). Henry indentured himself to gain passage on a 1609 voyage to Virginia; his contract of indenture was traded to the Algonquian. He lived with the Algonquian and became an interpreter.

➢ Polish King **Stephen** (1533–1586). Born Stephen Báthory. A very successful Polish king, he initially ascended the throne after King

Henry ascended the French throne and abdicated his Polish throne. In order to get a Polish and anti-Hapsburg king, a sister of a prior king, Sigismund II Augustus I, was elected queen and married to him. He was a successful military leader and eventually led all of Transylvania in addition to Poland. He knew Hungarian, Latin, Italian, and German but never learned Polish. His principle was that he was the king of bodies, and the Warsaw Confederation of 1573 was one of the first documents to guarantee nobility and freemen religious freedom. In fact, his wife's childless brother King Sigismund was also a champion of toleration.

➤ Oliver **St. John** (1598–1673). A member of Parliament in trouble in court from time to time. Friend of Lord Say and John Pym, investors in Providence Company. Married Jug, the daughter of Lady Elizabeth Masham by a prior marriage. After her death, he married Elizabeth Cromwell, sister of Lady Joan Cromwell Barrington. His final marriage was to Elizabeth Oxenbridge.

➤ John **Stone** (~1580–1634). A Virginia resident, who was a pirate and merchant transporting goods between New England, Virginia, the West Indies, and London. He was killed after taking advantage of the Pequot women on a stop he made on his way to Virginia after being banished from New England. He was accused of adultery, but no one could prove it. His banishment was therefore for drunkenness and public misconduct.

➤ Elizabeth **Stuart** (1506–1662). Eldest daughter of King James I. While her marriage to Frederick V, Elector Palatine, was arranged, the wedding was a two-month public party, and the couple fell deeply in love afterward. When he died, she did not eat or drink for three days. While they were married, he accepted the Protestant kingship of Bohemia, a risky venture at best. She was queen for a year and four days before she exiled herself voluntarily in anticipation of her husband losing the crown of Bohemia to Catholics. After the loss the couple fled to Holland. She had thirteen healthy children and was remarkable for her many letters from Holland. When her nephew Charles II was restored to the monarchy in England, she returned. Her daughter Sophia's son ascended the throne as George I in 1714.

➤ Claes **Swits** (circa 1570–1641). Swiss settler near New Amsterdam, a longtime trader with what he thought were good relationships with the Algonquians who killed him in 1641.

➤ **Tatobem** (1536–1637). Grand sachem of the Pequot. Had Steward ruler blood from the Narragansett wife of his grandfather Wopiguard.

➤ John **Throckmorton** (1601–1684). The Throckmorton family is on the passenger list of the *Lyon* in February 1631, though John was not able to become a freeman until 1638. Winthrop documents him as arriving with Williams, and his presence is referred to in 1635 by Hugh Peters, as Throckmorton was excommunicated from Salem at the same time as Roger Williams, for the same reasons.[16]

➤ Rebecca Farrand **Throckmorton** (circa 1615–after 1651, possibly after 1684). Rebecca, John Throckmorton's wife, lived on Hatfield Broad Oak, and may have worked at Otes.[17] While it is not known when they married, it would have been natural for them to marry after his scrivener's apprenticeship concluded. The two children listed as with her on the *Lyon* must not have survived. Their deaths, while unrecorded, would have been before the names John and Patience are reused, after 1643. Likely they died in the Siwanoy attacks that Winthrop records as killing whichever of the Throckmortons were at home. Since Rebecca had more children after this attack, she was clearly not at home.

➤ Arthur **Tyndale** (circa 1582–after 1631). Brother of Margaret Tyndale. Traveled with the family to New England but returned almost immediately.

➤ Margaret **Tyndale** (1591–1647). Third wife of John Winthrop Senior, produced seven children, though, of the later five, only one survived infancy. She was taught to read and write, and in the year she was in England while John Winthrop was in New England, the two wrote love letters back and forth. She was well loved by Mary Forth's grandchildren with John Winthrop as well as by her own children. John the Younger's second wife preferred Margaret's house to John's company and she, with his children, lived with Margaret until her death.

➤ William **Tynsdale** (1494–1536). Bible translator from Greek and Hebrew to English, executed by strangulation before his work was printed. The King James Bible relied on some of his translations. Two years after his death, it was central to a Coverdale translation sanctioned by King Henry VIII. Four years after his death, the Coverdale Bible was available at every church in England.

➢ **Uncas** (1588-1683). Mohegan Sachem.

➢ Captain John **Underhill** (1609–1672). Was sent to arrest Roger Williams. He was a leader at Block Island, the Battle of Mystic, and retribution against the Siwanoy, all battles with questionable outcomes, given later scrutiny. He arrived with the Winthrop fleet with his mother, took a Dutch wife, became an Anne Hutchinson follower, and was banished in 1640 over an internal military matter. He returned to England during his banishment, which was repealed in 1641 after a full repentance. Three months later he was acquitted of adultery. At age forty-nine he married as his second wife, Elizabeth Winthrop Feake, Hallett's twenty-five-year-old Quaker daughter, after the entire Hallett farm was burned in an Algonquian raid. He became a Quaker shortly before his death.

➢ Jane **Verin** (circa 1610–circa 1641). Wife of the rope maker Joshua Verin, she produced at least one son by him. They were one of the first Providence families. Her husband beat her nearly to death when she continued to attend church meetings at Roger's house/hill. The memory of the Verin incident, along with a treatise by John Milton on why divorce should be allowed, were catalysts for the liberal divorce laws written into the Rhode Island legal code. Jane Verin was also proof in the record that Roger was holding formal church meetings in English before the Baptist church was founded, even though no building was constructed as a common meeting place in Providence for many years.

➢ Joshua **Verin** (circa 1606–after 1650). Son of Philip Verin, a founder of Salem. He was a rope maker and the first person banished from Providence for the crime of beating his wife nearly to death.

➢ George **Villiers** (1592–1628). Successor to Robert Carr as the favorite of King James. He was titled the Duke of Buckingham. He had an arranged marriage with Sir Edward Coke's daughter Frances that ended badly when she ran off with the man she loved. Destroyed Francis Bacon by asking him to provide favors from the court and then not supporting him when he was accused of corruption. His crassness was blamed for the breakdown of the marriage negotiations of Charles 1 with the Catholic Hapsburg princess. He was a complete failure as a military leader because of inadequate planning, insufficient funds for the expeditions, and refusal to recognize his troops' needs.

➢ **Wampage** (circa 1614–after 1657). Siwanoy who executed Anne Hutchinson and afterward reclaimed her land.

➢ Mehitable **Waterman** (1626–1683). Richard Waterman's daughter.

➢ Richard **Waterman** (1606–1673). Salem resident who moved to Providence in 1638, an expert tracker and hunter.

➢ **Wawaloam** (1601–1686). Wife of Miantonomoh. Narragansett woman, alive in 1661 and giving testimony as to history of land ownership of Block Island. She would have had three names; her fictional childhood name was Oakana, and her fictional married name was Oonue. Wawaloam was her recorded name after Miantonomoh's death.

➢ **Weko**. Fictional name for the Narragansett wife of Yotan.

➢ **Weekan.** Fictional brother of Miantonomoh.

➢ **Weekan the Younger**. Fictional name for son of Miantonomoh.

➢ Jane **Whalley** Hooke (1610–?). Lady Joan Barrington's niece. Daughter of Richard Whalley of Kirkton Hall in Nottingham. First love of Roger Williams. Married William Hooke, a minister, in 1630. She lived in Axmouth until 1640, then migrated to Taunton, Massachusetts. She moved to New Haven, Connecticut, by 1645. She returned to England with eight children in 1654 and was known for her rare ability and habit of writing letters and was part of high society in London until her death.

➢ Francis **Weekes** (~1617–after 1656). Came to Providence as the lad of John Smith.

➢ **Wekeum** (~1533–~1636) Older brother of Canonicus, ancestor of Wopigaurd, who is ancestor of Sassacus but not Uncas.

➢ Alice Pemberton **Williams** (1564–1634). Mother of Sydrach, Roger, Robert, and Katherine Williams, as well as two children older than Roger and younger than Sydrach, who died as infants: Catherine and Robert. Alice was a landlord of a tenement called Harrows and some surrounding rentals. She also had three tenements adjoining her dwelling place.

➢ Robert **Williams** (1604–1680).[18] Married Sarah approximately 1617 abroad. Had two children. There was another Robert Williams brother to Roger born in 1599 who died in approximately 1603. At age fifteen, Robert apprenticed as servant to Viscount Montagu, and later he apprenticed to Sydrach, upon James Williams's death. Robert inherited his mother's tenement rental business, including Harrow and multiple other dwellings in 1634, though he must pay Sydrach for ten years, and Katherine and Roger for twenty years from the rent.[19] Robert migrated to New England and by 1639 was admitted freeman in Providence. Roger married Elizabeth in New England, and she was with him in 1672.[20] There was a lawsuit about property he improperly alienated in 1644. (Improper alienation means a lord has given you use of a feoff, and you have abandoned it improperly—i.e., without permission from the lord who has the grant from the king—to be managed by others.) At that time Robert was "beyond the seas."[21]

➢ **Ann**a Grace **Williams** (1625–?). Alice Pemberton Williams's will[22] left funds to an Ann Williams. She could have been Sydrach's daughter or Robert's. There was a ten-year-old Ann Williams on the *Abigail*, and there was smallpox on the *Abigail*.[23]

➢ Roger **Williams** (1603–1683). Roger obtained a charter for the colony of Rhode Island in 1644 as an explicit experiment with religious freedom. This charter was reinstated in 1663 when the English monarchy was restored. Roger was an original founder of the Baptist church in America.

➢ Roger **Williams** (1625 or 1638–1677). Sydrach's younger son by Anne Tyler Pinner or Tiller. See below the entry for Sydrach Williams for the discussion of the controversy around Sydrach's marriages. Roger eventually immigrated to Virginia. His mother was not the mother of James and Elizabeth, Sydrach's other children.

➢ Sydrach **Williams** (1595–1647).[24] Admitted by patronage at age eighteen to the Livery Company, a type of union, called the Merchant Taylor. Admission by patronage meant his father had been a member. He likely had three marriages. He married Ann October 10, 1623 (license October 1621). She died 1637(buried July 10, 1637). He married Judith Brown April 1638, and she died August 1638. He married Ann Pinner October 1638 … but her son Roger was born in 1638. In 1644 Sydrach had been in Italy for seven years, implying that he left before Roger was born. There is a discrepancy in that some have Roger born to the first marriage, yet he survived to 1677 and was not in Alice's will in 1634. Some have the marriage to Pinner as Sydrach's first marriage, but she was the mother of Roger, not of the other two children. It seems doubtful that the particular Ann Pinner they associate with Sydrach was actually his wife, as Sydrach's Ann Pinner likely removed with him to Italy and went to Virginia on his death in 1647, with no further records of her in England, whereas the Ann Pinner who was first married to Francis Pinner, who died in 1637. Sydrach's son Roger could not have been born in 1634, when Alice died, so his birth was after 1634. If he was Ann Pinner Williams's son, born between 1634 and 1637, there is no record of his birth in England, so perhaps he was born in Italy. The first records of Roger are in Virginia, but he likely was not born there.[25]

➤ Reverend John **Wilson** (1591–1667). Minister and teacher of the First Boston Church 1630 admitted freeman 1632. He returned to England in 1633 to retrieve his wife and children and had a third child in Boson in 1633. John Cotton stood in for him while he was gone. Upon his return in 1633 the church had grown and the position was split to John Wilson as minister and John Cotton as teacher. In 1634 he headed back to England and was nearly shipwrecked off the coast of Ireland. He returned in 1635. Anne Hutchinson was very critical of his theology, as she believed he bordered on a salvation of works. Never as popular as John Cotton, at one point he accepted a commission as chaplain on a military voyage to sit out the controversy. He was the archetype of the conservative Puritan minister and the cause of many a long punishment in the stockade.

➤ Ed **Winslow** (1596–1655). Third, sixth, and tenth governor of the Plymouth Colony. Apprenticed as a stationer in London, he abandoned it to join the Scrooby congregation in Holland, which was the congregation led by John Robinson in Leiden. He is a listed as a printer in London on his 1618 Leiden marriage certificate to Elizabeth Barker. She died in 1621, and he married Susanna, who bore him four children. He joined others in publishing pamphlets critical of the king, which were distributed in England. The king sent agents to Holland to seek Brewster's arrest, but he and his family evaded them and planned the pilgrim emigration to America instead. Winslow was Massasoit's primary liaison to the English. Winslow returned to England for the English Civil War and served Oliver Cromwell. He died of yellow fever at sea during a naval encounter with the Spanish.

➤ Elizabeth Fones **Winthrop** Feake Hallett (January 1610–1673). Henry Winthrop's wife, with subsequent marriage to Robert Feake.

➤ Forth Winthrop (1609–1630). Third child of Mary Forth and John Winthrop. Attended Cambridge and transferred to Exeter. Returned from Exeter, where he was studying, and died. His fiancée was Ursula Fones, cousin to Martha and Bess.

➤ Henry **Winthrop** (1608–1630). Adventurer and investor. Invested in a plantation in Barbados, but the tobacco was blighted, and he returned to England to recoup and try again with his father and the Massachusetts Bay Company, founder of the Massachusetts Bay Colony. He married Elizabeth Fones and had a surviving child, Martha Johanna, with her, and died a day after reaching New England.

➤ John **Winthrop** (1588–1649). Leader of the Great Migration expedition fleet of eleven,; emigrated on the *Arabella*. His spouses were Mary Forth, Thomasine Clopton, Margaret Tyndale, and Martha Rainsborough. Original investor in the Massachusetts Bay Company and architect of its independence from England. Second, sixth, ninth, and twelfth governor of the Massachusetts Bay Colony. When he took over from Endicott, the decision-making council was moved to New England, and the site of the colony seat was moved from Salem to Boston. He spent his fortune to make the Massachusetts Bay Colony solvent, and he never fully recovered his finances or his health after the recession in Boston induced by the Hutchinson banishment.

➤ John **Winthrop the Younger** (1606–1676). Secretary to sea captain in the battle of La Rochelle in 1627, then traveler to Turkey to make merchant tailor connections, married Martha Fones. Stayed behind to care for business when his father migrated on the *Arabella*. He followed, arriving November 1631 with the rest of the Winthrops. The code he used in his letters with Martha Fones was so complex that it was not broken for 300 years. [26] Owner of salt works and iron works, famous for medical remedies he freely provided. [27]

➢ Martha Fones **Winthrop** (1611–1633). First wife of John Winthrop the younger. Younger sister of Elizabeth Fones Winthrop.

➢ Stephen **Winthrop** (1619–1658). Margaret Tyndale's eldest child with John Winthrop Senior.

➢ Ed **Wightman** (1580?–1612). Well-respected merchant tailor. He denied the veracity of scripture to claim that Jesus was not the incarnate Son of God. King James as the head of the Anglican Church had him burned in Lichfield, and he was the last man burned at the stake in England.

➢ Robert **Wightman** (?–1629). First husband of Katherine Williams, Roger Williams's brother-in-law. Merchant tailor. Katherine married Robert in 1627, and he fathered her eldest three children. Robert's cousin was Ed Wightman.

➢ John **Woodbury** (1587–1641). John was one of the original planters of Salem, and Agnes, his second wife, joined him in 1636.

➢ **Yotaash** (1602–?). Miantonomoh's little brother. Best known for slaying Sachem Pequot Puttaquappuinckquame and taking his elaborately decorated canoe, which an Englishman, Mr. Stoughton, confiscated.

➢ **Yotan** (1584–1643). Canonicus's eldest son (fictional name). Died sometime before Roger Williams left for England the first time. The story he tells is a traditional Narragansett legend. [28]

ENDNOTES

1   Winslow, Ola Elizabeth Winslow,. *Master Roger Williams*. (New York: Macmillan, 1957), p. 45.

2   Williams, Roger. *The Complete Writing of Roger Williams*, Volume 6, ed. John Russell Bartlett, "Letter to John Winthrop, October 24, likely in 1636" (Paris, Arkansas: The Baptist Standard Bearer Inc., reprinted in 2005, originally printed in 1867), pp. 7–13, paraphrased and modernized.

3   https://books.google.com/books?id=8t8UAAAAYAAJ&printsec=frontcover&source=gbs_ge_summary_r&cad=0#v=onepage&q=canonicus&f=false

4   Grail, Peter. "Austin Friars and the Puritan Revolution: The Dutch Church in London" (EUI PHD Dissertation." Thesis submitted to the European University Institute, September 30, 1983), p. 421.

5   Grail, Peter. "Austin Friars and the Puritan Revolution: The Dutch Church in London" (EUI PHD Dissertation." Thesis submitted to the European University Institute, September 30, 1983), p. 421.

6   Grail, Peter. "Austin Friars and the Puritan Revolution: The Dutch Church in London" (EUI PHD Dissertation." Thesis submitted to the European University Institute, September 30, 1983), p. 157.

7   http://www.packrat-pro.com/ships/abigail.htm

8   Grail, Peter. "Austin Friars and the Puritan Revolution: The Dutch Church in London" (EUI PHD Dissertation." Thesis submitted to the European University Institute, September 30, 1983), p. 80.

9   Grail, Peter. "Austin Friars and the Puritan Revolution: The Dutch Church in London" (EUI PHD Dissertation." Thesis submitted to the European University Institute, September 30, 1983), p. 435.

10 http://archive.org/stream/britishcommittee00andrrich/britishcommittee00andrrich_djvu.txt

11 Grail, Peter. "Austin Friars and the Puritan Revolution: The Dutch Church in London" (EUI PHD Dissertation." Thesis submitted to the European University Institute, September 30, 1983), p. 17.

12 http://imageserver.library.yale.edu/digcoll:3730/500.pdf

13 The Sussex Archeological Society. *Sussex Archeological Collections Relating to the History of the County,* Volume 7, ed. John Russell Smith, "A Booke of Orders and Rules of Anthony Viscount Montague in 1595" ed. Sir Sibald Dave Scott, Bart. (London: E. Tucker, 1854).

14 Fisher, Julie A. and Silverman, David J. *Ninigret, Sachem of the Niantics and Narrangansetts: Diplomacy, War, and the Balance of Power in Seventeenth-Century New England and Indian Country.* (Ithica and London: Cornell University Press, 2014), Kindle Location 3.

15 http://images.library.yale.edu/walpoleweb/footnote.asp?db=a&id=14

16 Williams, Roger. *The Complete Writing of Roger Williams,* Volume 6, ed. John Russell Bartlett, "Letter to John Winthrop, June 2, 1637" (Paris, Arkansas: The Baptist Standard Bearer Inc., reprinted in 2005, originally printed in 1867), p. 27, footnote 3.

17 http://www.branches-n-twigs.com/genealogy/getperson. php?personID=I155&tree=allfam

18 http://familytreemaker.genealogy.com/users/m/i/c/Sue-Mickley/WEBSITE-0001/UHP-1153.html

19 http://familytreemaker.genealogy.com/users/m/i/c/Sue-Mickley/WEBSITE-0001/UHP-1153.html

20 Williams, Roger. *The Complete Writing of Roger Williams,* Volume 5, ed. Rev. J. Lewis Diman, "Introduction", Footnote 1 (Paris, Arkansas: The Baptist Standard Bearer Inc., reprinted in 2005, originally printed in 1867), p. xlii.

21 http://homepages.rootsweb.ancestry.com/~sam/williams2/roger.html

22 http://www.genealogy.com/ftm/m/i/c/Sue-Mickley/WEBSITE-0001/UHP-1153.html

23 http://www.packrat-pro.com/ships/abigail.htm

24 http://www.genealogy.com/ftm/m/i/c/Sue-Mickley/WEBSITE-0001/UHP-1153.html

25 http://www.genealogy.com/ftm/m/i/c/Sue-Mickley/WEBSITE-0001/UHP-1153.html

26 http://www.cslib.org/gov/winthropj.htm

27 Waters, Thomas Franklin and Winthrop, Robert Charles. *A Sketch of the Life of John Winthrop the Younger* (Cambridge, Massachusetts: University Press, originally printed 1899), p. 25. Digitized by Google.

28 http://www.native-languages.org/narragansett-legends.htm

Teresa was born in Houston, TX, raised in Utah, Kansas and Texas. She lives in New Jersey and Arizona. She trained to be a chemist until the last semester of undergraduate school when she realized she would graduate more quickly with a degree in Mathematics. Now she satisfies her chemical curiosity cooking in the kitchen, sometimes to the chagrin of her kids. For years she worked in a large corporation where she met many memorable brilliant people from all over the world pursuing the American Dream.

When her five-year-old son reviewed the family tree kindergarten assignment spanning fourteen generations in multiple lines, he crumpled his brow in study for a long pause. The poster size tree included shipwrecks, soldiers on both sides of the civil war, religious activists, English Colonists and American pioneers. He had one comment. "Mom, I was just sure Chuck Yeager would be in there somewhere."

After the death of her first husband, Teresa used exercise to combat grief. She became an endurance athlete, eventually completing the Iditasport a 100 mile race over ice and snow.

Teresa is a follower of Jesus Christ, though flawed—in other words just like his other followers. As such, she is utterly reliant on the grace of God, which she finds in the Roman Catholic, Baptist, Moravian and non-denominational traditions.